NIGHT WATCH

NIGHTHAWK SECURITY - BOOK FIVE

SUSAN SLEEMAN

EDGE OF YOUR SEAT BOOKS, INC.

Published by Edge of Your Seat Books, Inc.

Contact the publisher at contact@edgeofyourseatbooks.com

Copyright © 2021 by Susan Sleeman

Cover design by Kelly A. Martin of KAM Design

1

"Mom didn't kill herself." Kennedy Walker fisted her hands on her hips and glared at her younger sister, Finley. "And she sure wouldn't accidentally overdose on her medicine. Detectives and medical examiners are human too. They can make mistakes."

"Argh." Finley rubbed her face dotted with freckles. "Mom's been gone for almost a month, and you haven't proved foul play in her death. It's time to give up and move on."

Move on. Right. The very idea was ludicrous.

Kennedy strode to the wall of windows in their mother's floating home, where Kennedy had been staying since the funeral. She watched as the Columbia River crashed along the back deck and adjusted her stance for the sway that high winds and fast-moving currents could bring. A sharp gust fluttered curtains on a nearby window, cooling the August heat.

"Staring out over the river isn't going to change anything." Finley joined Kennedy, her tone softer now. "Mom wasn't murdered."

Kennedy glanced over her shoulder at her sister, who

resembled Kennedy in so many ways. They both had shoulder-length hair in an outrageous shade of red and an excess of freckles that they'd inherited from their late father. Finley had more than Kennedy, but Finley covered hers with makeup. Kennedy had never gone in for the girly things in life. She was a self-professed tomboy and glad of it. As kids, Finley had held tea parties while Kennedy had embraced their mother's interest in science and concocted wild and crazy experiments.

"I'm afraid you're going to burn out trying to prove something that doesn't exist," Finley said. "Once you get something in your mind, you don't ever let it go."

"Why should I let it go?" Kennedy snapped. "Mom had everything to live for. She'd finally gotten over losing Dad and loved living in this place. Plus, she was poised to make a breakthrough in her research project. And she was a scientist, for goodness' sake. She was meticulous with everything in her life. Every little thing. She would never accidentally take too much blood pressure medicine."

"You weren't here." Finley got in Kennedy's face. "You didn't see the stress she was under. She wasn't sleeping. Or eating. She lived in that lab or at the college. Came home only to feed Oreo."

As if Oreo heard her name, the cat crossed the room and wound in and out of Kennedy's legs, purring like a lawn mower. Kennedy scooped up the black creature with a white nose and paws and hugged her close, her soft fur tickling Kennedy's face. Oreo was missing her owner just as much as Kennedy missed her mom. Desperately.

Kennedy took a breath to keep from arguing with her sister again. They'd had this conversation before, but this was the first time Finley had brought up Kennedy's living in Virginia, where she worked as a forensic diver for the FBI. Maybe Kennedy should have moved back to Portland to help her mother with her research. If she'd had any idea things were so bad, she'd have come home.

But Kennedy hadn't seen any sign of this stress. "I talked to Mom every couple of days, and she didn't appear to be stressed."

"She didn't want you to feel like she needed you here. She wanted you to embrace your new career and live your own life." Finley stroked Oreo's head. "But she *did* need you. Badly. I don't want to think she snapped under pressure and ended her life. I think it was an accident. She was tired and worn out. She made a mistake, one that cost her life."

Finley's face contorted with pain, and she broke out crying.

Oreo meowed her concern, her focus fixed on Kennedy.

Kennedy's heart split at the pain in Finley's expression and tears begged to be released. She sucked in a breath, then another and another to stop them. She had to keep it together to help her sister. Five years younger, Finley was still trying to become a responsible adult, and Kennedy needed to cut her some slack while she was still grieving the loss of their mother.

Kennedy cinched her eyes closed until she gained control. "Tell you what. I'll keep working on Mom's project until it's completed, but I'll cut back a little on digging into the potential murder if that will make you happy."

Finley dabbed at her eyes, but it did nothing to stop the mascara running down her cheeks. "It's not about making me happy. I just don't want to see you stuck in limbo."

Kennedy released Oreo and drew her little sister into a hug. Sure, Kennedy wanted to offer comfort, but she needed some too. "Don't worry about me. I'll be fine."

Finley pushed back. "When you say cutting back, you don't mean dropping the murder investigation, do you?"

Kennedy shook her head.

Finley gave an angry swipe at her tears. "Then maybe you should get some help."

Kennedy eyed her sister. "What do you mean?"

"Erik Byrd and his brothers left law enforcement to form a protection and investigation agency. Nighthawk Security. You should call him and finally end this."

"No!" The word shot out of Kennedy's mouth like a bullet, before she could swallow and take control of the sudden burst of emotions. "My breakup with Erik was a mess. You know that. I can't even believe you'd suggest it."

"You hurt him. Big time. But now that Mom and Dad are both gone, you can explain. I'm sure Erik will understand. And if for some reason you're right, and Mom was murdered, he'll have to know about WITSEC."

"No." The word held less force this time. Truth was, Kennedy had wanted to tell Erik about her dad testifying against a pyramid scammer and taking his whole family into witness protection. Not that Kennedy had known her family was in the program. Not until her last year of college, when she'd found her parents' legal documents under a different name hidden in the garage. Their dad wasn't supposed to keep anything from his prior life, but he'd broken the rules. Thankfully, no one else had caught him.

She'd confronted him, and he explained about WITSEC, but forbid her from telling Erik. Her father's life depended on her keeping his secret so of course she couldn't tell. Wouldn't tell. But every time she looked at Erik after that, she felt like she was living a lie. No way she could live a lifetime of lies and deceit. Now, the tumultuous breakup was behind them, and they'd both moved on. No point in going to see him and bringing it all up again.

"It took me years to get over Erik." *If I even am.* "And I'm not going to reopen that old wound."

"Not even if he can help you prove your point about

Mom?" Finley crossed her arms. "Or are you afraid he'll do the opposite and side with the ME's findings?"

A vision of Erik came to mind. His dishwater blond hair. Wide jaw. Fit body. Those strong arms holding her. His ready smile that evaporated when she'd told him she didn't want to be with him. And then she'd walked out without an explanation. "Not for any reason."

"Fine." Finley tightened her arms. "Be that way. You always were too stubborn for your own good. I don't know why I thought you moving away for a few years would change that."

Kennedy took her sister's hand, her skin soft but cool from the night breeze.

"I don't want to argue with you anymore," Finley said. "Mom wouldn't want that. We should be sharing our memories of her and celebrating her life."

"You're right." Kennedy tried to sound cheerful but wasn't sure she accomplished it.

"Why don't we look at some old family movies?" Finley grabbed the TV remote and popped a DVD into the player and it whirred to the beginning of the first recording.

Kennedy settled next to her sister on the beige sofa in the small living area with an equally small L-shaped kitchen at the far end of the room. Their mom had moved into the floating home less than a year before, about two years after their father's passing, and Kennedy had only visited a handful of times. The small place that moved with strong winds and currents didn't feel solid like the home she'd grown up in, and she was still getting used to living on water.

A video from Finley's first birthday started playing. She sat in her high chair, and their mother was placing a small cake in front of a very chunky Finley. She plunged her fingers into the cake, and a wide grin brightened her chubby face.

"I thought this would be a good idea, but now..." A sob stole Finley's words.

Kennedy put an arm around her sister and held her close as tears rolled down her cheeks too. "Maybe we should hold off before watching more of these."

Finley punched the remote button, blackening the screen, and shot to her feet. "I need some air."

"We could sit on the deck."

"I need to head home and run this off." She started for the door to the street.

"Okay." Kennedy knew running was the way her sister often dealt with stress. As long as her sister was dealing with stress, maybe Kennedy could help. "I was wondering if you'd be willing to take Oreo."

"Like adopt her?"

Kennedy nodded. "I'm working so many hours while I'm here, leaving her alone a lot of the time."

"She's used to it from Mom working so much."

"Maybe, but I think she's really lonely. And when I go back home, I'm not around much either. Plus I travel a lot so it wouldn't be fair to Oreo. And if you took her, you could snuggle. Maybe that would give you some comfort."

Finley looked at the cat curled in a ball on the sofa, her white paws covering her cute white nose as she slept.

Kennedy didn't want to give up the sweet cat, but if Oreo could help Finley, Kennedy was all for it. "How about trying it for a few days, and if it doesn't work, you can bring her back."

"Okay, but don't get your hopes up."

"Let me get her things together for you." Kennedy raced around the house gathering toys, a bed, food, and dishes. She scooped the litter box so it was fresh for Finley. "Go ahead and take this stuff to your car, and I'll get Oreo into her carrier."

Finley picked up the bags and marched out the door.

Kennedy let out a long sigh. Things shouldn't be this hard between sisters, and she really did hope the cat would bring Finley comfort and allow her to let go of her grief. Maybe then she could consider how important it was for Kennedy to look into their mom's death.

"Come on, sweetie." Kennedy scooped Oreo up and took her soft purring body to the carrier. The precious kitty didn't even fight going into it, just turned and looked up at Kennedy with big, sad eyes, tugging at Kennedy's already raw emotions.

Finley returned, her expression tight, and picked up the carrier. "I'll let you know how it goes."

"Call me later today, okay?" Kennedy asked. "I want to make sure you're all right."

"Sure." Her sister spun and left, leaving the door open behind her.

Finley was still upset. The last thing Kennedy wanted. She could hardly fathom having lost both of their parents within three years of each other. She needed her sister right now. Desperately.

Kennedy closed and locked the door to keep out the racing wind, then paced the room. She stopped at the patio door to look at the gray skies. Rain was rare in the Willamette Valley in late August, but not unheard of, and she'd love to stand by the window and watch, but Finley spurred Kennedy's need to look through their mom's things again. She'd searched this place a dozen or so times to no avail. She was missing something. She was sure of it.

She climbed the spiral staircase to her mother's bedroom. Her floral perfume still lingered in the room. Kennedy opened a drawer and riffled through the clothing.

Tears wet her eyes again, and she blinked, trying to keep them at bay. Such an invasion of privacy to paw through the belongings of the woman who'd raised and cared for Kennedy every day of her life. She'd been an amazing and supportive mother. Always sacrificing to put Kennedy's and Finley's needs first.

Kennedy shoved the drawer closed. She couldn't do this now, not after arguing with Finley. Kennedy should have been more understanding and supportive of her sister. As the older sister, Kennedy should do everything in her power to take over for and emulate their mother and be sure Finley was okay.

"Oh, sis," Kennedy whispered as the tears finally came. She tumbled onto the plush bed, grabbing a pillow with her mother's lingering scent and curled around the soft fabric. "I'll do better next time. I promise."

Hugging her knees, she cried until her head ached and she could no longer keep her eyes open. An image of Erik Byrd came to mind, and her brain floated into college memories and thoughts of the man she once thought she would spend her life beside. Until her father's news ruined that.

She sighed, and sleep beckoned. Her eyelids grew heavy, and she drifted off.

Kennedy dreamed of trying to save her mother from a faceless fiend and woke with a start. Daylight had faded to dark. A shaft of moonlight pierced the open curtains, flapping uncontrollably in the brisk wind and highlighting the familiar bed, dresser, and floral wallpaper.

She was in her mother's bedroom.

A scraping sound on the first floor grabbed her attention.

What was that? Couldn't be Oreo.

Just water lapping on the deck, right? Or the wind? Maybe Finley had come back.

Or was it more?

Listen to her. Thinking something was going on when it was just the creaking and groaning of the home. She'd heard it plenty of times in the three weeks since she'd been staying here. She hadn't wanted to live here, and she'd started out bunking with Finley, but they hadn't been able to get along enough to share her place.

Kennedy closed the window against the threatening rain, and her stomach grumbled. She headed for the stairs. The top step squeaked under her weight.

A figure cloaked in shadows spun in the family room to look at her, the person's hand resting on the drawer handle for the sofa table.

"Finley?" Kennedy asked.

"What the heck?" The man ground out the words between clenched teeth then growled. A deep male growl, and stepped out of the shadows.

Not Finley. A big burly guy with a mask over his face and a stocking cap on his head. He was dressed in a green T-shirt and camouflage pants, and his eyes bored into Kennedy.

She glanced at the table holding her purse and gun. Her phone lay silently next to it. She couldn't access either item.

The man marched toward her, drawing a gun on the way.

A gun! Ohmygoodness. Ohmygoodness.

Her throat closed. She couldn't speak.

Think. Act. Do something.

She bolted back into the bedroom and twisted the lock, but it wouldn't hold him for long.

The dresser.

She rushed across the room and pushed it toward the door.

The door shook. The handle rattled.

Her heart raced. Nearly burst.

A thump sounded against the door.

He was trying to break it down.

She couldn't possibly get the dresser over there before he broke down the door. The only way out was the small patio. She bolted for the sliding door and flung it open. On the patio, she looked around for something to grab. Anything. To lower herself to the river-level deck and escape the gunman.

Nothing. Nothing at all. She searched her neighbors' properties, looking for lights. For help. Darkness greeted her. Why was no one home?

No. No. Not tonight.

She had no hope other than to leap into the water. Then she could hide near the small ski boat moored at the deck. Hopefully, the intruder wouldn't see her and think she'd succumbed to the current and cold water.

She climbed onto the rail. Issued a silent prayer. And leapt.

The water enveloped her body. Cold and breath stealing, She clamped her lips closed to resist gasping.

She got her bearings and swam toward the boat. She slid between the slippery fiberglass and the deck, the water roiling under her.

The intruder raced out the bedroom onto the upper deck, his solid footsteps sounding in the night. He remained in the shadows, but she knew he was looking for her. She wished she could see his face. How she wished that.

She tried not to move—not a fraction of an inch—but her body shivered.

Please go away. Please.

His feet pounded over the deck, heading back to the house.

Now! She had to move now before he got down the stairs and out to her location.

She tried to scoot free but couldn't move. The boat had shifted in the current and wind, pinning her against the dock.

She shoved against it, the fiberglass cold under her already chilly hands. The boat bounced up and down, splashing water, but didn't move away from the dock.

No. No. This couldn't be happening.

Footsteps sounded nearby. Feet came into view. Big feet wearing military style boots. She caught a glimpse of a crooked nose through the mask and a narrow face.

He gripped his gun with confidence as if trained to use it. No. Not just trained. Experienced.

His boots came closer, looking elephant-sized in her eyes.

She slid further under the boat.

Water lapped at her mouth. Her nose.

Please, don't let him find me. Please. Please. Please.

2

Erik was a glutton for punishment. Otherwise why would he
be in his truck headed to Kennedy's floating home? So she
could rip his heart out again? Probably, and unless he liked
pain, which he didn't think he did, this was a stupid move.

And yet...

He lifted his foot from the gas pedal and whipped into
the marina parking lot, holding tight to the wheel in the
strong wind. Maybe he should turn around. Ignore Finley's
phone call. Sure, Kennedy was struggling—burning out as
she tried to prove her mother's death was foul play, but that
wasn't life threatening. It wasn't as if Kennedy had any proof
that her mother had been murdered and the killer had
Kennedy in his sights. She didn't need his protection.

He let out a long breath and took another as he ignored
his good sense and pulled into a parking spot near a foot-
bridge leading down to a long line of floating homes. He got
out and clasped the steel railings on the bridge that were
warm in the night, and the moon above had broken through
heavy clouds. Stars sparkled in another nearby clearing. A
magnificent August night.

The vibrant blue, white, and orange homes shone

brightly, the river below angry from the approaching storm. Floating homes. He'd always called them houseboats, but he'd since learned that these homes didn't fit the term. A houseboat was a live-aboard boat with a motor and could navigate bodies of water. Floating homes were homes built on floats, moored to a semi-permanent location, and had to be moved with another vessel.

A man dressed in an army green T-shirt, camouflage pants, and boots darted onto the walking bridge. Head down, he slammed into Erik, glanced up, and kept going.

"Watch it!" Erik snapped and turned to follow the guy's progress as he raced across the parking lot and disappeared in the line of trees abutting the highway.

People jogged at all times of the day, but this guy wasn't dressed for jogging, and with a storm approaching, running was foolishness. If he were a resident of the community, he would get into a car and drive off, not bolt into the scrub.

Kennedy! Was she okay?

Erik charged toward her floating home, his heart pounding.

The lights were all out, the home illuminated only by the moon. Maybe she was asleep. Or maybe something had happened. He crossed the short gangway to the house, quickly adjusting to the subtle movements below his feet.

The front door stood open, heavy pry marks on the jamb.

A break-in. Someone broke in. Was it the guy he'd rammed into in the parking lot?

Erik's gut cramped hard.

He drew his gun. He wanted to call out Kennedy's name, but he couldn't signal his approach to any intruder. He slipped past the small kitchen immediately inside the door and entered the attached living area. Her purse and phone sat on a table. So she *was* here.

He noted a spiral staircase to an upper level but moved past it to the back wall with a sliding door. The latch was closed and locked.

All clear. No one on the back deck.

He turned to the twisty metal staircase. He'd be an easy target on those stairs.

So what?

If Kennedy was in danger upstairs, he would move heaven and earth to get to her. Even after she hurt him more deeply than any person had ever done.

He cocked his head, listening. Only heard the river lapping against the deck and the wind howling outside. He started up the steps. The first one creaked.

Father, please protect me. Protect Kennedy too.

Gun raised, he wound slowly up, his breath shallow, his heart thudding. Step by step. Up higher. One by one. He popped his head above the landing and peered down a hallway. No movement. He quickly took the last few steps.

Slow down. Be careful. You can't help her if you're dead.

He emerged onto the second floor. The first bedroom door stood partially open. He pressed on it. The wood slammed into a dresser someone had shoved almost all the way in front of it. Almost, but not enough.

Had Kennedy been trying to keep an intruder out? Had he gotten in and killed her?

No. Oh no. Please.

Heart in his throat, he entered. His breath left him at what he might find on the other side of the bed.

Fighting for air now, he eased forward. Glanced around the bed. No one. But the patio door was wide open.

He stepped onto the small deck. No sign of Kennedy.

He started to return to the bedroom but heard whimpering.

"Kennedy?" he called out. "It's Erik."

He stepped closer to where the sound had originated.

"Erik Byrd," he added in case she'd forgotten all about him.

"Erik. Oh, thank God. Is he gone?" Her words came out between chattering teeth. "The intruder?"

His heart swelled at hearing her voice. "There's no one here. I'm coming."

"I jumped," she said, her unsteady voice setting a blazing fire of anger in Erik's gut. "Hid. Got stuck and can't move. Too much pain. Oh, please hurry. Down here. So cold."

He bolted for the stairs, swallowing choice words as he tried to maneuver the confounded circular thing in a hurry. River temps at this time of year would be in the sixties, too cold for a swimmer not wearing a wetsuit. He had to move.

At the bottom, he flew across the room but paused at the door. He was ready to leap into the water but took a moment to shed his boots and some clothing. Especially his over-shirt, which he wore to conceal his gun. The suspect bumping into him could've left touch DNA on the fabric that they could use to identify this creep.

Erik charged across the deck in his bare feet, anger burning like a hot coal in his gut. No, Kennedy didn't need to see that. She was already frightened enough. He dug up the professional protector mode that he used on the job to keep his cool.

"Where are you, honey?" He shone his phone's flashlight ahead at the side of the deck where he'd thought her voice had sounded.

"Here. I'm here."

He fought the wind to swing right and kneel, searching with the flashlight beam between the deck and a small ski boat, where the water beat against the deck. Near the bow, Kennedy's large brown eyes locked on his. Her disheveled and shivering state, from cold or maybe fear, hit him like a fist grabbing his heart and squeezing.

"I'm here," he said, doing his very best to keep anger and pain from his.

He ran the light over the area, looking for the best way to free her quickly. "I'll untie the boat and then hoist you up. If I can't do it from the deck, I'll get in the water and hold onto you so you can pull up on the deck."

"Thank you." She sounded so forlorn it deepened the ache in his chest.

He pocketed his phone and released the closest mooring line, then gave the boat a shove with his foot and held it out against the choppy river waves.

Kennedy scooted out of the way. "I'm free. Oh, thank you." She shook her head. "I don't know how I got stuck, but I wasn't thinking clearly after the guy pulled a gun and came after me."

"He was carrying?" Erik heard his high-pitched words echo down the river. "That changes everything."

"We should call the police," she said.

"Getting you out of the cold water's top priority." He leaned over the edge, the wind beating against him. "Grab onto me, and I'll pull you up."

She raised her arms, and icy fingers clamped onto his shoulders. His anger over her suffering doubled. "Ready?"

"Yeah." The word carried a heaviness that reminded him of his heart the day of their senior year of college when, after two years of what he thought was blissful togetherness, she told him she didn't want to be with him anymore.

He raised her up until their bodies connected. He held her longer than was necessary, taking in a long draw of her coconut scent that hadn't changed over the years. She didn't try to break free.

Oh, man. To have her in his arms again. Pure joy. And heartache. She wasn't his anymore.

Would never be.

Face facts, man. Years had passed. Six years. And his reaction said he wasn't over her. He could resume their relationship right now. If...if she hadn't left him with no explanation. No reason. Just good-bye and a backward glance that left him wondering all those years. But that wasn't all. His latest girlfriend had cheated on him. Two strikes and he wasn't going for the third one. He couldn't trust a woman again. Never again.

He eased away from Kennedy before he did or said something he regretted. "We need to get you inside and into a hot shower and dry clothes."

She gave a sharp nod, but behind her eyes he saw turmoil. From the hug? From the attack? Likely the attack, as she was the one who broke things off in the past. She was the one who didn't want him. Pure and simple. He had to remember that.

"Thank you for coming." A tentative smile crossed her lips, and she gently touched his cheek. "For the rescue. I don't know why you're here, but thank you."

Her soft touch set a fire burning inside of him. He backed away and secured the boat. "Finley called me."

Kennedy frowned. "She shouldn't have."

Right. Kennedy doesn't want me here. "Let's go in and talk about it once you're warm."

She went in through the patio door and straight to the stairway. He followed but stopped in the family room.

"While you change, I'll get the police looking for the intruder." He held up his phone. "Did you get a good look at him?"

She shook her head. "I can give you a few things though. Big guy. Six feet plus. Maybe two-twenty. Big army boots and camo pants. His face was in the shadows, but I did see a crooked nose and a long face."

Like the guy he ran into in the lot. "I'll call it in and stay until an officer arrives."

She looked over her shoulder. "You don't have to stay. I'm—"

"I know you don't want to have anything to do with me, but the guy was carrying, and I'm not leaving you alone in case he comes back. So you'll just have to deal with me being here." His words came across as harsh, but come on. She was hurting him all over again.

"I didn't mean it that way." She grabbed a thick strand of wet hair and twisted it around her finger, something stress always had her doing. "Not at all. I just didn't want to waste your time."

Could he believe that? She seemed earnest enough. "Guess I'm a little amped up on adrenaline." Add some heart-wrenching memories of rejection to his wild emotions, and he was cranky.

"I'll be right back." She climbed the stairs and, though he should look away, he watched the fluidity in her body evident under the soggy pale blue knit pants and top clinging to her curves. She'd always worked out to stay in shape for underwater diving, and her sleek form attested to her keeping up the work in the years since he'd seen her.

She disappeared up the stairs.

He quickly dialed the Portland Police Bureau dispatch. Most people would call 911, but as a former PPB officer, he knew to reserve the 911 board for real emergencies. He'd cleared the house, and Kennedy was unharmed. There was no emergency here. Other than his need to put his feelings for her back into the folder where he'd stowed them years before—and do it before she came back down those stairs. He wasn't going to go crazy over her again. No way.

Erik resisted firing off a smart comment at Sarge with the Portland Police Bureau and ended the call. It wasn't sarge's fault that they didn't have the necessary resources to investigate every break-in that occurred in the city. So Erik would be on his own, and he phoned his sister, the forensic expert at the Veritas Center, a highly rated and respected local lab.

"Hey, baby brother," she answered cheerfully.

Erik nearly groaned at her use of the word baby, but she was a new mom and had babies on the brain, so he would cut her some slack. He described the situation.

"Kennedy?" Sierra's voice rose, and Erik could imagine his sister lurching to her feet at the news. "Seriously? And how are you doing with seeing her again?"

"I'm fine."

"Uh-huh. Sure. Then why do you sound like a strangled cat?"

"What?" He laughed at the vision.

"There's a tightness in your voice. Maybe others wouldn't hear it, but then I'm not others. I'm your only sister and changed your diapers. Fed and burped you. So I know you, little brother. Know you well."

"Okay, then. Moving on. Can you send someone out here to process the place?"

"I'll do it."

"You're on maternity leave."

"Reed can handle Asher for the couple of hours it'll take to process a floating home."

"You don't have to do it."

"Are you kidding?" Sierra's voice rose. "Miss out on seeing Kennedy again? No way. Give me the address, and I'll be right over."

Erik knew better than to argue with his sister. Once her

mind was made up, disagreeing with her was like fighting with a bull, and he couldn't think of a time when he'd come out on top.

He shared the address and ended the call when footsteps above caught his attention, and he turned toward the stairway. Kennedy's feet, covered in thick slipper socks, appeared, and she descended slowly. She'd put on black sweatpants and an oversized hoodie with the FBI emblem on the chest. The sweet smell of her coconut shampoo drifted across the room.

"What?" she asked. "No police yet?"

"They don't have the resources to send someone out for a break-in. But Sarge will assign a detective if we can provide physical evidence." He met her gaze. "I should've asked before. Are you thinking the break-in is related to your mom's death?"

She nodded. "And I thought it might make them rethink their findings on her death. But then I shouldn't be surprised by the lack of response. Not after my years in law enforcement." She moved to the entryway table and grabbed her keys from her purse.

"Going somewhere?" he asked.

"I want to get going on finding that evidence, and my forensic supplies are in the trunk of my car."

"I called Sierra. She'll handle it."

Kennedy lifted her chin and locked eyes with him. "I'd rather do it myself."

He hadn't forgotten her stubborn streak, and he'd often found it cute. Not tonight. Not when the intruder could still be around. And he couldn't let her put her life in danger. "I get that you're like this super FBI forensic tech, but you're too close to this case. If this guy is arrested, we don't want the defense attorney to claim you tainted the evidence."

Her shoulders dropped. "You're right. But you need my

help. He tossed something into the water. I think it was the crowbar he used to break in. Diving isn't Sierra's forte, and I plan to go in after it."

"I don't know."

That cute chin rose even higher, and she crossed her arms. "You have any other underwater crime scene investigators in the area?"

"We could get someone from Clackamas County Sheriff's Dive/Rescue Team."

"Sure, they have divers, but none with the kind of experience I have. They can't afford anyone full-time. None of the agencies around here can. It would be auxiliary duty at best, so how qualified are they? I dive on a regular basis and have had years of experience doing the job."

She had a point. One Erik couldn't argue with, but he didn't know all the facts of criminal law either. If she collected this evidence, would that jeopardize the case? "We can't risk you blowing up this investigation because of your connection. We need to get some legal advice before you go hopping into that water."

"You must know some criminal lawyers we could call, right?"

"Malone Rice is our best bet. She's the sister of Sierra's husband, Reed. Malone specializes in helping teens and battered women, but she'll still know if this is a good move."

"Okay, give her a call then."

"Not until you tell me more about what's going on."

"No time to waste." She fisted hands on her hips. "The river's current could carry the tool downstream. I need to dive tonight so that doesn't happen."

"First you can bring me up to speed." He gestured at the couch.

Kennedy narrowed her eyes, drawing his attention to

her many freckles. He'd once spent hours tracing the invisible lines between them with his finger.

She suddenly shook her head and marched across the room. *Okay.* She would comply, but she clearly didn't like it. She flicked on the switch for a gas fireplace, and bright flames flared to life before she dropped onto the hearth and crossed her legs. "Before I start, don't waste your time telling me I have no proof of my mom's murder. Gathering evidence on the job has been my life for years, and I understand that I have no proof. But I also know my mother. She wouldn't take too many pills on purpose or accidentally. She just wouldn't."

"Her death involved an overdose?" he asked.

Kennedy nodded. "She was otherwise pretty healthy, so they did an autopsy to determine cause of death. The tox screen revealed a very high level of blood pressure meds in her system that caused a heart attack."

"So she OD'd on blood pressure meds," he said, more to think about it than to state new information. Her mother had a Ph.D. in pharmaceutical science, so it was either a coincidence or ironic that she'd died from a drug overdose. "As a scientist, she would know what taking an excess of these meds would do."

"Yeah. And that's why they're not ruling out suicide." Kennedy clutched her arms around her waist, and tears wet her eyes.

He stepped closer, wanting to comfort her, but settled for perching on the arm of a nearby velvet sofa. "Finley said your mom was stressed."

"Stressed or not, she wouldn't make a big mistake like that. She's just like me. We're methodical. Organized. You know that, right? Could you see me making such a mistake?"

"Not the woman I once knew, but she's older now."

Kennedy dropped her foot to the floor with a solid thud that reverberated around the room. "She worked tough research problems every day without a hitch. She wasn't mentally diminished. I know. I reviewed her work after I came back to Portland to finish her project. Everything was perfect. And before you say she had an assistant to do it for her, she'd worked alone in the lab ever since I went back to school for forensic science. She did have a part-time administrative assistant. Nora Rayburn. I laid her off after my mom died because I like to handle everything myself."

He wouldn't argue about her mother's mental abilities. Just as important to him was that Kennedy had said she was here to finish the project.

"Did you leave the FBI?" he asked.

"They've given me leave for as long as I need."

Surprising. "That's very generous. Especially for a federal agency."

"Qualified underwater crime scene investigators with my years of experience are hard to find."

Erik understood the special skills she brought to a forensic unit. She'd paired her love of diving with her work. He'd never seen her do a forensic dive, but they'd dived together many times, and he knew she would be good at the job and enjoy it. But for now, she was living here, not in Quantico, Virginia, where the FBI's main lab was located.

Here. Portland. His town. Where he'd thought they'd both live to a ripe old age together. But even if he could trust her not to hurt him again and they rekindled their relationship, she would finish this project and go back to her life in Virginia. No point in even thinking about it.

"So who do you think would want to kill your mother?" he asked.

"Someone who wanted to stop her research," Kennedy said. "She also taught chemistry part-time at PSU, but I honestly can't see anyone she worked with wanting to kill her. Or the students. And her fellow professors loved her. At least that's what they said when I attended a small memorial luncheon they had for her. It was really touching."

"What project was she working on when she died?" he asked.

"She was developing a first-of-its-kind technique to quickly yet accurately characterize illegal pharmaceuticals. And she was also pioneering a way to give law enforcement officers real-time access to this information."

In Erik's patrol days, he'd seen the harmful and even fatal effects of illegal or counterfeit medicines. These fake pills contained the right active ingredient, but it was often at the wrong dosage.

"Sounds like she was doing some important work," he said.

Kennedy nodded. "Illegally dispensed meds need immediate testing when they're discovered. And, if there's a serious threat to public health, there needs to be a method for rapid early warnings. She was also improving the process of collecting information about the product's manufacturing and supply chain. That's vital not only for law enforcement investigations but for criminal prosecutions too."

"Okay, so that's got to tick off a lot of lowlifes who manufacture and sell counterfeit drugs," he said. "Have you been looking into that?"

"As much as I can with my limited resources. I've called in a few favors in D.C., but I still don't know who the key players are in the area."

"This guy tonight. You think he's trying to stop you too?"

She shrugged as if the intruder didn't much matter, but the fear lingered in those expressive eyes. "He was opening a drawer when I first saw him, so maybe he was looking for something."

Erik had to fight the anger still smoldering in his gut to keep his tone even. "Would you normally be here at this time of night?"

She shook her head. "I always work at the lab until at least nine and most days later. But Finley wanted to meet with me, so I came home early. I planned to go back to the lab, but my conversation didn't go well with Finley and I ended up falling asleep on my mom's bed."

Pain flooded Kennedy's eyes, another thing to ignore or he might do or say something far too personal. "We have to imagine the worst case scenario, which is that this creep wanted to kill you. Do you know if the marina has security cameras?"

"Not that I've seen."

"If not, security here isn't top priority." He stood and paced a few steps, then locked gazes with her. "And in that case, because of the break-in, I want to offer our agency's protection services. We'll also help you investigate your mother's death."

She didn't speak for the longest moment. "That...us together. It's not a good—"

"Idea? Yeah, I get that." He didn't like hearing her echoing his feelings, but he agreed. "We shouldn't spend time together. Not with our history. But I'm not going to let you fend for yourself when there could be a killer out there turning his sights on you. So either hire a bodyguard or let us do this for you."

She watched him, her gaze mining for something, as she twisted her hands on her lap. "I'm on unpaid leave. I can't afford a bodyguard or your services."

"Then we'll do it for free."

"I can't let—"

"You owe me, Kennedy. For the way you dumped me. So make it up to me by letting me make sure no one hurts you." He knew that was a low blow, but if it was the only way to get her on board with protective services, he wasn't beyond striking.

"I...I just don't know."

"If you won't do it for yourself, how about doing it so you can keep working on the project? And if your mom really *was* murdered, then you can find who did it."

"Okay." She got up. "But we have to agree to keep this professional."

"Trust me," he said, not letting his gaze waver from the bottomless brown eyes that always made his heart flip-flop. "I'll be the perfect example of professionalism."

She held out her hand. "Then we have a deal."

He clasped her hand, and despite the lingering coldness, his heart fired with a million little sparks.

Right. Professional. Could he do it? Time would tell.

He let go, almost hurling her hand away. "I'll get Malone on the phone."

He dug out his cell and took a few steps back, as if moving away from Kennedy would change the unexpected feelings.

Thankfully, Malone answered, and Erik explained the situation.

"And you said the police don't want to send anyone out for the break-in?" Malone asked.

"If Sierra finds something, they'll take an interest. If not, we're on our own. Either way, if we wait to dive for any evidence, we risk it washing downstream. So the dive needs to happen tonight."

"Then exigent circumstances would prevail, and it should be fine. If you could have someone record the dive, that would be great."

"I'll ask Kennedy about that."

Hearing her name, Kennedy eyed him.

"Let me know if I can help in any other way." Malone ended the call.

Erik shoved his phone into his pocket and joined Kennedy to share the conversation. "So what do you think? Could I dive with you and record it?"

"Not necessary," she said quickly. "Not if we can find another forensic diver to be my backup."

"Backup?" He studied her. "But you said no one was good enough to do this dive."

"Not as the lead diver, but as a backup, it'll be fine. We just need to get someone out here in a hurry."

"Why do you need a backup?"

"Forensic dives are just like your foot grid searches. A lead diver holds onto a rope and searches in a straight line to a designated point. Then the backup diver will do a secondary search to see if I missed anything. Which I never have, but this is too important to risk not doing a secondary search."

Erik nodded his understanding. "Brendan used to be a deputy for Clackamas County. He might know someone on their team who'll volunteer to work with you."

"Great. I've got gear in my mom's storage closet outside. So get Brendan on the phone, but you should know." She fisted her hands on her waist. "Backup diver or not, I'm going in tonight."

3

Thankfully, Brendan's buddy Charlie was on the way to dive with Kennedy. She hated to admit it, but Finley's call to Erik was fortunate in so many ways. They now had forensics on site and soon would have that second diver. And she was safe under Erik's protective oversight.

She glanced out the window and spotted him striding toward the Veritas Center forensic van in the parking lot, where he'd gone to help Sierra carry in her supplies, the wind battering his shirt. Normally, Kennedy would be fired up to take a look inside the van, but she needed a moment alone to gather her thoughts before the dive.

Not only to get over connecting with Erik after so many years, but now Sierra too. In the two years Kennedy had dated Erik, she'd spent a lot of time with his family, and she'd come to love all of them. Sure, the five guys could be a lot to take in at once, but they each had generous hearts underneath their harder exteriors. His dad, Russ, was super supportive, and his mom, Peggy, was the kind of mom every kid dreamed of—except for when she interfered a little too much. She would've had Erik and Kennedy married after only a few months of them being together. Kennedy couldn't even imagine how Peggy would go mother bear on Kennedy if they ever ran into each other.

She shuddered at the thought. Or maybe at the thought of an intruder. Something she was trying hard to pack away and not think about. She was almost thankful for the turmoil over being here with Erik and Sierra as it gave her something else to think about. Almost.

Erik started toward the house carrying Klieg lights under his arm, Sierra behind him with toolkits in each hand. If truth be told, Kennedy's heart was overly happy to see him again. Beyond what she could've predicted. She wasn't over him. She should've realized that in all those years when her relationships went nowhere. She'd compared the men to Erik, and they never measured up. She'd figured it was because they lacked many of his character traits. She hadn't realized they didn't measure up because they weren't him.

He reached her gangway, and she stepped back from the window before he caught her watching him. She twisted her hands together and took several deep breaths.

"Where do you want the lights?" Erik looked back at Sierra, who hadn't changed much over the years.

"I'll want to start with the front door, so just outside." Sierra was a female version of Erik with dishwater blond hair. Where Erik kept his hair in a buzz cut, she had bangs, and her hair fell straight below her shoulders. She was nearly six feet tall and still slender, though she'd filled out some and was more curvaceous. Kennedy noted a wedding ring on Sierra's finger as she dug her disposable gloves from her pocket and stepped into the room.

Sierra's gaze went to Kennedy, and Kennedy waited for a look of disdain, but Sierra cocked her head and studied her. "Long time no see. How many years has it been?"

"Six." Kennedy tried not to gawk at Sierra for not sounding mad over the way Kennedy had dumped Erik.

Sierra tipped her head at her brother. "This bozo never told us what happened with the two of you. I won't pry, but it's good to see you again."

She shot Erik a look and found him carefully watching her. Color her surprised. It almost sounded as if Sierra blamed Erik for the breakup. Had he not said anything because he was protecting her reputation with his family? Or was it just too painful to talk about?

"Let's just get the forensics going," he said.

Sierra wrinkled her nose at him then looked back at Kennedy. "I hear you're a hotshot FBI tech."

Kennedy chuckled at the face Sierra was making. "Not sure about hotshot, but I am a fed. At least a fed on leave."

"I'm sorry to hear about your mom." Sierra rested a hand on Kennedy's arm and met her gaze.

A pang of guilt tightened Kennedy's stomach. This wonderful woman didn't know the truth of what Kennedy had done to her brother. If she did, she wouldn't be so kind. Not that she would be rude. None of the Byrds would do that. Their parents taught them impeccable manners, but Sierra would likely give Kennedy the cold shoulder.

"And you think this break-in is related to her death?" Sierra asked, leaving her hand on Kennedy's arm.

"I'm not sure, but I don't see why else someone would break in here."

Sierra squeezed Kennedy's arm. "Then you have the complete services of the Veritas Center at your disposal. No charge." She snapped on the gloves. "Feel free to watch, but you know you can't help, right?"

Kennedy nodded. "And I promise not to backseat quarterback."

Sierra smiled and stepped into the beams of light from the portable units Erik had turned on.

"How did Reed feel about you coming out tonight?" Erik asked.

"He's fine with it. As long as I'm home for the next feeding." Sierra looked at Kennedy. "Reed's my husband, and we have a two-month-old son, Asher. The new love of my life."

"Poor Reed's been replaced already." Erik grinned.

Sierra laughed, and Erik joined her. His face, with its wide jaw sporting a thick close-cut beard, lost the tension and lit up. Kennedy's heart catapulted, and she couldn't look away from him.

He caught her watching, and his cheerful expression evaporated. He turned to Sierra. "What do you need me to do?"

She got out her camera. "Move out of my camera range."

Of course, Sierra would start with scene photos. Kennedy should've thought of that and gotten out of the way, but she'd been too flustered by the armed intruder to think logically. Was still flustered and needed some air. She turned and nearly fled onto the back deck, sucking in air and holding onto the railing.

The river lapped against the floats, the sound soothing. The cloud cover had evaporated, letting the temperature drop, and the sky sparkled with a million little stars around the half moon.

If life had been easy right now, she would stay here for hours, admiring the night. The wind whipped across the deck, and the smell of rain freshened the air, but stars had broken through the clouds. The rhythmic sound of flowing water and the starry night could be so romantic with Erik, whose heavy footfalls sounded behind her.

"You can't be out here." His deep voice thundered through her. "It's not safe."

All thoughts of romance vanished, and she spun. "You don't think he's here, do you?"

"We can never be too safe." He gestured for her to precede him back inside.

She didn't argue but strode into the living room, staying just inside the door to keep out of Sierra's photos.

He slid the door closed and stood next to her, and she caught his distinct scent. She knew it so well. "I never thought your mom would choose to live on a boat."

Kennedy looked out the window. "After Dad died, she needed a change."

"I'm so sorry, hon—" He curled his fingers to his palms. "I can't imagine losing one parent, let alone both of them."

Tears burned for release, but she controlled them. She wouldn't add crying in front of Erik and Sierra to her night. "It's been tough—harder for thinking my mom was murdered."

"About that." He sounded reluctant. "Just in case you're right and she was murdered, I need you to leave your phone here so you can't be tracked when you leave. We'll give you a virtually untraceable phone to use. So if you need to export information, we should do that now."

She picked up her phone, but paused. If she gave it to him, she would be handing over a lifeline, and it put a hitch in her heart. When had she become so dependent on this device?

"Trust me," Erik said. "I get your hesitancy. My whole life is on my phone. But if you end up needing a new one, we can restore your information."

Would it be the same? No fun blue cover with periodic elements on it. Maybe not personalized with her ringtones. Might not include her mother's last few messages.

No. No. Kennedy couldn't lose those. "My mom's messages. Will they transfer too?"

He nodded. "Since you have an iPhone, I'll just back it up to the cloud, and we can download everything to a new device."

"I'm not losing this." She took off the cover. "I also left my backpack at the lab and need to pick it up."

"I don't want you going over there right now. Give me the keys, and I'll have one of my brothers get it."

She thought to argue, but why? Anyone could pick up the backpack, and if it made Erik feel better, then she would let him have his way. She handed her phone to him, working hard not to touch him.

He cupped it tightly. "I'll get to work on exporting the data while you pack."

"Pack?"

He planted his feet in a stubborn stance she recognized. "I've had a chance to think it over, and I won't let you stay here. It's too dangerous. You can stay at my condo. Much safer."

She flashed her gaze up to his. "Not going to happen. I've started carrying since I met you, and I'll be fine here."

"Carrying?" He eyed her. "What prompted that?"

"My job. I see the bad things that can happen." She had to fight off a shudder to keep from raising his concerns even more and maybe from letting her worry ramp back up too.

He kept his focus pinned to her. "You didn't have your gun tonight."

"It was here in my purse." She held up her hands. "I know. I know. Fat lot of good it did me down here. But when I went upstairs, I didn't think... I didn't plan to fall asleep. I know better now, and I'll be extra sure I have my gun with me at all times."

"I still don't like you being on your own here. I checked things out when I went to help Sierra. No security cameras. Zero. So even more of a reason not to stay here. And if you're worried you'll have to put up with me at my condo, don't be. I'll bunk with one of my brothers, and you can have my place all to yourself."

She shook her head more vehemently than needed, and she didn't like that either. She was over him, right? She shouldn't let seeing him again impact her so much. She swallowed to level her emotions. "I can't put you out of your place. Not on top of the protection and investigative services you're providing."

He took in a long breath, and she waited for it to whoosh out, but he let the air out in slow frustration. "What do you think protection services are?"

"I don't...well... I didn't really think about it."

"Then let me tell you. One of us will be with you twenty-four/seven until this guy is caught. Except at the condo. Security for our building is top-notch, so you should be fine on your own there."

"But I—we can't." She gestured between them and lowered her voice so Sierra couldn't hear. "Can't be together that much."

"Why not?"

"Our history. It's bound to be uncomfortable."

Another breath, this one held before blowing out in hurricane force. "A little discomfort is worth it to make sure you're safe."

"But I—"

"As far as putting me out," he said, "don't think that way. You'll actually be doing us a favor. We won't need as many guys on your detail while you're at Veritas."

"At Veritas?" Trying to figure out what the lab had to do with this, she blinked a few times. "I don't understand."

"Right, you wouldn't know. Veritas has two six-story towers. Sierra wrangled us a good deal on office space in the lab tower, and the other tower holds condos where we all live."

"All of the Byrds?" She gaped at him. Not because of the living quarters, but because it was actually sinking in that using their agency meant she would be seeing his brothers again too.

"Not my mom and dad. Our family is close, but that would just be weird." He grinned.

Despite her unease, she felt the corners of her mouth crooking up. No. She wouldn't get drawn in by his presence. She'd never been able to stay mad at him. Never. One look at those honey brown eyes, which could one minute bore to the center of her very being and the next minute dance with delight, and her anger evaporated.

"I'll go pack a bag while I wait for the backup diver." She strode toward the staircase.

"Put on booties so you don't disturb any evidence as you head up," Sierra called out but didn't look up from the doorway.

Kennedy should have thought of that. She was a professional, just like Sierra. But then Sierra hadn't just had an armed man chase her and wasn't captivated by the very attractive ex-boyfriend in the room.

Get a grip, girl, she told herself as she slipped on the paper booties. *Or before this is all over, you'll be in for a world of hurt.*

In the family room two hours later, Kennedy inspected the O-rings on the oxygen tank to make sure it formed a tight seal with the regulator, then connected her buoyancy compensator, which looked like a bulky vest, to the tank, making sure to pull the tank straps tight. It would be easier to do the prep work for her dive on the deck, but Erik had asked her to stay inside for as long as possible.

Not a big deal, really. Except his presence seemed to fill the room as he watched her every move, a longing expression on his face. He was fully trained in diving. It was something they'd enjoyed doing together. She had enough gear for him to join her, but she didn't need the distraction. Of course, she wouldn't tell him that he distracted her. She wouldn't tell him that seeing him caused these unexpected feelings.

Professional. That's what they were. She just had to focus on her task.

She took the dust cap off the regulator and attached it, along with her low-pressure inflator and alternate air source.

He moved closer. "I wish you'd let me dive with you."

"No point. Besides we'll have our cameras on and communications devices in the face masks so you can watch and listen in." She tested the air pressure. Good. She had a full tank of air.

Before she could reach the valve, he twisted it all the way open to test the regulator. Their hands brushed, and she snatched hers back.

Great. Way to hide your emotions from the guy.

"Would you mind checking to see if Charlie is ready to dive?" she asked, hoping to get Erik out of the room.

"No problem." He met and held her gaze. "Don't mind leaving now that I saw with my own eyes that your equipment is working fine."

She was an independent woman. More independent than a lot of people, but her heart warmed under his concern. He'd always been protective and caring, but he never took it to extreme measures. Still, diving could be dangerous if she didn't carefully check the equipment. She hated to admit it, but she enjoyed the fact that he'd wanted to be sure of her safety.

She went back to her buoyancy compensator while he walked out the door. She loaded the BC pockets with tools and evidence containers that she might need. She also added a folding tactical knife. Never knew what she might run into down there.

Perfect. She was ready. Pumped to be diving again, even if it was thanks to a less than positive situation, she grabbed lights, a mask, and fins and headed out to the deck.

Charlie, a tall lanky guy, stood waiting. "Ready?"

She nodded. "You're good with the plan?"

"I am." He put a headlamp on and slid into the water.

She glanced at Erik, whose eyes were narrowed.

"Relax," she said. "We'll be fine."

"I know, it's just..." He shrugged and gritted his teeth.

She didn't want him to finish that sentence, as it seemed as if his feelings for her might not be dead either, and they didn't need that kind of distraction.

She slipped into the river and swam out to the first rope just as big drops of rain hit the water. She followed the rope down and was soon surrounded by murky darkness. Some people would freak out in such a claustrophobic situation, but she found it comforting. All the troubles and sounds of the outside world disappeared.

"Everything okay?" Erik's deep voice sounded in her ear.

Right. The outside world was still there. "Good, but it's very hard to see."

"At the bottom yet?"

She adjusted her headlamp. "I'm descending slowly so I don't disturb the silt and further obscure my vision."

"Keep me updated, okay?"

"Roger that." She reached the bottom and began scouring with her hand, feeling for any object.

She and Charlie would each hold onto the rope while sifting through a foot of silt, mud, trash, and foliage. They'd marked off a small section where she'd seen the item go into the water, and they would move back and forth in straight lines—like mowing a lawn—and as soon as she completed a section, Charlie would search the same area. If they didn't locate the item, they would expand downstream.

She shone her light ahead and swept her hand through the silt while barely kicking forward into the darkness and gliding her other hand along the rope until she reached the end. She didn't know the exact time it took, but she guessed about thirty minutes.

"Man, it's dark," Erik said. "I can't see a thing on the camera."

"Yeah, totally going by feel here." She swam to the second rope. "You're good to go on one, Charlie."

"Roger that."

She started down the second rope, and they passed the midway mark, but she didn't look up as she didn't want to move her light. Her gloved fingers crept through the silt. Something sharp clamped onto her fingers.

She yelped in pain.

"What is it?" Erik asked.

She tried to free herself from the radiating pain that had her gritting her teeth. "Something on my... Charlie, help!"

He swam over to her.

"Snapping turtle," she said, finally making out the shape in the cloudy waters. "Won't release."

"Let me get behind him and grab the shell," Charlie said.

Pain shot through Kennedy's hand, radiating up her arm. The turtle continued to hold its grip. This wasn't her first bite, and at least it was a common snapping turtle. Not like the alligator turtles in the south. They rarely sought a person out, but accidental strikes happened when they surprised a diver from where they hid in the sandy bottoms of fresh water.

Charlie grabbed the shell behind the turtle's head. His movement was enough to surprise the turtle, and it's mouth relaxed. She jerked her hand free.

"Let me move him well out of our way." Charlie swam away, holding the turtle at his side.

"Come on up, and I'll bandage your hand," Erik said.

"No need. I can finish."

"You'll need to have it looked at."

"Yeah," she said, thinking Erik was sounding like his mother, who would insist on the same thing. Her mother would too, if she were alive. Kennedy suddenly missed being part of such a big warm family. Missed having parents.

She'd been so sentimental since her mother died. But now wasn't the time for that. She needed to let it go and get back to work. Pain radiated through her hand, and she felt a bit lightheaded but swallowed hard and drew in some deep breaths to keep moving forward.

Nearing the end of the second rope, her hand connected with something metal. She lifted it up to her light, her hand throbbing with the exertion.

"Got it. It's a crowbar." Excitement of the find burned in her gut, maybe not as brightly as when she searched for a murder weapon that the killer warned that she'd never find. She might only be searching out a crowbar here, but this search was personal. This was for her mother.

4

Erik paced the dock, rain beating down on him. No point in looking at the video Kennedy and Charlie were sending up. Sure, it would be good documentation for court, but otherwise, he couldn't see a thing. He didn't know why having her cruising the bottom of the river bothered him, but it did. Not that she was in danger, other than from a turtle, and a bite on the hand was hardly life-threatening.

In the past, he'd never been super protective of her. Sure, when they were together, he felt responsible for keeping her safe, as most men did with the women in their lives, but he never let it get in his way or stop her from doing anything.

So what was going on tonight? Why the angst?

She surfaced, and he let out a long breath, then watched her swim toward him, the rain slicing into the river. The evidence bag was clutched in her uninjured hand. The minute she shed her dive suit and handed the crowbar over to Sierra, Erik would take her to the ER to get her hand assessed. Bites could easily become infected. He wouldn't let that happen.

"You still have a thing for her," Sierra said coming up behind him and resting a hand on his shoulder.

He thought to claim his lack of feelings for Kennedy but thought better as he turned to look at his sister, who now wore rain gear. Unlike him, she wasn't getting soaking wet. "No point in denying it, but I don't want Kennedy to know about it, so keep it between us."

"Oh, honey, sorry. You're transmitting your interest loud and clear, and she couldn't possibly miss it."

"Then I'll have to figure out a way to hide it."

"Good luck." Sierra tipped her head at the water. "Did they locate anything?"

"A crowbar." Erik's attention went back to Kennedy. "You done here?"

"Yes. I'll log the crowbar into evidence and take off."

"Can you process it for prints right away and get DNA samples off to Emory? For my shirt too?" The center's DNA expert was used to working late hours, and if not, once Emory learned this was personal to Erik, she would come back to the lab to get the samples running.

"I'll need to feed Asher first, but then, sure. Glad to. And I'll text Emory too."

Erik flashed a smile of thanks but moved across the deck when Kennedy set the crowbar on the edge. Charlie swam up behind her.

Sierra picked up the evidence bag. "I'll call you guys with the results."

"Thanks again for coming out." Kennedy tossed her fins onto the deck and climbed a ladder to the water-worn wood. "Mind if I tag along to watch you work. I'd love to see your lab."

"No problem."

"You need to have that hand looked at." Erik tried to reply without emotion but ended up sounding controlling and domineering.

"Good point. I'll do that." Kennedy flexed her injured

hand then looked at Sierra. "Can I come check in on you at the lab afterwards?"

"Perfect. That'll give me time to feed the baby." Sierra spun and gave Erik a pointed look before going into the house.

Terrific. He was being that open-book she claimed he was being. *Cool it.*

He gestured at the patio door. "We should get inside too."

Kennedy looked like she wanted to argue, probably because she was dripping wet, but she stepped ahead of him and stripped out of her wet suit and down to her compression shirt and neoprene shorts.

Charlie poked his head inside. "I'll head out around the outside so I don't get your floor all wet."

"No problem," she said. "As you can see, I'm already dripping everywhere and so is Erik."

Charlie ran his gaze over her, and Erik didn't like the interested look in the guy's eyes.

"Are you sticking around for a while or headed back to Quantico?" Charlie asked.

"I'll be here for a month or so."

Charlie cocked his head and studied her more deeply. "Maybe we could get together and do some recreational diving."

"Sounds great." She cast a beaming smile in his direction.

Erik nearly shouted at her to stop encouraging the guy, but she could encourage any guy she wanted to. Just not Erik. First, he didn't need any encouragement. Second, it was a bad idea overall. Even if he could start trusting women again, Kennedy would be leaving town as soon as she finished the lab project, and he was committed to his brothers and the business. And honestly, he loved living here with his family. Especially since he was now an uncle and would likely have more of his siblings' children to spoil in the near future.

"I've got your number from the callout," Kennedy said to Charlie. "I'll be in touch when this all settles down."

"Looking forward to it." That self-satisfied smile crept across his face again, grating on Erik.

Why couldn't the guy be an uggo? Why did he have to be so dang good-looking?

Charlie departed, and Kennedy looked at Erik. "Mind stowing my gear while I get changed?"

"No problem." He resisted demanding to see her hand up close.

She didn't need him turning into the mother she'd just lost. He didn't need that either. Though he had to admit with his mom, he'd seen enough mothering cast in his direction and could probably do a good job of it.

He carried the gear to a hose on the deck and washed everything with fresh water, then took it all to the outside storage closet. He hung her wetsuit on a special hanger, careful not to tear the neoprene. Her tank went on a shelf, and he hung the hoses to dry too. By the time he finished, she was downstairs wearing jeans and a body-hugging knit shirt in an emerald green that made her hair almost glow.

She tossed him a bath towel.

"Thanks. I washed everything off and stored it, then locked the closet," he told her before he made a huge mistake and complimented her on how well those jeans fit her curves.

"Thank you."

His focus went to the white gauze she'd wrapped around her hand. "Does it hurt much?"

"Yeah, but that's not going to stop me from finding my mom's killer. Nothing will."

And there it was. The thing he hadn't been able to put his finger on while she was diving. The thing that had him pacing the deck. The thing that he had to figure a way to work around or he might just fail her when she needed him most.

~

Kennedy flexed her hand in Erik's truck, cinnamon air freshener spicing up the air. Why she wanted to move her fingers, she didn't know. The wound hurt like crazy, and moving it only made it worse. Maybe she believed she deserved some pain. Perhaps as a consequence of hurting Erik. She'd always known she'd hurt him, but knowing it and seeing his pain were two different things.

Please help him to heal.

"Home sweet home," he said as he turned into the Veritas Center parking lot.

Kennedy had always wanted to tour the Veritas lab but with Sierra on staff, Kennedy had stayed away. How she hadn't heard about Nighthawk Security forming and officing out of the place was a small miracle with the way news traveled in law enforcement circles.

She was curious enough to drive by the building before, so even if Erik hadn't told her about the two towers gleaming in the moonlight, she would've known what to expect. They rose up into the night, two columns of hope for people seeking answers about parentage and relatives, and hope for law enforcement officers desperate for leads to close their investigations. A skybridge connected the towers at the top as did a building on the ground floor. But Erik didn't park in the lot out front. He wound his truck up the ramp to the sixth floor of the parking structure.

He got out without a word and opened the door to the

44

building by pressing his fingers on a biometric reader mounted outside the door, then took her down to the lobby to get a security pass before boarding the elevator again to join Sierra in her lab.

"You weren't kidding about security here," she said as he punched the button for the fourth floor where the trace evidence lab was located.

"The Veritas staff needs tight security to protect evidence," he said. "And also people who don't get the answers they were expecting with DNA can sometimes get out of hand."

"I can imagine."

"Just remember to wear the pass at all times and don't go anywhere in the building without one of us escorting you."

She nodded her understanding and they fell silent for the ride.

In the hallway, she glanced around, impressed with what she could see through lab windows. "I've always wanted to tour this place. We keep hearing people compare the labs here to ours, and you know we're the best."

He feigned an exaggerated gasp and turned to look at her. "Don't let anyone around here hear you say that." The playful grin she could hardly resist spread across his face again, and her heart somersaulted.

Great. She'd meant to waylay the lingering tension, and she had. At least outwardly, but not in her heart.

Not seeming at all affected by having her nearby, he led her to the back of the building, where a sign mounted on the wall read *Trace Evidence and Fingerprint Analysis.*

More fingertips pressed on a reader, and he opened the door then stood back. "After you."

She entered the spacious lab, the air tainted with a chemical smell despite what she knew had to be high-priced exhaust hoods. She stopped just inside the door to take a good look at Sierra's set up. The top-of-the-line equipment lining the walls and sitting on counters so fascinated Kennedy that she forgot all about the pain in her hand. She was surprised she wasn't drooling.

She shifted to take in the stainless steel lab tables filling the middle of the room, where techs wearing lab coats hunkered over them even at this time of night.

Sierra sat behind the table closest to the wall and waved them over. "Glad you could come by."

"Wow." Kennedy approached. "This place *is* as high tech as the FBI lab. I thought the gossip was exaggerated."

"Of course not." Sierra grinned, looking very much like Erik.

"You have something for us yet?" Erik asked.

"A few things." Sierra grabbed a black gel lifter like the ones Kennedy often used. The high-quality elastic sheet of rubber had a low-adhesive gelatin layer on one side made especially for lifting latent prints and dust impressions.

Sierra shone a bright light on the lifter to display a subtle dusty footprint. "I lifted a few of these prints from the deck surface before the rain hit. They're likely from male boots, size twelve or so."

"Unless my mom had a guest who wore boots, which I doubt, it's from my intruder." At the thought of the threatening male standing over her with the gun while she was pinned and helpless, Kennedy's legs went weak, and she dropped onto a nearby stool. "He wore combat boots. Khaki, I think. Large feet. So this matches."

"And he was dressed in camo," Erik added.

"Could be former military," Sierra suggested. "Or a paid assassin."

Kennedy gasped.

Erik ground his teeth, but he didn't look surprised by the comment. "I agree on the military, but assassin? If so, he likely wouldn't have given up on finding Kennedy and stayed to finish the job."

Kennedy shuddered. "Maybe he saw you coming."

"I was too far away." Erik tilted his head. "Was your mom connected to any extremist groups?"

"You're kidding, right?" Kennedy shook her head. "My mom was such a rule follower that she wouldn't even consider driving a mile over the speed limit."

Erik's eyes narrowed. "Then we need to look into military connections."

"I don't know of any," Kennedy said.

Erik stared over her head for a long moment before focusing on her again. "I don't want to speak ill of your mother, but I do want you to keep an open mind about what we might locate in our searches. Everyone has secrets. Even our parents."

Uncomfortable under his study, Kennedy moved her attention to Sierra. "I assume you'll have your staff try to identify the boot make and size. Maybe we can narrow down suspects that way."

"Not my staff. Not for you." She planted her hands on the edge of the table. "I'll do it personally."

"But your leave."

"Reed's still on leave too, and I can easily run up to feed Asher when needed or if I can't stand to be separated from him." She grinned.

Kennedy never expected Sierra to do this for her, and maybe once she learned why Kennedy had broken up with Erik, she'd regret offering her time. "Thank you."

"No problem. You're family. Or almost were anyway." Sierra jutted out her chin and looked up at Erik.

"What else do you have?" he asked, but his eyes had darkened.

She looked at Kennedy. "I lifted a single stray hair from

47

under the table where you spotted the suspect. It doesn't track with anyone in your family. Plus, I processed prints. Lots of them. But if our intruder's a pro, not likely his prints. I need to take both of your prints for elimination purposes. Finley's too. Also, Emory will need a DNA swab for you, Kennedy. She's our DNA expert, and I might as well take it while you're here. And Emory will need the same for Finley. If you could get her over here as soon as possible so we can get her DNA running and I can review the prints, that would be great."

"They're sisters," Erik said. "Can't you identify unknown samples by comparing to Kennedy's profile?"

"Not really," Sierra said. "Siblings share only about fifty percent of their genotype, so we need samples from both."

"I'll give her a call and get her over here as soon as possible," Kennedy said.

"I'll let my staff know to expect her, so if I'm not here, someone else can do the prints and swab." Sierra reached under the table and lifted up a biometric fingerprint reader.

Kennedy recognized the model that was smaller than a toaster flipped on its side. The model tenprint and rolled fingerprint scanner provided liveness detection and was top-of-the-line. Not surprising. Everything Kennedy had seen so far was the best quality.

"Nice machine," Kennedy said.

Sierra stroked it. "This baby is so new it's almost a virgin. Put your fingers on the screen to see how the advanced optical system captures plain fingerprint images and rolled fingerprints. Takes only a second."

Kennedy rested her fingers on the screen, and the prints instantly displayed on Sierra's laptop screen.

"We good to print the hand with the turtle bite?" Sierra asked.

Kennedy held out her hand. "Bite is higher than the pads."

"How's it feeling?" Sierra asked.

"Painful," Kennedy said but didn't belabor the point, as Erik was looking at her as if he took it personally that she'd been hurt on the dive.

Sierra grimaced. "I've had my share of injuries while working scenes, including animal bites, but never a turtle."

Erik frowned at Kennedy. "I wish I could convince you to call it a day and get some rest."

Kennedy ignored him and gingerly placed the fingers of her injured hand on the screen. Her behavior might be rude, but they'd already discussed resting due to the injury, and she'd told him she wasn't going to be babied. Sure, she might have difficulty performing normal tasks without full use of her dominant hand, but she needed to be involved in this investigation, and if she knew Erik, he wouldn't be going to bed. He would hunker down behind his computer and start researching.

Sierra looked at Erik. "You're up."

"That really *was* fast." Erik rested his fingers on the screen.

"Beats the equipment you were used to seeing in PPB booking." She faced her computer. "Okay. Perfect. Other hand."

He switched. "Now tell me that you think you recovered some viable prints."

"I lifted several latents from the table we think the suspect touched." Sierra leaned back and looked at Kennedy. "Your mother's prints would've been taken at her autopsy, but they wouldn't include them in your copy. Means we'll need another way to get them for elimination purposes."

"I wonder if they'd release them if I made a request," Kennedy said.

Sierra shook her head. "A detective would have access if we wanted to persuade them to ask. Still, I lifted a lot of similar prints at her house, and since she was the former resident, I think we can reasonably determine which ones are hers. But it won't hold up in court, and we'll need something official for that."

"I wish I had connections around here so I could get them, but I don't," Kennedy said.

"We'll need to get help from a detective," Erik said. "I'll check that out."

"I recovered touch DNA, too," Sierra said. "I've given it to Emory, and she's rushing the tests for you." Sierra put the reader back on the lower shelf. "She'll have the results in twenty-four hours or so."

Sierra looked up, a frown on her face.

"Why the frown?" Erik asked.

"I also recovered prints from the crowbar, but that or the DNA really does us no good. We can run them against our limited database, but we can only query law enforcement databases with official approval from law enforcement. As much as you want to keep this in-house, it's time to get PPB involved."

Erik groaned. "Odds are good that they'll confiscate the evidence and not share the results."

Kennedy stared at him. "So we could be left in the dark?"

"Yes." He curled his fingers into fists at his sides. "If so, let's pray that my prior service on the force can sway them our way."

5

Kennedy had to get out of Sierra's lab and do so now. Before she blurted out why she left Erik. Kennedy had always gotten along well with Sierra and confided in her in the past. But now? No. Kennedy couldn't share why she'd left Erik, and the longer she stayed in the lab, the greater the odds that Kennedy would say something about witness protection.

Besides, Erik deserved to be the first to know. The break-in could be related to WITSEC so she had to tell him and not in front of his big sister. Or his brothers. Alone.

In the hallway and after the door closed soundly behind them, she faced him. "I need to talk to you before the meeting."

He clenched his jaw. "That sounds ominous."

"It's about our breakup, and it could be relevant to what happened to my mom. Your brothers will need to know too, but I need to tell you first. You deserve that." She didn't know what she expected him to say or do, but his expression didn't change at all.

"We can stop at my condo." He gestured for her to precede him down the hallway to the elevator. On the way, she fired off a text to Finley to ask her to come over for the DNA and prints, and her sister replied right away.

Kennedy stowed her phone to board the elevator. "Finley will stop by before work, and I'll also give her all the details then."

"Perfect," he said, but his mind seemed elsewhere. They were quiet until they reached his condo.

Once he had the door open, he looked at her. "I should warn you. I adopted a dog this year. I named him Pong. He's very well trained and won't bother you, but I'll still take him to Drake's place with me."

"You named him after a video game." Vintage games had been his favorite way to let off steam, and it looked like that hadn't changed. "I should've known you'd do that."

Erik grinned, a cute little boy grin that melted her heart. "He's a golden lab, and he's trained as a sniffer dog for electronics."

"Oh, wow," she said. "Interesting. I've read a few articles on dogs like that, but haven't seen one in action."

"He's something to see." Erik's eyes lit up with a sparkle they'd once held when talking about their future together. "I can have him demonstrate for you if you want."

"Sure. I'm always glad to learn more about forensics work."

He flipped a light switch and stepped back. "Excuse the mess. I wasn't expecting company."

Curious about his home, she stepped down a long hallway that opened into a great room with an open kitchen boasting contemporary wood-toned cabinets. It smelled like toast and coffee.

She heard the dog whimpering from the living room and peeked to see him dancing to get out of his crate. The far end of the room held a big dining table, and the largest remote control model helicopter she'd ever seen sat on top of it.

She looked back at him. "I see you've upped your RC helicopter game."

"Don't you know it." That grin appeared again, and memories of how she'd once hoped to have children who had the same smile haunted her. "That baby is one of the biggest on the market. Blades alone are twenty-six inches."

Eyes lit with joy, he went to the crate, and Pong darted out the moment Erik opened the door. "Sit."

Pong's expression said he objected, but he sat and remained sitting in that spot when Erik came back to the table.

She set down her small suitcase that Erik had offered to carry, but she'd declined, and went over to look at the orange-and-neon-green remote control aircraft. "And you can really get this monster off the ground?"

"Sure thing." He patted the body. "I've been giving it a tune-up and was going to take it up this weekend. You should—" He shook his head and faced the other way. "I'll take Pong out for a quick break and then pack my things and change the bedding. Once that's done, we can talk and head up to the office."

"What can I do?"

"I got it." He jerked a thumb at the kitchen. "Help yourself to anything you want. Drinks. Snacks. But remember to stay in the condo."

Kennedy nodded but didn't move as he hitched up Pong's leash and exited the condo. Her thoughts went to his family. Soon she would see Aiden, Brendan, Clay, and Drake for the first time in years.

She chuckled. Without realizing it, she automatically ran through their names in alphabetical order. She'd always thought it was cute the way their parents had named them, but Erik? Nah. He'd gotten tired of it. Still, the brothers often did things in order without thinking, like lining up or choosing who went first.

Just the thought of seeing all the brothers together had her dropping sideways into a nearby chair and resting her arm along the back. She was going to have to tell them about WITSEC. She didn't think a pyramid scammer like the guy her father testified against would kill anybody, certainly not by administering excess blood pressure medicine, but then who did such a thing? More likely it would be someone with access to pharmaceuticals. People like the thugs who wanted to stop her mother's research.

If the break-in hadn't occurred, Kennedy might've started to believe Finley and the medical examiner and let it go. But now she'd gotten Erik and his brothers involved, and they would help her figure out what happened to her mother once and for all.

She closed her eyes and rested her head on her arm.

Please. Let us find the answers I need. And keep everyone safe.

She lost herself in prayer, completely focusing on God and the power He held over her life.

"We're back," Erik's voice startled her. "Sorry. Didn't mean to scare you."

"It's okay. I was just praying."

"Praying is always a good thing, but if you're worried about your safety, you can trust us to keep you safe." His eyes narrowed as he assessed her.

She worked hard not to show her discomfort under his study. "I know you will."

"But?"

"No but. Can we talk first and then you do the other things?" She pointed at the chair next to her. "I really want to get this off my chest."

Forehead furrowed, he unhooked Pong. The lab looked at her. "You two should be properly introduced."

Erik dropped to the floor and urged Pong to step nearer to Kennedy.

She held out her hand. "Hey, fella. Good to meet you. I'm Kennedy."

Pong shoved his head under her fingers, and the silky smooth hair tickled her skin. She'd had a dog growing up, and she couldn't resist kneeling next to this one, even though she should be telling her story. "Is it okay to hug him?"

"He's a big old softie and loves hugs."

She wrapped her arms around his neck, and he scooted closer. She inhaled his pungent earthy dog smell. She relished the warm unconditional affection he was offering and used it to gain the strength to share her story.

She looked at Erik over Pong's head and decided to launch right into things. "My dad was once an accountant. He fell in with a really bad person named Harrison Waldron. He was running a pyramid scam, and my dad fudged the books for Waldron, which helped him scam thousands of people."

She paused for a breath and to wash away the thought of her dad being the man who could do something so callous. "My dad was arrested, and to keep from going to prison, he testified against Waldron. This guy had a violent rap sheet and threatened to get back at my dad, plus he was running one of the largest pyramid scams in history, which is why they let us into WITSEC."

"That's crazy." Erik leaned forward, bringing him closer. "You never mentioned it."

"I didn't know. Not until right before we broke up. I've been in the program since I was two, but my parents kept it a secret." Her mind flashed back to the day she'd confronted her father. Her emotions were raw, and she felt too close to Erik so she moved to the couch. "I was looking for something in boxes in the garage, and I found a hidden bin. It contained legal documents with my mom's and dad's pictures but under different names. I asked him about it and that's when he told me we were all in WITSEC."

"Witness protection. Wow." Erik shook his head as Pong settled at his feet. "Just wow. That's a surprise."

She nodded. "It's something I couldn't tell anyone. Not even you."

"No. Of course not." He got up to sit next to her, and Pong trailed and rested his head on Erik's foot. "That's how the program works."

"But when I saw you after Dad told me, I couldn't look you in the eyes. I felt like I was lying to you. I tried to make it work for a few days, but I just couldn't."

His fingers curled into fists on his knees. "That's why you ended things with me."

She started to reach for his hands to smooth them out and relieve his tension but stopped and wedged her uninjured fingers under her legs. "I didn't want to do it. You deserved the truth, and I couldn't give it to you. But now that both my parents are gone, I figure the threat to me and Finley is reduced, and we can share with select people."

Erik massaged his temples and narrowed his eyes. "Are you still in WITSEC or did you leave the program?"

"Finley and I are still in the program. But I just violated my family's agreement by telling you, and I'll need to call the deputy and let him know." She crossed her arms like a hug to protect herself from everything that was happening. "Finley and I haven't even talked about this, so I'm not sure if she wants to stay in the program or not. Or even if there is enough danger for us to remain."

Erik arched a thick eyebrow. "After all this time, you decided to violate the rules and tell me. Why?"

"I think you deserve to know. I really do, so don't take offense when I say this, but I wouldn't violate the rules today to tell you any more than I would have years ago. I'm telling you because maybe the person who killed my mom or who broke in tonight could be related to my dad's past."

"Yeah." He went silent for a long, uncomfortable moment. "Could be."

"If it's a possibility that they killed my mom, I needed you to know so you can investigate."

"I'll have to tell my brothers. You know that, right?"

"Yes."

He leaned back in his chair and stared at the ceiling, tapping his thumb on the armrests before dropping his gaze back to her. "You had a good reason for breaking things off, but it doesn't change anything between us."

"No. No. I didn't think it would, and that's not my intent in telling you at all. But maybe, now that you know why I did it...I hope you can forgive me."

"Sure...yeah...yeah, sure. I can do that." He picked at the cuticle on his thumb, his eyes the color of coffee darkening.

Pong perked up, his eyes alert, likely knowing his owner needed protection.

"But the pain of the breakup is still there," Erik said, lifting his tormented gaze to her. "If it hasn't gone away in six years, I doubt it ever will."

Kennedy sipped on a bottle of water and tried to act casual. Even with the drink quenching her thirst, it was hard to relax with three strapping guys looking at her with varying degrees of interest and tension. She assumed she was responsible for the unease in the room as they waited for Aiden to arrive to start their meeting.

Maybe they wanted to know why she and Erik had broken up. Or maybe they were just tired. It was nearing midnight, after all. She couldn't imagine being called out for a meeting at this time of night, but these guys acted as if it was no big deal.

She heard the entrance door from the hallway open and everyone looked in that direction. Aiden stepped into the room. He was tall with dark hair and had blue eyes, resembling most of the other brothers.

"Sorry I'm late." Aiden dropped into a chair at the end of the table. "Harper called, and it's hard finding a time when we can talk, so I didn't want to let it go."

He turned to Kennedy. "My wife's an Olympic downhill skier. She's out of town training right now."

"Sounds fascinating. And exciting." Kennedy smiled.

"Sometimes too exciting, even for our fearless brother." Erik cast a fond expression at Aiden.

Aiden shifted his attention to Kennedy. "How's the hand?"

She glanced down at the bandage circling her palm. "It'll be just fine."

Erik locked his focus on her. "The wounds are pretty deep, but the doctor left it open to heal. Less risk of infection that way. I'll be changing the dressing to keep the risk of infection down."

Drake snorted. "Nurse Erik. I can see the uniform now."

The brothers laughed, and the image playing out in Kennedy's brain had her half tempted to laugh with them, but she didn't want to hurt Erik.

He didn't laugh along, just rolled his eyes. "You all good to get started here?"

"I'm assuming you're taking lead." Aiden leaned back in his chair and cast a challenging look at Erik.

"Of course."

Aiden rested his elbows on the arms of the chair and steepled his fingers together. "Then you know what I'm going to warn you about."

"I do and no need to say it." Erik gave Kennedy a funny look that she couldn't decipher, but he clearly didn't want Aiden to say more.

Erik took a long breath and shifted his stance. "It's easier for discussion if we call your mom by her first name. But if you don't like it, we can change."

"Go right ahead," she said, actually glad they would do so. She never thought of her mom by her name, and hopefully, that would make this discussion easier to bear.

Erik stepped up to the whiteboard. "Let's create a timeline and take things in order."

Erik wrote *Silas Walker Death, Wanda Walker Death, Wanda Home Break-in* in large black letters. He turned to Kennedy. "Could you give me the dates for your parents' deaths?"

Her father had died about three years before, and her mother nearly a month before and she shared that information. He noted the details on the board as well as the dates for the other items.

"Do you think Kennedy's dad was murdered too?" Aiden asked.

Erik recounted the WITSEC situation. The brother's all swung their gazes to her, but thankfully their expressions didn't hold judgement of her dad, only curiosity.

"I looked Waldron up," Erik said. "He's serving time in a federal prison in Texas."

Clay swiveled his chair to face Kennedy. "What about

your father's death? Any reason to believe he was murdered?"

Kennedy shook her head. "He'd had a pacemaker installed after a heart attack a few years prior to his death. Before he died, he called 911 complaining of another heart attack. Our inspector at WITSEC didn't think there was anything suspicious about Dad's death, but he wanted to close the case without doubts so he ordered an autopsy."

"Did they do a tox screen?" Clay asked.

"A basic one, yes," Kennedy replied. "It included prescription medications and drugs of abuse. I haven't seen it, but my mom said it came back negative for any drugs that could've been his cause of death."

Erik zoned in on her. "If it was just a basic screen, there could've been other drugs, or even plants, used to cause a heart attack that weren't tested for. If your mom was murdered, maybe he was as well."

"You think so?" Kennedy rested her hands on the table as she gave it some thought. "I know of many medications that someone could've used to kill him, but Waldron's in prison. Even if he managed to locate my dad, he couldn't have done it."

"Does he have a wife?" Drake asked. "Or adult children?"

"Yes." She stared at her hands and one by one lifted her fingers and pulled them apart as the thought of her dad potentially being murdered sank in. "You think Waldron would ask her or his kids to kill him?"

"Could be, or she could have decided to do so on her own," Clay said.

"Poison fits with a woman's MO," Erik said. "They're more likely than men to use poison to commit murder."

Kennedy still couldn't believe they were really talking

about this. "So, you think she somehow found out where Dad lived and poisoned him?"

"It's a possibility we can't rule out," Erik said. "And we would be remiss if we didn't at least consider a correlation."

"So you think this pyramid scammer, what's his name— Harrison Waldron—might be behind all of this?" Brendan asked.

Erik shrugged. "We need to look into him, which might include visiting the prison and talking to the guy. And finding out who's been visiting him."

"I'd be glad to take a quick trip to Texas to do that," Drake said. "Can use some of my tricks from fugitive apprehension to see what I can find out about him and his family. And I can find out who's been coming to see him. Maybe he contracted someone for a hit."

"Pardon me for saying this." Brendan faced Kennedy. "But are you considering exhuming your dad's body for further testing?"

She gasped.

"It's too early to consider that," Erik said. "Even if we wanted to do it, we don't have any legit reason to do so."

"I don't know," Drake said. "I think a good lawyer could make a case for it to see if Silas had the same drugs in his system as Wanda."

"Let's first get the autopsy report for Silas to see which drugs were tested for and what else they found," Erik said.

"I have a contact at the county ME's office," Brendan said. "I should be able to get the complete report."

"Great." Erik noted that and added Drake following up on Waldron on the board in red ink. "Wanda taught chemistry part-time at PSU and did pharmaceutical research full-time." He changed his focus to Kennedy. "Go ahead and tell them about your mom's current research project."

Kennedy felt his eyes on her as she shared her mom's work. "I think this is more likely why she was murdered."

"*If* she was murdered," Drake said.

There was no good response to that. "I think it's a better line of inquiry than the WITSEC aspect or even her teaching."

"I don't know," Clay said, a half-smile on his face. "Plenty of students these days might think murder would be a good way to solve a grade issue."

"You joke, but there was a guy at UCLA who killed his professor over grades a while back," Aiden said.

Erik wrote *Motives* on the board and listed out three items beneath it. *Counterfeit Pharmaceuticals, WITSEC,* and *Bad Grades.* "These will be our investigative priorities until we find something to change them."

"Like, maybe the information on Silas's autopsy or on Waldron," Drake said.

"Exactly," Erik said. "Or the forensics from Wanda's place. We just came from Sierra's lab. She's recovered footprints and fingerprints plus a stray hair. As of now, we have no way to run them against law enforcement databases, so I'll be calling PPB."

Drake narrowed his eyes. "Hopefully they'll cooperate and run the prints for us."

"I'll do my best to make that happen." Erik drilled his gaze into Kennedy. "At this point, it's logical to assume the break-in at your mother's place could be related to either of your parents' deaths, and that's the direction I'll take this investigation unless we discover something to change our focus."

Kennedy nodded, but her stomach clenched. With her work on crime scenes, she could easily imagine the things that could happen to change the focus. Things that might include the intruder coming back and ending her life.

Erik sucked in a generous gulp of air outside Drake's condo before heading inside. Wouldn't do for his closest brother to figure out that Erik's emotions were whirling like the blades on the helicopters he liked to fly. Sure, everyone in his family would know he had to be uneasy, but they didn't need to know the extent of his lingering pain.

Shoot, *he* hadn't even known until he'd seen Kennedy again. After she split with him, she'd transferred to another university, and he hadn't seen her again. Except in his dreams. And honestly, most waking hours, too, for a very long time.

He'd be out in the quad and think he saw her. Charge over to talk to her and startle some unsuspecting woman. That went on way too long.

He didn't even date seriously again until recently, when Aiden's wife Harper set him up with her friend, Grace. They went out for a few months—until he discovered that Grace cheated on him. The breakup was painful, but didn't hurt as badly as it should've. Meant he didn't care all that deeply for her. Still, it told him women couldn't be trusted. At least not easily.

"Not a word about how I feel, boy," he said to Pong as he unlocked the door. He stepped in and saw Drake sitting on the couch watching TV. The buttery smell of popcorn filled the air.

"Whatcha watching?" Erik asked to focus the topic away from Kennedy.

Pong made a beeline for Drake, who tapped his remote to pause the show and ruffle Pong's scruff. "Documentary on gun control."

"And, let me guess." Erik set the bag containing Pong's food and dishes on the kitchen island and lowered a tote bag and computer case to the floor, then plopped down on the couch next to his brother. "You're hating every minute of it."

"Not all of it. I mean, I'm all for banning bump stocks and ghost guns." He frowned, and Erik knew, despite his brother's love of firearms, he didn't want devices that could turn a handgun into a rifle or gun parts bought on the internet that could be put together to make unregistered guns readily available.

Drake cocked his head. "So Kennedy, huh?"

Erik looked away to keep his very perceptive brother from reading his mood. "Yeah."

"How was it seeing her again?"

"Not what I expected." Erik left it at that.

"You good to work her protection detail?" Drake released Pong, and the lab scooted onto the couch between them, his head on Erik's knee.

"Yeah."

"I would suggest you back off, but I know you won't any more than I did with Natalie." Drake smiled when he mentioned his girlfriend's name. The agency had protected her not too long ago, and Drake had fallen for the compassionate social worker.

Just like all of Erik's older brothers. They were now off the market. Aiden and Brendan were married, Clay engaged. Drake was moving toward engagement, too, but Natalie was a bit skittish. Sort of like Erik, but for different reasons.

"So where is the love of your life?" Erik asked, hoping to change Drake's focus.

Drake peered at him as if he knew Erik had purposefully redirected the conversation. "She has a big day tomorrow in court, so she went home."

Erik stood before Drake could ask questions about

Kennedy, and Pong hopped down and gave Erik an expectant look. "I need to do that deep dive on Kennedy's mom before we meet in the morning."

"Let me know if I can help." Drake picked up the popcorn bowl sitting on the couch next to him.

Erik snorted.

"What?" Drake arched a dark eyebrow, looking very much like their father. "I can do it. My computer skills are just fine."

"For the superficial stuff, yeah, but you're better off sticking to weapons." Erik grabbed his computer case.

"Don't mind that. Don't mind that at all." Drake grinned and turned the documentary back on.

Wishing he had his more powerful desktop computer at his disposal, Erik unpacked his laptop onto Drake's dining table. Erik couldn't go back to his condo to work in his office, since he didn't want to spend any more time with Kennedy. This machine would have to do.

Pong dropped down on the floor and rolled onto his side to stretch out, and Erik opened a special program available to private investigators and entered Wanda's social security number, which he'd gotten from Kennedy. As he'd anticipated, the record for Kennedy's mother came up clean for any arrests or convictions. He printed out the report, containing her prior addresses. WITSEC created bogus records for their protectees, so he wasn't surprised to see address information, wedding and graduation dates, etcetera, for Wanda and Silas Walker going back to their births, along with Finley's and Kennedy's milestone dates.

While it printed, he accessed Wanda's financial records. Kennedy had given him online access to her mother's accounts before he left. A very good thing. Not working in law enforcement any longer made it nearly impossible to access that information. At least not using legal methods.

He studied the bank statements and found regular monthly payments made for items needed to maintain a floating home, such as utilities and moorage rentals. No rent or house payment though, so she must've owned the floating home. He found her income from the college along with large deposits for the last two months to the tune of twenty thousand dollars wired to her account from a company called inDents.

He sat back.

Twenty grand a month. Not chump change, but she wasn't using it to live on. Just growing her account. So what was inDents, and why were they paying her?

He entered the name in an internet browser. The only item returned was a domain registration but no website developed. He looked at the other registry information, but it was private.

Why would they register an internet domain name without that domain being associated with any services such as email or a website? Could be associated with illegal activity or could be innocent, and they just hadn't gotten to developing a website yet.

Erik tried to trace the deposits but quickly lost the trail. If anyone could track these deposits and find information on this company, it would be Nick at Veritas. Erik texted the computer and cybercrimes expert to ask him to look into inDents and trace the deposits.

Nick replied that he would fit it in as soon as possible. Knowing his schedule, it could be weeks, which Erik didn't have. He had to figure this out himself.

This large of a deposit suggested something illegal to him. Just his gut feel. Maybe blackmail, but that wasn't likely as those payments wouldn't be done via electronic transfer but in cash. Plus, the thought of Wanda being a blackmailer was absurd.

The deposits could just be insurance payouts, though information on an insurance company should be readily available. Maybe Wanda sold a patent and was being paid in an installment plan.

Erik just didn't know, but it seemed likely to him that if he discovered where this money was coming from, he would figure out who wanted her dead.

6

Early the next morning, Kennedy once again sat with the Byrd brothers in their office, and she had to fight twisting her hair to relieve the stress. If possible, they all looked more intense. Or maybe Erik had shared the information he'd learned about her mother's finances last night, and they were wondering if she and her mother were both involved in something illegal when that was the last thing either of them would do.

She wanted to sigh, but she held it in and waited for the brothers to grab coffee and bagels and take a seat. She loved coffee, but her stomach turned at the nutty scent permeating the air.

Or maybe it was churning over Erik's news. He'd told her on the way to the office that her mother had received twenty thousand dollars wired to her checking account for the last two months from a company called inDents. He asked her to think about where it might've come from so she was ready to talk about it at the meeting, but Kennedy couldn't come up with a logical explanation for such a large sum of money from an unknown place.

Erik stepped up to the whiteboard, his footfalls confident and sure. "First up, I left a message with the sergeant I spoke to at PPB about the break-in."

"Let's hope he calls back soon." Clay set down his mug with a thud. "But I wouldn't hold my breath when we're talking about a break-in."

"I was able to get Silas's autopsy report." Brendan slid a set of papers down the table to each person.

Erik grabbed a copy. "I was hoping you'd do this quickly."

Brendan brushed his knuckles over his chest. "Just chalk it up to my superhero status."

The others groaned, but a ball of dread formed in Kennedy's stomach as she flipped through the pages. "The report doesn't tell us anything that we don't already know."

Brendan swallowed a bite of his blueberry bagel, which he set on a plate. "But it also doesn't list the blood pressure meds your mother died from. Not surprising since it was a basic screening. My source told me that, if we want to know about those meds, a comprehensive test is necessary."

Kennedy sighed. "I don't want to have my dad's body exhumed."

"And I don't think we should just yet," Erik said. "I'll stick with my earlier recommendation that we wait until we have proof that your mother was murdered."

"Agreed." She took in his sympathetic gaze.

Erik gave her a tight smile. "Then let's get to work proving what happened to Wanda. I completed my deep dive on her finances. I found her PSU income, but didn't find any source of income for her current project." He shifted his focus to Kennedy. "Do you know how she was paid?"

Kennedy took a sip of her water. "All I know is that she got a grant from two big pharmaceutical companies."

"Did she keep the money in a separate business account that we haven't found yet?" Erik asked.

Kennedy shrugged. "I haven't looked for that information, but I would think it's at her lab. And yes, I would think she would have a separate business account."

Aiden cupped his mug. "Is her lab independent or part of another facility?"

"Independent," she said. "The big pharma companies provided the equipment, and they said I could continue to use it."

"This is unrelated." Drake eyed her with a quirk of his brow, an expression that she remembered would be followed with a challenge. "But do you really think you can finish the project on the counterfeit drugs?"

"It's been a while since I've done the kind of research my mom was doing." She sat up straighter. "But even if I'm rusty, I'll keep working until I succeed."

"Has the pharmaceutical company given you a completion deadline?" Drake asked.

"One month, but I assume if I haven't completed her work by then that, if I show progress, they'll extend it."

Drake's eyebrow rose even higher. "Don't you find it odd that they outsourced this project when they have so many researchers on staff?"

Kennedy shook her head. "They're far too busy creating the next drug to work on this. Besides, it's not just one company that's being ripped off by the counterfeits. The two companies funding the research are the ones who have the most to lose, but this will be used by other companies and law enforcement too."

"Guess that makes sense." Drake grabbed his bagel covered with strawberry cream cheese. "So where is this lab?"

"In a leased industrial space not far from my mom's house."

"There was no record of that in her accounts," Erik said. "Is the place leased directly by the pharma companies?"

"Yes, and the utilities and security system are billed directly too."

Erik passed out a handout. "If you check out my report on Wanda's finances, you'll see that she's been receiving electronic transfers each month from a company called inDents to the tune of twenty grand."

Clay whistled and eyed Kennedy. "Do you know anything about inDents?"

"Nothing," Kennedy said. "I couldn't bring myself to look through her accounts yet, and I've never heard of inDents."

"Seems suspicious," Drake said.

"I searched for a website or any information on the company, but the only thing I found is that the domain name is registered, but is parked at a domain registry site. All other registry data is private. I also struck out on tracing the deposits. Still, I sent the info to Nick to do his thing." Erik looked at Kennedy. "Nick's the Veritas Center's computer and cybercrimes guru."

Brendan tapped the report in front of him. "I was thinking retirement money, but this says you didn't find any retirement accounts. You've ruled out the logical sources, so now I really want to know who this company is."

"You thinking bribe?" Erik planted his hands on the table and looked at Brendan. "Maybe blackmail? 'Cause I sure am."

"Could be."

Kennedy wished Erik would look at her so she could make eye contact to dispute his thoughts, but he didn't. "My mom would never do anything like that."

Erik shifted his focus to her, and she didn't like the

distrust in his eyes. "You never know what someone might do when pushed."

Kennedy sat forward. "But she wasn't pushed financially. Her accounts show that. Plus the house was paid for, and she made money off selling the family home. And the pharma companies were paying her somehow. Maybe that money was coming from them."

"It's possible," Erik said.

"What about her will," Drake asked. "Who did she leave her money to, and who's the executor of her estate?"

Kennedy shrugged. "Finley's been pushing me to read it, but I haven't had the heart to."

"Seems like now would be a great time to do so," Aiden suggested.

"Yes," Kennedy said, though she still didn't want to read it. The act made everything seem so final.

"Let's go ahead and table this discussion," Erik said. "I'll head to the lab to check Wanda's files when we're done, and maybe I'll find more information."

"You mean *we'll* head to the lab," Kennedy said.

"About that." Erik planted his feet.

Uh-oh. Argument coming.

"I'd rather you stay here for your safety," he said.

He made it seem as if she had a choice when she knew she didn't. "With the short deadline, I need all the time I can get to work on the project."

"It's safer here."

"Do you keep all of your clients prisoner here?"

"No, but—"

"But you protect people in danger, right?" She issued him a nonverbal challenge with a lift of her chin. "So you must have a protocol you can follow to allow me to go to work."

"We do. But you're...you're not just any client." Erik crossed his arms.

"We can do recon on the lab," Aiden said. "And find a way to let her work."

Erik shook his head.

"Let's go ahead and do a risk assessment," Aiden suggested. "And then we can decide if transport is safe."

His brothers murmured their agreement.

"Fine." Erik was still looking at her, but his jaw wasn't clenched now. "I'll do an in-person evaluation while you remain here."

"Okay." She wanted to get to the lab, but she didn't want to unnecessarily risk her life or cause Erik additional grief. That was going to happen as they spent time together, and on this, she was willing to compromise.

Instead of sitting around waiting for Sarge to call back, Erik and Clay headed out to evaluate Wanda Walker's lab. It sat across the road from the river, and Erik focused as he drove into the lot that abutted a large single-story building painted a drab yellow. One side held loading docks, and a sign offered space for rent.

"Separate entrance and exit from the lot," Clay said.

"Good." Erik slowed to take a careful look around. "Gives us two options for a fast getaway if needed."

"And good visuals for the entrance. Plus, Brendan could take a stand on the roof. Not only to keep us informed of any movement, but he'd have good line of sight for a shot." Clay sat back. "Unless there's a problem inside, I'd put this at a low-risk situation."

Erik wouldn't call anything that involved Kennedy's safety a low-risk situation. Sure, Clay was right so far, but

Clay hadn't once loved this woman more than anything. Clay's gut wasn't tied up in knots over it.

"Let's take a look at the lab entrance." Erik drove closer to the building until he found the entrance to Suite G, which held the lab. He parked in front, scanning the vehicles and nearby suites. They were all small manufacturing companies. "No red flags here."

Erik's phone rang, and he saw the PPB ID, so he tapped the screen and answered.

"Your message said you have some unknown prints and DNA from Wanda Walker's home," Sarge said in his usual gruff tone. "Still not sure that's enough to open an investigation here."

"I get that." Erik concentrated on breathing evenly instead of snapping at the guy and losing even more hope of getting his buy-in. "But you have to know the prints and DNA are meaningless to us unless they can be run through law enforcement databases."

"Yeah, that's a problem. But there's a lot of paperwork and time involved in one of my detectives opening an official investigation that will likely go nowhere."

"Can't they run them unofficially?"

"You know they can't." Sarge's deep voice pounded through the phone.

Erik focused on that calm breathing. "What can I do to make this happen?"

"Tell you what," Sarge said. "I'll go to my guys and ask around. See if one of them will do all the paperwork for this. If I get a bite, I'll contact the Veritas Center and give them my approval to run the prints and DNA. 'Course the results will come to us, and depending on what we see, we might not be able to share them with you."

"Trust me, I get it," Erik said. "Can you text me if one of the detectives steps?"

"Sure thing." Sarge sounded positive on the surface, but there was a cautious bent to the undertone.

"And make sure you tell them one of their former officers is asking for the help. Maybe that will help me."

"Wouldn't count on it." Sarge disconnected.

"Let's hope we get someone who doesn't hate an officer who moves to the private sector." Clay slid out of the truck.

Erik removed the keys and got out, forgetting about the call and keeping his head on a swivel for their suspect. He unlocked the suite door, flipped on lights, and tapped the security alarm code on the keypad.

Erik spun to take in the entire space. "No windows or doors."

"Makes protecting Kennedy easier."

"Once we get her safely inside."

Clay gave a firm nod, and Erik turned to look at the back wall. Made of glass, it divided the large space. A small reception or maybe administration area sat in front of the wall. A desk, tall metal file cabinet, and side chair took up the space. A business phone, computer, and stack of unopened mail sat on the tidy desk.

Clay strode to the glass wall and looked into the lab area. "Some of the same equipment Sierra and Maya use, but I have no idea what anything is."

"I'm sure Sierra's told us, but..." Erik shrugged. Not a one of the guys had ever had any interest in science when she'd been all over it since grade school.

A glass door opened to a small vestibule, which then led into the lab space. A shower was set up in the corner, and a sticker on the door read, *Authorized Biosafety Level 2 Lab.* Even with the set up, he could still smell chemicals lingering in the air.

"Level four's the top and most restrictive rating." Clay

joined Erik. "At least I think that's what Sierra said. Who knew they needed such a high rating for this lab?"

"They're dealing with counterfeit drugs, and they can be cut with anything. Even fentanyl, which can be fatal just by touching a small amount."

"Yeah. Right. Makes sense. Fentanyl's nothing to mess around with."

Erik turned to the side wall, where he found a small bathroom and a second exit. "We have two exits here too."

"I don't see anything that would stop us from letting Kennedy come to work."

"Yeah, me neither," Erik grumbled.

"Hey, it's good news. Don't sound so disappointed." Clay eyed him. "Right. You still have a thing for her."

"Maybe," Erik admitted.

"If your disappointment in this assessment says anything, it's not a maybe." Clay led the way to their SUV.

Erik climbed into the driver's seat. "I can control it."

"Can you? 'Cause, man, with the way I felt about Toni, if her life was in danger, I couldn't."

Erik gunned the engine. "I'm not going to be told to stand down."

"I'm not telling you that. Just wanting you to admit that you have an issue so you can deal with it."

Erik pulled out of the parking lot, spitting gravel behind him. His brother was right, but Erik wasn't ready to accept that he wasn't over Kennedy. That gave her power over him when he didn't want to be so vulnerable. Not ever again. But he also wouldn't turn his back on her or let his brothers take charge. He felt a personal responsibly for her safety, and he would see this through to the end no matter the cost to his emotions.

≈

Kennedy sighed contentedly. This was right. The place she was meant to be when she wasn't in the water. The lab. Her second home. Both places sealed out the public and left her on her own. Even the chemical odors comforted her. Sure, Erik was just on the other side of the glass wall going through the files and computers. And he'd also emptied the mini fridge and trash cans for food and drink containers that could've potentially been used to give her mother the overdose of medicine. He'd loaded the items in their vehicle, and he would have Maya analyze it all.

Kennedy hoped Maya located the meds so the question of whether her mother was murdered or not was answered. She also hoped Erik would find the information he sought on her mom's contract, and it would explain everything about her finances. What he wasn't going to find was any evidence that her mother was corrupt. Of course not.

Or was she?

Had her mom been involved when her dad had handled the accounting for the scammer? Kennedy had never asked. Why would she? There was no point twenty-plus years later. Her family had been upright citizens. Some might say a model family. And look at her doubting her parents. She had no reason to. No reason at all. There would be logical explanations for the money.

She shook her head to clear out the doubts and focused on her work. She'd inserted her arms into holes in a glass-fronted class 3 biosafety containment cabinet. Long, heavy gloves were attached to the holes inside the cabinet. She also wore a positive pressure personal suit for protection from powders, a face shield, and non-porous gloves inside the outer protective gloves attached to the suit. All to keep her safe from the drugs she was evaluating.

Overkill for sure, but all it took was seven hundred micrograms of fentanyl to kill, just a half dozen grains or so.

Plus, fentanyl sold on the street was almost always made in clandestine labs. It wasn't as pure as the pharmaceutical version. Meant the effect on the body could be more unpredictable.

A knock sounded on the glass behind her, and she swiveled to see Erik holding up a yellow envelope. He pressed the intercom button. "This was in the mail. Addressed to your mom. The colored envelope caught my attention."

"Do you think it's something I need to look at?"

He nodded. "We should open everything in the mail. I just brought this one to your attention because it seems like it might be personal. Want me to bring it in to you?"

"I'll come get it. Meet me at the inner door." She pulled her arms free and pushed her chair back. She wouldn't be leaving the room, so she didn't need to remove her protective clothing or take a shower.

She opened the door just a fraction, and Erik gave her the envelope.

"Thanks." She immediately closed the door to keep from spreading any contamination from her work and looked at the envelope. The bright yellow color would be hard to miss in the mail. The flap was taped closed.

She stared at it, uncertain about whether she wanted to open it and see personal information her mother didn't want her to know about.

"We won't know what it contains if you don't open it," Erik said.

"You're right." She glanced at him through the glass.

Her fingers were a bit clumsy due to the turtle bite, and she was double gloved even when using the large gloves in the biosafety containment cabinet. As with everything in this lab, her precautions were probably overkill, but better safe than sorry.

She took the envelope to a lab table and slit the top open with a scientific spatula. She looked inside and lurched back.

No letter.

"What is it?" Erik asked.

"Power. White powder." She looked up at him. "Stay there and don't touch anything. There could be powder on the outside of the envelope, and you need to be decontaminated."

"What do you think it is?" His voice was strained and high.

"Ricin maybe." Heart pounding, she looked at him. "But my gut says anthrax. These are both the most common biotoxins sent through the mail. Either way, I feel certain we're looking at a deadly substance sent to kill."

7

Erik froze in place, his mind racing to remember what he'd touched. Had he put his hand by or on his mouth? Could anthrax or another biotoxin go through his skin? He had no idea, and he didn't even want to ask. Better to wait for Kennedy to tell him what to do so he didn't do the wrong thing.

"I need you to shower," she said. "But you can't come in through this door without risking further contamination as it could be airborne."

He'd read about anthrax and the different forms. "So if it's anthrax, it could be the inhalation kind."

"Anthrax is anthrax. There isn't more than one kind, just different means of infection by the spores. We could be dealing with cutaneous—skin—infection if you touched it, or you could've inhaled it." She removed one of her outer latex gloves and set a test tube on the table far away from the envelope. She wet a swab with water from a vial and stuck it in the envelope.

"What are you doing?" His voice rose, worrying even himself. "You shouldn't be touching that stuff."

She looked up. "We want to know what's in here, right, and know on a timely basis?"

He nodded.

"Then we need to get a sample to the Veritas toxicology person. They have proper PPE to deal with this so it'll be safe." She sealed the tube then placed it in a screw-top canister and affixed a red biohazard label on the outside.

The label and her precautions raised his concern even higher. "Is there a way to be tested for my exposure? Like a blood test or something?"

She shook her head. "Nothing to determine if you carry the bacteria."

His heart dropped. "But I remember hearing about tests."

"Nasal swabs and environmental tests are done, but not to determine if an individual should be treated. They only determine the extent of exposure in the building. Same is true of ricin."

Oh, man. He could die. She could die. They both could. As could others who were exposed to the envelope before now. His head started swimming, but he balled his fists to control his emotions so he didn't make this incident more emotional for Kennedy.

She set the envelope on the floor. "Don't want it to accidently spill and spread."

"Good thinking," he said and meant it. He needed to put his trust in her and follow her directions. She'd been trained on infectious protocols, and she would do her best to keep him safe.

"Okay, then, I'll go first in the shower then let you in." She removed the other outer glove and left it on the table then went to the sink to wash and wipe down the outside of the canister in a bucket. Then she cleaned her still gloved hands with soap and water.

Seriously? This stuff, whatever it was, could be lethal, and she was using plain soap and water. Maybe it was a special soap. He wanted to know, but he didn't want to distract her by asking. He clamped his mouth closed.

He'd questioned her about the necessity of the suit and respirator when she'd put them on earlier, but now he could only offer a prayer of thanks for her protection, especially since she had open wounds on her hand from the turtle bite.

She stepped into the shower and set the canister on the far edge then used a handheld showerhead to clean her suit. She took the canister into another small area and shed the suit, which she hung up. Then she grabbed the sample and moved into another portion of the space with a floor tray filled with liquid and a small sink. She sealed the canister in a large bag with a big warning label on the side and cleaned her feet and hands again.

Finally, she put on a fresh mask and opened the door before disposing of her gloves in a biohazard bin. "You'll need to go in this way and try to avoid the final decontamination bath on the way in. I think you can get in without touching anything by stepping on the sides."

"Sure. I can do that."

She clutched the sample to her side. "Then head into the shower and shed your clothing. Scrub down any area that was exposed, and be careful not to cause any abrasions where an infectious agent could gain access."

He nodded.

She tilted her head. "You wouldn't happen to have a change of clothes in the SUV, would you?"

He nodded. "We all keep a set just in case we need it."

"Good." She let out a long sigh. "Before you remove your clothes, I'll have Clay give me your things to set outside the shower, and then I'll step out with him."

Erik opened his mouth to object. He didn't like her going outside and into potential danger, but he respected her need for decency, and the only real danger to her life would occur in the distance from the door to the SUV. "He'll put you in the vehicle for safety. It has bulletproof doors and windows."

"Fancy."

"More like lifesaving."

She nodded. "Wait to strip down until I bring in your bag."

"And here I thought you were just trying to get me out of my clothes." His joke barely cut the tension, but even with the mask on, he could see a smile in her eyes.

The good mood immediately evaporated as she spun for the door. She poked her head out and explained the situation to Clay.

Erik couldn't hear his brother's words, but his tone was sharp and pointed. A moment later, Kennedy brought Erik's tote bag to the shower door.

"Be sure to focus on your hands first," she said. "And use lots of soap and water."

"No special liquid needed?"

She shook her head. "Recent research says soap and water work as well as, if not better than, other chemicals. Just be sure to wash well, but again don't break the skin."

"And your hands are okay? Especially the one with the punctures from the turtle?"

She nodded. "No worries there, but if it makes you feel any better, I'll get treated for exposure too."

"How bad is this?" he asked, unable to resist.

"If you don't have any open sores, washing it off should take care of any cutaneous exposure."

"I've always got a cut or two from the job, but I don't think any of them are open." He gave his hands a thorough

83

inspection, finding nothing worrisome. "And if I inhaled it?"

"Then the doctors will start you on antibiotics, and we'll have to monitor you carefully for symptoms. If it's anthrax, just a few spores inhaled is enough to make it replicate, as it likes the moist warm areas in the lungs."

He swallowed. "But I'm not going to die, right?"

"Not if we get treatment for you right away."

Her tone continued to hold concern, and her hands were trembling. Not a good sign.

"You should get started. The sooner you disinfect, the better. And put on a mask before exiting, just in case." She gave him a tight smile and marched to the door.

She stepped outside, and he slipped through the foot-bath area and into the shower. As he shed his clothes, he hated that she wasn't in view, and his gut ached to protect her. He trusted Clay. All of his brothers for that matter, but she was special. Far more special than he was willing to admit.

He understood the physical attraction to her. She was a beautiful woman. But was it more? Was he still in love with her?

He shook his head, sending water flying, and focused on cleaning his hands, arms, and face. Washing once. Twice. Three times for good measure and looking to see if he had any open cuts. He didn't find or feel anything, but he couldn't be certain a small one didn't exist.

With no towels in sight, he moved to the foot bath and washed his hands in the small sink too. Then stood to drip dry, trying his best to keep his mind off Kennedy, but she seemed to consume his brain.

It had always been that way with her. She fired off senses and thoughts in him that no other woman had before or since. He knew he subconsciously compared all other women to her.

The door opened a fraction, and Erik felt totally exposed. Not because he was naked but because he didn't have his weapon.

Clay, mask on his face from the SUV's emergency kit, looked in. "Dude. Get dressed and let's get out of here."

"Working on it." Erik reached for his clothing, and still damp, he struggled to get the fabric over his wet skin.

The moment he was dressed, he headed outside, making sure to give the desk a wide berth. This whole place would need to be decontaminated before Kennedy could work again.

He huffed a laugh in his mask. He'd gotten his way. She wouldn't be working in the lab after this. He just didn't know coming here would potentially cost both of their lives.

After a trip to the ER, Erik and Kennedy climbed the stairs at Veritas, heading for Nighthawk Security's office. He was glad Kennedy agreed to take the stairs as it gave Erik a moment to take a few deep breaths before he met with his brothers. Wouldn't do to let them see him so rattled. They might lose confidence in his leadership ability and ask him to step down as lead. No way he was doing that. No way.

He blew out the bad air. He'd been stressed since Kennedy opened the envelope, and that increased with the arrival of patrol officers to secure the building. Clay had taken off with the potential anthrax sample for Maya to test for the biotoxin. He also took the food and drink containers from the lab's reception area to Sierra to fingerprint and then give to Maya to test for poisons. She would pay special attention to protein drinks that Wanda loved.

Aiden had arrived at the lab with a vehicle to transport Erik and Kennedy to the ER, and they'd been treated right away. Physically, he felt fine. The first round of antibiotics was administered via IV in the ER. He'd be taking tablets while they tested the powder. If indeed it was anthrax, he would stay on the antibiotics. For cutaneous exposure it required a course of seven days, but sixty days for inhalation, as anthrax could take that long to appear.

The ER doctor started Kennedy on antibiotics, too, but they weren't as worried about her exposure, not even with the open sores on her hand. She'd been well protected. He was thankful she was nearly in the clear.

Nearing the fourth floor landing, he heard Kennedy stop behind him.

"I'm glad we took the stairs," she said. "Helped to release some of this terrible stress. I feel like I'm drowning with it."

He took a good look at her. "I was wondering how everything was affecting you."

"It's not just me." She rested a hand on his arm. "We might not be together now, but that doesn't mean I'm not seriously concerned for your health."

"Yeah, I get that," he said. "But I can't spend two days worried about it. I just have to trust God and know that He'll make sure whatever happens is the right thing for me. And the same for you too."

She gave him careful study. "You always were so much better at trusting Him than I was."

She was giving him too much credit.

"I don't know about that. I'm obviously not trusting Him about relationships." He started up the stairs again.

He heard her footsteps behind him. "Are you avoiding all relationships?"

He looked back at her. "Our breakup was bad. Left me reeling. I didn't date for a long time. Then when I did, I had a girlfriend cheat on me. Kind of lessens your faith in women."

"I hope you know how sorry I am for my part in fueling that distrust."

"I do now." They reached the sixth floor, and he opened the door to the hallway. "I also know you were doing what you had to do, and you couldn't tell me. I get that. But it also tells me that something like this could happen in another relationship. Not WITSEC per se, but something that would cause a woman to step back after I was fully invested. Not sure I could handle that."

"You're very strong, Erik." She stopped in front of him. "You could survive that and so much more."

"Shh. Don't let God hear you say that or He might give me more things to handle." He chuckled, trying to lighten things up and end the conversation too. It did no good to speculate on what might happen if he got involved because he wasn't going to be getting involved. Period. End of story.

They walked to the office in silence. His brothers' voices carried from the inner room, and their receptionist, Stella, shook her head, her shoulder-length hair swinging with the motion. "They're in rare form today."

"Just today?" Erik chuckled and introduced Kennedy.

"Nice to meet you," Stella said. "The guys will fix whatever problem you're facing."

"I sure hope so," Kennedy said, not sounding all that sure of their skills.

Erik could understand that. After all, he was the one who'd suggested she open the envelope, and even if she was wearing the proper protective equipment, he felt bad for her potential exposure.

"After you." He led her into the conference room and glanced around the table. He wasn't surprised Drake was missing, as he was still in Texas.

"You don't look like you're on death's door," Aiden grinned. "When do you find out if you're infected?"

Erik appreciated his brother's lighter tone that downplayed the seriousness of their exposure. "Maya will know what we were exposed to tomorrow or the next day."

Aiden shifted his gaze to Kennedy. "And you're sure you're fine?"

She nodded. "Thanks to Erik, I opened the envelope when I was wearing my PPE, and it very likely saved me from exposure. I'm on an antibiotic, too, just in case."

Wow. She didn't blame him at all. Guilt ate at him anyway. "Go ahead and have a seat."

She took a side chair, and he went to one of the whiteboards and wrote the word anthrax with red marker. "Okay let's discuss the envelope to see if we can figure out who sent it."

Clay faced Kennedy. "Question is, was the envelope meant for your mother or for you?"

Kennedy rested her hands on the table looking relaxed, but Erik could see the strain in her eyes. "It was addressed to her but mailed after she died."

Brendan arched his eyebrow. "The sender might not have known she died."

"He would if he's her killer," Clay said.

"True that," Brendan said. "But maybe she made more than one person angry."

Kennedy's fingers tightened into fists. "That's entirely possible with the number of counterfeit drugs she was threatening to expose."

"My question is"—Erik tapped his marker on the whiteboard—"who would have access to anthrax or other biotoxins?"

"Terrorists are a given," Aiden said. "But I see no indication that we're dealing with terrorists here."

"So someone in the scientific community," Kennedy said.

"How is that even possible?" Brendan asked. "Anthrax has to be highly controlled by the government, and so are other deadly toxins, right?"

"Yes and no." Kennedy rested her injured hand on the table. "Getting a sample isn't as hard as you might think. A scientist engaged in legitimate research can apply for a certificate of registration with the feds. Once this person is designated as the Responsible Official, they can legally request samples of toxins and agents on a Select Agents list."

"Select Agents?" Brendan asked.

"Sounds like law enforcement, but it's not." She smiled. "We're talking about a list of biological agents and toxins that the Federal Special Agent Program determined to have the potential to pose a severe threat to human, animal, or plant health or to animal and plant products. To be approved to handle these agents, a security risk assessment is done by the attorney general, and then the applicant still needs approval by the HHS secretary or administrator."

"That doesn't sound easy," Aiden said.

"It's not, but once they're approved, they can order the microbe from wholesale supply houses. We call them reference laboratories. They keep large inventories of some of the deadliest organisms known to man. Those materials are normally shipped as freeze-dried samples via regular U.S. mail or through a commercial shipping company from the reference labs to the scientists."

"So, the shipment could be intercepted," Erik stated.

"Yes, but I've never heard of that happening. The more likely route to obtaining it illegally would be stealing some of the freeze-dried samples that are converted into live organisms and stored in sub-zero freezers until needed. An employee could simply use a cotton swab to scrape a minute portion of the culture from a stored vial, then start the process of multiplying the bacteria or viruses themselves."

Erik shook his head. "That's something I wish you hadn't told us."

"Sorry," she said. "Scary stuff, but I thought you should have the details."

"So," Erik said, "we're most likely looking for someone in the scientific community with connections to your mom. Maybe one of these Responsible Officials."

"Can you get us a list of these people?" Aiden asked.

"I'd think one exists, but I don't know if it would be in an accessible database. I can check. In the meantime, most of you have federal contacts who might be able to get this list. Ask them. Plus I'll ask Malone and Reed. Even Piper, Devon, and Hunter."

"And these people are?" Kennedy asked.

"FBI agents married to the Veritas partners. They can all look into it."

"Would be far easier if Sierra could process the envelope for prints or Emory could lift DNA from it," Clay said.

"If it's contaminated with a toxin," Kennedy said, "there's no way law enforcement will allow her to do that."

"What do you think the odds are that it isn't?" Brendan asked.

"With my mom's connections to the scientific world, I think it's very likely that we're dealing with a deadly substance." Her eyes narrowed. "I could be wrong about it being anthrax, though. Could be ricin or another substance. We'll have to wait for Maya's tests to confirm."

"If it is a poisonous substance," Erik said, "I would think the sender would be smart enough to wear gloves. So even if Sierra is able to process the envelope, it'll probably only hold prints from postal workers. Maybe we'll get prints or

DNA from the food containers that I grabbed before all of this happened."

"What we really need right now is Wanda's personal and professional contact list," Aiden said. "Then we can investigate everyone to see if one of them might've been angry with her."

"With the potential anthrax scare, her computer will be taken into evidence, if it hasn't been already," Clay said. "And her phone, if it's at the office."

"Already ahead of you." Erik grinned. "I started an image of her hard drive to upload to our server while Kennedy was working in the lab. I left it running and just checked it. The file completed. I'll review the data as soon as I can. No phone or copies of Wanda's contract at the lab, though."

"Her phone is at the house," Kennedy said. "I brought it home when I first got to town."

"Then Sierra probably fingerprinted it, and we need to upload the contents before PPB asks for it." Erik met Kennedy's gaze. "With your permission, I'll head over to your place after we finish here and do that."

"Sure," she said.

"I can also check Wanda's personal computer and email while I'm there."

"No personal email," Kennedy said. "My mom didn't believe in communicating via email except at work, and even then, she did it sparingly. Same is true of texts."

"Then we'll just have to depend on her call record and contacts." Erik didn't like that they'd have fewer leads in this investigation, but he'd have to deal with it. "And we all need to watch out for any military or militia-type connection to Wanda. Not that we think she's involved in anything like that, but the intruder was dressed in camo and combat boots."

"We also need to do a deep dive into Wanda's assistant,"

Aiden said. "I'll get started on finding the basics. If we need more, you can take it from there."

"Sounds good," Erik said. "She could be in on this, and we need to talk to her, but let's get the background on her first. Could help us formulate the right questions."

Erik looked at Kennedy. "We also need to remember that the break-in might be more a case of the intruder looking for something and not expecting to find you there. Means we should try to determine what he might be after."

"You think that's likely?" Aiden asked.

Kennedy nodded. "It seemed like he was searching for something when I first saw him."

"Then I'll do a thorough search of the place too." Erik looked at Kennedy. "Anything else I should get at your house? What about Wanda's personal records?"

"I don't know." Kennedy stared at her hands. "I haven't been able to bring myself to go through her things. I'm sure her will is there somewhere. It would be great if you looked at things while you were there. Feel free to search anywhere. Oh, and she has a printer with a copier, so make a copy of anything we could need."

Erik was thankful for her cooperation, but it came with a dose of sad resignation, and he didn't like seeing her this way. "You're sure you don't mind me going through her things without you?"

"Mind?" Kennedy stared across the room at the windows, then swung her gaze back to him. "Yeah. Probably. But you could've been exposed to anthrax, and I will do anything to bring the perpetrator to justice. Anything."

8

Kennedy didn't like sitting around in Erik's condo, but she couldn't do anything to help. At least nothing other than remaining in place where she was safe and Erik didn't have to worry about her.

A knock sounded on the door, and she jumped. Erik wouldn't knock on his own door. Should she answer it?

She strode down the hallway and glanced through the peephole. A tall, striking woman stood there. Sierra was with her and held a baby. He had bright blue eyes, and a smile on his adorable face.

Curious about the woman and the visit, Kennedy opened the door.

Sierra stepped forward. "This is Reed's sister, Malone. She's an attorney, and Erik thought it might be helpful for you to talk to her."

Surprised, Kennedy tilted her head and studied the woman more closely. She wore a black suit with glinting gold buttons. The sharply tailored blazer and the way her hair was perfectly twisted up in back brought to mind the words timeless elegance—a look Kennedy couldn't pull off even if she had a personal stylist. Her look was more flats, comfy knits, and jeans.

Kennedy shook hands with Malone. "I know he called you about the dive. Is that what this is about?"

Sierra shook her head, her hair brushing the baby's face. "He said it was about the reason you two broke up. That you might want to discuss whether sharing that information was legal or would get you into trouble."

She hadn't thought that there would be any legal issues with telling someone about her parents' WITSEC, but if Erik sent Malone, maybe there was something Kennedy didn't know. "Okay, sure. Come in, and I'll run everything past you."

Malone trained her gaze on Sierra. "You want to wait with us, or should I call you to come back and escort me to the door?"

"Oh, wait. For sure." Sierra looked at Kennedy. "That is, if you don't mind me hearing what's going on."

"All of your brothers know. What's one more person?" Kennedy forced out a laugh and stepped back for them to enter.

The pair went straight to the sofa and settled down as if they'd been there many times before. Kennedy wasn't surprised by Sierra, but what kind of a relationship did Malone have with Erik? Friends? Family? Girlfriend?

Kennedy doubted the last one, as he'd said he didn't trust women enough to have a relationship. He hadn't said that he didn't date, though. She glanced at Malone's perfectly manicured fingers but found no wedding or engagement ring.

Uncertain under the attorney's watchful gaze, Kennedy dug up a smile. "I don't know what Erik has to drink, but I can offer you some water."

"Nothing for me." Sierra shifted the baby, who had

chubby cheeks just begging for a squeeze. His dark hair was thicker on the top and shaped like a baby mohawk.

"Me either." Malone took a notepad from her expensive leather briefcase. Her shoes and suit looked pricey, too, but then that wasn't surprising for a lawyer.

Kennedy took a seat in a well-used leather recliner. "What do you need to know?"

"Start at the beginning of your story, and I'll ask any questions I might have along the way."

Kennedy gave Malone as many details as she knew about her father's criminal past and her family's time in WITSEC, including sharing their WITSEC inspector's name, Deputy Tyrone Kruse.

Malone jotted down notes, and Sierra's already large eyes grew rounder.

She shifted the chubby baby in her arms, who looked up at her with large blue eyes. "And this is why you broke up with Erik?"

"Yeah. It suddenly felt like I'd been lying to him—to everyone—my whole life."

"Wow. Just wow." Sierra jerked, and the baby startled with her movement. She lifted him to her shoulder and shushed him as he rested his head in the crook of her neck. "Erik had no idea. Poor guy."

"I know I hurt him, and I would give anything not to have been in that position, but if I had a do-over, I still would end things." Kennedy lifted her chin. "I couldn't live that lie any more today than I could've back then."

Sierra gently patted Asher. "I'm not blaming you. Just understanding why Erik was so impacted. He's never really recovered from it. He says he has, but his sporadic and awkward dating history says he hasn't."

"Maybe knowing the reason will bring him closure now." Malone tapped her pen on her notepad.

Kennedy hoped so, but he still seemed hurt and distrustful. She focused on Malone. "So, am I in any kind of legal trouble for telling people about WITSEC?"

"You're definitely in violation of your family's agreement with the agency, which is just cause to boot you from the program."

"With both of our parents gone, I don't even know if there will be any residual danger to me or Finley. I'm sure Tyrone will do an assessment, and then we'll have to decide if we want to remain under their program. I'm definitely leaning toward leaving it."

"Here's the thing you're forgetting," Malone said, her tone all official and lawyerly. "If you leave and continue to use your name, and Finley stays in the program, she'll have to be relocated under a different name and sever all ties with her past."

Kennedy's heart skipped a beat as the implication sank in. "That includes me. She'll sever ties with me, and I'll never see my sister again."

~

Erik took his time going through Wanda's things while the image he was taking of her phone completed, but she had very little to search, so he was back at the condo by lunchtime. He planned to discuss what he'd found with Kennedy over a meal. Hopefully the relaxed setting would soften the blow when he told her what he'd discovered.

He reached for the knob, but his phone rang. Seeing Sarge's name, Erik answered.

"Thought you should know." Sarge's gruff voice came through loud and clear. "We're forming a task force with all the appropriate agencies for the potential deadly toxin at the lab. You need to keep the investigation to yourself for now. We'll be requesting the prints and DNA from the break-in at Ms. Walker's home as well as any other evidence, including those food containers. We'd appreciate it if the Veritas scientists provided their findings as well. And Detective Frank Johnson will be calling you to get a statement from both of you on what transpired on the night of the break-in."

"Now you're interested in the break-in," Erik muttered. He felt his anger rising to the surface, and he had to swallow it down to remain levelheaded and not make an enemy. "I suppose any chance in our seeing the results from DNA and fingerprint database searches is now out of the question."

"Yes. We have no reason to believe the two incidents are related, but you know what I say?"

"You don't believe in coincidences."

"Exactly. So Johnson will want a full accounting of any leads you've run down so far."

"And if I don't cooperate?" Erik could barely contain his frustration over the one-way street.

"You know the answer to that."

"I'll be issued a subpoena or you might even have enough probable cause to get a warrant to search my place and office."

"Exactly. Don't make me do that."

"Can the Veritas experts continue working on the evidence they're evaluating?"

"I'll check in with the task force leader and get back to you." Sarge ended the call.

Erik refrained from punching the wall. He didn't want to share their information, but they didn't have much to share. They'd mostly struck out anyway.

He made a group call to Sierra, Emory, and Maya. Once they were all on the line, he brought them up to date on the new development. "PPB detective's name is Frank Johnson.

I've worked with him before, but he was in a tough spot back then so he was defensive. I hope he'll cooperate now."

"They'd be foolish not to let us continue with what we're working on," Maya said. "But I know how politics in a multi-agency task force work. You get FBI agents in the mix, and they'll likely want everything to go to Quantico."

"We've seen that happen often enough," Sierra said. "I'll rush what I can while we wait for a verdict. Let me know if I can do anything else."

"I really can't rush anything," Emory said. "It's all running right now, and the machines will need to complete before we can analyze the data."

Erik swallowed down his frustration. No point in letting them know how much this was impacting him. He thanked them and ended the call. He stowed his phone along with his negative attitude and opened his condo door. Voices floated down the hallway as the patter of doggie paws headed his way.

What in the world?

He'd expected Kennedy to be alone.

His mom's voice sounded above the others asking Kennedy if she was dating anyone.

Crud. His feet stuttered to a stop. What was his mom doing there? His dad was likely with her. Who let them in the building then escorted them to the condo? Sierra or any one of his brothers. One or more of them had probably told their mom about the anthrax. Not that he blamed them. She always managed to discover when one of her children was in danger or sick, and she always came running. He both loved and disliked that about her.

And she'd likely badgered Kennedy about their breakup. If he knew his mom—and he did—she was probably already trying to get them back together.

He didn't want to deal with that. He needed to focus on

finding the creep who drew a gun on Kennedy, but he would never leave Kennedy to fend for herself with his mother. Never.

Pong reached the door and gave a sharp bark of greeting. Even if Erik wanted to bail, his best friend had outed him. He strode down the hall, Pong rushing ahead, and prepared for his mother's inquisition. She was seated between Kennedy and Erik's dad on the sofa, but caught sight of Erik and propelled herself off the plump cushions.

When she approached, Pong eyed her as if he might need to protect Erik the way many working dogs might do.

"Sit," Erik commanded.

"I know you don't mean me." His mom smiled and looked him over. "I get that you never want any fuss, but I just had to see if my baby was all right."

Worse than he thought. "Baby? Come on, Mom. I'm not a child."

"You'll always be my baby. You'll understand someday when you have children." She cupped the side of his face then gave him a good once over. "You don't look any worse for wear, but Kennedy tells me we really won't know anything for a day or so."

"So far, I feel fine, so you don't have to stay."

"Nonsense." She waved a hand. "I brought lunch, and your dad is starving, so we'll all eat together. I'll just set the table."

"Can I help?" Kennedy asked.

"You're so sweet to offer." His mom stopped next to Kennedy and squeezed her shoulder. "You've been through a lot. Relax while I get the meal ready."

His mom didn't look mad at Kennedy, so she obviously didn't blame her for breaking up with him. Had Kennedy told his mom about WITSEC? Or had his mother believed all those years that, since Erik wouldn't talk about the reason he split with Kennedy, he must be at fault?

Kennedy met his gaze, and she didn't have the frightened-deer-in-the-headlights look that he'd expected. But she knew his parents pretty well and knew what to expect from them. Knew that his mom might whirl around like a tornado sometimes, but she always, always had her family's best interest at heart.

Kennedy sat up straighter on the couch. "Sierra brought Malone over to discuss that thing we talked about."

Okay, so she hadn't told his parents about WITSEC or she wouldn't be so cryptic in her word choice.

He felt his mother's gaze burning into him, but he continued to look at Kennedy. "I hope it was helpful."

Kennedy gave a vigorous nod. "She's going to make some calls for me, and I need to talk to Finley. Do you think she could come by today?"

"We're settled in here for a while, so sure."

"Then I'll give her a call." Kennedy headed toward the hallway.

Erik patted Pong to soothe his worried behavior and looked at his dad. "You're not planning to stay beyond lunch, are you?"

"Good to see you too." He laughed.

"Sorry. You know I like seeing you guys, but we have work to do, and I have information to share with Kennedy."

"Speaking of..." His mom glanced at him as she set plates on the table. "Everything okay with the two of you?"

"It's fine," Erik said. When his mom's eyes lit up, he wished he'd said they were on the outs.

"I'm glad." She smiled. "I always loved that girl, and it's so good to see her now all grown up, and a forensic scientist, of all things." She shook her head. "It's really something, isn't it? Working for the FBI. Traveling all over the country, diving in strange locations? What an exciting life."

Erik didn't know if recovering a corpse from a body of water fell under the label *exciting*. More like gruesome.

"Stay," he told Pong and crossed the room to her. "What's for lunch?"

"Chicken salad, fresh fruit, and homemade rosemary bread."

"What can I do to help?"

"Pour the water and set the silverware while I bring out the food."

Obviously, she didn't think his day was as hard as Kennedy's, as she was allowing him to help. When his mom came back into the room, bringing with her the savory smell of her famous rosemary bread, Erik put his arm around her shoulders and squeezed. "Thanks for coming, Mom. You're the best mother a guy could ask for."

Her mouth fell open. "What's wrong?"

"Nothing. Just thinking about Kennedy having lost both of her parents, and I'm still blessed with two wonderful ones. Figured it was time I said something." He looked at his dad. "You're great too, Dad."

"Well, sure. I knew that." He blew on his fingers and rubbed them on his chest as he gave a deep belly laugh.

Erik laughed with his dad and appreciated lightening up for a minute, just like Erik was sure his dad had planned. As a former detective, Erik's dad had experienced many difficult situations, but Erik could only remember a few times when he'd brought any of the turmoil home with him. And the times he did, he'd sequestered himself in his bedroom.

"We need to take Kennedy under our wing." His mother's gaze drifted to the hallway. "Give her the emotional support she needs. Maybe she should come stay with us."

"More secure here."

"But—"

"No buts, Mom. Her life is in danger, and we have to do our best to protect her. That means remaining right here where security is top-notch."

"I could stay with her."

"She's calling her sister to come over, and they'll need time alone."

"You never mentioned why the two of you broke up." His mom called the words over her shoulder as she went to the kitchen island to retrieve a large bowl.

"Not something I can talk about." He tipped the pitcher over the nearest glass and listened to the ice tinkling as it spilled out. Made him think of how his life had tumbled into uncertainty since he'd connected with Kennedy again.

He lifted Kennedy up in prayer. To ask God to remind her of His faithfulness and enduring love. To remember His promises and the way He'd been there for her in the past.

That would help to get her through this. Sure, his family could help, but when the big twists and turns of life assaulted a person, only God could provide the support needed to make it through to the other side. Hopefully, she would rely on Him and not try to walk this road alone. She didn't need to have all of it figured out. God did. Every little detail. She just had to trust Him.

His mother set the bowl on the table. "You can tell me anything, son."

"Not this," he stated directly and maybe with too much force.

She held up her hands. "Okay, but if that changes, just know I'm here for you and praying for you both."

"Thank you." He gave her an earnest smile.

She kissed his cheek and returned to the kitchen.

Erik saw the sympathetic look on his father's face. Each of the guys in the family had a special relationship with their dad, and they often confided things in him that they might not say to their mom. Their dad didn't pry. Their mother hadn't gotten that message yet.

Erik finished pouring the water, and Kennedy returned to the room, shoving her new phone into her jeans pocket. The jeans fit her like a glove, and he had no idea how she even got the phone into the pocket.

"Finley will come over after work tonight. I told her we could order pizza and talk. Is that okay?"

"Sure. I'll bring her up and then head to Drake's condo."

"Thank you." She squeezed his arm, firing off nerve endings.

He had to swallow to hide his growing interest in her. Not only from Kennedy, but from his mom. If she caught sight of how he was feeling, he might never get her to leave the condo.

"Uh-huh." His mother looked at him with a twinkle in her eyes. "Just as I thought."

"What's that?" he asked.

"Oh, nothing." She grinned, a Cheshire cat grin. "Lunch is ready. Let's all sit down and get reacquainted."

That look. The one that came from Matchmakers R Us, a term they jokingly applied to their mom and claimed she was a card carrying member, flashed in her eyes. Erik swallowed a groan and sat next to Kennedy.

He offered a quick prayer for his mom to behave. There was no point in talking about something that would never happen. It would just add anxiety to Kennedy's already stressful life. Even if she had hurt him, he had no wish for her to suffer any more pain.

9

Kennedy sat on Erik's sofa and listened to him say goodbye to his parents at the door, tears burning in her eyes. She swiped at them and took a few cleansing breaths. Pong was eyeing her from the end of the couch as if she might need his help. She'd take it. She was feeling very lonely right then.

Seeing Peggy's love for her family was so uplifting, and Kennedy missed her mom even more. The ache cut so deep that she could hardly get through the hours when she wasn't busy working. Not only did she want to finish her mother's project, but Kennedy needed to fill her time. With the anthrax scare, she couldn't go back to the lab until the scene was decontaminated and released. What was she going to do with her days until then?

Not sit here and brood, that was for sure. She wasn't a brooder. She was a doer. She would ask to be involved in the investigation. No, demand it. She had to. For her own sanity. And to finish her quest to find her mother's killer.

Erik strode into the room, a pensive expression on his face. He'd had the same look off and on since he'd come back from her mom's place. Was it what he'd found or because of his mom? Peggy had always been pretty aggressive, but not in a bad way. She just loved her children so much and wanted them to be happy. She'd hinted several times during lunch about Erik and Kennedy getting back together.

"I'm so glad you survived the meal." He rolled his eyes and sat between her and Pong, who immediately shifted to rest his head on Erik's thigh. "My mom can be a handful."

"I've always liked her, but I can see where it might be tough for a guy to handle."

His expression sobered, and he sunk his fingers into Pong's coat. "I shouldn't complain about her. Right now, I'm sure you'd be glad to have any kind of mom, and I don't want you to think I don't know that."

"I would. I really would." Those incessant tears wet her eyes again. She gave them an angry swat.

He leaned forward and clasped her hand. "If you need to cry, then cry. Anytime. No one will judge you for it. We just want to offer any comfort we can."

She tried swallowing and changing her focus to stem the tears, but they came fast and furious, rolling down her cheeks.

"Aw, honey. Come here." Erik moved closer and drew her into his arms.

She went willingly, giving Pong no choice but to move out of the way, and laid her head against that solid chest, which had once felt the imprint of her head day after day. His solid arms curling around her broke the final straw in her resolve, and she let go. Sobbing. Wetting his shirt.

He gently ran his fingers over her back in rhythmic circles. "Tell me what to do, honey. How to help."

Don't call me honey. I don't deserve it after the way I left you.

Exactly. She didn't deserve this comfort and support from him, and that was all it took to stop her tears. She needed to push away and put some distance between them before she did something like kiss him.

She pressed her hands against his chest, and he relaxed his arms. But before she could completely lean back, he ran his thumb over the tears lingering on her cheek. Her heart took a tumble into infinity, and she realized she could easily fall in love with this man again. If she wasn't still in love with him. This wonderful, considerate man who'd always respected her, loved and cared for her. He'd treated her like a princess, and she'd left him like an ogre. Sure, she had to do it, but he hadn't deserved the hurt and pain she'd caused.

His hand slid into her hair, cupping the back of her head. He leaned closer, as if he were going to kiss her.

Oh, man, what should she do? Her heart longed for the kiss. Her brain warned her to push back. She should move away. Quickly. But her heart was winning, and she couldn't budge even an inch.

But more than anything, she knew even if she *could* move, she didn't want to. Didn't want to at all.

What in the world was Erik doing? Kissing Kennedy. He had to be certifiably crazy. Completely and totally crazy. And yet...he couldn't stop. Didn't want to stop. Her lips were warm and insistent. She wanted the kiss as much as he did, fueling his passion even more.

He drew her close. Closer. Remembered all the times he'd held her. The good times. When he'd been head-over-heels in love with her. And now? What now? Was he leading her on?

He felt like an icy wind blew through his condo, chilling his desire. He jerked back before the cold wind froze him in place.

"I'm sorry." He ground out the words between deep breaths. "I shouldn't have done that. It was wrong."

Pain constricted her eyes. "Why exactly?"

"Because it can't go anywhere. It's wrong to make you think I'd changed my mind when I haven't."

"About forgiving me?"

"No. Not that. Not that at all. I've forgiven you, and I would never take that back." He curled his fingers tight against his palms to keep from touching her. "But I'm not interested in a relationship with anyone."

"I see." She crossed her arms.

He pointed at her arms. "That's exactly why it was wrong. Now you're mad or your feelings are hurt, and I didn't want that to happen. We agreed on professionalism, and we need to follow that agreement. I need to keep my hands and lips to myself."

"I'm not mad." She let her arms fall. "I'd be lying if I said I wasn't still attracted to you. I have feelings for you. But after the way I hurt you, I don't blame you. Not at all."

She touched his arm, her soft skin setting a fire burning in his gut again, and he had to resist bolting away and hurting her even more. His best bet was to shift their conversation back to the investigation. That discussion would put a damper on their emotions.

He jerked to his feet. "Why don't we sit at the dining table and talk about what I found at your mother's place. Then you can share it with Finley to see if she has any explanations."

"That sounds dire."

"It's concerning."

She blinked a couple of times. "Now you're scaring me."

"I don't mean to. I'll grab the information." He all but ran to snatch up his bag, which he'd set on the floor near the kitchen island. Pong trailed him, but he didn't want the distraction. He pointed at the dog's crate. "Go to bed, boy."

Pong gave Erik a sad look but did as he was told.

Erik felt Kennedy's eyes tracking him, but he had to be strong. Just like he'd been raised. Set a goal. Focus on it. Achieve it. Yeah, that was it. Focus on the goals. He had three of them right now. Keep Kennedy safe—top priority. Then find her mother's killer, if she was indeed murdered. And achieve the first two without causing either Kennedy or himself emotional distress. So, professional it was.

He remembered his search, and the fire for Kennedy evaporated. He headed back to the table, where she was looking up at him expectantly.

He set the folder on the table next to his phone, which he'd used to take pictures at her mother's place. "Before we start, I wanted to tell you I got a call from Sarge. A detective is going to call us for statements about the break-in. Plus, they're confiscating all the evidence, and they formed a multi-agency task force."

"All of this is because of the potential anthrax, right?"

He nodded. "They also want to see what we've learned. Even though the sharing won't go both ways, we'll cooperate."

"Of course."

"Let's start with your mom's phone. I only glanced at the data after I imaged it, but her call history has been cleared. Not a single call listed. Same for the internet. Why would she clear it if she didn't have anything to hide?"

Kennedy held his gaze. "She wouldn't. At least, I doubt she would. She hated technology. Well, except for work.

Even then, she had her assistant do most of the data entry. And her phone?" Kennedy shook her head. "She didn't know how to use it for more than making calls and had no desire to learn anything new. I doubt she'd have any idea how to clear the history. Is this a big set back?"

"Pretty major. Besides seeing who she'd been communicating with recently, we could've compared the calls to the phone numbers on the Responsible Official's list. If we get it."

Kennedy pursed her lips. "I could contact the phone company and get her information."

"They might give you access, but the problem is, it's a lengthy process to get paper copies."

"I can just ask for access to her online account."

"I doubt the phone company will give you that. Even if your mom made you executer of her estate. As such, her will gives you rights to certain assets, but there's been recent legislation regarding digital access."

"Why do you know about this?"

"You know how I geek out over anything digital." He flashed a quick smile. "Anyway, she doesn't specify digital assets, like her online phone account, in her will. Digital assets are different and are subject to federal and state laws. In Oregon, if the will doesn't specify them, it falls to each service providers' terms of service agreements. I checked the company's agreement, and it guarantees user confidentiality even after death."

"I've never heard of this. Are you sure?"

"Positive," he said. "And something people should really be thinking about when they draw up wills these days."

She crossed her arms. "So is there anything I can do?"

"Our best bet is to search her computer and try to obtain passwords." He settled back in his chair. "I haven't done that yet as there are other priorities right now. Like this photo of what's inside your mother's safe." He scrolled through the photos to the correct picture and displayed it for Kennedy. "You're looking at roughly forty grand in cash."

Kennedy gaped at the screen. "But I...we..." She shook her head. "Why would my mom have that much cash?"

"That's what I was hoping you could tell me. There's no evidence of any money being withdrawn from her checking account so I have to believe the cash was given to her."

"No. No." She shook her head hard. "Maybe Finley will know where it came from."

He didn't like what he needed to say next, but he had no choice if he wanted to figure out what was going on with the money. "Often when this much cash is found in relation to a murder, the money was gotten by illegal methods. I don't really think your mom would do anything illegal, but we can't rule it out."

Kennedy's eyes flashed wide open. "But how can we know?"

"I'll review older bank records that I haven't looked at yet. Maybe she cashed out proceeds from selling her home instead of leaving it in her bank."

"But why cash?"

"Did she ever express concern about keeping money in banks?"

"Never to me." Kennedy grabbed a legal pad and pen he'd left on the table and scribbled a note. "I'll ask Finley about that too. Maybe it's from before. From when my dad broke the law."

"Can't be. The bills are Series 2003 which are the current bills in circulation today. So too new. Have you given more thought to your dad working in something illegal or even hooking back up with the scammer from his past?"

Kennedy shook her head so hard her hair slapped in her

face. She swiped it away with a frustrated hand. "I can't imagine him doing it the first time let alone another."

"I don't think your dad would've done that either, but if I learned anything in my years on the police force, it's that people often do unpredictable things."

"Yeah, but not my dad. He was solid. Loved his job. Loved my mom and their life. Why go back to the old life?"

"That will be up to us to find out."

She sighed. "It seems like I knew very little about my mom's everyday existence."

"You really can't know anyone," Erik said. "You think you do and then wham. They can pull the rug right out from under you."

Kennedy gasped. She'd gotten his underlying message. He shouldn't have said it. Hated himself for needing to say it. Clearly, he wasn't over the pain she'd caused. Another good reason to keep things professional with her.

"I'm sorry." Erik wished he could take his words back. "I know that hurt. I shouldn't have said it."

"Feel free to say whatever you think. You always did, and I loved that about you."

"I thought you were the same way until that last day." He swallowed away his pain. "I get that you had to do what you had to do. There's nothing you could've done differently. But as I told you before. It still stings. Maybe by the time we wrap up this investigation, things will have changed."

"I hope so. I'd like us to be friends."

Friends. Not likely. He didn't say that though. No point in hurting her more. He swiped to the next photo on his phone. "I took pictures of your parents' wills. When your dad died, your mother inherited everything, and her will divided everything she had between you and your sister. And as I mentioned she named you executer. I don't see anything odd in that, do you?"

Kennedy shook her head. "She told us she was going to do that."

"I hate to ask, but does Finley have money issues?"

She cocked her head and studied him. "Not that I know of. She has a great job. She's a graphic designer and well paid. She lives in a modest one-bedroom apartment, so it seems unlikely. Why do you ask?"

"I found this letter from your mother to you. It wasn't sealed so I looked at it." He handed Kennedy the phone and watched her expression as she read the letter he'd photographed. In it, her mother asked her to watch out for Finley so she wouldn't blow her entire inheritance on frivolous items but instead put it to good use. Maybe buy a home or invest it.

Forehead furrowed, Kennedy looked up. "Finley takes after my dad. She's more of a daydreamer, more erratic than me and our mom. But still. I doubt she has money issues. It's just my mom wanting to be sure she's okay. Finley's the baby of the family, and my mom worried about her. You get that, right?"

He grimaced. "Unfortunately, I do."

"Please don't ask me to question my sister about this. We're walking a fine line right now, and I don't want to make things worse."

"We need to know." He watched her until she nodded her agreement. "And I'd like to do a deep dive on her background. Just to be sure."

"I don't like that." Kennedy chewed on her lip.

"I'll be doing one on you too. No stones unturned and all of that."

"But I..." She let out a noisy breath, and then a look of resolve passed over her face. "Go ahead. I've worked enough investigations to know it's important to be thorough. It's often things you don't expect that provide a lead in an investigation."

She was right, but he prayed that his deep dive on Finley wouldn't implicate her in anything wrong. He doubted Kennedy could handle her last remaining family member having been involved in either parent's death.

10

Kennedy's stomach threatened to expel the pizza she'd eaten for dinner with Finley, and the tangy spices lingering in the air didn't help. Kennedy hadn't a clue why her gut was tied in knots. Was it because Erik kissed her or because she needed to ask her sister uncomfortable questions?

She touched her lips, the kiss still a vivid memory. Kissing him had been great. Awesome even. She'd liked the softness of his lips on hers. The passion behind his touch. The hope for reconciliation she wished the kiss included. She honestly liked all of it. Way too much for her own good.

Thankfully, Erik had broken it off, and after escorting Finley to his place, he'd taken Pong to Drake's condo.

Except she wasn't really thankful. She'd wanted the kiss to go on and on. To feel like she had in the old days when love for a man was part of her everyday life.

She'd dated in the last six years but had never found *the one*. It was starting to seem like Erik might be that guy. If so, she was destined for a lifetime of loneliness because he wanted nothing to do with her, and she wasn't going to settle. Not when it came to a partner for life.

She glanced at Finley sitting next to her on the couch and scarfing down her pizza as if she hadn't eaten in a week.

Great. Kennedy was going to ruin her sister's evening with tough questions. Maybe damage their relationship even more. Then where would Kennedy be? Totally alone. But she had put off her questions long enough. She opened her mouth to speak, but Finley got up with her water glass and headed to the kitchen.

"So you and Erik. I caught the tension between you. Did you tell him about WITSEC?"

"I did."

"And?" Finley gave Kennedy a pointed look.

"If you're thinking we're going to suddenly get back together because he knows why I broke up with him, don't." Kennedy made sure her tone left no room for questions. "He appreciated the information but made it clear that will never happen. Not after the way I dumped him. Plus, another woman cheated on him. He's leery of all women."

Finley returned with ice clinking in the glass. "But if he was game? Would you be?"

"Too much time has passed. We're different people."

Finley dropped onto the sofa and drew her legs up to face Kennedy. "You didn't answer my question."

"I don't know."

Finley's eyes lit up. "I thought so."

"Don't get excited. Even if I did want to pursue something with him—and that's a very big if—he's not interested." Kennedy took a long pull on her water. "I had a reason for asking you to come by, and it wasn't to talk about Erik."

"What's up?"

"I talked to a lawyer today about WITSEC, and she asked what you want to do. Have you thought about it at all?"

"A lawyer?" Finley's volume rose.

"Erik's friend. Just a casual talk to see if I'm in trouble for telling his family about Dad."

Finley let out a relieved breath. "I haven't thought about it. Other than I want to talk to Tyrone, to see if he thinks that we're still in danger."

Kennedy agreed that they should speak to their WITSEC inspector too. "That would be a good thing to ask. Problem is, telling Erik and his brothers is a violation of our agreement."

"They won't tell anyone." Finley's eyebrows narrowed, creating a furrow that was already starting to become permanent, unusual for a twenty-five-year-old.

"Yeah, but I feel too guilty not to tell Tyrone."

That furrow deepened. "You have to do what you have to do."

"Go ahead and call him soon so you can make a decision," Kennedy said. "Who knows? He might kick me out, and it could be a moot point."

"If you tell him, and he lets you stay in the program, he'll relocate us." Finley locked gazes. "If so, you'll have to walk away from Erik again."

Kennedy's heart dropped. "If you stay in the program, so will I. I could never spend the rest of my life without seeing you and knowing you were okay."

"Me either." Finley grabbed Kennedy in a hug and quickly released her to stare into her eyes. Kennedy found only sincere concern looking back at her. "I don't want to argue with you. I'm glad Erik and his brothers are going to answer your question about Mom once and for all."

"And about that." Kennedy took a breath and planned her next words carefully. No way she wanted to sound like some freaked-out novice instead of a practiced professional. "There was an incident at Mom's lab this afternoon. A letter that held a suspicious powder was delivered there. I think it could be anthrax or ricin."

Finley's mouth dropped open. "Are you okay?"

"I was wearing PPE, so I'm fine. But Erik might've been exposed." Kennedy didn't tell her there was a tiny chance that she'd been exposed. Finley didn't need another thing to worry about.

"You must be so worried about Erik."

"I'm trying not to be until we confirm the substance. The doctor's started him on antibiotics so if it's anthrax, he should be fine. We'll know in a day or two if the powder contained anything dangerous." She'd done her very best to keep her tone level and emotionless, but tears were fighting to break free. She looked away until she had them under control. "I gave Erik permission to go through the house to look for any leads."

"And?" Finley planted her hands on her knees.

"And he found forty thousand dollars in cash in the safe."

"Oh." Finley's relaxed expression didn't change.

Not the response Kennedy expected. "Did you know about it?"

"Not exactly."

"But you're not surprised?"

"No."

"Come on, Finley. Why would Mom have that much cash? It makes no sense."

Finley shrugged.

Kennedy wouldn't let it go at that. "Did Mom ever express concern about keeping money in banks?"

"Not to me, no."

Kennedy searched her sister's face for any hint of what she was really thinking. "Okay, what gives? Why are you being so laid back about this? It's forty grand. That's a boat-load of money."

"I don't know anything about it."

"Then why aren't you surprised."

She squeezed her knees. "I don't want to say bad things about Mom. You know. With her dying and all."

"It's okay. You can tell me."

"It's just, you know how obsessed she was with her work. She often forgot to do the basic things of everyday living, like banking. Stuff piled up. It got so bad that even I couldn't stand it anymore and had to nag her or she would've had her utilities cut off. So maybe she kept the cash so she could access it at all times of the day."

"But you can access an ATM at all times of the day too. And you can't pay bills with cash unless you go into offices, and that would take even more time. So that doesn't make sense to me."

"You're right." Finley looked away. "I don't know then."

"What are you thinking?"

"Could it be illegal money from Dad's past?"

"The cash is newer than that."

Finley crossed her arms. "If you're thinking Mom was up to something illegal, you're wrong. She would never break the law."

"I agree." Kennedy sighed.

"What do we do about it? Do we spend it?"

"For now we leave the money where it is because the police will need to see it."

Finley frowned.

Kennedy took a breath before asking her next question. "Do you need money?"

Finley's eyes opened wide. "What? Why would you ask that?"

"You seem eager to get it."

Finley raised her chin. "I was just asking. We have to deal with it eventually."

"Right now, we just have to pray that Erik figures this out and hope that Mom didn't do something bad to get this cash."

"I wish I'd never called him." Finley pouted. "Then we'd be the only ones who knew about the cash."

"We'd still have the same questions about it, and this way we'll get an answer."

"Maybe one we don't like." Finley tightened her arms and slumped down.

"FYI, Erik will be reviewing your finances."

Finley jumped up. "You think I'm lying about something?"

"He's checking my finances too," Kennedy said. "He doesn't expect to find anything. It's just a task that an investigator needs to check off and move on. But if he finds something questionable, he'll dig and dig until he gets the answers he's looking for, so if he's going to find something, tell me now."

Finley's face paled. "He won't. I want to go home now."

Again, not the reaction Kennedy expected. Was she wrong to trust her sister? She didn't think she was making a mistake, but only time would tell.

Erik left Pong crated at Drake's place and returned to his condo from escorting Finley out of the building. Kennedy was sitting on the couch and looking even more upset than when he'd departed with Finley. Half an uneaten pizza congealed in a box open on the coffee table next to paper plates, and the air smelled like pepperoni.

He wanted to ask what Finley had to say about the

money, but with the strain in Kennedy's eyes, he didn't want to push. He also wanted to tell her what he'd learned about Finley but that wouldn't help Kennedy either. So he dropped onto a chair by his computer to patiently wait for her to share. Time ticked past like painful pricks from porcupine quills, but she didn't speak. Not a word.

Tick. Tick. Tick. Minute after minute. Five. Ten. Thirty.

Okay. Enough. His patience evaporated.

He got up from the dining table and joined her at the couch, where she was staring at her iPad. She glanced up, her eyes glistening.

His heart constricted, and his focus changed. Just like that. He would do anything to make those tears go away.

She turned the tablet to face him. "I shouldn't be looking at family pictures when I'm already upset, but I miss my mom. So very much. I think each day should get easier, but so far it hasn't. Something happens, and I keep thinking I should call her and tell her about it, but then it hits me. I'll never be able to call her again. Never."

Her chin quivered, and tears rolled down her cheeks.

"Aw, honey." He took her good hand and held it. "I want to take your pain away, but I know I can't. I wish I could find a way to help you through it."

Her eyes widened, and she took her hand back to swipe at her tears. "I wouldn't expect that. Not with the way I hurt you."

He'd felt like he'd made her feel bad since the moment they'd reconnected, and he didn't want that. Maybe at first. Maybe he'd wanted her to feel how much she hurt him, but not anymore. "You had to end things like you did, and it's forgiven."

"But I—"

"Stop." He tucked a strand of hair behind her ear and

held her gaze. "It's over. Let's move on and leave it in the past."

She blinked, her expression questioning. "Does this mean you might consider a relationship with a woman again?"

He let his hand fall. "I haven't come that far yet."

She nodded, but a sad resignation lingered in her eyes. "So I still ruined things for you."

He wanted to offer a comforting answer, not add to her pain, but he couldn't. "I'm not going to lie and say you didn't play a part in it, but it wasn't just you."

She took a breath and slowly let it out. "Did you come over here for a reason?"

Her change of subject didn't come with a change in her expression. He'd hurt her again. But he would move on. "It's Finley. She's in a lot of debt. She just opened and maxed out two credit cards, and she's a month behind on her rent."

"Not good. Not good at all. We're not allowed under WITSEC rules to open credit in our names. They issue us a card and track our expenses."

"I'd heard they did that. Kind of big brotherish."

"It's to keep us from drawing attention in a credit search, and of course becoming so desperate for money that we might do something stupid." Kennedy rubbed the palm of her good hand down her leg. "When I told Finley about the money in the safe, she seemed eager to spend it. She's probably embarrassed about the debt."

"Likely so."

Kennedy tilted her head, her sleek red hair sliding over her shoulder. "But how does that relate to my mom's death?"

"We don't have enough information to draw a conclusion yet. It's just a piece of the puzzle."

Kennedy lifted her shoulders. "Finley would never kill our mom, so don't be thinking she would."

"I didn't think that, but she could be in debt to someone who would." He wished he didn't need to say that, but he always had to speak the truth. "Maybe she knew about the cash and told someone, and they were trying to steal it."

"If she knew, why not take the money herself and pay off her debts. I was thinking more like she owed money to a loan shark." Kennedy took several exaggerated breaths, her gaze flitting around the room as if seeking answers. "But in that case, if Finley was the one who owed the money, why kill my mom?"

"They couldn't kill her or they would never get their money back. But it's also a stretch to think they would kill your mother. Hurt her, yes. With something obvious. Maybe a broken bone. Not something to cause a heart attack. I'll get one of my brothers to look into it."

"Why don't I just ask her about it?" Kennedy grabbed the strand of hair that had fallen over her eyes and twirled it around her finger.

"You can, but she might not tell you the truth."

"Sadly, that's probably true, but I'll ask anyway." Kennedy released her hair and gripped the arm of the couch.

"Right, now, I'm going to call my brothers and let them know about the money. See if they have any ideas on how to investigate it." He placed a video conference call, and when all except Drake were connected, he scooted closer to Kennedy and held out the phone, giving her a clear view of the screen.

Erik didn't waste any time. "In my search of Wanda's place, I found forty thousand dollars in cash in her safe."

Aiden let out a low whistle. "That's some chunk of change. You thinking she cashed out a few of those monthly deposits?"

"No," Erik said. "I've reviewed her financial records and

the cash didn't come from her checking account. And before you suggest that it's from Silas's past before WITSEC, the bills have a 2003 issue date."

Aiden scratched his neck. "So where would she get that kind of cash?"

"That's what I was hoping you all could help with," Erik replied.

Clay's eyebrows pulled in. "Maybe Silas started working on some illegal scheme again."

Kennedy lifted her chin, and her nostrils flared. "I can't see that happening. I really can't. Still, I know it's possible. One thing I've learned on the job, is that people do unexpected things. Maybe he desperately needed the money."

Aiden stared into the camera, his gaze penetrating. "If so, wouldn't he have spent it instead of socking it away in a safe?"

Clay cleared his throat. "He could've died before he had the chance to."

Kennedy's gaze shot to him. "But then wouldn't my mom have paid for whatever it was?"

"Perhaps with your father's death, the problem went away," Clay said.

"But if he owed money to someone, wouldn't they still come after my mother?" Kennedy asked.

"Logic says they would," Aiden said. "But we don't always deal with logic."

Clay propped his elbows on the desk in front of him and leaned on his hands. "He might've gotten more money than he needed."

"I want to look into his finances," Erik said. "Wanda didn't have records going back to when Silas was alive, and it'll take time to find anything. So let's move on for now. Any other thoughts on the money?"

"Not from me," Aiden said, and the others murmured their agreement.

Erik gave each brother a pointed look. "Give it some thought and let me know if you come up with anything. And would one of you look into Finley's potentially borrowing money from a loan shark?"

Clay arched an eyebrow. "You think that's likely?"

"No," Erik stated firmly. "But she's in debt, and I'm just checking all avenues to see if her money problems might've spilled over to Wanda."

"I'll do it," Clay offered.

"Let me know what you find." Erik's phone dinged and a text displayed on his screen. "Text coming in from Nick. He didn't locate anything else on inDents or the deposits."

"Whoever set this up knew what they were doing, then," Aiden stated. "If Nick can't find anything, no one can."

"Exactly," Erik said as he gave it some thought. "I'll give the info to Detective Johnson and encourage him to get a court order for the domain registration information."

Erik thanked his brothers and ended the call. At Kennedy's deep frown, he wanted to share something positive for once. "Your background check came back clean."

"That's not a surprise." Her forehead remained furrowed.

"I'm just about to start on your mother's older bank records. Would you like to go through them with me, or would you rather I take my things and head over to Drake's condo?"

Her finger started spinning in her hair, twirling a strand tight. "I don't want to go through her finances. Not at all. But I don't want to be alone either. So stay. Please."

He'd offered to work with her, but should he really stay? What with her emotional state and all? He should probably head over to Drake's place before he found other ways to comfort her, ways that weren't in their best interest.

He started to get up, but she pleaded with those gorgeous brown eyes. No way he could go, so he dropped back down onto the cushion.

About time he realized that he was powerless to refuse her anything. A fact he was certain would be his downfall again.

11

Kennedy crossed the large room to Erik. He'd come over from Drake's condo an hour before, bringing bagels for breakfast. She hadn't showered, so she'd gone back to his room to get ready and put a fresh bandage on her hand while he continued to work at the table, Pong resting at his feet.

Erik looked fresh in his work polo shirt and cargo pants. The dark black shirt highlighted his lighter hair. He glanced up from his computer, and with just one look, her pulse slipped into warp speed. She could too easily imagine waking up in the morning with him at her side. She'd often pictured it in the past, but now it seemed even more personal. Maybe because they weren't a couple anymore.

He smiled and lifted a large mug with big letters that read, *NO I WILL NOT FIX YOUR COMPUTER.* "There's coffee in the kitchen. I put a mug out for you. Help yourself to the bagels."

"Thanks." After a rough night filled with pain from her hand and bad dreams that kept her tossing and turning, she could use a gallon of the stuff. She hurried to the kitchen to fill a mug. She chose a plain bagel and slathered strawberry cream cheese over the surface. She hadn't eaten much of the pizza, and the scent of strawberries had her mouth watering as she took her plate and mug to the table.

She closely looked Erik over. "Any symptoms?"

"I feel perfectly fine." His gaze was earnest, and she believed him.

"It's likely too early for symptoms to occur anyway, but keep an eye out for anything unusual." She set down her mug and tapped his pill bottle sitting by his computer. "And keep taking these antibiotics."

"Yes, Mom." He laughed.

She settled in a chair and grinned back at him, but his eyes smoldered with an intensity that kicked up her heart rate. No. Not good. Keeping up this flirting—or whatever it was—would only lead them in the wrong direction.

He pointed at her bandage. "How's the hand?"

"Sore but manageable," she said, though the pain was bad enough that she'd been tempted to take the pain meds the doctor prescribed. She didn't. Not when she needed a clear brain.

"And you're feeling—?"

"Fine. No sign of illness." And no reason to linger on her health. "Have we learned anything about the DNA from my mom's place?"

"A text from Emory said the DNA from the print on the drawer matched my shirt, so the intruder definitely bumped into me. Too bad I didn't know that and stop him."

"You couldn't have known."

"I knew something was wrong." He leaned back and frowned. "Should've followed my gut. His DNA didn't match anyone in the Veritas database, so Emory will have to get Detective Johnson to run it through law enforcement databases."

"Speaking of Johnson, any word from him yet?"

"Not a peep, which is surprising, but maybe he's running down more promising leads." Erik sat forward and took a sip of his coffee. "I finished reviewing your mom's computer files last night and printed out a contact list from her phone." He slid a piece of paper across the table that held names, phone numbers, and emails. "Recognize any names?"

Kennedy scanned the list. "Mine, of course, and Finley's and Nora's, but otherwise? None." She reviewed the list again and looked up. "The email addresses could help. Since my mom only used it for work, they would all be work related. College and lab both. They're the people most likely to have access to biotoxins."

"Then I'll have the guys look into them."

"Sounds like a good way to start."

Erik set his cup down. "Do you know if PSU would have access to anthrax? Should we be ramping up our investigation into her fellow professors?"

She shook her head. "Most college labs aren't equipped to handle the list of Select Agents and toxins monitored by the feds. To be approved, they'd need a biosafety level 3 lab, and most colleges don't exceed BSL-2. I do know OHSU and OSU both have or at least had level three labs, but the last I'd heard, they didn't deal with Select Agent research. My mom's lab is a level two, but she insisted on several of the requirements for a level three for added safety, which is why I was wearing the right kind of PPE."

"But the scientists who work in these college labs might know how to get a sample of anthrax, right?"

"Yeah. It's not a bad idea to look in that direction."

"Let's talk about it at our next meeting and get my brothers' take on it."

"If terrorists can get Select Agents on the black market, counterfeit drug manufacturers likely could too. Especially the large operations working out of Mexico." She picked up her bagel and took a bite, the creamy strawberry flavor melting on her tongue.

"Something else we can't lose sight of. I should also mention that your mom had one credit card with a very low limit and it was maxed out. All the charges were for dining, which is odd, considering she had plenty of cash in the safe to spend and she only paid the minimum balance due on the card."

"That's odd." Kennedy washed down her bite with a sip of the strong black coffee. "My mom always preached about saving and money responsibility. I know she kept that credit card for emergency purposes or for the times she was required to have one for car rentals and such. So I don't know what's going on here. Or with Finley. I called her after you left last night. She said the only debt she's carrying is what she's racked up on her credit cards."

Erik held his mug just shy of his mouth. "Did she sound believable?"

Kennedy chewed another bite of bagel and swallowed it as she considered his question. "I'm not sure. I can tell when she's lying when I see her, but over the phone it's hard to do. I'll ask when I see her again." She nodded at his computer. "Did you find anything else?"

"Your mom's checking account was opened shortly after your father died. The initial deposit was only two hundred dollars. Kind of low, but since then there are monthly deposits of five thousand dollars from PSU."

"Her salary," Kennedy said.

He nodded. "And just like the twenty K deposits, she didn't really touch this money, and the balance in her checking account was building."

"This all seems off."

"Agreed," Erik said. "Maybe we could learn something from her college things."

Kennedy shook her head. "Finley has them at her place."

He leaned forward, enthusiasm lighting his eyes. "I think it's time we review them too."

Great. More personal things Kennedy really didn't want to look through. "The boxes are in Finley's storage room. I have a key, so we can pick them up whenever we want."

"Then let's get over there after we finish this." He looked at his computer screen. "Also odd if your mom practiced what she preached, is that she had no savings. Zero. Or at least I can't find any. Her checking account has been growing with the big deposits, but she wasn't socking it away in savings."

Kennedy shook her head. "My dad was big on saving too, and he should've left her well prepared for an emergency."

"Well, if he *was* saving, it would have to be in a separate account in his name, and your mother didn't inherit it. At least not via electronic transfer or a cashed check."

"Could she have cashed out a savings account and put it in the safe?"

"Sure, but forty K is far less of a balance than recommended for their age, and it sure wouldn't gain any interest sitting in a safe. But I didn't see any financial records for your dad at the house. In case I missed them, I've asked Brendan and Clay to go through your place today. With your permission, of course."

Kennedy didn't want even more eyes prying into her mother's past, but they would be discreet. "That's fine."

"Also in the computer files I uploaded from the lab, I found security footage for the past thirty days. I'd like to review the videos before I go get the files from Finley's place.

And then I want to see the logs and any files for a few months before that to see who's been logging in and out of the lab. Problem is, we don't have access to those files because the pharma company is paying for it."

"Do you think they'd give it to me if I asked?"

"It's worth a try."

"I'll do it right now." She picked up her phone, hoping this time she would actually be able to help move their investigation forward.

Kennedy was on hold for far longer than it took to make her request and get off the phone. By the time she finished the call, Erik had his face buried in his computer.

"The lady didn't even ask why I wanted the information," Kennedy said. "She can't do anything without talking to her manager."

He frowned. "That's a start."

She nodded at his computer. "Since I can't work at the lab, I'd like to help review the videos."

He took a long swig from his mug and grimaced. "Cold coffee. Yuk. I have hours of footage to go through, so that would be a big help."

She got her iPad out of her bag. "This is the only device I have with me. Will it work?"

"We could make it work, but I have a few machines sitting around that would do a better job."

"Just a few?" She grinned at him.

He smiled broadly, and her pulse responded with a jump. "Okay, maybe a dozen or so in various forms and ages."

She worked hard not to keep up the flirtatious tone that had surfaced again. "You never did like to part with a computer, even after you upgraded to a newer one."

"What can I say?" He eyed her, his light mood completely gone. "I believe in long-term commitments."

She didn't miss his double meaning but wouldn't bite and move to anything personal. "Seems like you do the computer work for the team."

"For the most part, but the others know their way around a computer for basic research purposes. And speaking of that, my plate is full, so Aiden is running a background check on Nora. Since Harper's off training, he's fine with long hours right now."

"Being an Olympic downhill skier sounds like an interesting career."

"She loves it. I think you'd like her."

Didn't matter. Kennedy wouldn't be around long enough to meet Harper. "And your other brothers? Married? Single."

"Brendan is married. His wife, Jenna, is a stay-at-home mother. She has a five-year-old, Karlie, who Brendan adopted right after he married Jenna. Clay's getting married in less than two weeks to Toni. She's an FBI agent, and Drake's seriously dating Natalie, a social worker. And you know Sierra's married with a baby."

Kennedy remembered the large Sunday family dinners with his parents. How did so many fit in their dining room now? But it was just what his mom had always wanted and not so subtly hinted at. "Your mom's dreams are coming true."

He chuckled. "I'm her only holdout. Means she's focusing a lot of attention my way. When she isn't spoiling the baby or Karlie or the three kids she and Dad are fostering."

"Three more kids?" Kennedy couldn't even fathom it. "Even more people for Sunday dinner. If you all still do that."

"We do," he said, his tone reserved now.

Maybe he thought she was going to ask for an invite. Not

a chance. She wouldn't want to insert herself into his family any more than she already had.

He lurched to his feet. "Let me grab a computer you can use."

Yeah. He was acting strangely, all right. Gone was the earlier companionship.

He headed for the doorway to his second bedroom that he'd set up as an office. Or more like computer central. If not for eating breakfast out here, she suspected he would be tucked in there working and not come out until he found something or lunchtime, whichever came first. She'd often had to pull him away from his computers in college, but the nice thing was that once she broke through, he gave her his full attention.

Not something she wanted now, thank you very much. She focused on finishing her bagel, barely tasting the strawberry cream cheese. She was swallowing the last bite when he returned with a laptop.

He plugged it in but set the machine in front of his spot at the table. "I'll get you logged into our network and queue up the next video for you."

She watched him for a moment, loving the sideways quirk of his mouth. She'd seen it more times than she could count when he was working on computers or homework. She'd often wondered why he didn't go into computers as a professional, but he said it would no longer be fun for him. Plus, he loved law enforcement even more. He claimed it ran in his blood.

"Why did you leave law enforcement?" she asked.

His head popped up. "For Aiden. Dad needed a kidney transplant, and Aiden donated one of his. At the time, he was an ATF agent. We were worried he would get into a shoot-out or confrontation and lose his only remaining kidney. So we formed the agency to keep him safer."

Ah, family trumped everything in Erik's life. Which was why he'd often taken her home on weekends for family dinner and why he frequently talked about getting married after they graduated. Oh, if that had only been a possibility, she would have his and his family's loving arms surrounding her after the loss of her mother and their kindness and wisdom supporting her.

He brought the laptop to her. "I've got it all queued up. Happy viewing."

She caught a whiff of his masculine scent, a mix of musk and mint. The same basic scent as he'd had in college, and her mind traveled back there again. Back to him holding her. For that moment, every problem receded and she believed she could overcome all obstacles.

"Something wrong?" he asked from the chair across from her.

She hadn't even noticed him move back to his seat. She had to do a better job of letting the past go.

"I'm good." She started a video and cupped her hand at the side of her eyes to keep her focus pointed at the computer. The big white bandage on her hand helped, and she managed to review file after file until she was tired from sitting. She was about to get up for a glass of water when, on her screen, a guy ran furtively across the lab parking lot in the dark and stopped in front of the lab door.

She paused it. "Look at this!"

Erik rushed around the table, but she kept her eyes pinned to the man, noting details. He wore dark clothes—maybe black. Heavy boots and a stocking cap. "He fits the build of the intruder at my mom's place."

"He sure does." Erik moved closer to the screen.

She looked at the date stamp. "Nine-fourteen p.m. on the night before my mom's funeral. During her visitation at the funeral home."

The man produced a key from his pocket and slipped into the lab's door.

"Who is he, and why does he have a key?" Kennedy waited to hear the alarm go off, but it didn't. "She would never give a key to a counterfeit drug maker. If he works for them, he would've had to steal it."

"Let's keep watching." Erik leaned over her, and for once, she barely noticed how close he'd come to her, but she did see Pong slink off and settle in his kennel. He kept an eye on them though, so maybe he was picking up on the tension.

The video played for nearly an hour without any action and finally the man exited.

"He's not carrying anything so if he took something it must be small," Kennedy said.

"He had to have the security code too, or there would've been a police response." Erik's voice came from close behind.

"Look." She tapped the screen on the main warehouse entrance, where a uniformed guard stepped out. He yelled something and ran toward the intruder.

The intruder bolted back through the lot toward the river and out of camera range.

"The main warehouse has their own cameras," Erik stated. "They could've captured additional footage. Rewind and zoom in on the guard's uniform so I can see which company he works for."

She rewound the video. "Shouldn't we just go straight to the warehouse manager?"

"If it's the company I think it is, I have contacts there. I should be able to get the video."

She zoomed in and froze the screen on the guard's chest. The patch read *Steele Guardians*.

"Perfect." Erik stood back. "I know Londyn Steele, and

her family owns Steele Guardians. She should be able to get us a copy of the video and do it far faster than going through the warehouse manager."

He pulled out his phone and stabbed the buttons, then lifted it to his ear. "Londyn. Good. It's Erik Byrd. I have a favor to ask."

Kennedy watched him as he described their need, his enthusiasm not waning as he listened to Londyn's response.

"Perfect," he said. "You know anything about the potential anthrax investigation?" He tapped his finger on the table as he listened. After a moment, he said, "Can you ask around?" A deep frown marred his usual pleasant expression. "Yeah, I get it. You can't tell me anything, but thanks for your help on the video."

He looked like he was going to lower the phone but then said, "Of course not. I don't want to get you in trouble." His frown deepened. "Thanks. Have Mackenzie call me ASAP."

He lowered his phone but kept it in his hand. "I forgot to mention Londyn's a detective with PPB. She can't share anything about the investigation."

"But the video?" Kennedy asked.

"She's going to have her cousin Mackenzie give me a call. If only Londyn had caught the anthrax investigation, we might know more about what's going on from their side."

"Wouldn't the police have looked at this video by now? I'm surprised they haven't asked if I know this guy."

"Maybe they haven't seen the footage yet, but trust me." He met her gaze and held it. "The minute they think you can help with their investigation, you'll be hearing from them."

12

Erik hung up with Detective Johnson. It was almost as if the guy had known they were talking about him, because he'd called just a few minutes later. Erik shared the information about inDents, but Johnson wouldn't promise to follow up on it. On the bright side, Johnson did confirm that the Veritas staff could continue with their evidence evaluations as long as they reported to him and him alone.

Erik wanted the results. How he wanted them. But he'd rather the evidence remained in-house and was properly processed more than anything else. So he notified Sierra, Maya, and Emory, then he and Kennedy continued reviewing videos. She hadn't said a word, but a few loudly expelled breaths and a tight expression told him she hadn't found anything else.

She looked up from across the dining table, catching him watching her. He thought to look away but held her gaze.

"While we wait for the files from Mackenzie, I'm going to move on to reviewing the GPS data from your mother's phone," he said.

"I doubt she used GPS. Not with her avoidance of most technology."

"She wouldn't have to do anything. Many phones default to on for frequent locations, so if what you say is true about her not being proficient in technology, she most likely didn't turn it off. Means we'll have a list of the places she'd recently visited."

Kennedy shook her head. "I didn't realize that, and I'm sure my mom wouldn't have either. So I doubt she turned it off. I sure didn't help her do it, but Finley might have."

"We'll soon see." He turned his attention back to his computer and navigated to the files he'd uploaded from Wanda's phone to run a JavaScript he'd gotten from Nick at Veritas. "GPS is on. We have a long list of addresses. We'll have to check them on a map to find out what's at each location."

"Can I help?" She stared at Erik with eyes wide and vulnerable.

"Sure." He was already creating a secure text to her so he didn't keep looking into those enchanting brown eyes. "I'm texting you a link on our server for the spreadsheet with the data. I sorted by location. You can open it on your computer, and we'll share the document in real time so we can see each other's work."

She clicked on her keyboard and looked up. "The first is the lab."

He noted the location and filled in all the correct cells on the spreadsheet. "Go ahead and take the first half, and I'll do the second. Enter the place that she visited in the spreadsheet, and then we can review them."

She focused on her screen with a deep intensity. An adorable little line formed between her eyebrows, and she pursed her lips. Working with her had been great so far. Another surprise for sure. He didn't expect to ever enjoy her company again, but the silence in the room was easy. Not at all forced, as he might have guessed it would be. More like the easygoing days when they sat across a table doing homework in college.

He flashed back to those times. The work was often interrupted with kissing. Sometimes he'd initiated those kisses. Other times, it had been Kennedy leaning across the table.

Lips locking. Work forgotten.

No. This is just torture. He shook his head to clear her from it. That was not going to happen here. No way.

He dragged his focus back to the computer and entered addresses into a map program. The first locations were places he would expect. Grocery store, post office, home. And frequent stops at restaurants for very short periods of time. Likely takeout.

"Done," Kennedy said an hour later. "Man, she got a lot of takeout, which I guess her credit card confirms."

"Indeed." He scanned the completed list. "Only two unexplained stops. The one in Tigard, which she visited often. It's an apartment complex."

"That's Finley's apartment."

"Okay, so that leaves one location in question. It's in Sherwood. Let me map it and take a look at the place." He entered the address in the map program and clicked on the street view. "It's a house. Know anyone out there?"

"Maybe Finley does. I'll text her and ask." Kennedy sent the text.

"While we wait for a reply, I'll get started reviewing the image I took of your mom's computer."

Kennedy sighed and started twirling her hair.

He met her anxious gaze. "What's wrong?"

Her hair twisted tight, she wiggled her finger and let it go, only to wrap it around her finger again. "I don't like invading my mom's privacy like this. What if we find something she wouldn't want us to see?"

He could see Kennedy's point, but they couldn't stop. "You mean like the money?"

"That and more." Kennedy let go of her hair and nibbled on her lower lip, worrying it hard with her teeth.

He didn't like seeing her upset and started to reach for her bandage free hand. A knock sounded on the front door, and he snapped his hand back.

"Probably one of the guys." Erik charged to the hallway, thankful for the interruption.

Pong came running from his crate and trotted alongside, his footfalls a rhythmic clicking on the hardwood floors. He might be a trained search dog, but he was also just a dog who wanted to protect his owner at every turn, and Erik wanted to hug his little buddy for that. But he also didn't want Pong to lose his training and paw everyone who came to the door.

"Sit," Erik said at the door. Pong immediately complied. "Good boy."

Secured building or not, Erik glanced out the peephole and found Aiden standing in the hall.

Erik opened the door.

"Got the information on the assistant." Aiden tapped his foot. "Thought you would like it right away."

Erik eyed his brother. "You could've emailed."

"I could've, but one of us needs to keep an eye on the two of you." His tone was joking, but his expression held a note of warning, as if Erik needed to be reminded to remain impartial in this investigation.

Erik rolled his eyes and stepped back.

Aiden entered, stopping to scratch Pong behind the ears. "Besides I need to make sure you aren't suffering any anthrax symptoms."

"We're both fine."

Aiden looked up and locked gazes. "You're acting awful cool about this."

Erik lowered his voice. "I don't want to worry Kennedy any more than she is. So please don't say anything to her."

"Your wish is my command." Aiden mimicked zipping his mouth closed and marched down the hall.

Erik followed, wishing everything with his strong-willed brother was as easy. Erik took a few breaths to let out his concern about the anthrax and offered a prayer that Aiden wouldn't say anything that would make Kennedy uncomfortable.

Aiden greeted her and pulled out a chair across the table to straddle it. "How well do you know Nora?"

"Not well," Kennedy said. "I only saw her a few times. She seemed very efficient."

"Especially for her age, right?" Aiden asked.

Kennedy's eyebrows went up.

"I'm not one for age discrimination, but I was surprised to learn that she was over seventy."

"My mom hiring Nora surprised me too. First that Nora was still working at her age. But my mom wasn't very social, and she said she wanted someone closer to her age who she could relate to. I worried Nora wouldn't have the computer experience the job required, but I was wrong. Nora has great technical skills."

"Good enough to erase your mom's phone?" Erik dropped onto a chair by Kennedy and explained the empty call log to Aiden. "Nora was the only other person with access to the lab so it could've been her."

Kennedy tapped her chin. "I suppose she could've done it."

Aiden rested his elbows on the back of the chair. "She was the one who found your mother. Means she had the opportunity to erase it before she called the authorities, but what motive would she have?"

Erik gave it some thought. "Maybe Nora knew Wanda was up to something that she didn't want anyone to know about."

"Could be, I suppose," Kennedy said. "Even more reason to talk to her."

Erik looked at his brother. "Did you find anything suspicious in her background?"

Aiden nodded. "There seems to be some question about why she left her last job. Money went missing, and then she was fired."

"Doesn't mean she took it," Kennedy said.

"True." Aiden patted Pong, who sat between him and Erik. "But the detective who investigated the theft was suspicious because she was one of the few people who had access to the cash."

"Still, if charges weren't brought, we have no proof," Erik said.

"No charges." Aiden continued scratching Pong's head as if the movement was helping him work this puzzle out. Pong rested his head on Aiden's thigh looking content.

"Even if she did steal money," Kennedy said, "it wouldn't mean she tried to steal from my mom, much less kill her. I doubt Nora had access to my mom's medicine."

Aiden returned his arm to the chair back. "She could've lifted Wanda's keys while she was working in the lab and had a copy made. And if she needed money, she might've given the key to someone else. Like the drug counterfeiters who wanted to stop your mom."

Kennedy pinned her focus on Aiden. "I don't know about Nora, but my mom was usually so focused on her work that she didn't notice much of what was going on around her. Nora could easily swipe the keys and get them copied."

"But there's the matter of getting your mother to take the extra doses," Erik pointed out.

"My mom's schedule was like clockwork, rarely deviating. She took three breaks a day and powered down protein drinks in each of them. She kept them in a small refrigerator in the reception area, where Nora would have access. And my mom didn't allow food or drinks in the lab due to potential contamination, so she took her breaks in the reception area. In fact, she frequently had lunch with Nora when she was there as Nora often picked up carryout on the way in."

Aiden sat up, his eyes alight with enthusiasm. "So she could've crushed the tablets and mixed them in the food, though that might be too gritty. Better to dissolve them in the liquids."

"Still, what's her motive to kill my mom?" Kennedy looked at Aiden, then at Erik as if she really expected them to answer her.

"Men and women commit murder for different reasons," Erik said. "For men, it's often jealousy, revenge, arguments. Women, on the other hand, are more likely to be involved in gain homicides."

"Gain?" Kennedy asked.

"They gain something from the killing. Money, the end of abuse, making life better for their children for various reasons, etcetera."

Aiden tapped his finger on the chair. "I would think the only thing that works for Nora on that list would be money, but then I don't know her."

"She *is* still working at her age, so maybe she doesn't have enough savings or social security," Erik suggested.

Kennedy frowned. "Or she just likes to work. At least she seemed glad to be there when I saw her."

Erik was starting to like Nora as a suspect. "Think of her from the counterfeit drug manufacturers' point of view. If she needed money, it's not farfetched to believe they approached her and offered a payoff to help them stop the research."

"Sounds possible," Aiden said. "And maybe Nora learned about the safe, but she didn't have the right combination so she sent the guy to the house to find it."

"Why not just do it herself?" Kennedy asked.

Erik leaned forward. "Age. Insecurity. Maybe she's working with this guy. A son maybe?"

"She does have five children," Aiden said. "Three are male."

Erik lifted the lid on his laptop. "Then we need their pictures to see if they fit the profile of our intruder. If they do, are they even in town?"

Aiden stood. "And if so, we'll need to interview them and check their alibis for each incident."

"I don't know." Kennedy grabbed that dangling lock of hair and swirled it around her finger. "I want to go on record as saying this seems pretty unlikely."

"Unlikely or not, we have to follow up on every lead." Erik looked up from his computer. "Starting with paying Nora a visit right after we pick up Wanda's college files. Hopefully, we'll get some answers to our many questions."

13

Kennedy was thankful to be riding in the backseat of the Nighthawk SUV with Aiden driving and Erik riding shotgun. Erik hadn't wanted her to come along to Nora's place, but Kennedy persuaded him by pointing out that Nora would likely be more open to talk with Kennedy present. Still, she had to promise to follow his directions and wear a Kevlar vest. Plus, he'd done a thorough risk assessment and brought Aiden along for additional protection. Erik clearly took his job seriously, and she was impressed with the many skills he'd learned over the years.

On the way to the house, they stopped at Finley's apartment to pick up the college records, and now Aiden was pulling into the driveway of Nora's small bungalow near the city. He wore reflective sunglasses, hiding his eyes and mood, but his body was alert for any potential danger, as was Erik's.

Erik's cell rang. "It's Drake. I'll put him on speaker."

"Yo, bro," Drake said. "Just left the prison. Waldron's wife was the only person who visited him, and she stopped coming ten years ago when she divorced him. According to Waldron, it wasn't an amiable divorce, and she married his

145

best friend. He's bitter about the whole thing. Said she poisoned his son against him, and he won't have a thing to do with him anymore. I'll stop by the ex-wife's place on my way back to confirm, but I just don't see her or the son trying to kill Silas or Wanda. And Waldron worked this scam alone, except for Silas's accounting help, and the people he knew in the investment community have turned their backs on him. He really does seem to be on his own."

"Do you think he was telling the truth?" Erik asked. "He is an expert liar, after all."

"You can't fake the bitterness he displayed. Or the hatred of Silas that Waldron still feels. But the only way I can see him taking Silas out would be by paying for a professional hit, and the feds seized all of his assets when he was arrested. He's broke and couldn't possibly pay for it."

"And what about how he feels about Kennedy and Finley?" Aiden asked.

"I don't see any danger there," Drake said. "His hatred is pinned to Silas. I could see him wanting to hurt Wanda to pay Silas back if he were still alive, but with Silas gone, there's no point for him."

"Okay, let us know what the wife says. We're about to interview Nora." Erik brought his brother up to speed on what he'd missed at the meeting.

"Hope she can shed some light on things. We could use a solid lead." Drake ended the call.

"Let's not be too quick to dismiss this angle." Erik ran a hand over his hair. "Waldron could get one of his fellow inmates to act for him, and we don't want to be blindsided by that."

Aiden looked at Erik. "There's a brotherhood in prison so it could happen, and you're right. We need to keep it as one of our lines of inquiry."

"Wait, what?" Erik stared at his brother. "I'm what?"

Aiden rolled his eyes. "You're right."

"Could you say it again? I don't hear it often enough."

Aiden socked Erik and climbed out.

Erik's good humor vanished as he swiveled to look back at Kennedy. "Okay. The rules again. Don't leave the vehicle before I get out. Don't get ahead of or behind me or take off in any direction. Stay by my side at all times. And if I or Aiden tell you to take cover, do it immediately. Don't ask questions. Just move."

"Aye aye, captain." She saluted him to lighten his mood.

He reached back and clutched her knee. "This is serious, Kennedy."

"Don't worry." She smiled but she could feel her chin tremble. "I'll do as you say."

He held her gaze for a long moment, then released her knee and got out. She waited in the vehicle, taking in the freshly painted home, which looked recently updated. Kennedy didn't know how long Nora had lived at this house, but if she'd been a long-time resident, she'd put some money into the place.

Erik stopped outside Kennedy's door and looked around, then gave a sharp nod as if cementing something in his mind. Maybe he did this for all his clients, but she liked to think he was taking this extra step because he cared about her. She was a very independent woman, but she really liked his protectiveness.

He pulled the door open. The minute her feet hit the walkway, he slid an arm around her back and snugged her up against his body. He whisked her past Aiden, who had a hand on his weapon, and Erik's gaze was like a constant radar blip, moving over the area.

They hurried up the porch stairs, Aiden coming behind them. Erik stood to her right side, the wall to her left, and Aiden remained behind. She might be exposed to potential gunshots, but these guys would take the hit first, and she figured their vests were up to the task.

Erik pounded on the door, and footsteps sounded on the other side.

Kennedy took a breath to prepare herself as Nora opened the door and ran her gaze over them. Her eyes hooded, her sagging lids narrowing even more. Thankfully, they'd all hidden their vests under shirts, but the bulkiness probably gave them away.

"Kennedy?" Nora pinned her focus on her. "What's going on?"

Kennedy smiled to try to relax the older woman. "These are my friends, Erik and Aiden Byrd. We're looking into my mom's death and wanted to ask you a few questions."

"Me?" Nora clutched the front of a flowery blouse she'd paired with dressy black slacks. "But what can I tell you?"

"Why don't we come in, and we can talk about it?" Kennedy didn't give Nora time to think but stepped over the threshold. The small room she entered had formal furnishings and held the thick floral scent of Nora's cloying perfume.

Nora held the door handle while Erik entered.

"I'll be staying out here, ma'am," Aiden said, taking Kennedy's attention. "Go ahead and leave the door cracked open."

Nora eyed him for a very long time then left the door ajar. "Go ahead and have a seat. Would you like some coffee? I just brewed some. I have fresh raspberry Danishes."

"Nothing for me, but thank you," Kennedy said.

Erik leaned against the wall. "I'm good."

"Your hand. What happened?" Nora asked, sounding concerned.

"A turtle bit me while I was diving." Kennedy smiled to

play it down and spotted a family photo on the sofa table. She lifted it and studied it. "Are these your children?"

Nora perched on the edge of a stiff, mauve high-backed chair. "It's nearly five years old now, but yes. It was taken the year before my husband passed."

"Do they live in the area?" Erik asked.

Nora swung her head to look at him. "All but my youngest daughter. She's in Denver. And all are married now with children of their own. I have six grandchildren." She smiled and smoothed her gray hair that she'd pulled back in a severe bun.

"What do they do for a living?"

Nora's eyebrow went up. "Are you here to talk about my family or your mother?"

"Both, I guess," Kennedy said, but Erik made a brief slashing motion across his neck. *Okay.* He didn't want her to talk about Nora's sons. "Mostly my mom, I guess."

Kennedy returned the frame to the table and sat on the beige-and-blue camelback sofa across from Nora.

Erik dropped down next to Kennedy and focused on Nora. "Did you believe the ME's findings that Wanda either took her own life or accidentally took too many blood pressure pills?"

Nora laced her fingers together in her lap. "Not really, but it was the only logical explanation." She looked at Kennedy. "Sorry, sweetheart, but I also don't think Wanda was murdered. I just don't see any reason for that."

"What about the counterfeit pharmaceutical dealers?" Kennedy asked. "They would have wanted her to end her project without completion."

"Sure, yes, I suppose, and they probably have access to drugs that could be used. Still, she didn't get any threats or odd contacts. At least not that I knew about, and we were friends. She shared se—she would've told me."

"What were you going to say?" Erik asked.

"Nothing. It's nothing." Nora clamped her hands on her bony knees. "It's just…how would they give the pills to her? They would've had to force them down her throat, but there was no sign of struggle."

"Perhaps they had help from someone close to Wanda?" Erik pinned Nora with such an intense gaze that she flinched.

"Me?" She lifted her hand to her chest again. "Are you thinking I did it? Why would I want to hurt Wanda?"

"Money," Erik said.

"I don't need money."

"Then why work at your age?" Erik asked.

Anger flashed in Nora's eyes. "I enjoy the challenge and stimulation. Not that it's easy to find a job. Age discrimination is prevalent. I can't prove it. Everyone's too careful for that. Still, God willing, I plan to work until I drop dead." She ran her gaze over them. "Something you young things wouldn't understand, but feeling useful is what makes me tick."

"How long have you lived here?" Kennedy asked.

"Moved in after my husband passed. I liked it because it was all updated." Nora jutted out her pointy chin and crossed her arms. "Why is that relevant?"

"Just curious."

"Do you or any of your sons own a gun?" Erik asked.

"My sons?" She tightened her arms. "Why is that any of your business?"

Kennedy leaned forward and cast a sympathetic look her way. "I'm sorry that we have to ask. But someone broke into my mom's house and threatened me with a gun."

"Oh, my dear." Nora reached out but dropped her hand before touching Kennedy. "I'm so sorry."

Kennedy tried to smile, but she couldn't dredge one up.

"If you're involved in my mother's death, you might've asked one of your sons to break into the house."

"Oh, for Pete's sake." Nora rolled her eyes. "They know nothing about this except that your mom died and my job ended."

"What about your last job?" Erik asked. "Why did that one end?"

"Sounds like you already know. And so did Wanda." Nora pulled her shoulders into a hard line and cast Erik a disgusted look. "Petty cash that I was in charge of went missing. They couldn't prove who stole it, but they fired me for negligence. Let me tell you, it was obvious they thought I was guilty. But why would I risk being arrested for five hundred dollars when I don't need money? Fools. That's what they are, and good riddance, I say. I don't want to work for anyone who would think I was a thief."

Erik nodded as if he believed her, but Kennedy knew Nora was holding something back and it was making Kennedy mad. What could Nora be hiding and why was she hiding something?

"Do you know what Wanda did outside of work?" Erik asked.

"When did she have time to do anything but sleep?" Nora stood and glared down on them. "I think we're done here."

Interesting. What about Erik's question set Nora off?

Erik didn't stand, just leaned back as if getting comfortable. "One more question. Did you do anything with Wanda's phone when you found her in the lab?"

She didn't answer right away but stared down at Erik. "Like I said. We're done here."

"We've fingerprinted Wanda's phone. Will we find your prints on it?"

"I helped Wanda manage her phone, but she kept it clean, so probably not."

"Would you come in to the Veritas lab to be finger-printed?"

"If the police request it. Such an invasion of my privacy." Nora eyed him. "Now if you'll excuse me, I have a job interview I need to get to."

Kennedy stood. "I'm sorry we had to ask these questions."

Nora offered a sad smile. "I was friends with your mother, and she would be so disappointed to hear I'm being treated as a suspect."

"Please don't take it personally." Erik got up but he didn't take his penetrating focus from Nora. "The person who finds a body is always suspected of involvement in a homicide until ruled out."

Nora sniffed. "The police didn't think I had anything to do with Wanda's death."

"Because they didn't think she was murdered." Kennedy widened her stance and didn't bother hiding her frustration. "But I'm going to prove that she was, so if you *did* have anything to do with it and you're not telling us everything, you should know I'm coming for you."

Nora blanched, but guilt flooded her face.

"*We* are." Erik stepped up beside Kennedy, his stance firm and unmoving. "If you're involved, *we are* coming for you."

~

Erik got Kennedy safely ensconced in the SUV, and Aiden merged into traffic. He'd pulled the older brother card to drive them home, but all he'd had to do was ask, since Erik wanted to be free to protect Kennedy if the need arose.

Erik glanced at his brother. "Do you have time to look into Nora's sons and get those alibis?"

"Sure thing."

They both let their gazes rove over the area close to the city made up of older buildings with retail on the ground floor and apartments above. They had a job to do, even if the vehicle had full bulletproof protection. No one could hurt Kennedy right now unless they planted a bomb or rammed a vehicle into the side where she sat. The first was unlikely. The second was possible. Once they turned the corner ahead and merged into traffic Erik would relax. A bit anyway. He wouldn't fully relax until they walked into his condo again.

And then he had a whole new threat to deal with—his growing attraction to Kennedy. That might not be dangerous to her, but it was to him.

"Did you notice how Nora clammed up when you asked her what my mom did outside of work?" Kennedy asked.

"I did." Erik glanced over the seat at her. "Do you think your mom could've been dating?"

Kennedy gaped at him. "I can't imagine it. But then I've never considered it. She lived for work."

"We have to remember the money in the safe." Aiden peered at her in the rearview mirror. "Maybe Nora's behavior was more about your mother being involved in something illegal. I could hear everything you guys said, and it seemed like she was evading answering about the phone."

"She could've deleted the files," Erik stated. "But what would she have deleted?"

They fell silent as they pondered the questions, and Erik continued watching out the window, looking for anything unusual.

At the corner, a shimmer of light coming from a two-story building caught Erik's eye. He grabbed his binoculars and searched out the window as Aiden approached the intersection to prepare for a left turn.

The shimmer moved. "Something fishy at three o'clock. Above the drug store. Don't know what. Sunglasses, maybe, but I don't like it."

Aiden shifted to look. "Building has an apartment For Rent sign."

"Could be a shooter hunkered down in a vacant building," Erik said.

"Let's not hang around to find out." Aiden couldn't barrel into incoming traffic but he eased into the intersection against the light, horns honking at them.

Erik spotted a rifle being lifted into the open window.

"Gun. Get down." He tossed the binoculars to the floor as bullets peppered his and Kennedy's side of the SUV. Each round sounded like underwater explosions as the glass splintered but held fast.

"Get us out of here." Erik plunged over the seat, scooped Kennedy into his arms, and hit the floor with his shoulder to sustain the brunt of the impact. His shoulder wrenched, but it would take far more than that little bit of pain to make him let go of the woman he'd once loved.

"Truck blocking the intersection." Aiden laid on the horn. "I have to maneuver around him."

The vehicle swerved to the right. Metal pinged. Glass popped. Exploded. But the SUV held tight—the safety features doing their thing to protect them, as Aiden moved them through traffic.

"What's happening?" she cried out.

"Assault rifle trained on our SUV. The bulletproofing should hold."

"Then why tackle me?"

Why indeed? "I'm not taking any chances."

The barrage continued, bullets flying. They suddenly stopped. The silence deafening. The shooter likely emptied his magazine and was reloading. Took only seconds before the *pop-pop-pop* started again, their vehicle feeling like a tin can downrange at rifle practice.

"Finally!" Aiden snapped then floored the gas, and Kennedy trembled under Erik's body. She was scared and in danger. His fury exploded inside him with the same force as the bullets trying to pierce the SUV.

Aiden wound in and out of traffic. He must've managed to dial 911, because suddenly Erik heard the emergency dispatcher through the speakers. Aiden reported the shooting while Erik's only job right now was to use his body as a human shield.

The spray of bullets stopped. The windows were marked with spidery webs of broken glass, and he couldn't see through them.

"We should be out of range now," Aiden said. "Dispatch is sending units to the area. They'll come to the office to take our statements."

"Don't you want to turn around and stop whoever did this?" Kennedy's high and stressed tone sounded shrill. "He killed my mom!"

"Of course we do." Erik adjusted his position to take his weight off her. "But our number one goal is to make sure our protectee remains unharmed."

"And that's me? I mean, what you think of me?" She squirmed around to look at him, her eyes wide and dark with terror. "A protectee?"

He brushed a strand of hair away from her cheek, keeping his emotions in check and tamping down the desire to kiss away her fear. "You know that's not all. And if you keep looking at me like that, I'll do something that might take my focus off the job."

She blinked a few times. "How am I looking at you?"

"Like you're one step from losing it." Like she needed him to hold her close. Which he could easily do considering his position. Just because he *could*, didn't mean he should.

"I've never had anyone shoot at me before. And I've never even heard a machine gun." She shuddered.

His control evaporated, and he drew her close, holding her as if her life depended on it. Erik would need to thank Aiden later for insisting on adding the armor to their SUV.

Erik had never been shot at before either. Not once as a police officer. And certainly never in a hail of bullets like today's attack. This guy was serious. Dead serious. Did he believe Kennedy or Erik could identify him? He must.

The situation gave Erik a new appreciation for the second chance at life he'd just been given. *Thank You!*

He was going to take a long look at himself. Was he living his best life? Living the life God wanted for him. Or was he shutting out the woman who'd been the best part? Had God brought them back together for a reason? Erik never wanted to live outside of God's will. So a great deal of soul searching was in order. Until then, he needed to release Kennedy and keep his hands to himself.

14

In the Veritas parking structure, Kennedy's legs wobbled like a newborn colt trying to get up for the first time, and she wasn't sure she could continue to stand. She would, for Erik. The tension oozed from him as he and Aiden assessed their vehicle, and she didn't want to add to his unease.

She rested her good hand on the vehicle for support. Weakness invaded her muscles while adrenaline consumed her body, but she held firm, even when taking in the spidery circles of crushed glass on the windows. The sharp holes in the vehicle's body—too many to count. Yet not one of the bullets had penetrated the vehicle.

Thank You for protecting us!

"Let's get inside." Erik sounded strong and in control, but his shoulders were tight, his eyes narrowed and piercing.

Aiden gave a sharp nod, putting up a good front as well, but Kennedy could see in the rigid set of his jaw that the attack had shaken him too. And he, like Erik, felt responsible for the bystanders who'd been shot. They would recover, but still had the pain to endure now, and then there was a tremendous amount of property damage. None of it was the fault of anyone in this garage, but guilt ate at them all.

They took the hallway to the Nighthawk Security office, and Kennedy didn't even notice the view from the skybridge. Inside the office, they marched straight through the reception area to the conference room.

She'd barely made it and feared she might crumple to the floor, but she wasn't going to ask for any help from Erik. Not after the hug. She couldn't have him touch her while she was so vulnerable. Not now that she knew her feelings for him ran deep. Deeper than she wanted. If they didn't find the intruder-turned-attacker soon, she was going to fall hopelessly in love with this fine man.

And maybe that was supposed to happen. Maybe that was what God wanted for her. For Erik. Or not. She didn't know how to interpret the shooting. Should she even do so? She was so confused.

Please. If I'm to learn something from this, make the lesson clear.

Until she had clarity, avoiding close contact with Erik would be best. She turned to Aiden instead. "What now?"

"Go ahead and have a seat." His words were tight, clipped. "I'll get the others."

Erik pulled out a chair for her, his gaze locked on her.

"Thanks." She dropped onto the chair.

Aiden strode to the far side of the room where his brothers were working in cubicles. She remained close enough to reach out and touch Erik, whose focus was riveted to her, but she would keep her gaze pinned to the whiteboard on the wall ahead of her until all the brothers dropped into chairs at the table. Including Erik, who sat down next to her.

She scooted her chair away, earning her a raise of his

eyebrows. She looked away before he asked what was going on.

"FYI," Drake said as he approached the table with his brothers, and Erik looked happy to have him back. "Waldron's ex confirmed his story. No question. She really does hate the guy."

Erik went to the whiteboard and slashed an angry line through Waldron's name and spun to run down the attack with them. "How in the world did the shooter know where we were?"

"I might be able to shed some light on that," Brendan said.

Everyone's focus swiveled to him.

"Spit it out," Erik demanded.

"Let me put this picture up on the screen." He tapped his phone a few times, and a photo appeared of a small square gray plastic piece that read "Tile" on it.

Erik shot his brother a look. "Where did you find it?"

"In the lining of Wanda's purse," Clay said. "It was lodged up against the cardboard bottom, and it freed up when I shook the purse upside down."

Erik's jaw clenched. "I should've done that."

Kennedy was totally lost. "What is it?"

"A tracker," Erik said. "They're often put on keychains and other items that might get lost. But an unscrupulous person could put one in a purse or bag and track another person without them knowing about it."

"Couldn't she just have bought one to keep track of her purse?" Aiden asked.

"As I said before, she wasn't into technology," Kennedy said. "And if she put it in there, why hide it in the lining of her own purse?"

"Someone was tracking her," Clay stated.

"Can you trace trackers like this back to the owner?" Aiden asked.

"Perhaps," Erik said. "With access to Tile's records, we could figure out who's following it. The thing is, without a warrant, we would have no luck in accessing those records. Plus, I'd guess a bogus email account was set up for this item, and even with Tile's records, we won't find who put it there."

"But you'll try?" Kennedy asked.

"Of course. And because this was in your mother's purse, it's possible there's one in yours. We should check."

"Mine?" Her heart dropped. "But when could he have put something in my stuff?"

She could almost see the thoughts pinging through Erik's head, and he grimaced. "While you were sleeping. Working in the lab concentrating so fiercely you didn't see him enter the waiting area. Anywhere in public that he could brush up against you or access your purse. Maybe even at your mom's funeral."

Her stomach clenched. "And that's how he knew where we were."

Erik nodded. "Probably. And if he was nearby, he would've had plenty of time to set up for the shooting."

"I doubt it would be in my purse. I brought it to my mom's place, and the tracker would have placed me there. If he'd known I was there, he wouldn't have broken in."

"If the person who's using the tracker is the same person behind the break-in," Drake pointed out.

"For the moment, let's assume it is," Erik said.

"Then let's check my backpack. I usually shove my purse in it and carry both with me, but I left my pack in the lab the night the intruder broke in." Heart thumping, Kennedy jumped up and hurried across the room to grab her backpack. She dumped the contents onto the table and combed through the items. "Nothing here."

"What about the zipper pockets?" Erik asked.

She slid them open one by one, taking far longer to do so than normal, as she had to use her left hand. Her pulse raced, and she fumbled even more. Erik looked like he wanted to take the pack from her, but if someone was tracking her, she wanted to see it for herself.

In the smallest of pockets, one she never used, she felt an object about the right size. *No.*

She looked up at the brothers, who were all watching. Waiting. She pulled her hand free then unfurled it to display the tracker on her palm.

Erik's sharp intake of air said it all.

Someone had been tracking her movements, and she had no idea who or for how long.

The office door opened, grabbing Kennedy's attention from the worried brothers' faces and from the deathly silence in the room.

Sierra walked in, shoving her hands into the pockets of her lab coat and running her gaze over the group. "What's with all the tension?"

"We took fire from a machine gun near Nora's house." Erik's words were flat, as if his life hadn't been on the line. "And we just learned someone was tracking Wanda and Kennedy."

Her gaze swung from face to face. "Everyone okay?"

"We're fine but you should see the SUV." Aiden tsked.

"Thanks to your planning ahead, we *are* fine." Erik peered at his brother. "Thanks for saving our lives, bro. I can never repay you."

"Yes, thank you," Kennedy added.

Aiden's eyes narrowed, but he gave a firm nod. "Going forward, we need to assume this attack wasn't only meant for Kennedy."

"How so?" Sierra perched on a chair.

"I figure if the guy was looking for something at Wanda's place and thought Kennedy wouldn't be there because her tracker was displaying at the lab, that he didn't intend to harm Kennedy. He could be thinking Kennedy saw him. Erik did too. So he must think you can ID him."

"Which means you're now a protectee as well," Clay said.

"What?" Erik snapped his chair forward. "What? No. You aren't going to lock me up here. I have an investigation to work."

"We can handle it," Drake said calmly, but his hands were tightly clasped on the arms of the chair.

"No." Erik shook his head. "No. No way."

"All I'm suggesting," Clay said, "is that we do a risk assessment before you leave the building, just like we'd do for Kennedy. Then take proper precautions."

"It's going to be more of a challenge since we're now down to one SUV," Drake added. "Or at least I assume we are."

"I'll put up a picture of the damage for you." Erik tapped his phone, and an image of the bullet-riddled SUV filled the TV mounted on the wall.

Sierra gasped.

"Whoa." Brendan leaned forward. "Amazing that it held."

"It would still probably be useable, if we could see out the windows." Erik changed the picture to another view, this one of the windshield.

Sierra lurched to her feet and hugged Aiden. "I thought

you were mad for spending so much money on those SUVs. You were very wise."

"As usual." He grinned over her shoulder.

She eased free and swatted at him, then turned to hug Erik. "I'm glad you're fine."

"Don't worry so much," Erik said, but his voice cracked.

"I can't help it when you guys all decide to work in professions where guns are needed." She moved on to Kennedy and leaned down to envelope her in strong arms.

The hug was warm and sincere, but instead of relishing it, Kennedy felt like a fraud in this tight-knit family. She wanted to be part of the group again, but she had no right. Would never have the right.

She pushed free and smiled up at Sierra. "Thank you."

"Of course. You're one of us again." She gave Erik a pointed look before addressing the group. "I just dropped by to tell you about the evidence before I turn it over to Johnson."

"Won't that get you into trouble?" Kennedy asked.

"I haven't gotten his signed contract yet, so I'm walking a fine line." Sierra wrinkled her nose. "All but one set of the prints I processed matched Kennedy, Finley, or the prints I believe are Wanda's, due to the quantity and locations."

Erik eyed his sister. "Only one set?"

"Yes, which is kind of odd, unless Wanda didn't have visitors."

"She only lived there for about a year and wasn't a social person," Kennedy said.

"Still, I would expect a print or two from the former occupant," Sierra said. "Unless your mother fastidiously cleaned the house before moving in."

"She was a neat freak, so it wouldn't surprise me." Kennedy couldn't stem the smile at the images arriving in her brain. "Not only did I see it growing up, but I worked

163

with her in the lab long enough to know the lengths she took it to."

Erik nodded at the evidence bag. "I want that back after you print it."

"Won't take long." Sierra took a small plastic evidence bag from her pocket and scooped the tile tracker into it.

"You know most sisters carry tissues or lipstick in their pockets, but not ours," Drake said.

"Have evidence bag, will travel. That's my motto." Sierra reached into the other pocket to pull out a small container. "And maybe a pacifier for good measure."

They all laughed, and Kennedy didn't know how they managed it, but it had to be a defense mechanism so they didn't burn out.

"The hair you recovered at Wanda's place is a good lead, though, right?" Brendan asked.

"It definitely isn't a match to any of the people we'd expect to be at the house," Sierra said. "But again, it's odd that there weren't more unidentified prints."

"Are you thinking the home was wiped down to eliminate prints?"

"Yeah. Maybe. Sure." She shoved the evidence bag into her pocket. "I lifted a large number of them, but not for the size of the space. So if Wanda was murdered by someone she knew, maybe the killer visited her house in the past. Then went back to wipe down things he or she touched. But keep in mind that they'd have to know what they were doing or I could still have found remnants of the prints."

"Or he wore gloves," Drake said.

"He didn't the night I saw him," Kennedy said. "So seems like he wouldn't have when he visited her."

"We might never know what happened." Sierra planted her hands on her waist. "There were two different prints on the phone I found upstairs. One is Wanda's and the other one doesn't match the one I found by the drawer. So now we have two unknown prints."

"That's my mom's phone," Kennedy said. "So the one print matching hers makes sense."

"We need to get Nora's prints," Erik stated. "See if it matches the unknown one."

"Get her in here, and I'll handle it," Sierra said.

"She already said she wouldn't come in unless the police requested it," Kennedy said.

"If that changes, I'll be here for you," Sierra said. "That's it for me, except I should tell you I'm also going to examine the hair by microscopy, but that will take some time to produce helpful information."

"And what will that tell us?" Erik asked.

"It can help establish whether the hair is diseased, was forcibly removed, or was treated with hair dye or another artificial substance. When we have the suspect in custody, I can compare a hair sample from the suspect and this one next to determine if they share similar characteristics and came from the same person."

"I am so thankful for your advanced skills," Kennedy said.

"Glad someone in the room appreciates it." Sierra grinned at her brothers. "That's all I have for now. I assume you'll suggest that they let Grady evaluate the bullet and casings used in the assault."

"Grady?" Kennedy asked.

"He's our ballistic expert," Sierra replied. "No way PPB has the abilities to do the same work. They'd have to send the bullets and casings recovered at the scene to the state police. Grady will get the information faster."

"What about the apartment where the shooter took his stand?" Drake looked at Erik. "Think we can have a look at it or get Sierra in there to process it?"

"Doubtful," Aiden said. "I called it in and was already warned to stand clear. I'm expecting a call back from the detective who caught the case. A Brynn Frost. Though I think they'll likely decide it's all related to the lab scare, and the task force will take over."

"Not if we get there before they do." Erik stood. "We'll head over there and persuade Frost to give us access to the scene. She's fair and impartial, so I think we have a shot."

"As the family mediator and resident smooth-talker, you're the guy to do it." Aiden grinned.

Erik was quite the charmer. Kennedy had fallen for him the first time they'd met. He was smooth but not slick and insincere. If any of the brothers could do this, he could, but that didn't mean he should go back to the crime scene. "Won't it be dangerous? The shooter could be there."

"I doubt he's anywhere in the area, considering the police presence such a shooting will bring." Erik held her gaze. "Of course, I can't let you come along."

"Don't worry," Kennedy said, the memory of the shooting flashing in vivid colors in her brain. "I wasn't even going to ask."

15

Despite Erik's assurances to Kennedy, the brothers were still vigilant as they arrived at the drugstore where the shooting had occurred. Yellow tape fluttering in the soft evening breeze circled the property and closed off the usually busy thoroughfare in both directions. Bullets littered the pavement, shocking Erik at the number that had been fired.

He scanned the onlookers. Seeing nothing out of the ordinary, he got out of the SUV to join Aiden, Grady, and Sierra. She'd insisted on coming along after she fed Asher.

Brynn Frost stood near the perimeter of the large scene with other bullet-ridden vehicles parked where the drivers had stopped. She spun to look at the team as they approached.

Erik tried not to look formidable, but his days as a patrol cop left him with a certain swagger that he'd never lost. He'd worked with Frost before, and at one point, she'd thanked him for being one of the few single patrol officers who didn't hit on her. Little did she know he'd thought about it. She was an attractive woman, but with his trust issues, he didn't think there was any point.

"Detective Frost," he called out and waved. "Erik Byrd. One of the intended victims in this incident."

Her big eyes widened, and recognition flashed on her face. She wore black slacks with a white blouse open at the collar that fit her trim figure well. She crossed the pavement and stuck out her hand to Erik.

"Good to you see you again, Officer... er, Mr. Byrd."

He shook her hand, not surprised at all by her firm grip. "Just Erik."

"I was surprised to learn you'd left the force, but then I heard it was for your brother's health. Admirable."

"I'm the brother in question." Aiden offered his hand. "Aiden Byrd."

As she shook hands with Aiden, Erik introduced the others.

She gave them a tight smile. "Not sure why you brought your forensics team along."

"We wanted to offer our services for no charge," Sierra said.

Frost tilted her head, her bluntly cut hair swishing over her shoulder. "Why would you want to do that?"

Sierra stepped forward, her shoulders back, her expression like their mother's when she was determined, and Erik almost felt sorry for Frost. "Because I'm also a Byrd, and someone tried to kill my brothers. I need to do everything I can to make sure the shooter is found."

"And because we have better facilities to process the evidence than your local lab." Grady held up a hand. "And before you think I'm insulting your criminalists, I'm not. I'm just stating a fact."

Frost eyed him. He'd seen the look before as she examined crime scenes. "So you really did leave, didn't you?"

"Is that a problem? I know some officers don't like dealing with those of us who go out on our own."

"Not for me. Not at all. And I'd be glad for the expertise you're offering, but I can't authorize the Veritas Center's services even if they *are* free."

"But your LT can, right?" Erik knew her lieutenant would be the one to make the call. "Would you ask? Then my brother and I can give our statements from the shootings while these guys get to work."

She ran her gaze over all of them again, and Erik was sure she was going to say no.

He couldn't let that happen. "I'm not at liberty to say why, but this investigation is going to become top priority for your department." He was thankful that he was told not to mention the potential anthrax to anyone else. If he did, she would immediately call the task force, and he'd have no hope of getting a look at the scene, much less processing it. "A proactive response that could get you noticed for all the right reasons. Could be a career maker."

"And you can't say why?"

"Sorry. No."

She watched him for a long time. His former officer days told him she was running all the information she possessed through her filter before acting. Officers did that most every minute of their shifts, though their decisions could often be life-threatening, whereas on a case that was bound to be high-profile, hers could simply be career suicide.

"Fine." She rested her hands on her waist. "Wait here. I'll give him a call."

"Thank you."

"Don't repay me by trying to force your way onto the scene."

"I wouldn't do that," Erik said.

"Yes, you would. We all would." She walked across the road, digging out her phone. She stopped just down the street from the drugstore that was an old-fashioned pharmacy with a soda fountain.

The two-story building was a drab beige stucco. Big picture windows held old-fashioned advertising signs, and the customers and staff were staring out the windows. But what Erik really cared about was the open window above where their shooter had taken a stand and fired off more bullets than Erik could count.

Grady stared up there too. "If you guys didn't have the bulletproofing, you'd all be toast."

Sierra jabbed him. "Do you always have to be so blunt?"

"Sorry, but it's true. From that range, he would've taken everyone out."

Erik spun to face him. "Don't let me catch you mentioning that to Kennedy. She doesn't need to hear that."

"No worries. I can be discreet."

Sierra snorted. "At least you can try."

"So if we assume the shooter hunkered down behind the open window, while we wait, we could take a walk to find the apartment entrance."

"What part of 'wait here' don't you get?" Erik asked.

"She meant the crime scene," Aiden said. "We're free to roam anywhere we want outside of it."

"I agree," Grady said.

Erik looked at the pair. "We don't want to risk making her mad or she could change her mind."

Grady shook his head. "When did you become so obedient?"

"It's not obedience but wisdom, man. Do what every woman wants or risk her wrath." He wiggled his eyebrows at Sierra to lighten the mood.

She punched him, and he stifled the urge to knuckle her head. Exchanging barbs with his siblings was always guaranteed to brighten things up, even if they were acting like teenagers again.

"Doesn't matter," Grady said. "Here she comes."

Frost strode across the street, but her face was a mask of stoicism and Erik wished he knew what she was going to say.

She stopped and planted her feet.

Uh-oh.

It didn't look good—not good at all—and Erik offered a prayer as he braced himself for the answer.

"My LT has worked with Veritas several times, and he's glad for the help," Frost said, surprising Erik. "He just asked that you send over that standard contract, and we'll move forward."

"I'll do it right now." Sierra got out her phone and tapped the screen.

"So what are we looking at here?" Erik asked.

"Apartment over the pharmacy is vacant and has an exterior entrance on the back of the building. The shooter jimmied the lock and slid a table over by the window, where we think he rested his weapon." She looked at Grady. "I'm sure you can confirm that once you do a trajectory analysis."

Grady nodded. "With the number of rounds fired, I'm sure to find bullets lodged in multiple locations, and I can easily make an official determination."

Frost unfurled her hand to reveal an evidence bag holding bullet casings. "From the apartment. Any thoughts on what kind of weapon we're looking at here?"

Grady took the bag and studied the contents. "Looks like 9×19 mm Parabellum ammo. Which won't likely be any help. It's the world's most popular submachine gun cartridge. It's also the caliber for the most widely used military and police handguns."

"So too common to be unique?" Frost asked.

"Exactly." Grady ran a hand through his sandy-red hair and fixed his blue-eyed gaze on the detective. "Best we can hope for on the casings—other than using them for trial when I can match the bullet to the weapon if we recover it— is to find that the subject transferred his DNA when the bullets were loaded into the magazine."

"If the shooter cast his own ammo instead of using factory cast ones, he'd likely leave prints on the bullets, right?" Frost asked.

"Sure, but not in this case." Grady turned a casing over. "These are from jacketed rounds, which individuals can't cast."

Frost narrowed her eyes. "Well, shoot."

"Hold on," Grady said. "You might not be able to cast FMJs at home, but the casings *can* be reloaded, and we might gather prints that way."

Frost took a step closer. "So you can tell they're jacketed rounds just by looking at the casings?"

"In this case, yes," Grady said. "And if you want some good news, I've seen two case types in this bag so it's likely they *are* reloads. I'll know more after I look at additional casings. The more case types I find, the more likely they're reloads. If you have anyone else collecting bullets, which I hope you won't, they should pay extra attention so they can be processed for prints and DNA."

"I'm almost certain the bullets came from a submachine gun," Erik said. "At least that was the sound pattern."

"Though I didn't hear the gun, I would agree," Grady said. "You can't always determine by looking at casings whether or not they were fired from a sub-machine gun rather than a different semi-auto pistol or carbine. However, I'm pretty confident I already know the gun we're looking for here."

"You what?" Frost gaped at him.

"Way to bury the lead, man." Aiden rolled his eyes.

"So what are we looking for?" Frost asked.

"An H&K MP5. Pretty much all H&K guns leave a fluted marking on the case that quickly identifies the gun they were fired from. These casings have that telltale fluting. Plus, the H&K prefers FMJ over pretty much anything, so that's another tipoff."

"You're amazing." Sierra gazed at Grady with respect.

Grady waved a hand. "You do the same thing only with other evidence. And of course, this is a specific science just like your forensics are, and my immediate determination is an educated guess based on the markings and the amount of casings as well as their fall pattern. I'll take all the evidence back to the lab and confirm the weapon used."

The detective kept steady eye contact. "I've heard the Veritas experts could do things we don't do in our lab. You all keep proving it."

"We do for sure." Grady frowned. "But I'm not going to pull a rabbit out of a hat. In general, unless the shooter was grossly inept or wanted to be discovered, it's going to be extremely difficult to find any markings to give you a lead on his identity."

"But not impossible, right?" Erik asked.

"Not impossible." Grady shifted the bagged casings in his hand. "And of course, if we find bullets that aren't too mutilated and with good markings, we can run them through the federal firearms database." Grady looked at Frost. "With your official approval, of course."

Just like running prints and DNA in databases, the National Integrated Ballistic Information Network—NIBIN —database managed by ATF was limited to participating law enforcement agencies. It stored over four million pieces of ballistic evidence, providing a nationwide network of ballistic data for firearms to be shared, researched, identi-fied, and cross-referenced.

Frost's phone chimed. "That's my LT. Let me see what he wants. Be right back."

She strode across the street again.

When she was out of earshot, Erik looked at Grady. "Anything you were holding back?"

Grady snapped off a glove and scratched his close-cut beard, the color matching his red hair. "I might've played down my ability as the best firearms examiner outside of the FBI's lab." He grinned. "Let me get to work on taking these casings into evidence for them. Gonna take a while with the quantity."

He'd brought a large plastic case much like Sierra's, and it contained some of the same tools. Markers to denote bullet locations. Camera to document items found. Tweezers to remove bullets from any kind of substance they pierced. And bags to collect all the evidence, which he would take back to his state-of-the-art firearms lab, a place Erik and his brothers took every opportunity to visit.

Frost came back. "LT got the form, so we're good to go. But before you leave here, we'll want an evidence list and your scene photos."

Sierra started to pump her fist but must've thought better of it, as she lowered it. "Sure thing."

"Same with you, Houston," Frost told Grady.

Grady gave a tight smile. "You got it."

Sierra looked at Frost. "So we're good to go?"

"Not inside," Frost said. "I still need to tell our criminal-ists to stand down. They're not going to like it, but you can get started out here with wide shots of the scene. Just sign in with the officer of record. I'll tell him on my way past that you're officially welcome."

"Thank you," Erik said.

She let her penetrating gaze linger. "Just don't do anything to make me regret my decision."

She marched away and stopped by a patrol officer holding a clipboard.

"Making friends and influencing people." Sierra laughed. "But on the bright side, I doubt the criminalists are fond of me to begin with. Despite me telling them that they're super good at their jobs and they just don't have all the cool toys."

"Don't sell yourself short," Grady said. "You've got mad skills and experience that they don't possess."

"Well, yeah, but I thought that would sound too cocky to say aloud like you do." She laughed and lifted the camera that hung around her neck. "I need you all to wait here so I can take scene photos. And move your kit, Grady, so it's not in my pictures."

"Did I mention bossy, too?" Grady laughed.

"Hey, you've only had to deal with it for a few years." Erik slung his arm around Sierra's shoulders. "I've been bossed around by her my whole life."

He loved that he could tease her, and she went with it. Most of the time. But right now he was more thankful for those mad skills Grady mentioned. Maybe she would recover something that would produce the lead Erik was desperately looking for. No guy threatened Kennedy and got away with it. That wouldn't go unpunished. The creep could count on that.

Erik stood back and contemplated leaving after he and Aiden had given their statements. He wasn't needed here. Grady and Sierra would do top-notch work, and all he could really do was get coffee. But he wasn't ready to go back to his place, where he'd have to fight his feelings for Kennedy. The shooting had really done a number on him, bringing up all the old feelings for her. Maybe cementing them in his heart again. And it seemed like she felt it too. Or maybe he just wanted her to.

It would be a lot easier to stop thinking about her—about the way he was starting to feel again—if he hadn't once known what it was like to be wholly loved by her. But he did. And it had been exhilarating and calming at the same time. An impossible contrast, but there it was. Kennedy. He'd never been able to put his finger on why he was so drawn to her, but he was leaning toward surrendering to it again. Lock, stock, and barrel.

He started to sigh but stopped when Sierra glanced at him. If she got even a hint of his returning interest in Kennedy, his sister would start asking questions. She must not have seen anything interesting in his expression because she returned her focus to her work. He watched her, taking a moment to appreciate his family. And thinking about how Kennedy was almost alone. Just a sister left.

Frost returned, grabbing his attention. "Let me show you inside so you can get started on the evidence."

Sierra had finished taking her shots, so Frost led them to the back of the building and up worn wooden stairs with plastered walls to a landing with two doorways. One of them stood open.

She stepped through it into a single room that was made up of a living, bedroom, and kitchen space. The table she'd mentioned sat in front of the open window, shell casings scattered across the floor.

"Let me snap pictures, then we can get to work," Sierra said, already lifting her camera.

Frost focused her attention on Aiden. "I'll take those statements now. You know the drill. One witness at a time. So if you'll wait downstairs, I'll talk to Erik first."

"It'll give me time to look around outside." Aiden jogged down the stairs and out the door.

Frost drew a small notepad and pen from her pocket. "Tell me what happened."

As Grady tapped his foot and watched Sierra, likely jonesing to get to the casings, Erik launched into a description of the incident.

Frost asked a few follow-up questions, then closed her notepad. "I'll just talk to your brother and let you know if I have any more questions."

"Thanks again for letting us handle the forensics."

"Just remember. They're not being processed for you but for PPB. I'll decide if and when I'll share any information."

Erik nodded, and she started down the stairs. She was right. The evidence was confidential, but if Sierra or Grady discussed something they discovered and Erik overheard the conversation, all the better.

"Here! Look!" Sierra's excited tone broke into Erik's thoughts.

He moved closer to her. She was holding up a white vinyl wristband for Grady to see, but she cast Erik a subversive look. She knew he was listening, but wouldn't acknowledge it.

Erik focused on the bracelet similar to ones handed out for admission to theme parks, waterparks, and bars. Large black letters were embossed on the band, as were tiny red hawks. Erik tried to read the writing but couldn't make it out.

"Where's it from?" Grady asked.

"Hood to Coast relay race dated this year." Sierra turned the bracelet in her fingers. "The race ends today."

"You're kidding, right?" Grady took the band with his gloved fingers and studied it. "A guy runs the world's largest relay race and then stops in to shoot at an SUV. Not likely."

"Maybe his leg of the race was done earlier," Sierra said.

"But if his leg was done, and he came here to commit a crime, why keep the band on?" Grady asked.

"Bragging rights?" Sierra looked at Erik. "Our family ran the race one year, and we were so thankful to finish. Nearly two hundred miles. We told everyone who would listen."

Erik thought about the two-day race with over a thousand teams of eight to twelve members who ran or walked a course that started at Mount Hood, wound through Portland, and ended at the Pacific Ocean. Registration for the iconic event filled on opening day for the past thirty years. But Erik didn't comment as it would be an acknowledgment that Sierra shared evidence with him.

"They didn't give out bracelets when I ran it in 2001," Grady said.

"Not when we did either," Sierra said. "That was in '05, but I guess things could've changed. Or maybe the team had them made. Or a vendor was selling them as a souvenir. But if that was the case, I don't get the red hawks on it."

Erik's sister was in tune with him, as that was his thought as well.

Grady glanced at Erik. "If it was a team thing, we should be able to comb race videos to identify the team by the bracelets."

Sierra nodded. "That would bring us down to twelve suspects. Well, plus the people on their road crew."

Erik's parents had served as their road crew, driving the support vans that picked up and dropped off the runners and gave them a place to sleep and hydrate along the route.

"Still, I don't see our shooter yanking off the bracelet and leaving it behind," Grady said. "But I suppose the band could've distracted him while he was shooting. Depending on the weapon, and if he was holding it right, it could've even brushed against his arm or chest and irritated his skin."

"Or it's not from him," Sierra said. "A hitman would never leave his brass behind, much less something as easily identifiable as this."

"He did leave brass here. Lots of brass." Grady looked around. "Looks like he fired off a couple of magazines, and each one can hold up to thirty rounds. We might be looking at sixty casings here. Probably too much for the shooter to pick up before the police arrived. He didn't want to risk getting caught."

"Then you guys should get back to it," Erik said, finally unable to keep quiet. "I'm going to search the web for information on Tile trackers to see if we can figure out who used them to track Kennedy and her mom. And then I'll search for Hood to Coast pictures of teams who might be wearing those bracelets. Hopefully, we'll find our suspect's group and narrow it down to him. And once we have the shooter, we'll use Grady's expertise to put him away for a very long time."

16

Kennedy appreciated Drake's escort down the sixth floor hallway, but she could no longer keep up the conversations they'd been having. She needed to go to bed. Not that she would. She hadn't heard from Erik except for a text telling her that he, Grady, and Sierra had not only been given access to view the scene, but that the Veritas Center would collect and process evidence, meaning they would be at the scene for hours. And a later text that said they'd found a bracelet for the Hood to Coast race, giving them a direction to proceed.

She imagined him persuading the detective to accept his help, and her feet slowed at the image. The detective likely had no chance against Erik's persuasive personality. When he'd turned his charm Kennedy's way, she'd rarely been able to ignore him. If he decided he wanted to be in a relationship with her again and started to pursue her, what would she do? Would she cave? Resist? She suspected she was leaning much closer to caving than resisting, and oddly that was less terrifying than it had been just a few days before.

"Coming?" Drake paused at the skybridge and glanced back at her.

"Sorry. Got lost in my thoughts."

He gave a pointed nod, then took long strides, and she hurried to keep up over the gently swaying bridge. He'd been very attentive while they waited for news in the Nighthawk office. He'd even tried to keep her mood up by telling her childhood stories about Erik, and she didn't want to take up any more of his time.

A text sounded on her phone, the ping echoing off the glass enclosed space.

"It's from Erik," she said. "He's in the parking structure with Grady recovering slugs from the vehicle."

"And you want to go out there." Drake's statement was followed by a lopsided grin.

"Is that a problem?" She shoved her hand into a pocket to keep from busying her fingers with a lock of hair.

"Nah. It's just going to take quite some time to document and recover all of the bullets, and I thought you wanted to rest."

"I might be able to help."

His eyebrow went up, and he cocked his head.

"What? You don't think I know how to recover evidence that isn't in the bottom of some body of water?" She crossed her arms. "Because I do. And I'm very good at it too."

Drake held up his hands. "Not questioning your skills. Just wondering why you'd want to hang out in the parking garage when you could be comfortable in Erik's condo."

Because I want to see Erik. There. She had to admit her real reason. After the shooting, she wanted to confirm again that every hair on his head was fine.

"But to each his own." Drake crossed the remaining distance to the door. He opened it then looked out. "We're clear."

She took the last few steps and paused at the open doorway. Erik, Grady, and Sierra stood near the battered SUV, their backs to Kennedy.

Erik spun, his sharp expression softening when he locked eyes with her.

"Ah, so that's your real reason." Drake's snarky grin irritated Kennedy, but he was right on target.

Sure, she wanted to help if she could. She really did. She also wanted to make sure Erik was all right. But she hadn't seen him in over six hours, and she missed him. She didn't know what was going on with him. With her. With them.

Oh, she was pitiful. Her mind was a mess. Waffling one minute and the next, desperate for something that would never happen again.

She steeled her resolve to hide her feelings and shifted to stare at the terrifying-looking vehicle as she approached him. They'd been inside the SUV that now sported bullet holes too numerous to count. She had the urge to touch one of the cavities, just to be sure the shooting had been real, but the terror deep in her soul told her it was real. Told her that someone tried to murder her and Erik.

She wrapped her arms around her stomach and faced him.

"You didn't have to come out here," he said, but he didn't sound like he was unhappy with her presence.

"That's what I told her." Drake cast her another snarky look.

She ignored him. "I wanted to see if I could do anything to help."

"I appreciate that." Grady gave her the same warm smile he'd offered when she'd met him before he'd left with Erik. "But with the armor plating, the removal is going to be tricky, if not impossible, without taking the vehicle apart."

"It's probably going to be an all-nighter." Sierra yawned. "And I, for one, am not going to help. Asher awaits me."

"Thanks, Sis." Erik bit his lip as if he wanted to say a whole lot more.

"I'll get the slugs to you for printing and DNA before I analyze them and obscure anything," Grady said without looking up from his camera. "But I have to say, I can't guarantee I won't smudge anything with how embedded some of them are."

"You recovered what?" she asked. "Over sixty casings? If the guy left his prints or DNA, we should be able to get what we need between the bullets we recovered and that quantity of casings." She picked up her case. "Okay. I'm out of here. Night all."

"Thank you for your help, Sierra," Kennedy said.

"Any time, but please don't go out and get shot at again." Sierra wrinkled her nose and pressed her fingers on the biometric reader by the door, which popped open for her. She disappeared inside the building.

"If you don't need me to babysit Kennedy any longer," Drake said. "I'll take off too. Need my beauty sleep."

"No amount of sleep is going to fix that ugly mug." Erik chuckled. "But seriously, thanks, man."

Drake gave Erik's shoulder a playful punch and strode off in the same confident way all the Byrd brothers moved. Their dad had the same way about him. They'd also picked up a sensitive side from him, not that a one of them would admit that. Well, except Erik when they'd been together. He'd often been tender. Mix that with the assuredness and protectiveness, and it was a trifecta of attraction that left Kennedy's heart pounding.

"You two should take off too," Grady said. "There's really nothing you can do here. I need to remove these slugs."

"I'm trained to remove bullets," Kennedy said.

"Sorry, but I'm a control freak. Especially in a tricky situation like this one. And one that involves people we care about. So..." Grady shrugged.

"I could help take the vehicle apart," Erik offered.

"I can handle it." Grady shifted his gaze between Erik and her. "Besides, you look like you've got something you might want to talk about."

If Grady was picking up on her emotions when he was busy doing the thing he loved the most, she wasn't hiding her growing feelings for Erik very well.

"Then we'll head out," Erik said. "Call me if you need me. Or if you want to stop by, I'm bunking with Drake."

Grady's rust-colored eyebrow rose, but he quickly turned his attention back to his work.

Erik spun, and Kennedy headed for the door. In the hallway, he strode past her to the elevator keypad to call the car.

"It's going to take a boatload of cash to fix the SUV," she said, preferring to keep the charged atmosphere in control by sticking to business.

"Aiden assures me that our insurance will cover most of it." The elevator car arrived, whooshing open, and he held the doors for her.

"I'd like to cover any deductible." She entered and leaned against the back wall.

"That's not necessary." He joined her and stabbed the button for the second floor.

"But if you weren't protecting me, you wouldn't have incurred the damage."

"It's all part of the business."

She didn't want to be even further in their debt. "Are you sure your brothers agree with that?"

"If they don't, my mom will set them straight." He laughed.

Despite her desire to keep things calm and neutral

between them, she laughed along, remembering the past when he could easily go from serious to playful.

He sobered. "We were once really good together, weren't we?"

And back to serious just as quickly. She didn't know how to reply, so she simply nodded and hoped it didn't encourage this topic to continue when she was so uncertain of her feelings.

"I wish I could let go of how I feel and we could try again." He held her gaze. "If I could, would you want to do that?"

Oh, man. She shouldn't answer, but she couldn't hold back. "Want to? Yes. Would I? Not unless I knew without doubt that you really had let go of the pain and hurt I caused. I couldn't get serious with you again, only for you to bring that up all the time."

"Yeah." A pensive look consumed his face. "Yeah, that would be important."

The bell for their floor dinged, and when the doors opened, he held out his hand. "I don't know if I can do that."

"I didn't think it would be easy," she replied as she passed him.

He gently took hold of her arm and pulled her close. He smelled masculine and like the outdoors, and she wanted to step into his arms and cling for dear life. But she froze and waited for his cue as to their next move.

"But I want to," he whispered in her ear, his breath warm against her neck. "I really want to."

Her heart skittered, and she looked up at him. The searing intensity in his eyes burned to her soul. She should say something. Do something. But the words or actions wouldn't come.

His phone buzzed. He let out a long breath, but instead

of answering it, he slid his fingers into her hair and cupped the back of her head.

"I'm going to kiss you again if you don't stop me." His phone buzzed again. It had to be important, and she suspected he would regret not answering it. He was just giving in to the moment. He hadn't let go of the way she'd hurt him. Maybe he never would.

"You should answer that," she said, regretting the words the moment they came out.

He let her go and muttered something under his breath as he lifted his phone to his face. "This better be important."

She heard a male voice on the other end of the call say it was. She watched Erik's face but couldn't tell if the news was good or bad.

"I was just walking Kennedy to my place. We'll be right there." He hung up and shoved the phone into his pocket.

"What is it?" she asked.

"Clay located the race team that wore the hawk bracelets. He'll meet us at my place. Maybe you can ID one of the men on the team as your intruder."

Erik opened the door to his condo, and Pong came running, his tongue hanging out, his eyes alight with what Erik believed was love. Before Erik had left his condo, he'd crated Pong as he usually did, but Clay must've let the dog out.

"Sit," Erik commanded. He didn't want Pong to forget his obedience skills just because he was retired and was doted on by Erik and his family.

Kennedy entered the condo and stopped to ruffle Pong's ears. She was rewarded with a sloppy kiss. "Aren't you just precious?"

Erik groaned.

She looked at him. "What?"

"Precious?" Erik feigned a gulp. "He's a former working dog and has his standards to uphold. Fierce is a much better word."

Kennedy chuckled. "Sorry, no can say." Kennedy ruffled Pong's ears again. "You're precious, aren't you, boy?"

He yelped his agreement.

"See. He knows who he is." Kennedy gave Erik an impish grin, then chuckled and headed into the condo.

Erik wanted to tug her into his arms and tickle her like he'd often done, tickle her until she surrendered and their tussling turned into kisses. But even if Clay wasn't waiting for them, Erik wouldn't touch her again. Not now. Not when he didn't know who he was anymore since he'd reconnected with her. Maybe he should take lessons from his dog, who was confident enough to let her call him precious.

Erik sure wouldn't like that, but honestly, Kennedy once could have called him anything, and he wouldn't have balked. The thought had him smiling as he followed her into his home, his dog on his heels.

Clay was sitting at the dining table, laptop open in front of him. He looked up, excitement burning in his eyes. "We may have found our shooter."

Erik wasn't as excited. Sure, finding the person who wore the bracelet was a good lead, but he couldn't see the shooter ripping off the bracelet and leaving it behind as evidence. Not under any circumstances. Still, they needed to follow the lead.

"The team call themselves the Redhawks which makes sense with the wristband and the fact that they're former Oregon Air National Guard 142nd Fighter Wing." Clay narrowed his eyes, looking so much like their dad that Erik felt like Clay planned to scold him for doing something wrong. "Have a look. There are a few guys on the team who fit your intruder's build, but one in particular that I'm really liking for this."

Erik would've expected Kennedy to race over to Clay, but she dragged her feet as if they were encased in wet cement. He got it. She was nervous about seeing the man who'd likely chased her with a gun and fired a hail storm of bullets at their vehicle.

Erik followed her, and they both stood behind Clay to look at the big picture on the computer screen. Erik eased closer to Kennedy, and their fingers touched. She glanced at him and offered a soft smile. He should let go as he'd just sworn off touching her, but her smile encouraged him to lace his fingers with hers.

She clung tightly and leaned over Clay as Pong came to lie on Erik's feet and look up at Kennedy, his expression worried. Erik had known he was falling for her again, but he hadn't expected his dog to fall in love with her too.

The picture showed nine men and three women wearing camouflage T-shirts and black shorts standing in front of a fighter jet and holding a banner that read *Redhawks Fly Through the Hood to Coast Race.*

Clay tapped the screen on one of the men. "This guy seems to fit the build of your intruder best. He our guy?"

She squinted. "Could be, but why did you choose him over the guy behind him? They're about the same size and build."

"Guy in the front is missing his wristband."

Kennedy sucked in a breath. "He is, isn't he? He would've had to leave the race, set up the shot and get back in time for this picture."

"It's a stretch, but it could happen and he could be our shooter or at least know something about it," Erik said. "And it wouldn't be any stretch to think a guy with the skills former military might have could shoot at us. Far more likely than the wife of a scammer, a college professor, or a student."

"Agreed," Clay said. "And the suspect at Wanda's place was wearing military boots and camo. Could be another point in this guy's favor."

Erik nodded. "You have any names to go with the picture?"

Clay shook his head. "You're the internet guru. Figured that would be your job."

Clay leaned back, forcing Kennedy and Erik to separate and step back.

"I'll get started on it right after I look through Wanda's college records," Erik said.

"But you just said this was more promising." Clay closed his laptop.

"I think it is in regards to the shooting, but Kennedy and I were discussing who would have access to anthrax or another Select Agent, and it could be someone in the science department at OHSU where Wanda taught. So I'll start there as I assume Kennedy will want to look through the boxes, and if I search for the name first, she'll have to wait on me to review the boxes." Erik looked at her. "Do you?"

"Want to look through them? No." She bit her lip. "Will I do it? Yes."

"You guys want help?" Clay asked.

"It's only a few boxes," Erik said. "And it's getting late. I figure you might need to check in with Toni to go over wedding plans."

"That would be good." Clay smiled widely. "Fourteen days and counting. There must be some crisis or other that needs my help. Or maybe she just needs moral support. Especially if Mom's been trying to be too helpful."

"I don't mean to be thankful for Toni's distress," Erik

said. "But the wedding sure has distracted Mom from bugging me in person about the anthrax scare. Not that she hasn't texted a million times a day. Guess weddings trump anthrax." Erik laughed.

Clay snorted. "I think weddings trump everything in Mom's life. At least until she has us all safely married. Then she'll probably start on our spouses' siblings. Malone ought to watch out. Or maybe she'll change her focus to increasing the number of grandchildren."

"Congratulations on the upcoming wedding." Kennedy gave Clay a luminous smile. "I'm so happy you found someone who makes you smile like you do when you talk about her."

"Oh, he's hooked all right." Erik laughed.

"And proud of it." He punched Erik in the arm. "Time you took the same plunge."

Erik opened his mouth to protest but Clay started across the room and down the hallway.

"He really looks happy."

"He is. As are all my siblings right now. Family gatherings are almost enough to make you want to gag," he said, but honestly, he enjoyed seeing everyone happy.

Odd that he really hadn't been jealous until that moment. Until Kennedy came back into his life. But that wasn't something he would dwell on.

"You should know," Erik said as he went to the end of the table and lifted two of the three boxes onto it. "I researched Tile trackers while Sierra and Grady did their thing and found out that they don't have serial numbers, just a Bluetooth ID. Once we know who put the device in your bag, we can tie the account to that person via that ID, but it won't allow us to trace the trackers back to the owner now."

"Another dead-end then."

"For now, yes." He slid one of the boxes over to Kennedy. "Let me grab gloves in case we find something important." He dug in his computer case for two pairs, then handed one to Kennedy.

She opened a box, and he lifted the lid on the one next to it. He started digging to find it contained mostly awards, desk supplies, and old journals, which he set on the table. In the bottom of the box, he found a leather-bound book that raised his hope for a lead.

"Calendar and diary," he said to Kennedy and sat down to look through it. He set the book on the table and it opened in the middle.

"See this." He pointed at the paper near the spine. "Someone ripped pages from the book in the diary section."

"My mom could've done it."

He met her gaze. "Yeah, or someone who didn't want anyone to read what she'd written."

"What's before and after the missing pages?"

He turned back a few pages. "Before it are notes about student labs she wanted to include in her curriculum."

"And after?"

He flipped more pages. "She was going to propose a research project for her advanced students. She's made a list of pros and cons she would use to get her supervisors on board with it."

"Does she say what they would research?"

"Medicinal chemistry and blood cancers."

Kennedy rubbed a hand on her forehand. "I didn't know she was interested in that."

"Did she know anyone with a blood cancer?"

"Not that I know of."

"Do you think she might've had cancer?"

Kennedy's eyes flashed open. "Wouldn't they have found that in an autopsy?"

He shrugged. "That's a question we need to ask a medical examiner."

Kennedy shook her head. "Surely if she was sick, Finley would've seen it. It's too late to ask her about it tonight, but I will first thing in the morning."

"And speaking of morning, we need to get to work so I can get at least a few hours of beauty sleep before interviewing the guy in the photo." Erik chuckled.

Kennedy's narrowed eyes said she found no humor in his comment. "You don't even know his name."

"I will by morning."

"That's overly optimistic, isn't it?"

"Nah. With the former military connection, I can find him."

She locked gazes with him. "Then I'm coming with you to the interview."

She looked ready for a fight, but it wasn't needed. "You're the one who might be able to identify him, and I didn't plan on stopping you. But we won't rush off. If he's our guy, he's already tried to kill us and Aiden. So the team will do recon at the guy's house then meet to formulate a plan."

Erik's phone rang, and he answered. "Good evening, Maya."

"I wish it were a good one. The toxin came back positive for anthrax."

He was glad he was sitting or he might drop to his chair. For the first time since he'd been exposed, he had a valid reason to be concerned for his life.

17

Kennedy couldn't think of a better way to start her day, even if the entire Byrd clan sitting around Erik's dining table was a bit intimidating. With spouses and significant others and new children, there were so many more of them now. But then she was more self-assured than she'd been as a college girl, and she knew she could hold her own.

They'd streamed a Sunday morning worship service online and were now having breakfast in lieu of Sunday dinner. Peggy changed things up because Kennedy was having dinner with Finley that night. Kennedy couldn't believe Erik's mom would change her plans so Kennedy could be included, but she had. She seemed eager to talk to Erik.

Kennedy stabbed a bite of the fluffy scrambled eggs lying next to crisp bacon and a mix of melons. There was also homemade bread toasted to a crisp brown, just the way she liked it. The scents of bacon and toast twined together and reminded her of breakfast at home with Finley and their parents.

She chewed the eggs, resisting falling into the sadness of grief, and smiled at Peggy, who was watching her from where she stood behind the table. "Thank you again for breakfast. It's a great way to start the day."

Peggy beamed at her as she rested a hand on Logan's and Willow's shoulders, the foster children seeming to fit right into the family. "You're most welcome. I wish I could say it was because I just wanted to be nice, but—"

"Here we go." Aiden grinned, and his brothers groaned. "The real reason we're all gathered together."

Peggy ignored him and grabbed a pile of papers from the counter. "I brought a schedule for each of you boys, and I need you to follow it."

"What in the world have you got planned?" Erik took a long pull on his steaming mug of black coffee.

She gave a piece of paper to each of his brothers except Erik.

"Why am I excluded?" he asked, looking half amused and half offended.

Aiden glanced up from his page. "Because you're the subject of our assignment."

"What?" Erik shot a look at his mother. "What's going on?"

"I know how you all get when you're working on behalf of your clients," she said. "You get so wrapped up in it that you forget about everything else. Especially when the client is someone you care very deeply for."

"Yeah, so?" Erik said.

"So now that the test came back positive for anthrax, you need to be sure to take the antibiotic as scheduled and pay attention to any symptoms that might arise." She glanced at Kennedy. "You too, sweetheart."

"Of course," Kennedy said. "But my risk of exposure is far less than Erik's, so don't worry about me."

"I'll be praying for you both until you're in the clear."

She stepped next to Erik and placed her hand on his shoulder. "I need you to be extra vigilant."

"I will be." He squeezed her hand. "Promise."

Peggy pinned her gaze on him. "I'm not so sure. You'll get busy digging up some information on your computer, and you'll forget all about the anthrax. So I want your brothers to keep an eye on you and let me know how you're doing. Same goes for Kennedy."

"Mom," Erik said, his patience seeming to evaporate. "This is crazy, even for you."

"You could die from this, son." She pulled her shoulders back in a hard line. "I won't let that happen."

"Fine, then if you want a play-by-play report, I'll set an alarm on my phone and check in with you on a regular basis."

She shook her head hard, almost violently. "No. No. I've thought about this. I can see you with your face glued to a computer screen, hunting down valuable information. Your alarm rings. You turn it off, planning to look at it in a minute, but then you forget."

"I won't—"

"Dude," Drake said. "You totally will."

"But I—"

"We all know you will," Sierra said.

"And your mom's right," Kennedy said, wishing she didn't have to be on the opposite side of what Erik wanted all the time. "Our health has to come before anything."

Erik gritted his teeth and glanced around the table. If he was seeing what Kennedy was seeing, it was the determined set of his brothers' and sister's faces. He might want to argue, but there was no point. After all, that was what made these people so special. They would stop at nothing to protect a family member, and the same held true with a client, which right now meant her. Five men and one woman who would do anything to help her. Anything.

Oh, man. She was so blessed. So very blessed. Tears wet her eyes.

"Kennedy, honey." Peggy's fierce mama-bear gaze zoned in on Kennedy. "What's wrong?"

"I'm just feeling very blessed to know all of you, and so thankful you don't hold the way I broke up with Erik against me."

"About that." Peggy dragged her chair next to Kennedy. "Sounds like everyone knows what happened but me, and don't you think it's time I'm in the loop too?"

Erik groaned, but Kennedy didn't mind telling Peggy about the breakup. Kennedy had already blown her WITSEC agreement, after all. And she wanted this special woman to know that Kennedy didn't abandon her son without a good reason. Why keeping Peggy in the loop was so very important to Kennedy, she didn't know, and she wasn't going to analyze it, because if she did, she might not like the answer.

Erik stowed the conversation from breakfast. He couldn't think about how well Kennedy fit in with his family and still keep her safe as he drove her and Drake to their interview with the Hood to Coast racer. Didn't take Erik long the night before to learn the guy in the picture's identity, plus the identity of the other people on the team. Not surprisingly, the guy was a former pilot and major, Mick Hess. He lived in a four-story apartment building near the Portland Air National Guard Base, which was located adjacent to the Portland International Airport.

A commercial jet soared overhead, and Erik glanced up.

The sun beat down on the area, and the snowcapped peak of Mount Hood fairly glowed, but there wasn't a fighter jet in the sky.

"I was hoping to see the jets." Kennedy peered out the window in the backseat. "But maybe you can't see them from here."

"You can," Erik said. "They fly in formation in this area, but I've only ever seen them in the afternoon."

It wasn't uncommon to catch one of the F-15C Eagles the guard exclusively flew, roaring out of PDX on an almost daily basis. The Air Guard was a reserve component of the Air Force, performing both state and federal missions. And seeing the jets soaring through the sky in formation was a remarkable sight.

Kennedy's eyes narrowed. "Then we won't likely see them today."

"Probably a good thing," Drake said from the seat beside Erik. "Could be a distraction."

Erik loved everything aeronautical and would be stoked to see the jets, but his brother was right. They couldn't afford to be distracted by anything. He needed to keep Kennedy's safety first in his mind.

Which was why they'd done a thorough threat assessment before coming here. Low risk, but still not no risk. He pulled into the parking lot and searched the area for danger. A few commuters heading to work but otherwise it was calm and quiet. Their other brothers had come ahead of them to do additional recon, and Aiden saluted Erik from the sidewalk.

Good. Everything was okay for their early morning knock and talk. *If* Hess let them in. A big if. Especially if the guy was their shooter. But Erik was going to get in that door no matter what happened.

He parked next to his brothers' rental vehicle and

turned to look at Kennedy. "Hang tight while I get the lay of the land." They'd reviewed aerial footage, but he wanted a firsthand look before he allowed Kennedy to step out of the safe bulletproof environment.

He joined his brothers.

"We're clear." Aiden planted his feet on the sidewalk. "Apartment's at the end of the first floor hallway. We confirmed exits include the apartment's patio door and the front door with exits on both ends of the hallway, plus a stairwell and elevator."

Erik lifted his hand to block the sun as he surveyed the building. "So Aiden will take the closest end of the hallway, Brendan the far end. Clay has the patio door, and Drake's with me for the suspect's apartment."

"Exactly." Drake's droll tone said he wanted to move on.

Erik looked at the SUV where Kennedy waited. No way he'd rush this. He had more at stake here than his brothers. Erik was falling in love with Kennedy all over again, and he was powerless to stop it. In fact, he didn't even want to try anymore. He just wanted to focus on her well-being and forget the past. Forget the hurt. And keep her safe.

Erik jerked his head at the SUV. "I'm going to do a quick pass of the first floor then I'll meet you at the vehicle to escort Kennedy inside."

"Understood," Drake said.

Erik strode off. He heard his brothers talking but couldn't make out their words. They were probably discussing the fact that he had the least amount of experience in law enforcement. It was true. He did. But he'd been an exemplary police officer and trained with Blackwell Tactical to improve his skills. The whole Nighthawk team had, but Erik had gone to Cold Harbor for one-on-one training with Blackwell's owner. A former SEAL, Gage

Blackwell was the best trainer in the area, and Erik had learned a lot from him.

But he hated the thought that kept niggling at his brain with each footstep. Today they might just find out how much he'd learned about protection skills.

~

The Kevlar vest was bulky and hot as the sun shone brightly in the morning already approaching eighty degrees. Kennedy kept tugging it down under her blouse as they waited outside Hess's place for him to answer the door. She wished her dominant hand weren't bandaged and she could grab her gun if needed. But Erik and Drake were carrying, and they could stop any threat. Erik had pounded on the metal several times, but no answer. Hess was home. That was certain. The brothers had watched the place all night. They'd seen Hess go in and never come out.

Finally, heavy footfalls sounded on the other side of the black metal door.

"About time." Erik waved his hands at Kennedy in a shooing motion. "If he's our shooter and feels threatened, he could open fire. I don't want you taking a bullet."

She swallowed and moved back from the door. She knew visiting this man unannounced was dangerous. Not only had Erik and his brothers told her several times, but the bulky vest reminded her with every move. Suddenly the danger seemed real. Very real.

The door opened a crack, and a man matching Hess's picture poked his head out. He ran a sharp gaze over them with penetrating brown eyes. "Yeah."

He didn't show any sign of recognizing her or Erik, just a hint of frustration in his large wide-set eyes. He had near-black hair cut military short. He was tall and wore an over-shirt on top of a blue T-shirt and khaki tactical pants. His body was toned—maybe too toned for the suspect she'd seen at her mother's place.

But what really caught her attention was the bump on his nose and the long pointy chin. He could be their guy, all right, or just another active guy who'd broken his nose at some point in his life. He was wearing a long-sleeved over-shirt in summer, and she had to think he was using it to hide a weapon on his hip. She didn't see a bulge, but she'd keep an eye out for it as she assumed Erik and Drake would do. Especially Drake. Erik explained that his brother would hang back, and his main focus would be protection so Erik could question Hess.

"Are you Mick Hess?" Erik asked, though he had to know from the race pictures that they were looking at Hess.

"Who wants to know?" Hess clamped his hand on the door and fired a challenge Erik's way with his lifted chin.

"I'm Erik Byrd with Nighthawk Security. This is my brother Drake and forensic specialist Kennedy Walker. We're working an investigation where the Hood to Coast race may play a part. We have some questions about the Redhawks race team."

"Not sure how I can help you. You're probably better off talking to our team leader."

"Maybe so," Erik said. "But since we're already here, would you mind us coming in for a few minutes?"

He glanced at his watch. "I can't be late for an appointment."

"We won't take long." Kennedy said, smiling, hoping to ease the suspicion in his expression. "Please. It would be a big help, and I'd really appreciate it."

She was flirting, and Erik cast her a dark look. When Hess smiled back at her, she let her grin widen. Based on his ease, she didn't think he recognized them. Maybe he was just the grunt man and had been told to shoot at the car without knowing who rode inside. She glanced at his shirt again and spotted the holstered gun this time.

Her ease with the guy evaporated.

"Fine." Hess stepped back. "But you've only got five minutes."

Kennedy went first and kept her smile in place.

The apartment was sparsely furnished, the living room holding only an overstuffed black leather recliner and a matching couch along with a coffee table and the prerequisite huge TV with surround sound. Nothing on the walls but white paint.

Kennedy sat on the couch, realizing that, unlike a lot of bachelor pads, this place was sparkling clean. Maybe from his military training as his shirt and pants were pressed. Erik leaned against the wall next to the couch, and Drake remained just inside the door.

Hess looked at Drake. "You're a jumpy one."

"Yep," Drake said, his expression remaining neutral.

Hess closed the door and took confident strides toward Kennedy. He stood near the end of the sofa, his focus on Erik. "So what did you want to ask about?"

"Your team wore wristbands with hawks on them," Erik said.

Kennedy kept her focus on Hess, who didn't seem at all troubled by Erik's comment.

"Our leader used to work in the public affairs department on base, and she went all out when she put our team together. She had uniforms, a banner, and the bracelets made. We didn't want it all, but once she gets going, you can't stop her."

"Do you still have your bracelet?" Erik asked.

Hess didn't answer right away, so Kennedy tried to look beneath his stone-faced expression. Maybe he was using tactics he'd learned in the military if he were ever captured to convincingly evade questions.

"Trashed it after the race," he finally said.

"Trashed it or lost it?" Erik clarified.

"Trashed. Near the finish line." Hess folded his arms over a broad chest, showing the first sign of being uncomfortable. "What's this all about, anyway?"

"Do you own any weapons other than the Glock at your side?" Erik asked.

A hint of surprise raised Hess's eyebrows, but he quickly dropped them and patted his holster as if confirming Erik's assessment. "A few."

Erik pushed from the wall and planted his feet, his chin out. "Name them."

"Not that it's any of your business, but I've got a Remington 870 pump shotgun and a Sig Sauer P320."

Erik lowered his chin. "No semi-automatics?"

"I'd love one of those bad boys." He grinned. "But no reason to own one, and I don't like to waste my money."

With the sparsity of his furnishings, Kennedy could believe that. "Do you have any friends who might own one? Someone you might borrow one from?"

Hess turned his full attention on her, and she could easily imagine him in the cockpit of the million-dollar fighter, checking the dash and aiming his sights on an enemy. It didn't take much more to imagine him behind the weapon that was fired at her, and she had to work hard not to shrink back.

"Not that I know of," he said.

"Couching your answer," Erik stated, his gaze firm.

Hess lifted his shoulder, his mouth curving up in a half smile.

Erik's nostrils flared. "You won't be smiling if we determine you were the person who open fired on our vehicle yesterday."

Hess took the news in stride, not even a flash of surprise. So did he know about the shooting? Was he involved? The shooter?

"Didn't touch a gun yesterday," he said, his tone flat. "Not even this one." He tapped his Glock. "Couldn't. Not with the race."

Erik rested his hands on his hips, looking as threatening as Hess. "So exactly where were you at eleven-thirty A.M. yesterday?"

"In Seaside having lunch with the team and celebrating finishing the race."

"And you were never out of your team's sight?"

He crossed his muscular arms. "I had to go to the can, but otherwise? They'll confirm I was there."

Erik nodded slowly. "Then how do you explain that one of your team wristbands was found in a vacant apartment in Portland, where a shooter hunkered down to take us out?"

Hess flexed his jaw muscles a few times. "I didn't put it there. The band irritated my arm from the minute I put it on." He held out his left wrist. A red rash circled it, perhaps confirming his comment. "I'm a team player and kept it on until the finish. Then, like I said, I trashed it near the finish line."

"And before the team picture was taken," Erik stated.

"You noticed that, huh? Suppose I'll get heat from our leader. She was all about uniformity. Military precision and all of that." He shrugged, looking confident and a bit smug. "I don't plan to run again next year. Too much crud for it to be any fun."

"I'll need a list of your team members and drivers and their phone numbers," Erik said.

Hess lifted his shoulders. "Don't see why. We were all

together celebrating, so none of us could've done what you think. And besides. I don't know any of you and I'm not going to give out my friends' info to just anyone."

"We're with Nighthawk Security." Erik held out his ID, feet flat on the floor, planted wide and glaring at Hess.

"I'll write down your phone number and have them call you." Hess eyed Erik. "Just let me grab some paper."

When he was out of earshot, she leaned closer to Erik and lowered her voice. "You know they're going to confirm his alibi."

He nodded. "But we need more proof than this guy's word that he was where he said he was."

18

Erik checked his email after a quick lunch in his condo with Kennedy. A message arrived from Mackenzie Steele, and he clicked it open.

"Got the video from Mackenzie," he said to Kennedy, who was sitting across the table littered with dishes from their takeout sandwiches and potato chips.

Kennedy hurried around the end of the table, and he started the video playing from the lab's main building. The security camera caught the man who'd gone into the lab scurrying across the parking lot, then darting over the highway, barely slipping in front of a semi-truck before racing down the bank to a small aluminum fishing boat moored in the river.

"Didn't expect that," Erik said as the guy hopped into the boat and propelled slowly away from the shore.

"Stop," Kennedy cried out. "He threw something in the water. Go back and zoom in."

Erik rewound to that location and enlarged the frame. "A handgun. He's pitching a handgun into the water."

Kennedy whipped her gaze to Erik. "He must not want to get caught with the gun."

Erik took a moment to calm his excitement. "Sounds likely. Attempted burglary is a class-three felony, but attempted burglary with a weapon is a class-two. Plus, he might've used that gun in another crime and doesn't want it connected to him."

"We need to get over there and recover it." She stepped back to leave.

"Hold up. Let's see if I can make out any boat registration details first." He rewound the file again and zoomed in on the information on the hull of the boat as it pulled away from shore. He squinted, but the writing was too blurry to read.

Kennedy twisted her hands together and then winced and rested her injured hand on the table. "We need to find that gun."

Erik didn't want her going down there, and he especially didn't want her heading to an area out in the open without a threat assessment. "It's been three days. Other than the gun, we'd have no way of knowing if he left any other evidence behind or someone else did. And the gun could've washed downriver by now."

"We have to at least look for it." She crossed her arms. "The area isn't heavily trafficked, so odds are good that if we recover evidence, it'll be from him."

"Fine." Erik stood. "I'll send Sierra."

"Someone has to dive for that gun, and that someone will be me. Plus, he could've dumped something else."

Erik had known this was coming. "We didn't see him dump anything else."

"You never know." She tightened her arms and narrowed her eyes.

He still didn't like this. "What about your hand? Is it a good idea to go into the water with open wounds?"

"I can wear neoprene gloves." She pled with her eyes.

"Go back to your law enforcement days. If you were investigating this case, would you find the best diver you could to do the search? If I wasn't doing the dive, would you call someone in?"

"Yeah," he said, wishing he didn't have to admit it.

"And you'd want the very best?"

He nodded.

"So let's go."

He lifted his hand. "Not so fast. I don't want to take you out there, but I will. To do it safely, we need to meet with my brothers and create a plan."

She sighed. "Every minute we wait is a minute evidence could be destroyed."

"And every minute we don't plan is a minute you could be killed." He planted his hands on the table. "This isn't negotiable, Kennedy. We do it my way or not at all."

She jerked her head toward the hallway. "I could just walk out that door."

"You could, but I know you're too smart to do that." Her eyes weren't softening at all. "Don't make Finley lose her only living relative."

"Ooh, you don't fight fair." She propped her hands on her waist.

"I'm only reminding you of what could happen," he said, trying not to sound frustrated.

"Fine." She crossed her arms. "We do it your way. But it would be better to dive in the daylight, so let's get your brothers together as fast as we can and get out there."

Kennedy clasped her seatbelt buckle, ready to click it open the minute Erik gave her the okay. After an hour-long meeting with the guys, then a thorough risk assessment, which took another hour, and finally another hour gathering supplies and loading the vehicles, she was jonesing to get into that river to locate the gun. Plus, see if there was any other item the suspect might've dumped but wasn't visible on the video.

Even with the plan, Erik was scoping out the area and talking to Sierra, who'd arrived an hour ago and set up a perimeter around the ground when the guy had run from the lab to the water.

Not that Kennedy could see what Erik or Sierra were doing. He'd put blinds—sort of like sunshades—on all the widows so no one could see in. And over the back, he'd installed a tent so he could leave the tailgate open for her to exit the vehicle without being seen. The vehicle was bulletproof, but he said he didn't want anyone to know she was in the SUV or they might be able to figure out she was planning another dive.

Brendan was atop the lab building, keeping an eye on the area through his rifle scope, and the other brothers were erecting a tarp tunnel that extended from the SUV tent to the large boulders at the river's edge. They'd recently started using these precautions when they protected a celebrity or any other person who might draw a crowd that they couldn't protect against. Celebrity or not, with their precautions, she wouldn't be seen by anyone but Charlie, who'd already strung ropes in the river for their perimeter.

Kennedy might want to be out there with Charlie in the worse way, but she'd agreed to play by Erik's rules. Problem was, at the time, she had no idea his rules would be so very restrictive.

Kennedy's phone chimed with a text, and she let go of her seatbelt to see a reply from Finley.

If Mom had cancer, she didn't tell me, and she didn't seem sick.

Thanks, Kennedy replied. *It was probably just something she was interested in.*

The tent zipper razored open behind her, and she turned to see Erik step inside and cross to the tailgate. She took in the fine form he made in his wetsuit, which he'd put on so he could swap out oxygen tanks to save time on the dive when they ran out.

He gave her a tight look. "We're good to go."

She climbed over the seat. Not an easy task in a wetsuit that wanted to stick to the leather. Erik had asked her to get ready at the condo to limit the amount of time she was in the tent. She supposed she could've climbed into the suit in the vehicle, but anyone who'd ever squeezed their body into a wetsuit understood such a feat would be harder to accomplish there.

She scooted to where her tank and remaining gear sat on the tailgate. "FYI, Finley replied to my text, and she said our mom never said she was sick and didn't act sick."

"Probably just a teaching thing, then, but I'll still ask an ME to let me know if it could be missed on autopsy."

"I sure hope it wasn't. I'd hate to think she had cancer and was suffering through it alone."

"You could request her medical records, but I don't know if you want to go there," he said.

"Let's see what the ME says first. If blood cancers can be missed at autopsy, I might want to get her files."

"Sounds good. But you should know that if she *did* have cancer, suicide could be an even more compelling explanation for her death."

Kennedy didn't want to think that way, but Erik was right. "Let me know when the ME gets back to you."

He nodded. "Let's get going. You'll go straight through the tent and tunnel and into the water. Try to remain above the surface for the least amount of time as possible. If you find the gun, send up a marker but don't surface. Bring it in while submerged."

He'd already run this plan with her a few times now. She got it the first time, but she also got his need to be extra careful. "Sierra find anything?"

"Washed out footprints. We've only had rain the one night since the guy tried to break in, so they're pretty well intact. But that doesn't mean it's our guy."

"But it could be."

"Yeah. Could be." He frowned. "Sierra's casting the prints, and she'll compare them to footprints she lifted from the deck at your mom's place."

"Not that it would move the investigation forward, but we would at least know it's the same guy."

"Okay, let's get started. Don't take any risks on your diving safety."

"Don't worry." She rested a gloved hand on his arm. "You guys planned this to the nth degree. Besides, God's watching over us."

"I'll try to keep that in mind."

"We all set?" Drake called from the tent entrance.

"Ready." She jumped down from the tailgate.

Erik pressed on the hearing device lodged in his ear, which connected him with all of his brothers. "We good to go, Brendan?"

She couldn't hear Brendan's response, but Erik's firm nod told her all she needed to know. She took a step, but Erik grabbed her up in an awkward hug, his arms and hands trying to find purchase anywhere but on her oxygen tank. She circled her arms around his neck and took a deep breath of his masculine scent then quickly pushed away before the hug turned to a kiss.

She started down the tunnel, the sense of danger pressing in on her like the darkness of the fabric surrounding her. She didn't think this creep knew she was there. Not since they'd eliminated the tracker from her backpack and Erik had given it to Nick at the Veritas Center. He'd put it in a Faraday room with specially lined walls to stop electronic devices from sending or receiving outside signals.

She put on her headgear and stepped onto a rock ledge in the water with her fins in her hand. The easiest way to put her fins on was to drop into the river with her buoyancy vest fully inflated so she would float and could easily strap them on by herself, but then she'd be exposed. She turned to look at Erik for the help they'd provided for each other on their many dives in the past.

Without a word he stepped onto the rock and braced his legs wide.

"Thanks," she said. It might not be a good idea to keep touching him, but since she really didn't have use of her dominant hand, being able to hold onto his shoulder with the injured one while she slid on her fins worked well.

When she was finished, he gave her one last lingering look. "Be careful."

She dropped into the water and dove. Sunbeams filtered into the liquid and spread out with circles of white, undulating light. The water was green and cloudy, but she could clearly see the silty bottom today. Charlie was waiting for her, and he gave her a thumbs-up. She grabbed onto the rope with her uninjured hand and pulled forward, keeping her focus trained down at the bottom.

She filtered through several beer cans, a fishing lure, even an old disintegrating wooden oar as she moved the full length of the first rope. Her hand hurt from dragging it along the bottom, feeling for anything, but she'd worked in more pain than this, and this dive was for her mother. She came up empty-handed and started down the other rope, passing by Charlie, who traveled behind her. Up and down she went until they'd covered their entire search area and her hand screamed for her to call it quits. But she wouldn't give in. She'd do another search downstream.

Together, she and Charlie relocated the rope downriver and continued swimming until her tank ran out of oxygen. She replaced it with Erik's help and went back to work, loving the silky smooth feel of the water as it glided over her body. She might have been enjoying the water, but hope faded with each fresh oxygen tank. But finally...finally...after four tanks and nearly as many hours, her hand slid over a solid metal object. Her injured hand throbbed too hard to grab the item, so she looped her arm around the rope and released the item from the silt with her good hand.

Ah-ha. A handgun. A Glock to be specific.

She anchored a marker next to it and signaled for Charlie to take photos with the underwater camera. When he'd finished, she bagged the gun and tucked the bag in her vest then swam one-handed for shore.

"Got the weapon, and I'm coming in," she announced over their communication device.

"Excellent." Erik's excited voice played through her ear. "Stay submerged at the rocks until I check with Brendan and give the all-clear."

"Roger that," she said, feeling like an agent, not a crime scene investigator.

She had to admit the adrenaline rush from the added danger pumped through her body and made her feel nearly invincible. But she wasn't invincible—not by half—and she had to remember that and listen to Erik's directives if she wanted to stay alive.

~

Erik let out a long breath through his teeth as Drake cranked the SUV's powerful engine. Erik sounded like a leaky tire as he released his adrenaline from watching Kennedy dive in an unprotected river. But now she was safely back in the vehicle, where no one could harm her.

"You okay, bro?" Drake asked. "No signs of the anthrax, right?"

Another thing to sigh over. The brotherly check-in.

"I'm fine." Erik tried not to snap.

"Then why the sigh?"

"It's nothing," Erik said, though it was everything to have Kennedy sitting safely behind him.

He swiveled to look at her, not surprised to see her biting her lip. She'd been wincing in pain since she'd surfaced with the gun.

Drake glanced up at the mirror as he shifted into gear. "No anthrax symptoms for you either? I hate to ask, but you know my mom." He grinned.

"She just wants to be sure we're okay, so feel free to ask me. I'm fine."

Erik appreciated her kind reply, especially when she was so stressed. Drake started to back out, but Sierra rushed their way, waving her arms.

Drake shifted into park, and Erik motioned for his sister to climb in the backseat so they didn't compromise the vehicle security by leaving a window open while they talked.

She slid in next to Kennedy. "Found something I thought you guys would want to know about right away."

Erik swiveled to look between the seats in time to see Sierra hand a plastic bag to Kennedy.

She studied the bag. "What is this?"

"A prickly caterpillar bean," Sierra said.

Kennedy passed the evidence bag to Erik. He'd never

seen anything like the reddish-and-white striped curly bean with tiny spikes running along the edge. He gave the bag back to Sierra. "How do you know about this, but more importantly, what does it have to do with our investigation?"

"I had to research the beans for a previous investigation. They aren't native to Oregon. The beans are a French heirloom, and the seeds are hard to come by. Likely only a very avid gardener or a plant collector would have this plant in their garden."

"Why do you think it was here then?" Kennedy asked.

"My best guess is it caught on the suspect's pant leg in his garden, and then it fell off near the river."

"Or it's not from him at all," Drake said.

"Or that." Sierra narrowed her gaze at their brother. "But the odds are just as good that it is from him. I found it near boot prints that I think match the prints I recovered from Wanda's deck. I won't know if I have a definitive match until the cast cures."

"Which will be when exactly?" Erik asked.

"Three days." Sierra and Kennedy said the words at the same time then laughed.

"We can't wait that long." Erik knew he was scowling at them, but come on. Three days of not having an answer when Kennedy's life was in danger was too long. "We'll go ahead and cross-reference gardening and biology against the list of Responsible Officials."

"I thought you didn't have that yet," Drake said.

"Not yet," Erik said, trying to sound optimistic. "But I'm sure someone will come through for us."

"Sure," Drake said. "We might get it, but it could take longer than the cast curing."

Erik clenched his jaw and wished his brother didn't feel the need to point out every problem. Erik worked hard not to snap at him. "Until we get the list, we can go back through

Wanda's contacts to see if we can find a gardening connection there."

"That sounds like a good plan, Erik." Kennedy fired a testy look at Drake.

Erik's mouth almost fell open. She was sticking up for him, as she'd often done in the past. In those instances, he'd always thought about what a wonderful partner and mother she would be. Championing her husband and children more than anything else. And he'd lost out on that when she'd said goodbye to him.

But you have another chance.

He shook his head, hoping the idea he wasn't ready to face would disappear, but it lingered. He turned his focus to Sierra. "Anything else, or can we get Kennedy back to the office?"

"That's all for now, but I'll have Grady run ballistics on the gun after I print it, and I'll let you know what I find."

Erik was thankful this scene hadn't been taken over by the task force, or Sierra wouldn't be able to share her findings. But it was just a matter of time before they discovered the same information and took over.

Sierra rested a hand on Kennedy's arm. "Keep up your spirits. We might not have anything concrete now, but we'll figure this out."

Kennedy smiled. "I know, and thank you for taking time from your leave to do this work."

"Are you kidding? I love my son, but I'm ready to get back to this."

"So you're going back to work, then?"

"Part-time at first. We've found a great nanny, and there are perks of living in the building, I can pop upstairs whenever Asher needs me. It's the perfect scenario."

"Sounds like it."

"Can we end the baby talk and get going?" Erik asked.

"Just wait until you have a child." Sierra grinned at him. "Then let's see who'll be wrapped up in baby talk."

She slipped out of the SUV before Erik could get out a rebuttal and marched back to the protected scene.

Drake finally got them on the road, and Erik tapped the dashboard to connect to his phone and send a group text to the people who were looking into the Responsible Official list to light a fire under them.

He'd tried to sound confident with Sierra and Kennedy before, but he hadn't a clue if they would ever get this important list that could point to the person who was trying to hurt Kennedy.

19

As Kennedy stepped ahead of Erik into the Nighthawk office late that afternoon, she wished she were still at the river working the scene with Sierra. Not that Kennedy didn't trust Sierra. She did, but there was nothing like having your own eyes on a crime scene to be sure nothing was missed.

Kennedy entered the main area to find Malone waiting for them, Stella sitting behind her desk. Malone marched toward them in spiky heeled patent leather sandals that had to have cost a pretty penny, as did her power suit.

"Hi, Malone." Kennedy smiled at the attorney.

Malone trained her gaze on Kennedy, but her smile was tight, and Kennedy was tempted to reach for a strand of hair. She curled her fingers instead.

"Mind if we step inside the other room," Malone asked, but headed through the doorway without waiting.

A ball of dread formed in Kennedy's stomach as she followed Malone into the other room. Once the three of them were inside, she closed the door.

"Please tell me you stopped by to give me a copy of the Responsible Officials list," Erik said.

"Well hello to you too." Malone rolled her eyes.

Erik took a breath and let it out. "We're desperate for that list. I'd hoped your contacts came through for you."

"I didn't even know you had contacts with the feds," Kennedy said.

Malone gave a sharp nod. "Former federal prosecutor."

"Oh, wow." Kennedy was duly impressed. "Why the change, if I might ask?"

Malone tilted her head, her striking blue eyes narrowing, but she didn't speak.

"It's okay," Kennedy said. "I was being nosy."

"No, it's not that. I don't talk about it often, so I was just figuring out what to tell you." She started to cross her arms then let them fall to her sides.

"You know attorneys." Erik grinned. "They always have to watch what they say."

Malone flicked a hand at him. "It's not that. I left because of the stress. You see all kinds of things as a federal prosecutor. I mean, all kinds of things. Many that are hard to handle. Especially when you can't do anything about them."

"That's the way it was in law enforcement too," Erik said, his tone somber now.

Malone smiled at him and took a breath. "One of the things I couldn't do anything about and couldn't get over was seeing battered women or suffering children. I had a particularly bad case, and it forced me into a change. I decided to devote myself to helping others. With Reed's support, I opened my own practice. My main focus is helping marginalized people, but I have to take on additional clients to pay the bills." She stuck out a foot. "And keep myself in shoes."

She laughed, and despite her polished appearance that had thrown Kennedy at first, it was clear Malone was down to earth and a good person to know.

"We're getting off track here." Erik's tone was gentle,

which Kennedy appreciated when she could see the frustration in his eyes.

"Okay, okay. I get it." Malone reached into her jacket pocket, took out a flash drive, and handed it to Erik. "The list. I wanted to drop it off in person so we didn't leave any electronic trails. Don't want to get my source in trouble."

Erik cupped the drive and pumped his hand in the air. "Thank you. Thank you. Thank you."

Kennedy smiled at his reaction and enjoyed his celebration with him. You'd think he'd won the lottery, not just received a list of people. He was fully invested in this case. Despite how Kennedy had wronged him, he'd overcome the rejection to do his very best to help her.

What a man.

The kind of man you don't let go once, let alone a second time.

"I have news for you, too, Kennedy," Malone said. "I checked in with your WITSEC deputy. He's not happy with you sharing with others without checking with him first. Given what's going on now with your mother's potentially suspicious death, he wants you and Finley to stay in the program. However, if you do, you would both need to be relocated."

Erik pocketed the flash drive. His jaw was clenched, and his shoulders tightened into a hard line as he stared over her shoulder at the wall. "Because she told us about it, you mean?"

Was he thinking the same thing as Kennedy was thinking? That if she stayed in WITSEC, they could never see each other again?

"Yes," Malone said. "I know that seems drastic, but it would keep you safe."

"It wouldn't solve the problem of who murdered her mother, though," Erik said.

Malone didn't bend under the intensity of his gaze. "Have you located proof that she actually *was* murdered?"

"Not yet."

"So it could still be an accident or—"

"Don't waste your breath saying it," Kennedy snapped. "My mom *did not* kill herself."

Malone held up her hands. "Okay. Okay."

"Sorry," Kennedy took a breath. "I'll talk to Finley about what she wants to do. Should I get back to you or call Tyrone directly?"

"Let's keep the communication going through me for now so I have a record of it." Malone smoothed back her already perfectly groomed hair. "Now if it's okay for Stella to escort me to your sister's place, I'd like to spoil my nephew before I have to go back to work."

"I'll go ask her." Erik left the room.

Malone rested a hand with perfectly manicured nails on Kennedy's arm. "Let me tell you what I tell all my clients. It's always darkest before a real breakthrough. So keep the faith and your spirits up."

Kennedy nodded, but she wasn't certain that was true. Kennedy's darkest hour had come when her mother died, and her father's death was a close second. No breakthrough had come either time, unless Kennedy considered seeing and falling for Erik again as a breakthrough. Because if she did, she'd really broken through, and that was a fact she could no longer dispute.

Erik printed the list of Responsible Officials and made copies for his brothers, and then he and Kennedy high-lighted a portion of the list for each of them to research. When his brothers arrived at the office and were seated in the conference area, he slid a copy down the table to each of them.

"Malone came through for us, but the Responsible Officials list is confidential." Erik's brothers knew how to keep things quiet, but Erik still ran his gaze over them to confirm their agreement. "I've assigned sections of the list to each of you so you can work up a background on the individuals. We're looking for people who might be avid gardeners and who would have a connection to Wanda."

"Gardeners?" Aiden looked up from the page he'd been reviewing.

"Right. You don't know." Kennedy explained the prickly caterpillar bean to the team.

Drake's eyes narrowed. "This sounds like a long shot."

"It is." Erik slapped his list on the table. "But the list is over a hundred people long. You have a better way to narrow it down other than by people connected to Wanda, which is a given?"

Drake snapped his chair forward. "We interview the gardeners first then go back to the others. I just don't want us to forget about the others."

"Hopefully, the prickly caterpillar bean will lead somewhere, but yeah, we can't forget about anyone connected to Wanda." Erik let out a breath. "You all get started on the list, and also look for potential anthrax connections. Does anyone have any questions?"

"Yeah," Brendan said. "Why are you so cranky?"

"I'm not—"

"Save it." Clay flashed up his hand. "You're the poster child for cranky right now."

They were right. His brothers were giving of their time to help and deserved civil responses from him.

"Sorry," he said sincerely. "We're not making much progress, and I feel like I'm failing."

Aiden held up the list. "But we have a solid lead now, and it's bound to turn something up."

Bound to? Erik wasn't quite so optimistic, but he wouldn't bring his brothers or Kennedy down with him. "You're right. I'll cool it. "

"At the risk of making you madder, my turn to ask about the anthrax for you two." Brendan split his focus between Erik and Kennedy.

"I'm good," Kennedy said.

"Me too," Erik said. "And I'm ready to get to work."

"Before we start," Clay said, "I wanted to update you on my investigation into Finley and a potential loan shark. If she's in debt to someone, I couldn't find it."

"Glad to hear that," Kennedy said.

"I had a similar bust on Nora's sons," Aiden said. "They're squeaky clean and all have solid alibis for the times in question."

Erik frowned. "These guys were a long shot at best. Let's get moving on the list. Kennedy and I'll first review Wanda's phone and email contacts for gardeners, then start on our portion of the list."

"Time to head to the cubicles." Drake got up and squeezed Erik's shoulder as he passed by.

Erik cast his brother a thank you look and the same with his other brothers as they went to their respective cubicles. Erik looked at Kennedy. "The list is on the server. Let me get a computer for you to use."

He grabbed a laptop from his cubicle, set the machine next to her, and logged her into the network.

"You really have a great support group, don't you?" she asked.

"It sure is hard to stay in a bad mood with them around," he said. "They'll work until they get you out of it."

"My mom was like that." She frowned. "Now, I need to

be the one to do that for Finley, but how can I from across the country?"

"You could just move back here."

"Not if I want to keep diving for the bureau," she said. "The Portland office isn't big enough to support such a position."

"Maybe they'd let you work from here but keep you on salary out of Virginia."

"I can't imagine they'd do that."

"But you're on the road for the job, so does it really matter where your home base is?"

"I suppose not, though Portland is a fairly expensive city to fly from on short notice. But when I'm not diving, I work in the lab, and that's not possible here."

She had him there. Why was he trying to talk her into moving back here? Was it for Finley or for himself?

"Besides, if Finley chooses to remain in WITSEC, this conversation is moot."

His mood had improved some, but her comment sent it diving again. "You'll go with her, of course."

"Yes." The word was so quiet, he almost missed it.

He'd hoped she wouldn't answer. Especially not so quickly. That she would say she had to think about it. But he knew she was making the right decision. Family was everything.

"I assume you'll talk to her tonight."

Kennedy nodded.

He grabbed his own laptop, logged into the network, and opened the file. "You take the first half of the list, and like we did when we worked the phone calls, enter any information you learn in the spreadsheet."

"Will do."

He turned his attention to the names. On the sixth one, he looked up. "Here's something. One of your mother's fellow scientists is a botanist. Judson Purvis. He's on faculty at OHSU, and he fits the intruder's description."

Oregon Health and Sciences University was one of Oregon's premier colleges.

"Botany could very well mean he's a gardener," she said, her face beaming.

"And since he's local, we can interview him."

"We should also talk to Oscar Edwards, the department chairman at PSU, where my mom taught. I met him at her memorial luncheon, and he was very sympathetic. "

"Does he fit the intruder's build?"

"No. He's short and round, but he might be able to give us a lead on this Purvis guy. Or maybe he hired a hitman." She shook her head. "Listen to me. A hitman. But you do hear of people hiring others to commit murder."

"You do indeed," Erik replied, because it was true, but he doubted that was the case here. He tapped the list. "You think Edwards might know Purvis?"

"PSU and OHSU share a science building, so it's possible."

"Then let's arrange an interview with both of them before they go home for the day." Erik let the excitement of a lead bubble up in his voice. "And maybe, just maybe, we'll find out what the prickly caterpillar bean means, and if it's related to your mother's death."

20

Nearing five o'clock, the sun still hung high and bright in the sky as Kennedy slipped out of the SUV and walked between Erik and Drake on a busy Portland street toward Portland State University. They headed straight for the science building.

The brothers had done their usual risk assessment, and finding minimal risk in attending this interview, they stationed themselves in various locations near the building. Kennedy couldn't pick them out, but she knew they were watching.

She felt the eager energy of the students they passed and nostalgia for an easier and less stressful time in her life—a time when both of her parents were alive. She missed them even more. She'd been back to PSU only a few times since she'd received her master's degree, and it felt odd to be on campus again. Her visits were back in the day when she once thought she wanted to be a researcher just like her mom, but after a year of research, Kennedy discovered she couldn't be inside all day. So she'd gone back to get a criminal justice degree too.

She reached the sunny atrium of the contemporary

steel-and-glass building connecting two tall towers. The south wing held administrative offices, which was where they were headed to meet with Professor Oscar Edwards. The department chair and her mother's former supervisor, was the only one of the two professors who'd returned their call.

Inside the lobby, Erik and Drake looked up.

"Wow," Erik said. "This place is something else."

"The walkways make me think of the many Portland bridges," Drake said.

"I've read that's what the designer had in mind." Kennedy tried to look at the wide-open space with polished concrete floors, glass walls, and suspended walkways through their eyes. "It's hard to believe this building houses research labs, and there's even a dental school on the top floor."

"You must've loved going to school here," Drake said.

"Sadly, this building didn't open until after I graduated, but I've had several tours since then." She tipped her head toward the south wing. "Come on."

She walked between them to a communal space designed for conferences or lounging. Professor Edwards, wearing a lab coat, stood by a group of plush contemporary chairs. Behind him was a gorgeous view of the river, and the sunlight streaming in reflected off the sixty-something's shiny bald head. He stiffly waved them over, the crisp white fabric of his lab coat flapping with the motion.

"Kennedy." Edwards awkwardly shook her uninjured hand before introducing himself to the others. "Now, sit down and tell me what I can do for you."

All but Drake obeyed Edwards' demand and sat in the gray fabric chairs. Drake stood, his gaze roving the area.

Erik leaned toward Edwards. "Would you have any

reason to believe that someone might've wanted to hurt Wanda?"

Edwards' gaze flew to Kennedy, alarm in his eyes. "Did someone hurt your mother before she died?"

Kennedy shook her head. "I'm having a hard time believing she took her own life or accidentally took too many pills. So we're looking into her death."

Edwards tugged the lapels of his lab coat together. "I know how hard it is to accept a parent's death, but if you're asking me if anyone around here would hurt her? No. She was loved by all. You saw that at the memorial luncheon."

"People can mask their true feelings," Kennedy said.

Edwards gave a vigorous nod. "Probably truer in academia than many fields, but not in this case. She helped others whenever possible. She never stepped on another professor's toes to climb the ladder. She had what she wanted in her own lab and didn't need to vie for tenure or a full-time position."

"And yet she still taught here," Erik said, sounding like he was fishing.

"She loved enriching young minds." He steepled his fingers. "I know it took a toll on her to do both jobs, but she didn't want to give up the teaching."

"Was she close to anyone on staff here?" Erik asked.

"Close?" He tapped his fingers together. "She didn't attend any social outings with faculty."

"There were notes in her journal about presenting a potential lab on medicinal chemistry and blood cancers," Kennedy said. "Do you know anything about that?"

"She never mentioned it."

"How about gardeners?" Erik asked. "Any professors in the department who are into gardening?"

He tilted his head. "Several people come to mind." He smiled, but she thought it to be forced. But then, his behavior had been stiff and formal so far, and he'd acted the same way the other time she'd met him. His first concern here was likely to put the best spin on his department for any questions posed to him, and she wondered if he was telling the truth about anything.

"Could we get a list of names?" Erik asked.

"I'll have to check with legal first," Edwards replied. "As department chair, I can't hand out information on our faculty without authorization."

"I don't suppose you can do that quickly," Kennedy said.

"I've never seen our attorneys work fast." He offered a patronizing smile.

She shifted in the chair. "Are you familiar with the prickly caterpillar bean?"

He tilted his head. "I've heard that mentioned, but I'm not sure where."

"Recently?"

He tapped his chin. "No, I can't say as I remember when or even where I heard about it."

"What about anthrax?" Erik asked. "Do you have it in any of your labs?"

"Anthrax?" He clutched his hand to his chest. "Oh, dear. No. No. We aren't conducting any research that would require anthrax." He flashed his gaze to Kennedy. "Was your mother involved with that? If so, I'd be very surprised. I didn't think her lab was a level three."

Kennedy started to answer, but Erik stood, and she took it as a sign that he didn't want additional discussion on the matter.

Erik peered at Edwards as if he were looking at the man through a microscope. "If I were to ask these questions of other professors here, would I get the same answers, or would I get the party line from them too?"

"I'm not sure what you mean. I've told you the truth, so

unless they lied to you, you would get the same answers." Edwards got up, resting a hand on his lower back as he stood. "I'm sorry that my answers don't seem to be to your liking, but it is what it is." He turned his attention on Kennedy and smiled. "Your mother was a wonderful person, and she'll be sincerely missed."

"One more thing, Professor," Erik said, seeming as if he was trying to catch Edwards off guard. "Do you know Professor Judson Purvis?"

Oscar's jaw tightened. "That pompous old fool. Yes. Everyone in our academic circle knows him."

"Why's that?" Erik asked.

"He's on the fed's Responsible Officials list, and he's the only one in the area. He believes that makes him superior to the rest of us, when any one of us could apply for and be approved if we had a reason to."

"And what's his reason?" Erik asked.

"Research involving Peronosclerospora Philippinensis. A downy plant mildew that causes great damage to maize and sugarcane around the world."

"Can you spell that for me?" Kennedy asked and jotted it down when he did. "So nothing that could poison an individual like anthrax?"

"No. Nothing like that. Which makes his posturing even more pretentious."

"Did he know my mom?" Kennedy asked.

"I don't know. He was a big schmoozer at parties, but since she didn't attend them, perhaps not."

"Does he have an office in this building?"

"Yes." He named the location. "Now, if that's all—"

"For now," Erik said.

Edwards walked away, a hitch in his step.

"I didn't much like that guy," Drake said. "Did you believe him?"

"It was hard to see through the smoke he was blowing to find the truth, so no," she replied.

"Let's head up to Purvis's office," Erik said. "See if we can surprise him."

The guys stepped next to her, and they checked the directory for his office location then, she led the way through the building to Purvis's closed office door. Drake pounded loudly, then stepped aside.

"Enter." The single word came from a haughty male voice.

Erik shook his head. "Sounds like he's the king of the castle allowing us entry."

"Edwards did say the guy was pompous," Kennedy said.

Drake parked a shoulder on the wall. "I'll stay out here and have your back."

Erik pushed the heavy door open, releasing a strong whiff of incense. He blocked the way as his head swiveled, then apparently finding it safe, he stepped back. Kennedy got her first look at a man with a full head of white hair sitting behind the neat desk. He had a thick neck and broad shoulders under his stiffly starched white shirt.

He stood and planted his big hands on the desk, and she imagined him wearing a stocking cap and breaking into her mother's place. He fit the build and seemed aggressive already, but his nose was perfectly aligned.

He eyed them both for a long moment. "And who might you be?"

Kennedy forced herself to relax to reduce his suspicion and reminded him of their phone message. "We were hoping you might have time to talk with us."

He lifted his hands from the desk, extending one to shake and offering her a sympathetic smile. "Is this about your mother? I heard about her passing, but I didn't know her, so I'm not sure I can be of help."

His grip was tight and painful, but she worked hard not to wince. "Would you mind if we just asked a few questions?"

He rolled up a perfectly pressed white sleeve and glanced at a pricey gold watch. "I have a lecture in fifteen minutes."

He settled into the high-back leather chair and rested his elbows on the padded arms, looking alert yet relaxed at the same time. There was something about him that was disconcerting, but she couldn't put her finger on it. Maybe it was the arrogance in the set of his jaw and his gaze. Or maybe she just wanted to see something negative in him because he was the same size as the guy who'd threatened her.

"You say you didn't know my mother, but Professor Edwards said you're very social. We wondered if you'd heard some gossip about her, or have any idea of who might want to harm her."

"Harm?" He cocked a thick black eyebrow. "I thought her death was an accident or self-harm."

"We have reason to believe otherwise," Erik said.

"Goodness." Purvis snapped his chair forward. "From what I hear, she was well loved. I have no idea of who might want to hurt her."

Erik pointed at a wall of potted plants. "You obviously love plants. Do you garden at home too?"

"Yes." His eyes took on a sparkle. "After research, puttering around in my garden is my next love. I find great enjoyment in trying new plants and cross-breeding them."

Erik leaned forward. "Would you happen to have a prickly caterpillar bean?"

"I once did. I just had to grow it to see the odd shape, but it didn't do anything for me. It's an annual so when it died off, I didn't plant it again."

231

"I'm assuming most everyone in your department has a home garden," Kennedy said.

"Most of us do."

"What about the chemistry professors?" Erik asked.

"A few that I can think of."

"Is Professor Edwards one of them?"

"Oscar?" Purvis lifted his chin. "He has a garden, but calling him a gardener is a stretch. At least a gardener at my level. He's an amateur."

"So you've visited his garden?" Kennedy asked.

"A long time ago."

Erik's eyes glinted. "At that time, did he have a prickly caterpillar bean?"

"Not that I saw, but the seeds were making the rounds around here for some time." He waved a hand. "They're rare and hard to come by, so they were snapped up."

"Could you give us a list of the people in the department with gardens?"

"If you give me your email address, I'll get to it as soon as I can."

Kennedy appreciated his helpful attitude, but he had this self-serving air, and she didn't trust him to be truthful if it didn't benefit him. "Do any of the labs here work with anthrax?"

He snapped his chair forward. "Anthrax? No. Why do you ask?"

"We're exploring many lines of inquiry," Erik said.

Purvis shifted his gaze to Kennedy. "Do you think your mother died of anthrax exposure?"

"No." Kennedy didn't feel a need to share the details of her mother's death with this man.

"But you are a Responsible Official," Erik stated, "and as such, you could request anthrax."

"I'm the only Responsible Official on faculty." Purvis

puffed up his chest. "I take that tremendous honor seriously and wouldn't try to procure any Select Agent that we didn't have a legitimate reason to request. We don't have a legitimate reason to ask for anthrax."

"So that's a no, then?" Kennedy prodded when he didn't actually answer the question. "You've never requested anthrax."

"Correct." He stood, his eyes narrowed into angry slits as if upset at being pushed to respond. "Like I said. I have a lecture, and I need a moment to prepare. Please close the door as you leave."

Erik placed a business card on the desk, tapping it a few times to get Purvis's attention. "Thanks for agreeing to email a list of gardeners. And if you hear anything unusual regarding Wanda, we would appreciate hearing about it."

Purvis gave a sharp nod then fired a pointed look at the door.

Kennedy stepped out before Erik and turned to him as he closed the door.

"He was either hiding something at the end, or he just doesn't like to be questioned."

"Could be either," Erik said. "But I think he deserves a deeper dive into his background. As does Edwards."

In his condo, Erik closed up his laptop, and resisted sighing. A few hours in research and he'd hoped to find something about either of the professors that would move their investigation forward. Or that his brothers had found viable suspects on the Responsible Officials list, but dinnertime had come and gone, and they were no further ahead than when they'd gone to interview the professors.

He looked at Kennedy, who was setting out silverware

for a late dinner with Finley, who'd arrived a few minutes before. Finley had brought three large salads, but Erik was going to take his meal to Drake's place to give the sisters time alone.

He piled the to-go container with a big cobb salad on top of his laptop, wishing it was a thick juicy steak with a steaming baked potato instead. He laid his phone next to it and looked at Finley. "Just call when you're ready to leave, and I'll escort you to the exit."

"Thanks." She lifted the lid from her taco salad, emitting a tangy scent.

"You sure you don't want to eat with us?" Kennedy asked.

"You need time alone."

"That doesn't sound good." Finley frowned, looking very much like a younger version of Kennedy. "You're not going to question me again, are you?"

Kennedy sat. "No. Just want to catch up."

"Okay, then." Finley's frown turned into a hesitant smile as she dropped into a chair.

"See you later." Erik resisted squeezing Kennedy's shoulder with his free hand.

For the last two hours as they'd worked side-by-side, he'd had the most overwhelming urge to touch her. He'd contained it, but he kicked up his speed to get out into the hallway, where he took a deep breath before heading toward Drake's condo, Pong at his side.

His phone rang, and he flipped it over on his computer to see an unknown number. Could be related to the investigation. He answered.

"Mr. Byrd, it's Nora." Her tone was frantic and curt.

"What is it?"

"I need your help. Please. I just got home. Walked from

the bus stop. There's someone in my house. I see a flashlight moving inside. I'm so afraid." Her voice broke with a sob.

"Don't go inside." He used his best former officer voice to gain her cooperation. "Move away from the house to a safe location and call 911."

"But you'll come too, right?"

No chance he wouldn't go. "I'm on my way, but a patrol officer will be able to respond faster than I can get there."

"Hurry. Please hurry!" Her high-pitched request pulled at his protective streak. "And come alone. I don't want Kennedy to find out about this."

21

Nora told Erik to come alone, but he wouldn't do so, even if the police would be on scene when he arrived. So he grabbed Drake and they took off, the drive made in silence. By the time Erik pulled up to the house, the sun had dropped behind the horizon, and he had to squint to see a patrolman haul a male outside through her front door. No sign of Nora in the shadowed darkness, but lightbars on two patrol cars twirled, the orbs casting red and blue light and disturbing the calm neighborhood.

Erik shifted into park and kept his focus on the action. "Maybe this's the guy who broke into Wanda's place too."

"Let's find out." Drake reached for his door handle.

"No. You stay here," Erik said. "Nora wanted me to come alone, and I don't want to spook her."

Drake was quiet for a moment. "If I see any threat, I'll be joining you."

"Thanks, man." As the guy in cuffs was hauled closer, Erik could see that he fit the intruder's description, from the crooked nose all the way down to the combat boots. *Oh, yeah!* Maybe their suspect had been arrested.

Erik waited for the officer to put the man in the car

before he got out of the SUV. He approached slowly until he could get a good look at the officer's face.

Excellent. Erik knew the veteran officer who was now staring at him.

"Smitty!" Erik called out. "It's me. Erik Byrd."

"Birdbrain." He lifted a fist to pound Erik's hand with a hard punch. "What are you doing here?"

Erik grinned at the old nickname. "I believe this guy is related to an investigation we're working on. Your department is investigating too and being handled on your side by Frank Johnson."

Smitty's eyes narrowed. "Tell me about it."

Erik gave a brief overview of the investigation.

"This is really odd." Smitty looked around, maybe checking to see where the other responding officer had gone, then stepped closer. "We found the guy stealing a denture plate."

"Denture?"

"Yeah, not a full set, but an upper plate."

When Erik and Kennedy were dating, Wanda had lost many of her upper teeth due to gum disease and uncontrolled blood pressure. She was a beautiful woman—an older version of Kennedy—but she couldn't do implants, so she'd had to have her upper teeth removed. Was this Wanda's plate and did Nora have it or did it belong to Nora?

"It's in a small brown box labeled inDents," Smitty added.

inDents. Alarm bells rang in Erik's head, but he wasn't going to share his knowledge with Smitty. Erik would save that for the detective. "That *is* odd."

"Yeah, there were plenty of pricey electronics in reach, so this guy must've specifically been looking for the denture." Smitty ran a hand over his silvery buzzed hair.

"You talk to the homeowner yet?" Erik asked.

Smitty shook his head. "Dispatcher told her to go to a café down the road to be safe. Was planning on heading over there after we wrap things up here."

As the first responder, Smitty had a bit of work to do before he could leave, giving Erik enough time to question Nora. "You'll loop Detective Johnson in on this, right?"

"Will do."

"And have him give me a call."

"You got it. Now back to your cushy private job while I do mountains of paperwork." Smitty grinned. "Seriously. Good to see you, Birdbrain."

"You too, man." Erik wanted to rush away, but he took his time heading back to his vehicle and slowly pulled away from the curb.

"Where we headed?" Drake asked.

Erik explained and just finished when he found the restaurant brightly lit and filled with customers.

"Let me guess," Drake said drolly. "You want me to stay here."

"And here I thought I was the smart brother." Erik chuckled and reached for his door handle.

Drake didn't laugh. "I might not be coming in, but I'll be right outside the door."

"Just don't let Nora lay eyes on you."

They both got out, and at the restaurant door, Drake stopped next to a pillar in a shadowed area.

Erik pushed open the door, the bells above tinkling. The old-fashioned diner smelled of burgers and fries, and Erik's stomach grumbled. Maybe he should grab some dinner here instead of eating the rabbit food Finley had brought to his place.

Nora sat at a counter facing the door. She spotted him, leapt from her stool, and ran across the room, barely missing a server in a short skirt and bright red apron, her arms filled with platters.

"Sorry," Nora tossed off the quick apology but didn't stop until she clutched Erik's arm. "Did you go to the house? Did they arrest someone?"

Erik nodded, and her shoulders sagged.

He held her up. "We should sit down and talk about it. Somewhere private. Like my vehicle."

"I've already paid for my coffee so I'm good to go." She bolted for the door.

Her behavior might be funny if not for the fact that it was borne from terror. He gave Drake a subtle gesture telling him to stay put, then unlocked the SUV doors, and they got in.

"Do you know who they arrested?" she asked as she closed her door.

Erik shook his head. "But he fits the build of the person who broke into Wanda's house."

"I thought it might be connected to that."

"Why would you think that?"

She bit her lip. "I haven't been completely honest with you."

"I thought as much."

"You did?" Her eyebrows shot up. "But I was so careful to hide my feelings."

"Not quite careful enough to fool a former police officer." He smiled. "What haven't you told us?"

"First, about Wanda's phone. I erased it." She flashed up a hand. "And before you judge me, let me tell you why. She was seeing someone. Dash Gordon. She didn't want Kennedy or Finley to know about him. So I had to do it. She would've wanted that. And I wasn't interfering in a murder investigation then."

Erik didn't bother to lecture her. The damage was done. "Why didn't she want her daughters to know?"

"Dash is only forty-five, and it was...well, it was just a fling. She'd been with their father since she was eighteen. One night when the two of us went out, we ran into Dash. He's a sales rep for one of the pharmaceutical companies sponsoring her project. He came on to her, and she might've been a little bit drunk."

"It's odd that we didn't find his prints in her bedroom, then."

"He wasn't invited over there. Finley had a habit of dropping in unexpectedly. And Wanda was worried someone would see them together and it would be construed as a conflict of interest, so Wanda always went to his place." Nora twisted her hands together. "I also took her overnight bag so the girls didn't ask why she had one at the lab. Plus, it had some suggestive lingerie in it."

He was glad that Kennedy and Finley had been spared seeing that. "Did the bag have an extra denture in it?"

Nora's eyes flashed open. "How did you know?"

"That's what your intruder was trying to steal."

"Seriously? Why would he want that?"

Erik hoped to find out the answer to that as soon as Detective Johnson called him back.

"Do you know Dash's address?"

She shook her head. "Somewhere out in the country on the east side. He traveled a lot and liked to live in the woods but be close to the airport. But if you're hoping to talk to him, he might be hard to find."

"Why's that?"

"He's on vacation. Took a full month off. That's why Wanda had a bag packed. She was going to take a few days off and spend them with him."

Erik nodded. "Is Dash his real name or a nickname?"

"Real."

Then he should be easy to find. "Wanda had forty thousand dollars in cash in her safe. Any idea where that came from?"

Nora shook her head, her eyes wide. "Surely, nothing illegal."

"Did she need money?"

"Yeah, for medical bills. She was recently diagnosed with a rare kind of lymphoma." Nora's voice broke, and she cleared her throat. "I don't know the details, but she'd just started expensive treatments. She didn't have insurance or enough money saved to pay for them."

Wow. This news was big. Huge. And Wanda had kept it from Kennedy. How was she going to take this? He would have to find a way to break it to her gently.

Nora's eyes glistened with tears. "She was worried about paying bills when they started rolling in."

"She could've asked Kennedy for help."

"No. Wanda didn't want her girls to spend their money on it. That's one of the reasons she wouldn't tell them. She knew they'd insist on helping pay for her treatments. She was saving as much money as she could, pretty much only spending on her meals."

"What about retirement savings?" Erik asked, glad to finally be getting some answers. "Didn't she have that to use?"

Nora snorted. "Silas lost every penny of their savings in a risky investment. He was conned by a scammer."

Sounded like justice, considering his past. Erik didn't know how much of this he would mention to Kennedy. He would have to give it some thought because he didn't want to hurt her or change how she thought about her mother. Before he made any decisions, he needed to talk to Wanda's boyfriend.

"I know this was hard to share." He gave Nora a sympathetic look. "Anything else you wanted to tell me?"

"Nothing, other than I'm sorry I didn't tell you right up front." Nora pressed her palms over her legs. "I was just trying to protect the girls like Wanda would've wanted me to do."

"Thank you for being honest," Erik said. "When the police officer comes to talk to you, you need to tell him everything you told me."

"But then it's going to come out, and the girls will find out."

"I'll talk to the detective on the investigation and ask him to be discreet." *But, I don't know if I can keep this from Kennedy. Not and have a relationship with her again.*

Wait, what? Where did that come from? Was he actually thinking of proceeding with a relationship?

And if he knew this and didn't tell her, the secret would eat away at him. Just the way the WITSEC secret would've done with Kennedy if she'd stayed with him. He would tell her. It was just a matter of when.

He caught sight of the patrol car entering the lot. "You'll want to go meet the officer. His name's Smitty, and he'll take good care of you."

The moment her door closed behind her, Erik got out his phone and plugged Gordon's name into a PI database. He found only one Dash Gordon in the Portland area. He lived on the east side, just as Nora had said. Erik searched for photos of the guy and found a few on Facebook. His build was right for the intruder, but he wasn't the guy Smitty just hauled in, of that, Erik was certain.

Drake slid into the vehicle and Erik brought his brother up to speed as he moved to his laptop and did a recon of the property to determine how many of his brothers he needed to call out for a knock and talk.

The large log cabin overlooked a small lake and was tucked behind tall trees and scrub. There was only one way into the property. Erik didn't like not having a second exit. Not at all. Could be an ambush waiting to happen. Not that Gordon would be expecting Erik, but Erik wasn't taking chances.

He grabbed his phone again and tapped in a group text to his brothers.

Aiden, remain at Veritas for Kennedy's security detail. Everyone else meet me at the I-84 exit 17 motel parking lot. We have a house to raid and maybe a murder suspect to detain.

~

Kennedy had asked Finley about the Tile tracker, which she denied and then they moved onto everyday life. Kennedy tried to listen to her sister describe her day designing a web ad for a local retailer, but Kennedy's mind kept drifting to Erik as she wondered what he'd been doing for the past few hours.

"Earth to Kennedy," Finley said.

Kennedy snapped her focus to Finley. "Sorry."

"You've barely been listening to me through the whole night."

"You're right," Kennedy admitted. "I don't mean to ignore you."

Finley's expression went from judgmental to kind. "I know you're worried about Erik."

"Yeah. Not only his health but I wonder what he's doing right now. We've pretty much shared every step of this investigation and I know he has to be working on something now, but I don't know what. I sure hope he's not going to keep it from me."

"Do you have reason to believe he would?"

Kennedy shook her head. "He hasn't kept anything from me so far."

"At least not that you know of." Finley's words had a bite to them.

Kennedy didn't like seeing her sister so distrustful, but her last relationship had ended badly when she'd found out the guy had been lying about his marital status. He wasn't divorced as he claimed, just barely separated.

But Erik wasn't like that. Kennedy was certain of it. "He's the straightest shooter I know. I doubt he'd ever lie to me or hide something."

"All men do. Even Dad did." Her voice rose a notch.

"That's mighty negative."

Finley crossed her arms. "I have experience to back that up."

"I think you're dating the wrong guys. The bad boy types walk on the wild side." Kennedy tried to forget about Erik to help her sister, who was obviously still very impacted by her breakup. "On the other hand, I always thought of Drake Byrd as kind of a bad boy, and he's a fine man. So even if you're attracted to that type, there's still hope."

Finley sighed. "I think I'm sabotaging my relationships."

"Why's that?"

"For the same reason you did with Erik. I can't spend a lifetime living a lie with the man I love."

"Yeah, that's a hard one." Kennedy wished she had a different answer.

"Still, I've decided what I want to do about WITSEC, and you're not going to like it."

Kennedy swallowed hard. "You're going to stay in the program."

Finley nodded. "I have to. You pointed out my debt. Well I'm swimming in it. I can't get out from under it. I talked to Tyrone. He says there's enough danger that he recommends we stay in the program. And they'll make all my debts go away when they relocate me."

Just hearing the word *relocate* put a pain in Kennedy's heart. "We could use the money from Mom's safe to pay it off."

"Not if Erik proves it was illegally gained."

"I don't think that's the case, but even if it is," Kennedy said, "I'll help pay your debts off."

"You don't have a lot of money either. And I know Mom's will forbids you from selling her home and giving the money to me. Plus, this isn't just about the money." Finley clutched Kennedy's hand. "It's about our safety too."

"I know," Kennedy said, wishing that wasn't true but it was and she didn't want to talk about it because it could be the very thing that separated her from Erik. "You said you didn't read Mom's will."

"Yeah, well, I didn't want you to know." Finley crossed her arms.

"That's got to hurt."

"It did. A lot. At least at first." Finley relaxed her arms. "Now, I know she did it to try to make me grow up. Which I plan to do with this second chance with WITSEC."

"And you'd leave and never see me again?" Kennedy's words were stated calmly, despite the hurt she felt.

"I know you'll come with me."

Kennedy hated being taken for granted, but Finley was right. Kennedy would go with her sister, and Kennedy would be the one doing the leaving. Not only leaving Erik and his wonderful family behind, but leaving her heart right along with them.

22

Nearing ten P.M., Erik and Drake arrived at the parking lot where Erik had arranged to meet his brothers and cruised through a nearly full lot to the back. He searched for his brothers but he and Drake had arrived first.

Erik shifted into park on the side of the two-story motel where he had a good view of the entrance. "I'm going to give Johnson a call to ask about the guy Smitty arrested."

Drake shifted to look at him. "You thinking he could be Wanda's killer?"

Erik nodded as he got Johnson's voicemail and had to leave a message. "We could rule Gordon out as a suspect if we know if this guy's prints match the evidence, and he killed Wanda."

"*If* indeed she was killed," Drake said.

Erik swallowed a groan. Day five since he'd found Kennedy shivering in the water, and he still didn't have an answer to that question. They hadn't located anyone with a motive to kill her. Lots of people had the means, but the *why* was perplexing. If she *was* murdered, someone obviously had a reason.

Anyone close to a murder victim was a suspect. A

boyfriend fit that bill. But why would Gordon want to have someone steal Wanda's denture plate?

"You sure you did a thorough search for inDents?" Drake asked. "Seems like we should be able to find something."

"Not only me, but Nick too. Without a court order we're not going to be able to break the domain privacy."

"Seems like if this guy went to all the trouble to break in and steal the plate, it has to be a key lead in this investigation."

"Yeah, that and knowing Wanda was sick and was trying to raise money to pay future medical bills." Erik needed more info and Drake was just sitting there so Erik dialed Maya, who answered despite the late hour. "Erik?"

"I'm with Drake, and you're on speaker."

"You sure do work late," Drake said.

"As apparently do you." She laughed. "How can I help?"

"I've just learned that Kennedy's mom had a rare kind of lymphoma," Erik said. "I have a call in to the ME's office, but I wondered if you might be able to tell me if a blood cancer like that could be missed in an autopsy."

"Sure." She sounded tired, and he felt bad for bothering her. "I'd have to have more details to be positive, but yeah. It could be missed."

"I'll try to find out more and get back to you. For now keep this between us."

"Will do." There was a long pause. "And FYI, I haven't found any sign of drugs in the containers from the lab. I know I'm not supposed to share results with anyone but Johnson, but I figured, since everything is negative so far, it can't hurt to tell you."

Another lead, dead. "Thanks for the info. We'll just have to keep looking."

"Or resign yourself to the fact that Wanda either made a mistake or chose to end her life."

Erik didn't want to admit that, but he didn't know what to think.

"Sorry for bothering you so late, but thanks for your help." Erik ended the call.

"So looks like Nora could be telling the truth," Drake said.

"But how it relates to Wanda's death is still up in the air." Erik shoved his phone into his pocket just as his brothers drove into the lot.

"The cavalry has arrived." Drake laughed and got out of the SUV.

Clay parked right next to the company SUV and Erik got out to join them.

The moon hung bright in the clear sky littered with sparkling stars. Good for seeing their target, but bad for being seen. A soft breeze did nothing to cool the eighty-degree-plus weather, unusual at this time of night.

His brothers piled out, and he held out his phone. The screen displayed a satellite view of Gordon's property. "Take a look at the place while I bring you up to date."

He gave his phone to Clay and told them about Wanda's boyfriend. "I haven't told Kennedy about this, so not a word to her. In fact, if one of you even hints at it, I'll deck you."

"Our baby bro taking charge big time." Brendan laughed.

The others joined in, and Erik gritted his teeth. He would always be the baby. He couldn't change that, but he could continue to work hard to change his brothers' perception of him. He wasn't angry or even hurt. He just needed them to see him as the man he'd become. "I know you all think it's funny, but I can hold my own and you know it. I'd appreciate it if you stopped with the baby comments."

Brendan held up his hands. "Touchy much?"

"Put yourself in my place for once." Erik faced his brother. "How will a client respect me if you don't?"

"We respect you," Clay said.

"Speak for yourself." Drake chuckled.

Erik was starting to get mad, but he swallowed it down.

"Seriously, bro, we do," Drake said. "But we're not here to get all touchy-feely, are we? We're here to find a way to keep this suspect from bolting so we can interview him."

He was right, and Erik let this go. For now, but he would continue to bring it until they took him seriously.

"Just a quick anthrax check," Clay said. "Mom's been bugging me to report."

"I'm fine." Erik turned his attention to Drake. "You've had a lot of experience bringing in criminals who don't want to be captured. Not saying this guy is even bad or that he'll balk, but we have to assume he will. So what do you suggest?"

"We get eyes on the place and determine if the suspect is on the premises. If he is, we cover all exits and windows, then move in." Drake dusted his hands together. "No biggie."

Erik didn't agree. "We need to assume he could be Wanda's killer and take precautions."

Clay nodded toward the back of the rental SUV. "We brought vests and rifles."

"Then let's load the equipment in the company vehicle and get going." Erik ignored the thoughts of the prior shootout and why it was important to take Nighthawk's SUV to help his brothers stow the bins in the back of the SUV. They all dressed out in vests and added their comms units, and Erik got behind the wheel. Drake took shotgun while Clay and Brendan climbed in the back. Even at their ages, they still paired up with the sibling closest in age, as they'd done when they were kids.

The drive took forty minutes, and they moved further from the city and deeper into wooded country.

"I keep thinking about the guy who was arrested," Drake said. "We know Wanda was paid by inDents each month, right? A big chunk of change."

"Yeah," Erik said. "But why? Was she doing research on the dentures on the side to make some money? Was she wearing them in a trial? If that's true, twenty grand a month is a lot of money. So research seems more likely."

"We should have the Veritas team look at the plate the guy tried to steal," Clay said. "See if it's special in any way and would warrant a twenty K a month payment to Wanda."

Erik nodded. "I'll ask Johnson about that."

"Back to the money," Clay said. "Nora said Wanda needed money for medical bills, right? So even if she had the forty thousand in the safe and was getting a twenty K deposit each month, the bills could be a whole lot more than that."

"No kidding," Brendan said. "If Dad's transplant and Aiden's bills are any sign, she didn't have nearly enough money to pay ongoing treatments she would need."

"Yes," Erik said. "But her finances are really confusing. There were only two small medical charges on her credit card four months ago. I didn't think anything of it, but maybe this was when she found out she had cancer."

"If she was having treatment, shouldn't there be a record of paying for it in her checking or credit card account?" Brendan asked.

"Nora said Wanda just started, so she likely hadn't gotten the bills. Or she could've used cash. Not her maxed out credit card, though."

"Why pay interest on credit card debt if you have the money?" Brendan asked.

"If she really *was* sick," Clay said, "she might've wanted to keep the cash for her medical bills."

Erik slammed a fist on the wheel. "We just don't know enough to form a logical answer to any of these questions. Hopefully Dash Gordon will help."

Drake shook his head. "I still can't believe Wanda had a casual boyfriend. She just didn't seem the type."

Erik glanced at his brother. "It's weird to me too. But people change."

"Has Kennedy changed?" Clay asked.

"Sure," Erik said, but he thought about all the ways she was still the same. Still kind. Still devoted to and fiercely protective of family. Still ambitious. She was a self-starter. Loving. Compassionate. All fine traits in Erik's eyes.

"You two going to kiss and make up?" Drake grinned.

Were they? He sure wanted them to. "The verdict's still out."

"Looks like you might be running out of time." Drake's gaze burned into Erik.

Clay leaned between the seats. "If Gordon gives us the answers we need to close this investigation, she'll be heading back to the East Coast or staying in WITSEC, and you'll be missing out on a terrific woman."

Erik knew his brothers spoke the truth, but that didn't mean he was ready for a relationship again, and as Drake pointed out, Kennedy lived across the country from Erik or could be staying in witness protection. Problem. Big one. He would never ask her to trade her dream job for him any more than she would ask him to leave his family.

"Driveway half a mile ahead on the right," Drake announced.

Erik slowed to a crawl, cut the headlights, and made the turn onto the long treelined drive. The wheels crunched over gravel, each turn emitting tiny pops of sound in the quiet. Erik spotted the house sitting a couple of football fields from the road and killed the engine.

He reached for the binoculars, but Drake already had them lifted to his eyes. "One light on, no sign of movement. Red Jeep Renegade in the drive."

"Give me the plate, and I'll run it." Erik pulled up on his phone one of the PI databases they subscribed to and entered the digits as Drake rattled them off. The result populated Erik's screen. "Belongs to Gordon. It's his only registered vehicle."

"So he's likely home," Clay said over the seat.

"Could've gone out with someone," Erik said. "But yeah. It's likely."

"I say we send out a scouting party before approaching," Drake said.

"You and I can go." Erik made sure the internal lights wouldn't turn on when they opened their doors and slid out.

He felt for his weapon and tucked his shirt behind it for easy access. Drake did the same.

The moon and stars illuminated the long drive. They needed to be careful not to be seen. He pointed at the trees along the drive and headed into them. He paused near a large flowering shrub scenting the air with a sweetness he found overpowering. He grabbed the binoculars from Drake to take a good look at the house.

"Still no movement," Erik said. "We need to get closer to the front porch to take a look."

"Risk being exposed."

"If you were hunting a fugitive, would you risk it?"

"Heck, yeah." Drake grinned.

"Then I'm going in. You stay here." Erik jetted across the drive and ducked low to make his way to the porch. He popped up, binoculars in hand, but couldn't get a good look through the big picture window.

The door was ajar.

Had something bad happened here?

He had to get a look through that window.

He started up the stairs to the porch. Reached the top and froze.

Man, oh, man.

He clamped a hand over his nose and mouth.

No point in going any further. The stench coming from the house told him everything he needed to know right now, and he backed away to call in a deputy.

Someone was dead in this house and had been for some time. Likely Dash Gordon.

Hopes ruined, Erik waited on the tailgate of the SUV for a local detective to arrive. Thankfully they'd parked far away from the house and couldn't catch the smell of death that was oozing out of the open door. His brothers hung with him, the tone oddly somber for the group. Erik had hoped Gordon would give them answers. Nope. Didn't happen. The guy created more questions.

The first responding deputy had gone inside the house to confirm what they'd suspected. Gordon had died. He'd taken two bullets to the chest at close range, and the house had been ransacked.

The deputy said Gordon appeared to have been tortured, his fingers mutilated. Teeth pulled. This investigation had suddenly gotten ugly. Very ugly. Erik couldn't be happier that Kennedy was safely settled in his condo with Aiden.

The deputy was young, and this was his first dead body. He was alone, freaked out, and needed to talk. So Erik told him that, as a former officer, he understood, and the kid unloaded every detail of the scene. Erik doubted he'd get any additional details from the responding detective when he arrived.

On the bright side, with Gordon obviously having been murdered, Erik finally had strong reason to believe Wanda had been murdered too. Different MO for sure, and maybe different killers, but this death cast a suspicious cloud over hers.

Erik's phone rang, and he answered the call from Sierra. "I'm putting you on speaker. Everyone's here except Aiden and Kennedy."

"I just got off the phone with Detective Johnson," she said. "He gave me permission to share the results for the evidence we turned in to him. Grady's done running ballistics on the gun we recovered, and I processed the prints for that and the bullets in the clip. Plus prints from the casings at the ambush. They all match, and they also match the unknown print I lifted at Wanda's place."

Erik let the information sink in. "So he's our guy, whoever *he* is."

"Yes, and Johnson now has all of the evidence, and he'll be running the prints through AFIS."

As a police officer, Erik had used the Automated Fingerprint Identification System—a database holding fingerprints from most law enforcement agencies and was managed by the FBI. "Anything else?"

"Two things. First, I'm still waiting on the footprints at the river to fully cure so I can make a positive determination. And second, the hair I recovered at Wanda's house was dyed. Less than a centimeter between root and color change suggests that the hair was dyed less than a month ago. I'm trying to determine the color and brand of the dye, but that could take some time. Also the sample had a flat-cut end, telling me he'd recently had a haircut."

"So our guy dyed and cut his hair." Erik came to his feet when he spotted an unmarked car pull up the drive. "Maybe as a disguise."

"He's a natural blond. Isn't it amazing what a single hair can tell you about a suspect?" Sierra's enthusiasm for her job shone through her tone.

Erik appreciated the information, but he couldn't get as excited about it. "Thanks for the update, but I gotta go." He stowed his phone and looked at his brothers. "Looks like it's showtime."

He started for the detective, but his phone rang again. *Perfect.* Detective Johnson.

"Please tell me Smitty got ahold of you," Erik said the minute Johnson came on the line.

"He did."

"Do you have a name for the suspect Smitty arrested?" Erik held his breath, hoping Johnson would cooperate, considering Erik and the Veritas team had been so forthcoming with him.

"You didn't hear this from me, but the guy didn't have ID on him. Still, his prints came back to a Jeremy Miller. Also matched the prints for the evidence your sister submitted."

"He's our guy then," Erik said.

"I'm sure liking him for it. He was arrested for drug possession and distribution about five years ago. I suspect we'll find a link between him and the counterfeit drug distributors. Not that he's admitted it. He's not saying a word. Not a single word. Not even 'I want my attorney.'"

"Drugs." Erik let the word hang out there for a moment as he processed the implications as related to the illegal pharmaceutical project Wanda was working on. "Why take Wanda's denture and nothing else?"

"Good question," Johnson said, in his low rumbly voice. "One I don't have an answer for. You recognize the name?"

Erik mentally ran through names on the Responsible Officials list and Wanda's contact list. "Nope. We need to get him talking to figure out his relationship to Wanda Walker."

"I'd like to get you and your client down here to see if either of you recognize him from the break-in."

Erik didn't mind looking at a sixpack of photos to try to ID the guy he saw in the parking lot, but he hated to put Kennedy through the stress. Even if she worked in law enforcement, this was personal and would be painful. Still, he knew she would want to go. "I can arrange that."

"Sooner rather than later."

"Roger that." Erik shared Gordon's death with Johnson.

"Well, isn't that something," Johnson said. "Who's the detective out there?"

Erik shrugged. Even if Johnson couldn't see it, it was an automatic reflex. "Just going to meet with him now."

"Since you don't know his name, give him my number and have him call me right away." Johnson's demanding tone held a determination Erik hadn't witnessed from the guy before. Likely the pressure from being on the task force. "You hear me?"

"I hear you." Erik hung up and strode toward the slim detective deep in conversation with the deputy.

Erik didn't know how this was going to go down, but one thing he did know that he hadn't been clear on before. He had to tell Kennedy about Gordon before the trip to the police station and Johnson mentioned it. Or this detective called her to ask questions.

Having the matter settled should have lifted a weight from Erik's shoulders, but it did just the opposite. He didn't have any right to keep the news of her mother's boyfriend from her anyway, and he wouldn't want to be left in the dark on one of his parents. Plus, she might recognize the guy's name, which could move the investigation forward.

More than anything, he didn't want to hurt the woman who was taking over his heart again. He wanted to commit to her and give her only the best and most joyous life, a thought that shocked him as much as finding Gordon's body.

23

Kennedy glanced across the sofa at Erik. He looked worried. Uncomfortable in a way she'd never seen before. And asking her to sit down so he could talk to her? He'd never done that before either. Her stomach coiled around the salad she'd eaten earlier and the spicy taco salad smell lingered in the air, making the nausea worse.

She tried to clutch her hands in her lap, but the bite was still painful, so she settled on clasping the wrist of her injured hand. She wished she could stop her mind from conjuring up all kinds of crazy ideas about where Erik had been for the past six hours, but she'd always had a vivid imagination.

He planted his hand on his knees. "I got a call from Nora. Someone broke into her place, and she asked me to come alone."

"Nora? Really?" Kennedy's heart fluttered as she tried to figure out why Nora might want to see Erik alone.

"Her first concern was the intruder, of course," Erik said. "The police were there when I got there and had him in custody."

"But why didn't she want me there?" Kennedy asked.

"She had some things to tell me about your mom that she didn't want you or Finley to know." His eyes were tight with a deep pain. "But I think you deserve to hear them."

She took his hand, feeling the rougher skin of a man who didn't sit behind a desk all day. "It's okay. Just tell me."

"Nora was the one who erased your mother's phone."

Phew. Not as bad as Kennedy feared. "Why would she do that?"

He swallowed, and his Adam's apple bobbed. "Your mother was seeing someone. His name was Dash Gordon."

Her mouth fell open. *No. Not her mom.* She said she never wanted to date. Kennedy snapped her mouth shut. "My mom. Seeing someone. That's crazy. But who is this Dash guy?"

Erik pulled back and stood to pace. She went after him and joined him by the floor-to-ceiling window overlooking rolling hills of dried grasses from a summer of little rain. Portland city lights twinkled in the distance.

She rested a hand on his shoulder. "What is it?"

He turned to look at her, the anguish doubled in his eyes. "Your mom had an overnight bag at the lab. Nora took it to her place."

Kennedy's stomach threatened to explode. "Ah. She was more than seeing him. They were sleeping together."

Erik nodded. "Nora didn't want you or Finley to know. He was much younger, and your mom thought you might judge her for having a fling with a younger man."

Kennedy ran her hand through her hair. The thought of her mother being someone Kennedy really didn't know was upsetting. But... "She deserved to be happy. I would've protested at first, but if this Dash person made her happy I would've come to accept it."

"There's more. Let's sit down again." He took her hand and started to lead her across the room.

She jerked him to a stop. "Just tell me."

He closed his eyes for a moment before meeting her gaze. "Your mom had a rare form of lymphoma."

Blood rushed to Kennedy's head, and she wished she'd listened to Erik. She dropped onto the nearest dining chair to wait for the feeling to pass. "She never said a word."

"She didn't think she would have enough money to pay for her treatments, and she didn't want to be a financial burden for you or Finley." He pulled out a chair next to her. "Or tell you that your dad lost all of their savings in a scam."

Kennedy's heart ached for all her mother had endured, and Kennedy hadn't been there for her. Not at all. She looked at her hands and worked hard not to cry. And her dad losing their savings? She had no words for that. Except he'd helped scam people out of their life savings, so it was fitting the same should happen to him. Unfortunately, her mom got stuck in the middle. Again.

"Also, you should know that the guy who broke into Nora's place was stealing a denture plate from your mother's bag. It was in a box labeled inDents."

She raised her head. "The company who was paying her the twenty grand every month? Was it for this denture plate? To wear it? Test it, maybe?"

"We don't know." Erik frowned. "The guy's not talking. His name is Jeremy Miller. He's not in any of the information we've reviewed. Do you know him?"

"I wish I did."

"He has a record for drug possession and distribution. Could mean he has a relationship with the counterfeit drug manufacturers. I'll do a deep dive on him to see what we can find."

"But why the denture? How would that be related to counterfeit drugs?"

"No clue. I'm going to ask Johnson if the Veritas team

can look at it."

"That would be good."

Erik shifted on his chair, looking even more ill at ease, and she braced herself.

He rested an arm on the table. "You should also know that we went to Dash Gordon's place to talk to him. He was tied to a dining room chair where he'd died of gunshot wounds to the chest."

She gasped and blinked a few times to process the news. "And you think his death has to do with my mom?"

"It would be a huge coincidence if it's not. Grady's over there now recovering bullets and slugs. Maybe they'll match bullets to the gun you brought up on your dive. The prints on both of those match the shell casings recovered at the shootout."

"Good news." *Finally.* "We're making some progress." She stared over his shoulder, trying to think about what was coming next, but thoughts of her mom suffering with cancer wouldn't stop, and she couldn't hold back her tears. She got up again, not sure of her destination, but she couldn't sit still with all the guilt piling on her shoulders.

"What is it, honey?" Erik stepped near her.

She wanted to walk into his arms as she'd done back in the day when something bad had happened. He would hold her tight and make it all go away. For that moment anyway. Even after he released her, she always felt stronger for the comfort he offered.

God was the same way. Once she gave up on what she could do herself and stepped out of her own way and into His loving arms, she was much stronger. So easy, yet so hard. She'd been fighting that embrace since her mother died. Maybe she was mad at God. Probably was and she wasn't sure if she even knew how to find Him again. What to do? How to look for Him?

"Kennedy?" Erik asked.

Her tears poured from her eyes. She wasn't ready to share her struggle with God. "I hate to think of my mom being alone with the cancer. If only she'd told me."

He took her uninjured hand, his big fingers enveloping hers, and she stared at them twined together. He drew her close. Closer.

"I wish I didn't have to tell you," he whispered.

"Thank you for not keeping it from me." She looked up and met his gaze. "No more secrets in my life."

Right. Like that was possible. A sob escaped, and she looked away.

"What is it?" He tipped her chin up.

"One more big secret," she said. "Probably for the rest of my life. Finley decided to stay in WITSEC, and we'll be relocated again."

"Why?" His voice rose.

She pulled back.

"Sorry. Why?" he asked again, his tone softer that time.

She told him about the danger first as that was the biggest reason, but then had to tell him about the money too.

He shook his head. "I'll pay off her debts."

"She's too proud to take money from me, so she'd never take it from you."

"But doesn't she know what she's doing to you? You'll have to give up a career you love. And I know you can't keep your former careers in the program or even do them as a hobby, so you won't likely dive again."

"She knows the rules." Kennedy's throat closed, and she could barely get the words out. "She's just looking out for our safety, and I have to go with her. I'm all she's got."

His eyes narrowed, but he didn't speak.

She raised her chin in solidarity with her sister. "You'd

do the same thing for your family."

He gritted his teeth. "My family wouldn't ask for such a huge sacrifice."

"You made one for Aiden," she pointed out.

"That's different. He didn't ask us to quit our jobs. It was our decision." Erik shook his head. "And here I thought *I* was going to give *you* the bad news. I don't want you to disappear from my life again. I want to..."

He shook his head and ran a hand over his face.

"You want to what?" she asked, not sure she wanted to know the answer.

He met her gaze. "I don't know what I'm feeling for you or even if I could be ready for a relationship if you were interested, but it doesn't matter now, does it? You're going away for forever."

Erik parked outside PPB's central precinct, clutching the steering wheel beneath his fingers and doing his best not to look at Kennedy. The last thing she needed right now was for him to let his fear of losing her make him try to convince her not to go into witness protection. He didn't want her to leave, but he had nothing to offer her. Not only couldn't he promise a long-term commitment at this point, but he could never replace a family member.

Drake got out of the vehicle and did a quick canvass before he crooked his finger at the SUV. Erik glanced around to confirm his brothers were in position. They pulled out all stops on the protection detail, even if visiting a police precinct was a low-risk situation. After discovering Gordon's body, Erik wouldn't take any chances with Kennedy's life.

He looked at her. "You remain between me and Drake,

and we go straight inside."

She nodded, but her focus was on the precinct doorway in the tall stone building.

"Don't worry." He did his best to sound comforting. "You won't see him. Just pictures."

"I know."

He resisted reaching for her hand and got out to open her door. Nearing two a.m., the temps had fallen some, but it was still a warm evening. He and Drake escorted her inside, and the desk sergeant called Johnson down to meet them.

Erik stood between Kennedy and the exit, noting the lingering scent of a fresh lemon cleaner on the recently mopped floors.

The elevator doors opened, and a short, pudgy guy poked his head out. "Come on up."

They boarded the car, and Erik introduced Kennedy.

"Thanks for coming down in the middle of the night." Johnson fixed his detective stare on Kennedy.

"I assume this will be a regular sixpack of photos," Erik said, drawing Johnson's attention.

Johnson nodded. "I'll put you in separate rooms and show each of you six photos. You tell me if you see the man who broke into the floating home."

"Sounds easy enough," Kennedy said, but her hand was trembling.

Johnson eyed her. "Just be sure you look at each photo carefully. And the session will be recorded for future criminal proceedings. I assume you're okay with that."

Kennedy nodded.

"I'm good," Erik said.

They exited on the detective's floor and passed a reception desk behind a thick bulletproof window. Johnson used his keycard to open a door next to the desk, which led to a wide-open area running the width of the building with cubicles and chest-high dividers giving privacy. The scent of popcorn filled the air, and several detectives were working, despite the late hour. Not surprising. Crime didn't stop for anything.

Johnson wound his way to a small conference room and pointed at a chair inside. "Have a seat, Byrd. I'll be back."

Erik squeezed Kennedy's good hand. "You can do this."

"I know," she said, but her hand was clammy and Erik knew she was thinking about the man coming for her, his gun aimed.

Johnson led her down the hall, and they disappeared around a corner.

Erik sat in the room, where a trash can was overflowing with disposable coffee cups, which accompanied a stale coffee odor.

Not five minutes later, Johnson returned, his expression not giving away if Kennedy had been able to identify the suspect. He dropped into a chair next to Erik and opened a folder. "Ready?"

"As can be."

Johnson turned on a video camera and did an introduction, then flipped over six photos on the desktop. "Take your time. Let me know if you see the man who ran into you in the parking lot outside Kennedy Walker's home on the night of the break-in."

Erik stared at the men in the lineup, one by one. It only took one look before he saw their guy looking back at him. Erik tapped the fourth picture. "It's him."

Johnson's expression remained flat. "Are you positive?"

He nodded. "Positive."

"Ever seen him before or after?" Johnson asked.

"Just when he was being arrested tonight," Erik said, his gaze pinned on the suspect.

"Okay, then we're done here." Johnson peered at the camera and gave a concluding statement before he turned it off and looked at Erik. "You chose Jeremy Miller."

Erik wanted to pump a fist, but he didn't want to seem unprofessional. "Did Kennedy ID him, too?"

"She did. I'll take you to her and escort you out of the building."

Erik followed Johnson down the hallway to another room, where Kennedy sat in a chair, her hands locked on her knees.

She looked up. "Did we identify the right man?"

Johnson nodded. "Both of you chose the guy we have in holding, and we ran his prints against the ones recovered from the shell casings at the shooting. They matched."

"Yes!" Erik pumped his fist. *At last. They had their guy.*

"We can't say he's the guy who tried to take you out, as we have no proof he fired the rounds, but he at least loaded the ammo."

Kennedy sat upright. "If his prints match that ammo, it means his prints also match the one lifted from the drawer at my mom's place."

"Indeed." Johnson let out a long breath. "We have proof that he's the creep who scared you half to death, and he's now behind bars."

"So this is it. The man who was after me—us—is locked up, and we're safe."

"Looks like it." Johnson smiled. "Miller will go away for some time, and you can return to your life."

"Not so fast." Erik looked at Johnson. "We still don't know if he killed Wanda or even if she was murdered."

Kennedy frowned at Erik then shifted her focus back to Johnson. "Did any of the prints lifted from the anthrax envelope match his?"

"They did. A partial, anyway."

Kennedy tilted her head. "So he somehow got a sample of the anthrax even though he's not a Responsible Official."

"We're working on that now, but agents tell me some of the militant groups have found ways to get samples. Foolishness when they don't know how to handle it properly. They're more likely to kill themselves than the people they're threatening."

Erik resisted grinding his teeth. "To recap, we have Jeremy Miller responsible for the break-in and loading the ammo for the bullets fired at our vehicle plus for handling the gun and crowbar recovered from the river and the anthrax envelope."

Johnson nodded.

"Did Sierra update you on the hair found at the Walker place?" Erik asked.

"She did. And you shoulda seen me in the interview room looking for blond roots in the guy's hair." Johnson laughed. "I'm pretty sure it was dyed. I wish I could just yank a hunk out, but you can't do anything these days without a warrant. And I couldn't even grab his glass for DNA collection."

Erik could imagine the interview scene. He'd been in plenty of small interview rooms, but trying to see the roots of a suspect's hair that had just been dyed? Would be a challenge without giving away what he was doing and providing Miller with information that Johnson wouldn't want to share.

"So he really is our guy," Erik stated as he let the information sink in.

"Yep," Johnson said. "We have evidence to connect him to every crime. With his history of drug sales, I doubt it will be long until we link him to the illegal pharmaceutical dealers that Dr. Walker's project would've put out of business."

24

The morning came too soon for Erik, and he leaned back from the dining table at Drake's condo to admire the brilliant reds and oranges of the sun rising over the Portland skyline. He took the final sip from his mug, the nutty scent of coffee lingering in the air, and his mouth protested at the extra acid as Erik had brewed the coffee strong the way his brother liked it.

Erik had gotten a few hours of sleep for tossing and turning over Kennedy returning to WITSEC protection today. He was going to drop her at her house to pack, then Deputy Kruse would transport her and Finley to their new home.

His phone chimed with a text, and he looked at the screen to find Grady's name.

Slug pulled from the wall at Gordon's place matches the gun Kennedy recovered from the river.

He should respond with a yay. But his heart said too bad. He just lost the argument he'd planned to use to keep Kennedy from going home today. He'd planned to tell her a man had been murdered in cold blood, and until they knew Miller was the killer, she still needed Erik's protection. But now she didn't. Not anymore. Not with this new information from Grady. Miller killed Gordon. At least the evidence indicated that, and Erik had nothing to keep her here. She had to do what she had to do. Once again. And once again it involved leaving him behind.

He typed a thank-you text to Grady and packed up his computer. Might as well not linger on the what-ifs and if-onlys. Better to get over to his condo to see if Kennedy was ready to leave. Besides, it would be good to get out the door before Drake got up, discovered Erik's mood, and fired questions at him.

He grabbed his overnight bag and laptop and Pong cast him an expectant look.

"Why not?" Erik said. "You can help me after she leaves."

Erik left the coffee pot on for Drake and stepped into the hallway. Pong traipsed alongside and Erik let them into his own place. He wasn't surprised to see Kennedy sitting on the couch, her packed tote bag by her feet and a mug of coffee in her hand.

"Good morning," he said. Man, who was this guy? He sounded pretty formal for a man who was in love, but he needed to keep a professional edge. It was the only thing that would get him through saying goodbye to her without begging her to stay.

She held up the mug. "I just made coffee."

He dropped his bag and set his computer on the island while Pong trotted over to Kennedy. "Looks like you want to get going."

"We have time for a cup of coffee together." She set down the cup and ruffled Pong's ears.

Erik didn't mind spending a little more time with her. He went to the kitchen to pour a big mug of coffee. He took a sip on the way back. She'd made it just the way he liked it. Medium strength.

He sat in the chair across from her. "Sleep well?"

"Yeah, I actually did. A lot of worry has been lifted from my shoulders, thanks to you and your family."

"Glad you're feeling better." He didn't know what else to say so took a long drink of the rich black coffee. "But even if you're safe now, we still need to figure out if Johnson's right and Miller was involved in your mom's death."

"I'd appreciate that."

"I suppose you and Finley will be leaving soon." He rested the hot mug on his knee, but he felt jittery and didn't think he could sit here drinking coffee with her when she was leaving him forever. "I can email findings to your WITSEC inspector so he can get them to you."

She frowned. "I hate leaving my mom's project unfinished."

Right. That was what she hated leaving. Not him. The pain of that truth felt like a lightning bolt to the heart, and he knew, then and there, that he *did* love her. He wanted her in his life. He wanted to fight for her. But he wouldn't. No matter what he wanted, he wouldn't come between Kennedy and her sister.

He stood before he caved in to his emotions and made things hard for her. "I'm caffeinated enough, and we should get going."

A flash of pain marred her face. Dare he hope it was because she didn't want to lose him either? Still, it didn't matter.

He crated Pong then grabbed her bag and led her to the SUV, where he got them out of the lot and on the road without a word. They made the thirty-minute drive in silence. Tortured, uncomfortable silence. Not at all like their usual easiness. He kept noticing her fresh coconut scent and wanted to take her hand to pull her close and be surrounded by it so he could remember the way she smelled and how she felt in his arms when she was gone.

Traffic was light, and he reached the marina in record time. In the parking lot, he climbed out into the breezy summer morning and grabbed her bag.

"I can take that." She removed it from his hand. "I know you have things to do, so I'll say goodbye right here."

He nodded, but he didn't know what to say or do. How did you say goodbye to the love of your life?

"Thank you for everything," she said, her words rushed and nervous. "I know I didn't deserve it, but I am very glad for your help. And tell your family how much I appreciate it too." She rose on her toes and kissed him on the cheek.

He caught a whiff of the coconut again and lifted an arm to draw her close, but let it fall. "I'm glad we were there when you needed us."

She smiled at him.

He stepped back and shoved his hands into his pockets. "I'm glad we had a chance to iron out our differences. I hope your new life is everything you want it to be."

"Goodbye, Erik." Her eyes flooded with tears, and she bolted for the bridge.

He grabbed onto the SUV's door handle to keep from racing after her. He stood there until he could no longer see her. His heart felt like she'd sunk a fishing hook in it and was reeling it along with her. The pain in his chest was nearly overwhelming.

He knew this exact feeling. Had felt it before, the day she'd left him in college.

His mind screamed to go after her, but he couldn't. Wouldn't. He rounded the vehicle and climbed in. He revved the engine, drawing the attention of a man standing by the marina's front door. Erik felt lost and needed something to focus on. Wanda's death was just the thing. Maybe this guy knew something about Wanda that no one had asked about. Sure, Erik was grasping at straws, but finding out what happened to Wanda was top priority now.

Erik killed the engine and jogged across the lot. The elderly man crossed his arms as if he was expecting a fight.

Erik introduced himself.

"Wayne Villanueva," the man said. "I manage this place."

"I think one of my brothers interviewed you." Erik handed him a business card.

"Right. About Wanda." He frowned. "I was sad to hear of her passing."

Erik held out his phone displaying one of Jeremy Miller's photos from Facebook. "Do you know this man?"

Villanueva studied the image. "Don't know him, but I did see him here before, sitting in his pickup for hours. Big black Ford F-450. Noticed it right off the bat as you don't see that many of the bigger Ford trucks. He just sat there, so I went to ask what was going on, and he took off before I could talk to him."

"Did you get a plate number?"

Villanueva shook his head. "Truck was too muddy. Only caught a G in the first few digits."

"When was this?"

Villanueva took a small notebook from his pocket, licked his finger, and paged through it. "Week ago Friday."

Before the break-in.

"He do something wrong?" Villanueva asked.

"Broke into Wanda's home, but he's been arrested." Erik pointed to the business card he'd handed Wayne. "If you remember anything else or hear anything about this guy, give me a call."

Villanueva gave a serious nod, and Erik went back to his SUV. Each step he had to force his feet to keep heading away from Kennedy's house. He took a minute to look up Miller's DMV records and found the truck Villanueva described.

During the drive home, Erik forced his mind to run through the case so when he got back to the office, he could spend his day reviewing every lead and holding the whip over his brothers to keep going with the Responsible Officials list.

Which he did, but they didn't uncover a single lead. The guys went home to have dinner with their significant others, reinforcing for Erik how alone he was except for his trusty buddy Pong.

Back in his condo that evening, after scarfing down a mediocre frozen pizza, he stood at the window overlooking the city.

So what if he was alone? It gave him time to do what he liked to do. No one depended on him, and he was free to spend his time however he wanted. Like keeping up with this investigation until he dropped from exhaustion so he wouldn't miss Kennedy.

He went back to the table and looked at Wanda's contacts and the Responsible Officials list. Not a single gardener other than Oscar Edwards, and not a bit of evidence pointed to him as having been involved in Wanda's death.

Should Erik interview him again? He didn't think he'd get any additional information, but maybe he should stop by the professor's house unannounced in the morning and ask for a tour of his garden to look for the prickly caterpillar bean.

A text from Detective Johnson dinged on his phone.

You wanted permission to have Veritas look at the denture. I got approval, and the denture is waiting at your front desk for you.

Thanks. Erik raced for the door and then the stairwell. He bolted down the steps.

Who should he have look at the plate? Sierra? Maybe. Or maybe Maya. Sierra should be home with Asher instead of working, so he would start with Maya.

He reached the lobby, signed out the denture, and rushed up to Maya's lab. Thankfully, she was still working at a machine on the back wall. Just inside the door, he stopped to catch his breath from jogging down the stairs.

She turned and smiled, but immediately frowned and crossed over to him. "You're not here because of your anthrax exposure, are you?"

"No."

"Phew. What can I do for you?"

He held out the denture plate. "It might be more Sierra's thing, but I've already bothered her too much on her leave."

Maya looked at the plate, and her eyes lit up.

"You've come to the right person." She smiled up at him. "I think I can help you prove Wanda was murdered."

Kennedy stood on the deck looking over the water, her heart heavy. She would be leaving with Finley tomorrow. One more night on the floating home, and she should've packed already, but stood out there looking at the moon slicing across the deck like a bright spotlight. She'd been useless all day, wandering around the house, touching everything she would have to leave behind. She started out deciding what to keep of her mother's things, but it didn't take long before she realized most everything she wanted she wouldn't be allowed to take.

No photos. No videos. No mementos that referenced her family in any way.

The enormity of her decision to follow Finley rendered her ineffective, and she'd done nothing but stare at her mother's things and the water throughout the day.

Her phone rang. *Finley.*

Kennedy dredged up a cheerful tone. "Hey, Sis."

"Tyrone says be ready at nine A.M. for transport."

"Nine?" The finality of her decision hit Kennedy. "No. Please. I want a little more time."

"No can do." Finley sounded eager and determined. "We're lucky I got him to back off until tomorrow by telling him Nighthawk Security was protecting you."

Kennedy opened her mouth to tell Finley that she'd left Erik and his brothers and was on her own tonight, she didn't want to hurry the process along. Kennedy would have one more night in the same city as Erik. Maybe he would come by again. Maybe she would go see him. Maybe, maybe, maybe.

She swallowed down a sigh. "I'll be packed and ready."

"With the little bit we can take with us, it's not like it'll take long," Finley said. "See you in the morning."

Kennedy ended the call before she snapped at her sister and blamed her for having to give up everything. Everything!

Kennedy didn't know yet where they would be relocated. Or what kind of job she would be doing. She was supposed to have called to quit her current job, but she'd put it off, and now it was too late for the day. She would do it first thing in the morning. Likely the last call she would make from this phone.

"Stop being such a big baby and suck it up," she muttered. "You've made the best decision for Finley. A decision Mom would want. So stop whining. It won't accomplish anything. Face it. You're going to have to once again walk out on one of the finest men you know."

Enough star gazing. Pack and get some sleep. That was what she needed to do.

She spun and headed into the house, but her feet stuttered to a stop just inside the door.

A man stood by the front door, cloaked in shadows. She gasped.

"Hello, Kennedy," he said. "Time for us to finish this once and for all."

～

Confused, Erik blinked at Maya. "How can you possibly tell she was murdered from her denture?"

"I'll bet we'll find that it contains the heart medicine the ME couldn't explain in her system."

He gaped at her. "In her denture? You've got to be kidding me."

"Not kidding at all. You wanted me to review Wanda's autopsy file to look at the toxicology report, remember?"

"Sure, but what does that have to do with the denture?"

"There was a photo of her plate, and I noticed it was unusual. It was 3-D printed, not traditionally made."

He shook his head. "Are 3-D dentures really a thing?"

"Yes." She rested her hands on her waist. "Printable dentures aren't common yet, but they could be the way of the future."

"Okay, makes sense, I guess, but the medicine? How's that connected?"

She crossed the room to a work table. "First, you need to know that nearly two-thirds of the denture wearers in our country suffer from frequent fungal infections. Needless to say, that causes a lot of issues for the wearer. Researchers want to solve that problem and have filled 3-D printed dentures with microscopic capsules that periodically release

276

an antifungal medication. These aren't available to the general public yet but are still in the testing phase."

"And you think someone put heart medicine in her plate instead of the antifungal?"

She nodded. "Not just anyone could inject the meds into an antifungal denture and expect it to work. And honestly, not many people even know about these dentures, so seems like a scientist is trying to develop them for heart medicine."

"Then they'd likely have to be connected to a research lab to have perfected these."

"Absolutely. It's not as simple as just putting tablets that you'd find at her house into the denture. It would need to be calibrated to dispense the right dosage. So if we find the heart meds in the dentures, we'll have a limited number of people who would have the right knowledge to pull this off."

He shook his head and smiled. "You are simply amazing, you know that?"

Color rose over her face, and she waved her hand to dismiss the compliment. "I just keep up on research and developments."

"Still, it's incredible that you thought of using the denture to look for Wanda's meds."

"Not sure incredible is the word." She wrinkled her nose. "More like a crazy way my brain sees everyday things and figures out how they can be used to commit a crime."

"Well, I for one, am glad you're crazy." He handed over the evidence bag. "I assume you can test for the meds here."

"Yes. If it's in the denture material, I'll find it." She pulled a sheet of white paper over the table and took the denture plate from the box. "I'll have to crack this open to see if it includes microspheres. They protect the drug during the heat printing process and allow the release of medication as they gradually degrade."

Excitement burned in Erik's gut. He'd finally be able to

prove that Wanda was murdered. She hadn't died of suicide or incompetence, just like Kennedy had asserted all along. "What if inDents was experimenting with this heart medicine, and Wanda was trialing it for the company? Then these microspheres degraded faster than planned and gave her a serious overdose."

"That's what I'm thinking." Maya looked up. "No offense, but I'll do this quicker if you don't watch me."

"I'll take off."

"I'll text you the second I know anything."

"Will it be tonight?"

She nodded but didn't look up.

He left the lab and took the stairs to his place. If Maya was right, he might still have time to tell Kennedy in person what had happened to her mother.

He opened his condo door and caught a faint hint of her coconut smell. His gut twisted, but then he heard Pong whimpering from his crate. The little fella would be a distraction from pain. The past few days, Erik had taken him out for bathroom breaks when needed but neglected the long walks the dog liked to take. That was going to change right now.

Erik opened the crate door. "Ready for a walk."

Pong danced then sat as if he knew dancing wasn't proper behavior for a trained dog.

Erik ruffled his scruff. "It's okay, boy. At least one of us should be happy."

Erik clicked on Pong's leash, and they were soon out in the clear night, temps in the seventies. Erik should be enjoying his walk, but with the lack of focus came more thoughts of Kennedy. He had to do something to clear his mind.

"Let's run, boy." Erik started off, his tactical boots heavier than the athletic shoes he'd left in his condo, but soon the miles disappeared beneath his feet to the sound of paws clicking on the sidewalk. Perspiration coated his body, and his muscles strained, the punishment feeling good. And no signs of illness from anthrax. He felt perfectly fine.

Please keep it that way. For Kennedy too.

His phone pealed into the night, disturbing the peace. He came to a stop, his breathing sharp and fast. Maya's name appeared on the screen, and he answered.

"I hope you have good news," he got out between deep breaths.

"We were right! The dentures contained Wanda's heart meds."

"Finally." He huffed out a breath and dragged in another. "An answer. So maybe she wasn't murdered, and it was all a horrible accident."

"If so, inDents needs to be held accountable for it."

"Yeah," Erik said, his focus on Pong, who was probably hot and thirsty. "I need to find out who they are and make sure they pay."

He ended the call and turned to race back home. Pong kept up beside him, the patter of his paws like a clock ticking away and matching the thoughts pinging through Erik's brain.

Could Jeremy Miller have been stealing the denture to keep anyone from discovering the medicine? Had Wanda's boyfriend known about the trial? Had inDents killed him to cover it up?

The police said the boyfriend looked like he'd been tortured. Maybe they were trying to get him to tell them where the denture plate was located after they searched Wanda's house and the lab and didn't find it. Then Kennedy and Erik saw him at Wanda's place, so he wanted to take them out too.

It was all making sense, everything fitting together and

tying up with a neat bow. Sure, they would have to get Miller to confess and tell them who was behind inDents, but Erik figured that would happen in time. Time Erik didn't have before Kennedy disappeared again. He needed to tell her about all of this now! Before she left town. If she hadn't already gone.

25

Kennedy recognized the voice and knew the identity of the man lurking in the shadows. Oscar Edwards. He stepped into the light from the lamp as she tried to figure out what he meant when he said they had something to end. She had no idea.

"How did you get in here?" she asked, trying to remain calm.

"Your mother used to hide a key under one of the pots." Edwards held the key out on his palm. "I guess she didn't tell you."

"Why would she tell you?"

He shoved the key into his pocket. "I had to meet with her every week, and we sure couldn't meet in public where video cameras are everywhere nowadays. And you know your mom. She often got bogged down in her research and forgot everything else. She was often late and gave me a key to let myself in."

Kennedy couldn't imagine her mother being so secretive. "Why were you meeting with her?"

He lifted his shoulders, and a cocky smile spread across

his face. "She was trialing a denture plate I've perfected to deliver medicines to the wearer."

Kennedy tried not to gape at the man, but what he was saying was crazy. "Medicine through dentures?"

He lifted his chin. "Researchers have been experimenting with 3-D printed dentures to deliver antifungal medicines to denture wearers. They were so shortsighted. Why stop there, I asked? Why not try other meds too? Just imagine it. The denture wearer—often seniors who forget to take their meds—will have them seamlessly delivered, and they only have to change out the dentures every so often." His shoulders rose, and he let out an arrogant huff of air. "I'm going to make a fortune."

Ah, now things were becoming clearer. "You're behind inDents."

"I *am* inDents." His shoulders rose even higher. "Every brilliant thought behind it."

"And you gave my mom her heart medicine that way, but it failed and killed her."

He frowned. "Once I get the dentures back, I can investigate the failure. Of course I also have to make sure no one learns of it."

In his dreams. "But you can't keep it a secret. My mom was buried with them, and the police have the spare set."

"No worries." He tossed off an easygoing shrug. "The pair your mother was buried with will soon be recovered."

She cringed at the implications behind his statement. "And the other pair? The one Jeremy Miller stole? Do you know him?"

"My sort of nephew." Disgust deepened Edwards' tone. "He botched things up one too many times. He's on his own, but *you* will get the pair back that the police are now holding."

So he did it. This man killed her mom. Sure it was an accident, but he was responsible.

She opened her mouth to spew her anger at him, but held it in check, curling her fingers into fists. This creep wouldn't get away with killing her mother, but anger would get Kennedy nowhere right now. She had to get the details from him. Then she would find a way to get free and see him punished.

"Sort of nephew?" she asked, surprised by how calm she managed to sound.

Edwards' lip curled as he rolled his eyes. "My sister once fostered a teen. Jeremy Miller. She always begged me to think of him as family. Not easy. Not when he was so rough around the edges."

Edwards shuddered. "The boy pushed the boundaries and got into trouble with the law too many times for my liking. Now, he's become fascinated with guns. He's one of those militia fanatics you hear about on the news. Disgusting, but just the guy I needed. He was more than glad to break into all the places where your mom might've kept her spare denture and recover it."

Oh, Mom, you trusted the wrong man. Totally trusted the wrong man. "You had a key and code for the lab too?"

"Your mother was kind enough to let me do my research there late at night. After all, dispensing drugs without going through FDA protocols isn't exactly approved."

Her mother really must've trusted him, as being generous with her lab wasn't common for her. "Which is why you paid her so much money. You both knew this trial could kill her."

He grimaced. "That's a bit extreme."

"Extreme!" Kennedy finally lost it and charged across the room, her blood boiling. She was going to grab her gun and... *Stop. Calm down and think.* "That's exactly what happened."

Edwards held up his hands and stood back. "We don't know that for sure."

Kennedy wanted to see this man suffer, but he was talking, and she needed him to keep giving her the information that would convict him and put him behind bars for the rest of his life for murder.

She took a long breath and let it out. "You knew it could kill her, which is why you're trying to cover it up. Did you purge the lab video too?"

"Video. No. Why? I haven't been there in months. Didn't have to go there while your mom was trialing the plate." He shifted on his feet, looking antsy.

She still had a few more questions for him, but then she was going for her gun and holding him here until the police could arrive. "You have a prickly caterpillar bean plant in your garden, right?"

"I never understood why you asked about that, but yes. It's quite the unique plant."

"One of the beans must've gotten stuck on Jeremy's pant leg. It fell off near the river after he broke into the lab."

"Ah. I have a nice thick stand of them. He probably brushed against them when he came to get his marching orders." Edwards shook his head. "Just between you and me, the guy could be more careful."

"But not you, right?" Her anger seethed under her words. "You're so careful that you put the Tile trackers in my mom's purse and my backpack so you knew when it would be safe to break in."

He grinned. "I had to track her just in case the plate did fail. Was easy enough. I hid the tracker in your mom's purse when she went to the bathroom at one of our meetings, and you left your pack sitting unattended at the church after her funeral."

Just the reminder of the day put a pain in Kennedy's heart and a flame to her anger, but she wasn't done. Not quite yet. "Did your nephew mail the anthrax too?"

"Of course, but I gave him the envelope. He wouldn't have access to that. *I* was the mastermind behind it. Behind everything." He eyed her. "Though you aren't showing any ill effects from it."

She explained what happened. "So you see. You failed. Again."

"Alas, it didn't work the way I had hoped," he admitted. "I thought you would see a letter addressed to your mother and be eager to open it. But I'll be ending your involvement today, and I have plans for your PI too."

"Once the police link Jeremy to you, you'll be charged. Assuming your sort-of nephew doesn't turn on you before then."

"Won't happen. Sure, he'll likely be charged with burglary, but he won't spill his guts about all of this once he knows you can't testify against him."

She forced a chuckle she didn't feel. "You obviously don't realize that we recovered forensic evidence that will tie Jeremy to my mom's house and a gun that he used to kill her boyfriend."

Edwards' eyes widened. "He killed the boyfriend?"

She saw a myriad of emotions race through his expression. "Jeremy went rogue on you, and you didn't know."

Edwards' face blanched, but he quickly recovered.

"This is all going to come out," she said, attempting to sound brave. "So no point in harming me or Erik. As accessory to murder and attempted murder, you're going to go away for a long time."

"They need proof for that, and you're going to help me

285

take it out of their hands." His eyes lost focus, and she thought he'd gone to an alternate place. He was clearly crazy in his obsession with his project. She really needed to get away from him, warn Erik, and then call the police.

"Now!" He jutted out his chin. "You're going to help me get those dentures before the police wise up and have them analyzed."

"No, I won't." She rushed toward her purse and shoved her uninjured hand inside. Her fingers curled around the weapon.

Edwards whipped the purse from the table.

"No!" She shot out her other hand to latch onto it, but the pain radiated up her arm and she instinctively let go.

He jerked the leather free and moved back to the open doorway. "Let's see what you're so eager to get to."

He plunged his hand inside the bag and came out holding her gun. There was suddenly a heavy, sick weight to the air surrounding them, and panic raced up her back.

"This is perfect." His lips curled in a revolting grin. "We'll just take a little trip somewhere more private where we won't draw attention from the neighbors while I persuade you to cooperate, and I can use your own gun to do it."

Erik didn't want to waste time with crating Pong in the condo. He loaded him into his truck and set off for Kennedy's place under the star-filled night with dark clouds on the horizon. As the miles flew past, his mind raced with questions. How would this news impact her? Would it change anything for them? He couldn't see how, but at least she would know her mother hadn't been murdered.

Kennedy would still leave him, still follow Finley. But at

least he'd get to see her one more time before she was gone forever. It would be painful and joyous at the same time. Hopefully the joy would outweigh the pain.

He pressed his foot to the gas pedal. Racing down the roads with little traffic, he made the trip in twenty minutes.

"C'mon, boy," he said to Pong, and they exited.

Pong had no idea where they were going, but he must've been picking up on Erik's excitement as he was pulling at the leash, which he rarely did.

A light was still burning at the marina. Maybe the manager was working late. Erik crossed the bridge and arrived at Kennedy's place to find the door slightly ajar. His heart rate kicked up. Their suspect was in county lockup, so what was going on? Even if Kennedy had already left with Finley, she wouldn't leave the door open.

He tied Pong's leash to the railing. "Stay." He drew his gun and pushed on the door. It swung inward with a groan.

Her purse lay on the floor, her phone on the table. She wouldn't leave them behind if she'd hadn't gone into WITSEC. He checked her purse. Her gun was gone.

Had something bad happened again?

He had to know. Find her. Now!

He didn't call out but moved room to room, up the stairs, each space empty and undisturbed just as it had been the night of the intruder. No sign of an altercation. Other than her purse on the floor and her missing gun.

A wave of fear washed over him. He rushed to the deck. The boat was gone. Had Kennedy taken it? No, she wouldn't take a leisure trip in the night, would she? She'd never been into boating other than using it as a way to reach her diving locations. Surely, she wouldn't go diving on her own. And especially not at night.

On the other hand, this could be her last chance to dive before going into hiding.

He raced to the outdoor closet and jimmied the lock open with his pocket knife. Her diving equipment was inside. Okay. She wasn't diving.

Where was she?

"Kennedy. Are you here?" he called out.

No answer. None.

"Kennedy." He cupped his hands around his mouth. "Kennedy!"

He shone his phone's flashlight along the edge of the deck, searching the water, the current moving faster than normal. He looked up. The clouds had shifted overhead. A storm was coming, and she could be in even more trouble.

He tapped the contact list until he found Finley's name and dialed. The call rang five times and went to voicemail.

He dialed the Veritas Center.

"Pete," Erik said when the guard answered. "It's Erik. Has Kennedy shown up there tonight?"

"Sorry. No."

Erik hung up and called Finley again. Still no answer. Were they together somewhere? Maybe at Finley's place? Or had they indeed been relocated already? But why did Kennedy leave her phone? True, she'd get a new one and new ID anyway, so maybe she didn't care.

He needed to be sure she was okay.

Finley's place. He had the address from their research. He'd go there to check.

He bolted through the house and grabbed Pong's leash. They hurried to the lot, but Erik made a detour to the marina door. The same guy Erik had talked to before answered his knock.

"You again," he said.

"My girlfriend is missing. Wanda's daughter. Kennedy. Do you know her?"

He nodded.

"You see her today?" Erik asked.

"In the morning. She stopped by to tell me she would be leaving and wanted to sell her mom's place. She said a guy would contact me about it."

"And you didn't see her after that?" Erik had to work hard to keep the panic out of his tone.

He shook his head.

"Anyone strange or unusual go through the lot tonight?"

"Not that I noticed. I don't know all the cars, but nothing suspicious."

"Did you hear a boat take off from the vicinity of her place?"

"Heard a motor, but it's hard to tell the location. Sound travels on the water."

"When was that?"

He tapped his chin. "I'm not sure. An hour ago. Maybe less."

"How long are you going to be here?" Erik asked. "In case I need your help."

Villanueva glanced at his watch. "I can hang around for another hour or so."

"I'm going to run to her sister's place. Give me your phone number so, if I find her, I can call you."

He handed a card to Erik. "And I got your card in case she shows up here."

"Thanks, man." Erik turned to go.

"Hey, one more thing," Villanueva called out. "I remembered seeing that guy you told me about another time. And he was with another fella. They were arguing."

Erik spun to lock eyes on the manager. "Did you hear the conversation?"

Villanueva shook his head. "Too far away, but I can tell you what he looked like. He was a big guy. Muscular. Wideset eyes. Black hair in a buzz cut."

Erik knew that description. He thumbed through the photos on his phone until he found the former Major Hess's picture. "This the guy you saw?"

"Yeah. Yeah. It's him all right."

Erik couldn't imagine how Miller and Hess were connected, but they were. This could account for them having found the team bracelet at the shooting.

"Thanks." Erik ran for the truck and texted Aiden to look into a connection between the two men. Erik darted through traffic as fast as he could to Finley's apartment and pounded on the door.

Pong sat and looked up at him, his body trembling. Erik's distress was causing the dog to worry.

"It's okay, boy." Erik squatted and stroked his head.

"Who's there?" Finley's voice came from the other side of the door.

"It's Erik Byrd. Is Kennedy here?"

Finley opened the door and scratched her head. "No. Why?"

"She's not at her place. She left her phone behind. Her gun is gone, and so is the boat. I'm worried someone might've forcibly taken her."

Finley's face paled and she stepped back so he could enter. The one-bedroom apartment was neat and tidy and smelled like vanilla. The minute Erik and Pong stepped in, Pong went into search mode. He charged across the room to a black cat with a white nose and paws that sat on the sofa, warily watching him.

"Sorry," Erik said. "Pong is socialized, and he gets along great with cats, but he hasn't seen one in some time."

Erik tugged on Pong's leash, but the dog remained firmly planted and stared up at him. "You don't have any flash drives or anything like that in the couch do you?"

"No. Unless a friend dropped one when they visited."

"Mind if I look so I can get Pong to stand down?" Erik explained about Pong's working dog status.

Finley waved a hand. "Knock yourself out."

Erik moved to the couch.

The cat eyed him and must've found him lacking, as it jumped down and strolled toward a scratching post in the corner. Pong followed the cat and sat next to it.

"That's weird." Erik joined Pong and knelt next to him. "What is it, boy?"

The cat circled around Erik's back, rubbing softly against him, and Pong made the circle with the cat.

"What *are* you doing, Pong?" Erik picked up the cat and something dangled on the collar, catching his attention. He flashed a look at Finley. "It's a mini flash drive. Someone put it on the cat's collar."

Finley hurried over to them. "Must've been my mom."

He removed the collar and jumped up. "You have a computer with a USB port I can use?"

"I'll get my laptop." Finley headed down the hallway.

"Good boy, Pong." Erik moved to a chair by the small breakfast table, and Pong trotted along. "I wish I had a reward for you, but I didn't expect to need your services tonight."

As Erik waited, he looked around the space. She'd packed two suitcases and a few boxes. His gut tightened. These items served as a reminder that when he found Kennedy—and he would find her—she would be leaving. Leaving him. But at least she would be safe in WITSEC.

Now? Now he just didn't know.

Finley returned and set her laptop on the table. Erik booted it up and plugged in the drive. It opened to reveal a document and a spreadsheet. He clicked on the document.

"It's a letter to you and Kennedy from your mom." He started reading, and she looked over his shoulder.

Wanda explained that she'd participated in a denture trial to raise money for medical bills. She wrote the letter in case anything went wrong so they would know about it and could make sure the company's owner was held accountable. She said the spreadsheet held daily records she'd made about her blood pressure for inDents.

And then she mentioned the owner's name—Professor Oscar Edwards.

"Edwards," Erik said. "I should've leaned on that guy harder."

Finley looked at Erik. "Do you think he has Kennedy?"

Did he? "I don't know who else would."

"But why?"

"Yeah, why? We have to figure the guy who was arrested is connected to Edwards, and maybe he doesn't want her to identify him."

"But you saw him too."

"Right. I did. So why else would he take her, and more importantly, *where* would he take her?" He met Finley's worried gaze. "Keep this flash drive safe. I'm going to call my brothers and one of them will be over to make sure you're all right. The rest of us will find Kennedy."

He looked at the dog. "Come, Pong."

Erik's furry buddy trotted over to him, his leash dangling. Erik picked it up, and they jogged to his truck. Erik dialed his brothers and got on the road as he waited for them all to join the call. He explained the situation. "I need one of you to provide a protection detail for Finley. The others gear up and grab the drone and my red helicopter with controller from my spare bedroom and meet me at the marina."

"I'll handle the detail," Brendan offered.

"Thanks."

"What do you have planned for Kennedy?" Aiden asked.

"Her boat is missing, and the manager said there was nothing suspicious in the parking lot. So I figure if someone took her, they went by boat. We don't know which way they went, and we'll need to scan both directions of the river. One of you can pilot the drone, and I'll command the helicopter. I mounted a camera on the base."

"That only gives us a limited range," Aiden said.

And not a very long range at that. "I'll see if the marina manager can arrange boats for us to use."

"We'll load up and be there as fast as we can," Clay said. "Don't do anything stupid."

Erik wanted to snap at his brother, but he was right. If Erik could think of anything to do, he would do it. Stupid or not. "See you there."

He dialed the manager.

"Did you find her?" Villanueva asked.

"No, and I need your help. Could you get two boats that I can borrow in the next half hour?"

"Boats? Hmm. Yeah, well. I have one. And I can knock on a few doors. Boat people stick together, so I'm sure someone will lend us another."

"Perfect," Erik said. "I'm on my way."

He disconnected and glanced at Pong. "So what do you think, boy? Is she still on the river or did they just take the boat to a boat launch and then travel by car to some destination where he plans to kill her?"

Pong whimpered.

"I know. Why do that? If he's going to kill her, why not just take care of her right there? Maybe he's trying to avoid being seen at the marina." Erik tapped his thumb on the wheel as he thought. "If that's the case there would be a vehicle at the marina. Unless he was dropped off."

Pong sat up, his face alert.

"If Oscar Edwards is involved, I can look up his registration and cruise the lot for his vehicle. Maybe see something inside to tell me what he's planning to do."

Erik arrived at the lot and idled his vehicle near the entrance to look up Edwards' vehicle registration information. Erik soon had the plate number for the guy's black Toyota RAV4, and Erik cruised through the lot to search for it. He spotted the SUV in the back, far away from prying eyes.

"Stay," he said to Pong and got out to look inside.

The wind had picked up, and it buffeted his body as he stepped up to the Toyota. The vehicle was empty. No weapons Erik could see. No restraints, tape, or ropes. But then if Edwards had taken Kennedy, he would have all of those items in hand.

Erik hurried back to his truck to search the internet for any social media information to give Erik a clue where the guy might take her. He'd added a family reunion photo to his page since Erik had last checked the professor out. A banner in the back said the event occurred a month ago, but Edwards must've just gotten around to posting the picture. Erik zoomed in on the photo and about dropped his phone. On the far left stood Jeremy Miller.

"See this, boy," he said to Pong. "Miller is connected to Edwards somehow."

Erik tapped on the photo that Edwards had tagged of Miller, which took him to Miller's Facebook page. Erik had looked at the page after Miller's arrest, but hadn't been searching for a connection to the professor. He scrolled down to a photo of a little cabin in the boonies on a property with a river flowing through it. Miller's house?

Could he live on the Columbia River? Could Edwards be taking Kennedy to Miller's place? Erik opened another database to locate Miller's address then mapped it. The property was located in a small county with very few marine patrol resources.

Erik could call the sheriff, but he wasn't confident in the smaller agency's response. Besides, Erik had no proof someone abducted Kennedy, and it would waste valuable time trying to convince a deputy to begin an all-out search. Erik could use that valuable time to look for her.

He drove straight to the marina office and got out with Pong. Erik and his brothers would still travel in both directions on the river, but after seeing Miller's connection to Edwards, you better believe Erik was heading toward Miller's place.

~

Kennedy searched her brain for an idea of how to escape, but she could hardly leave a distress signal or clue for anyone when she was piloting a boat with a lunatic professor holding her own gun on her. She had no idea where they were going, but they were heading east and upriver to a less populous area.

The wind bit into her face as her mind raced for thoughts of how to get away before he tortured or killed her. She could bail overboard, but she knew from the other night that the water was cold enough to become a problem in a very short time.

Could she swim to the shore before her body shut down? Especially with an injured hand? That would hinder her progress. Or could she do it before the professor shot her? The distance wasn't likely an issue, but the cold and a stronger than normal current were.

Plus, Edwards would just rev up the motor and come after her.

Unless she stopped him. But how?

She slowed to get a better look around and listened.

"Why're you slowing down?" he shouted.

"Watching for the sandbars," she lied.

She peered overboard and saw nothing but a few branches floating in the rapidly flowing water. Could she grab one and somehow jam the propeller so the boat would be rendered useless?

She'd have to get to the back of the boat somehow, but jamming the propeller was worth a try. After all, she was going to lose her life one way or another. Might as well be the way she chose.

26

While Drake piloted the borrowed ski boat with powerful motor, Erik ran the helicopter up the river. He'd outfitted most of his RC choppers with night vision cameras, so he had a good view of the water and river banks. They'd traveled ten miles, and he hadn't seen a sign of Kennedy and her abductor.

The skies suddenly opened up with a drenching rain, and he hunkered over the controller with his raincoat to keep it dry. On the screen, he watched the water flow under the helicopter, but his mind was elsewhere.

Oscar Edwards. A name Erik would never forget, no matter how this turned out. *No! Stop thinking that way.* It would turn out fine. He couldn't allow himself to contemplate anything else. He and Drake would reach the boat before Edwards hurt Kennedy, and they would rescue her.

"Can't you make this thing go any faster?" Erik shouted without taking his eye off his screen.

"Doing the best I can, bro." Drake sounded way too calm for Erik's liking, but Erik knew his brother's guts were tied up too.

Erik had to let God point him and his brothers in the right direction. He'd leave it all up to God and let Him take control.

Right. That was all. No big deal.

Kennedy had decided she would jump, but she had to find the perfect spot, and now with the pouring rain beating down on her, she had an even more difficult time seeing. River width varied significantly, and a narrower location could ensure that she made it to shore. And she needed a clear place on the bank where she could climb out.

"Stop!" Edwards shouted above the roar of the motor.

She lowered the throttle, and the motor's growl turned to a low-pitched rumble as the boat settled down into the current. She turned a bit, looking for anything to grab and knock him overboard before she had to enact her plan of jumping into the water. Other than the tote bag he'd brought aboard, all she saw were cushions and life jackets. And he'd asked her to stop in one of the widest parts of the river, she thought was nearly four miles wide. It would take her at least two hours to swim the distance, and no way she'd make it to shore before succumbing to the cold.

"Drop the anchor," he commanded.

"Here?" She couldn't keep the surprise from her voice.

"Yes, here."

"I think it's in the back."

"Then kill the motor and move." He gestured at the back of the boat with the gun and ran his hand over his polished head like a squeegee pushing the water to the back. "And no funny business. I won't hesitate to shoot."

She moved toward the boat's stern, climbing over seats

and being careful not to lose her balance as the craft swayed with the current. She heard a buzzing sound above and glanced up. Something moved high in the sky. She squinted. Was it a RC helicopter?

Erik?

She quickly lowered her gaze, so Edwards wouldn't notice.

"Quit stalling and hurry up," he yelled.

She found the anchor and started unwinding the rope. If the helicopter was above, Erik had to be nearby. Thankfully, Edwards didn't hear it. She'd always had sensitive hearing, and maybe the pitch eluded Edwards' older ears.

If she jumped now, she might be able to block the propeller, and Erik might be just downriver on his way to rescue her.

She got the rope fully untangled and climbed up on the seat to drop the anchor into the water. She let the rope slide through her hands, careful of the injury. She kept hold until the anchor made a solid clunk on the bottom. Now, Edwards couldn't move the boat without pulling it up, which would take both of his hands. He would need to put the gun down to do that.

Then maybe she could strike him with a heavy branch. She would have to play it all by ear.

Please, help me to get away.

She clamped her unbandaged hand over her mouth so when she hit the cold water she didn't reflexively gasp and draw water into her lungs and took the leap of faith.

∼

"I've got her," Erik yelled. He climbed to the back of the slippery boat as Drake continued upriver so he could talk to his brother without shouting. "They stopped in the middle of the river. She just dropped the anchor."

He shifted so Drake could see the live feed just as Kennedy leapt off the boat and into the water. She disappeared below the surface.

Erik's heart refused to beat.

"Water's too cold for her to last long," Drake said, his hand still on the throttle and powering their boat forward. "We need to hurry."

Erik had his focus glued to the screen and finally saw Kennedy battling the strong current near the motor. "She's okay."

"What in the world is she doing?" Drake asked. "Edwards has a gun, and he's making his way to the back of the boat. He could shoot her."

She disappeared under the water with the branch just as Edwards reached the back. He stood to survey the area, slapping the rain from his face and holding a hand over his eyes. He dropped to his knees on the seat and set the gun down to reach for the anchor rope.

"No time to call the coast guard," Erik said. "We have to hope Kennedy swims to shore. We'll ram the boat. Or shoot the guy. Move."

Drake pushed the throttle harder, and the boat lunged forward. Erik slid back on the slippery seat and, as the boat rose in the churning water, continued to watch the screen.

"She surfaced and is swimming for shore," he shouted. "We can hit the boat with no problem."

"Roger that," Drake said.

On the screen, Edwards pulled the rope, hand-over-hand. He'd soon have the anchor up. But too soon for Erik and Drake to take him out?

Erik didn't know. Wouldn't know until they were right up on the guy.

The cold water threatened to numb all Kennedy's muscles, the rain obscuring her view, but she could still save herself. She'd moved far enough away from the boat that she hoped Edwards thought she was swimming for shore, then behind him and out of his view, she cut back to the other side of the boat.

Her injured hand ached, but it seemed like the cold and adrenaline kept the pain under control. Near the boat, she located the perfect branch and rested it under her chin.

Choppy river waves lapped at her face and mixed with the rain. Gagged her. She coughed. Cleared her throat. Wanted to give up. The cold telling her body to give in.

No. Not today. Keep moving.

She fought the current. Fought the cold. Fought the desire to give in. She had so much to live for. Erik. Finley. Somehow, she would be with them both. They could figure it out. If he'd have her.

She reached the boat. Saw Edwards pulling up the anchor as she suspected he would do to come after her. He was off balance. Perfect. She surged up on the boat and hooked her elbows over the edge for support. With her good hand, she grabbed a branch from the water. She thrust it into Edwards' backside and sent him toppling over the edge as the force propelled her back into the water.

She let her adrenaline fuel her and pulled herself back into the boat. She lay in the cold bottom unable to move and prayed with everything she had that God would send someone to rescue her.

"Kennedy's something else," Drake said.

Erik agreed. She'd knocked a recently armed man from a boat and had gotten back in. "Pull up alongside, and I'll board."

"What about Edwards?"

"Drop me off in their boat and check on him."

Drake nodded and eased their boat alongside Kennedy's while Erik brought the helicopter in to land.

"But be ready if we need to use this boat to take Kennedy in. With the bigger motor, we'll get back to her place faster." Erik grabbed an emergency blanket from the kit that Villanueva had provided and leaned over to grab Kennedy's vessel.

He hopped into the boat toward the bow so he wouldn't risk stepping on her. His feet slipped on the slick bottom, but he grabbed a seat to stop his fall.

"Honey," he called out through the still pounding rain. "Are you okay?"

"Just c-c-cold."

His heart soared at her voice, but he didn't like how cold she seemed. He climbed over the seats, wanting to focus only on her, but kept his eyes out for Edwards. Erik grabbed Kennedy's gun and stuffed it in his pocket, then dropped to the bottom of the boat in the middle where he could see both sides.

He scooped Kennedy into his arms, and she snuggled against him. Her body quivered with the cold. He shook out the aluminum emergency blanket and draped it around her body, then hugged her tight, the fabric crinkling under his arms.

Thank You, thank You, thank You.

"You were very brave and ingenious." He kissed the top of her soaked head. "But please don't do anything that dangerous again."

"I hope I never have to." She shuddered under the blanket.

He wanted to say he would never let her out of his sight again. His heart shattered with the thought of her leaving him, but he wasn't going to say anything to her without thinking about it first.

"Yo," Drake called out. "I'm going for Edwards."

Erik nodded.

"He's responsible for my mom's death," Kennedy said.

"Her denture. I know."

"How?"

"Your mom put a flash drive on Oreo explaining the denture trial and why she needed the money. Johnson gave the spare plate to Maya for examination, and she found the meds."

"He wanted me to help him get that plate back for him." She shook her head. "I refused. He was bringing me out here to convince me to help him. I don't know what he thought I could do, but maybe it was just a madman's last-ditch attempt."

She shuddered again, and Erik pulled her even closer. She was an amazingly strong woman, and she'd taken it upon herself to perform her own rescue.

"He's connected to Jeremy Miller," Erik said, "but I don't know how."

"Edwards' sister fostered him when he was a kid. Edwards thinks of him as a sort of nephew."

Foster records were sealed, so there was no surprise to Erik that he couldn't find the link. "Hess is connected to Miller too. Aiden's looking into him. Unless Edwards mentioned that too."

"No."

"Then we'll be sure to keep digging. After we persuade Johnson to bring him in for questioning." Erik saw Drake stop his boat and reach over to haul Edwards onboard. The guy was limp and unmoving.

"We need to get him somewhere warm," Drake said.

Erik looked down at Kennedy, the rainwater rolling from her shiny blanket. "You able to transfer to the other boat? It has a bigger motor and can get us back faster."

"Yes."

"You'll have to sit with Edwards," he added.

Her shoulders rose under the blanket. "Great. I'll have a chance to glare at him and get rid of some of the anger burning in my gut."

Kennedy had done exactly what she'd said she would do. Glare at Edwards right up until the moment she reached her mom's place. Wasn't hard. The man killed her mother. Sure, it was an accident, but he shouldn't have been doing a drug trial in secret. She'd left Erik and Drake to deal with the creep while she took a hot shower and dressed warmly. By the time she got downstairs, the police had taken Edwards away, and Erik waited alone for her by the roaring fireplace.

"You feeling better?" he asked.

She nodded.

"Your hand feeling okay?"

She looked at the fresh bandage. "Seems like the cold water acted like an ice pack and let me use it more. Now it's throbbing."

"Johnson called and cleared up the mystery of Hess's involvement," Erik said. "He and Miller are buddies. Miller couldn't buy guns legally due to his felony conviction for drugs, so Hess was supplying Miller with weapons."

"So he'll go away for being an accessory to Gordon's murder."

"He will, and he's already been arrested so you're truly safe." Erik's brows drew together. "I'm sorry I wasn't here when you needed me."

"You couldn't know."

"But I could've insisted you stay at the condo until you left with Finley."

"I would've said no."

He took a step back. "Why?"

"If I'd stayed, I might change my mind about WITSEC, and Finley needs me. You don't."

He crossed the room, his expression blank, masking his emotions. He took her good hand and a flash of warmth lit his face.

"I do need you, honey." He cupped the side of her face, and she pressed her cheek into his hand, reveling in his touch.

"I still love you." His voice broke.

Her heart stumbled at the unexpected confession and she blurted out, "I love you too, I—"

"I know." His hand trembled. "You need to think of your sister. If there's one thing I understand it's family ties. When I thought I was going to lose you, I vowed to talk to Finley. To persuade her to give up on WITSEC and stay. But now that I've had time to think about it, I know I can't do that."

"Why?" Why wouldn't Erik fight for her? Why would he let her go so easily?

"I could never live with myself if I convinced the two of you to stay and then Waldron harmed you. I know it's a longshot, but if your deputy thinks the risk is real enough to keep you in the program, what I think needs to take a backseat to his experience and judgment."

"Yeah, I suppose." She didn't know what to think now. She'd spent her time in the shower planning to come down here, declare her love for Erik, and tell him she would persuade Finley to change her mind. But what Erik said made sense, and she couldn't be responsible for putting her sister in danger any more than Erik could. No matter how much Kennedy wanted to be with this amazing man for the rest of her life, she had to walk away.

27

Kennedy stood in Maya's lab at the Veritas Center, Maya and Sierra in front of her. Twelve days had passed since Kennedy's rescue, and she was pleased to be at the lab and not in some unknown town with a new name issued by WITSEC. All thanks to Tyrone's cooperation.

Kennedy had managed to change their WITSEC future, not by convincing Finley to stay in Portland, but by convincing Tyrone to give them time somewhere in seclusion while he did a comprehensive threat assessment on Waldron.

During that time, she'd secretly kept in touch with Sierra to be sure Erik didn't have any symptoms from the anthrax. Kennedy couldn't talk directly to Erik and get his hopes up that she might not go into hiding, so she'd chosen Sierra as her point of contact and sworn her to secrecy. The good news was Erik was in the clear so far and odds were in his favor that he wouldn't have any issues.

When Tyrone declared the threat level as negligible, their WITSEC days ended. It wasn't her decision or Finley's, but Tyrone's. They no longer needed the program.

"So have you decided?" Sierra asked.

Kennedy stowed her thoughts and looked at Sierra. "I don't want to accept a pity job."

Sierra tilted her head. "What do you mean?"

Kennedy lifted her shoulders. "Be honest. Tell me if you made up a job with Veritas so I'd stay close."

"First, the team would never go for that," Sierra said.

"She's right," Maya said. "It has to make sense for the business."

"And second," Sierra said. "It wasn't my idea. In fact, I was against it at first."

Kennedy had to work hard not to let her mouth drop open.

"She's right again." Maya chuckled. "I was the one who proposed the idea. With so much water in the Portland area between the river and the coast, we get calls for water recoveries all the time. I ran the numbers and figured, if we hired you out to the agencies along with using you for other forensic recoveries, we would have a win/win situation."

Kennedy shifted her focus to Sierra. "But you were against it?"

Sierra's eyes narrowed. "I've been queen bee in the forensics department around here for so long that I felt threatened by your credentials."

"Threatened? But why?" Kennedy gaped at her. "I'm nowhere near your level. I'm in awe of you."

"You're selling yourself short," Sierra said. "Don't do that, but you can keep on being in awe of me." She laughed.

She reminded Kennedy so much of Erik, whom she hadn't seen since the night of the rescue. Just the thought of him put an ache in her heart.

"And if travel is your thing," Maya continued. "I'm guessing you'll get enough regional travel to fulfill that need too."

Kennedy glanced between the women. "This isn't just a whim, and in a few months or even next year, you'll decide you need to eliminate the position?"

"Are you kidding?" Sierra asked. "We're expanding so fast that we can hardly keep up, and if Maya determined that we can afford you, we can."

"So, what do you say?" Maya asked. "Can we add you to the Veritas Center roster?"

It just seemed too good to be true. "Are you sure I'll be a good fit for the lab?"

Maya nodded. "We asked about you. Everyone sings your praises, and we know you have the standards we look for in team members."

"Then, yes." Kennedy wanted to pinch herself to be sure this was true.

Sierra grabbed Kennedy in a hug and swung her around. "When can you start?"

"I'll have to put in my notice. At least two weeks. Maybe more." Kennedy ran her previously injured hand over her face, thankful that the bites were healing well and she no longer needed a bandage. "I won't leave them in a lurch."

"But you don't have to do that today, right?" Sierra asked.

"No, why?"

"It's Clay's wedding, and I know Erik would want you there." Sierra's broad smile reminded her of Erik again.

She was so tempted to say yes, but... "I don't know. I wasn't invited."

"Only because we didn't think you'd be around." Sierra's earnest tone gave Kennedy hope. "But now you're not leaving."

Kennedy looked at her watch. "I don't have anything to wear."

"We have time. Trust me." Sierra got out her phone and tapped her foot as her call connected. "We need you, Kels.

Kennedy is here and needs something to wear to the wedding. Can she borrow something?"

A slow smile spread across Sierra's lips, and she hung up then clutched Kennedy's arm. "Come on, you two. Kelsey has given us free rein in her closet."

"Perfect," Maya said.

"Kelsey?" Kennedy asked as Sierra dragged Kennedy to the lab door.

"She's the only one of the partners here who's a clothes horse. She's guaranteed to have what you need, and she has impeccable taste. We'll find a perfect dress for you." Sierra got the elevator door open and punched the number five.

"No offense," Kennedy said. "But you're starting to remind me of your mother."

"Et tu, Brute?" Sierra mocked pulling a knife from her chest. "Seriously, maybe a little. But I want to see my baby brother happy, and you make him happy. If I have to nudge it along a bit, I will."

"I would've called him tomorrow," Kennedy said. "After all the festivities were over."

"But why wait when you can put on a dreamy dress. He'll be in his tux, and there'll be candlelight and moon-light and romance in the air."

"Erik in a tux." Kennedy fanned her face. "I can't think of a single reason why I shouldn't go to the wedding." She laughed, and when the elevator opened, Sierra dragged her down the hall past her own condo to the other unit on that floor.

Kelsey opened the door. She was a stunning woman, about Kennedy's height with black curly hair. She was dressed in skinny jeans and a dainty halter top and her face was perfectly made up. Kennedy suspected she would fit in Kelsey's dresses, but they would look so much better on Kelsey.

"I am so jealous," Sierra said. "You had Sophia three months before I had Asher, and I don't think I'll ever fit into skinny jeans again."

"Sure you will." Kelsey squeezed Sierra's arm. "I didn't do anything special, and it came off."

"But you don't love chocolate like I do." Sierra shook her head and put her hands on Kennedy's shoulders. "Enough about me. We're here to dress this beautiful woman. I suspect if the dress is right tonight, we'll soon be attending her wedding."

Sierra winked at Kennedy and laughed. Together, they went to Kelsey's room. Kennedy had never had many friends, and she could see these women becoming friends in the future. If Erik wanted her, that was.

"My closet awaits," Kelsey said. "But before I show it to you, I need you to promise not to judge me."

"And trust us," Maya said. "When you see the size of it and the contents, you'll want to."

Kelsey rolled her eyes.

"Scouts honor." Kennedy held up three fingers. "No judging, but maybe a little jealousy."

The four of them easily fit in the walk-in closet, which was the size of a small bedroom.

Kelsey held her hands out to encompass the space. "Since I had Sophia, I've cut back, but clothes have always been my therapy for the tough job I do."

"Kelsey's our forensic anthropologist," Maya said.

"Ah," Kennedy said. The woman dealt with bodies that were often nothing more than bones when recovered.

"Snuggling Sophia is better therapy." A dreamy smile crossed her face.

"I know what you mean," Sierra said. "But I didn't have a clothes addiction. Only a work one."

"It wasn't a—never mind." Kelsey shook her head.

"You're right, and the evidence is right in front of us. My evening wear is on the back wall." Kelsey stepped out of the way.

Kennedy stared at the full rack of brightly colored dresses. "I'm helpless with formal attire. Can you just choose something for me?"

A fire lit in Kelsey's eyes. "You know it. I have a few green dresses that would look amazing with your coloring."

She pulled down three dresses covered in protective plastic and returned to the bedroom. By the time Kennedy joined her, Kelsey had one of them uncovered and held it out. "Use my bathroom to try it on."

"I don't know. It's beautiful, but it looks too glamorous for me."

"No such thing." Kelsey put the dress in Kennedy's hands and gave her a push toward an open door.

"We didn't mention she's kind of pushy when it comes to fashion." Sierra laughed, and the others joined her.

Kennedy went to the bathroom with their joy ringing through the room and slipped into the halter dress with chiffon ruffles that draped perfectly along her shape. The dress left her shoulders and most of her back bare. She wasn't used to showing so much skin, but she had to admit it accented all her features, and the green was fabulous with her hair color.

But could she wear it? She didn't know. She wasn't even sure she could step out and show the other women.

A knock sounded on the door.

"How's it coming in there?" Kelsey asked.

"I have it on, but..."

"I'm coming in." Kelsey pushed the door open. "Let me zip it up for you."

Kennedy turned her back to Kelsey, and once the zipper was at the top, Kennedy looked in the mirror.

"Girl, it's perfect. Once we put your hair up, Erik won't be able to keep his eyes off you." Kelsey took Kennedy's hand and led her out to the bedroom.

"Oh, wow," Sierra said. "That's the dress. My brother isn't going to know what hit him."

~

Erik tied the confounding bowtie in his bathroom mirror, swiped a path free from his shower steam, and stood back to look at himself. He forced a smile, which he would need to keep plastered there for Clay's wedding and the reception. He was happy for his brother. He really was. But with Kennedy walking out on him again, he knew his heart would ache all day. Maybe for the rest of his life.

"Focus on being a groomsman and supporting Clay," he told his reflection. "That's all you have to do."

He adjusted the tie. He and his brothers all owned basic black tuxes for client protection details in formal settings. Toni had insisted on Clay having a special tux, but thankfully she agreed the brothers could wear the tuxes they owned. Meant no fittings or hassle of picking up and returning them.

Not like Erik didn't have the time. Since Kennedy had left with Finley, he'd been throwing himself into work and flying his helicopters to fill the days, but time still inched by as if in slow motion. He missed Kennedy more than he thought possible. Even more than when they'd broken up the first time. This time, he knew she loved him and they could be together if not for WITSEC.

A knock sounded on his door. He glanced at his watch. He was driving to the church with Drake, who was stopping by to get him, but not for thirty minutes. And the dude was never early. Maybe he had a problem with his tux.

Erik went to the door. "Need help with your bow—" But the words died at the sight in front of him. Kennedy. He stared at the green dress that clung in all the right spots. Her hair was swept up, little curled strands dangling by her face. Her freckly shoulders were bare. She was stunning, and standing in his doorway. He swallowed, tried to get some moisture into his mouth. "Kennedy?"

"Hi," she said softly.

"You look...wow...just wow. I don't have words." He blinked a few times to be sure he wasn't hallucinating. "You're here. WITSEC. What's going on?"

She smiled. "Can I come in and explain?"

"Um, yeah, sure." He stepped back and closed the door.

She brushed past him, leaving a pleasant flowery scent that he recognized from one of the Veritas partners, but he couldn't remember which person.

She went into the living room but didn't sit, and he took a minute to admire her legs accented by strappy sandals.

"You look amazing," she said. "I always figured you'd dress up nicely, but wow. That tux." She stepped closer and lifted a hand as if she was going to adjust his tie but then let it fall.

"About WITSEC?" he prompted.

"I asked Tyrone to find us a temporary safe house while he did a threat assessment. I thought, if the danger was minimal, Finley would willingly leave the program."

"What did he find?"

"Minimal risk, and he didn't extend our agreement. Finley and I'll live together to reduce costs and take care of her debt. We never did figure out where that cash in the safe came from, but it doesn't appear to be illegal so we'll use that."

"Will she be moving to Virginia with you?"

Kennedy shook her head, one of the strands of hair

crossing her cheek. He wanted to move it, but she swept it out of the way before he could. "I got a job here, and I'm moving after I give notice."

She couldn't have gotten a full-time position as a forensic diver. Not with the local agencies. "Where will you be working?"

"Right here. At Veritas. They offered me a full-time job as a forensic diver with a very generous salary."

He resisted gaping at her. "Let me guess. Sierra's doing."

"Actually no. Maya's idea. She thinks in addition to the work I can do for the lab, they can hire me out on other dives in the region, and my salary will basically pay for itself."

He shook his head. "Is this for real? You're staying?"

She stepped up to him and rested her hands on his shoulders. "I hoped you would want to start dating again. Was I right?"

"Are you kidding me?" He circled his arms around her slender waist and pulled her close, to inhale that perfume that was driving him crazy. "I want you right by my side now and forever."

She smiled, a sultry kind of smile that got his blood boiling. "Then let's seal this with a kiss."

He lowered his head, and their mouths connected in a bonfire of emotions. He could hardly think about anything other than how she felt in his arms, and that he would be able to hold her every day.

Every day.

His brain cleared, and he lifted his head. "Wait here."

He ran to his bedroom and opened the bottom dresser drawer, where he'd hidden the ring he'd bought for her back in college. He could only hope she would say yes to such a sudden proposal.

He raced back to the family room and got down on his knee.

She gasped. "Are you—?"

"Proposing?" He held out the ring box. "I know this is sudden, but I have never stopped loving you. I know we've just gotten back together, but you are the love of my life. Will you marry me, Kennedy?"

"Marry you?" She fanned her face and gaped at him.

He could hardly stand to wait for her answer, but he wouldn't pressure her. He did wiggle the ring just a bit for encouragement, and then he spotted the tears glistening in her eyes, and his heart dropped. Was she going to say no?

"Yes!" The word burst from her mouth. "Yes. Of course."

Her eyes glinted with joy and a wide smile crossed her face. A smile he couldn't wait to kiss away. He slid the ring on her finger. She held it up to the light, and the solitaire diamond sparkled, casting tiny prisms of light around the room.

She looked at him. "It's the one I picked out in college."

He nodded. "I never got that car I was saving for."

"I know how much you wanted the vintage Mustang. Makes this even more special." She drew him to his feet and threw her arms around his neck. "I love you too. So much. I'm so happy."

He twirled her around, and she giggled like a little girl, the sound cutting to his heart and lifting his joy to new heights.

A knock pounded on the door.

Erik groaned and drew back. "Drake is picking me up, but he's early."

He took Kennedy's hand and looked at the ring. "We might want to make this announcement after the wedding celebration so Clay and Toni can have their own special day."

"Then let's put the ring in the box, and you can give it back to me again after the wedding."

A flash of uncertainty lit in his gut. "You'll still say yes, right?"

"Of course."

"Come on, bro." Drake pounded on the door.

She slipped the ring off and gave it one last longing look before settling it in the blue velvet.

"Be right back." Erik pocketed the box and jogged to the door, his step so light he thought he must be floating. He opened the door. "Sorry. Was talking to Kennedy."

"Kennedy?" Drake's eyebrows went up. "What's she doing here?"

"She's not going into WITSEC, but will be working for Veritas."

"No wonder you're beaming." Drake pushed past him and strode up to Kennedy. "Congrats on the job. You'll love working and living in Portland again."

Kennedy nodded, her gaze locked on Erik, and he could hardly breathe for the love beaming his way.

Drake turned and locked Erik in a headlock. "And this guy's going to be sickeningly happy."

Erik laughed. "You mean like you?"

"Yeah. Just like that." Drake let go and chuckled as he looked at Kennedy. "Since you're all dressed up, I'm guessing you're coming to the wedding?"

"Sierra invited me and arranged for the dress, but I don't want to crash."

Erik took her hand. "I know when I tell Toni about you, she'll want you there."

"And if she doesn't, our mom will make sure you're wanted." Drake laughed again. "So let's get a move on. Don't want to stress Clay out any more than he is now."

The trio headed for the door, Erik holding firmly to

Kennedy's hand. He leaned close. "I hope you like weddings. I, for one, don't believe in long engagements."

28

The wedding was simple yet elegant, and Kennedy felt perfectly dressed. She'd had to be alone for some time while Erik performed his groomsman duties, but that was okay with her. She hid out in the kindergarten classroom until she heard the wedding march and knew that Peggy would be inside. Kennedy didn't want Peggy to see her and change her focus.

Once Toni was at the altar, Kennedy slipped into the back of the church and sat on the groom's side in a pew with big white bows and delicate white flowers decorating the end. She immediately connected gazes with Erik, and the smile he fired her way sent her heart fluttering.

Peggy must have noticed, as she turned and scanned the church, but thankfully missed seeing Kennedy.

Clay took Toni's hands, and she beamed at her husband-to-be. She had large icy blue eyes that were warm with love. Her ebony hair was swept up in a simple knot with pearl pins holding it in place. Her dress was an unassuming white A-line dress with lace shoulders and a banding of matching lace around her waist. Although floor-length, it had a very short train. Very much like the dress Kennedy might choose.

As beautiful as Toni was, it was the five Byrd brothers in their crisp white shirts and black tuxes who stole the show. Or maybe just the blond one on the end. They were lined up by age—minus Clay, of course—and their corresponding spouses and girlfriends stood in the same order on the bride's side along, with Sierra, whom Erik had walked down the aisle.

The couple exchanged vows and rings, and Kennedy thought about the ring in Erik's pocket and smiled at him. He returned that same combination of dazzling and secret burning inside smile, and she couldn't look away. Not even when Toni and Clay walked down the aisle arm-in-arm, a healthy dose of joy in their expressions.

As they passed, Kennedy made a mental note to later ask Toni where she got her dress.

Kennedy shook her head. Listen to her. She'd gone from potentially not seeing Erik again to engaged to him in a matter of days. She'd called Finley before the ceremony. Her sister was over the moon happy for Kennedy and happy that she was marrying a man who would never leave his family and Portland, so Kennedy was here to stay as well.

The bridal party made their way down the aisle, couple after couple. As Erik passed by, he gripped her hand for the briefest of moments. His parents followed, and Peggy's mouth dropped open when she saw Kennedy. She stopped to squeeze Kennedy's shoulder.

She mouthed, "We'll talk later."

Kennedy knew what was coming, but she didn't care if Peggy tried to matchmake. The match was already made. Though Kennedy had to play along because, if Peggy knew she and Erik had gotten engaged, so would everyone else.

The three children Peggy and Russ were fostering followed behind.

Kennedy waited for her turn to exit and found Erik

waiting for her. He grabbed her hand. "I have to go with the wedding party to the reception hall, but I asked Reed to give you a lift."

"Okay." She worked hard to hide her disappointment.

"I thought you'd never get out here." Erik drew her close. "We'll be next if I have anything to say about it."

He kissed her cheek and raced out the door to jog across the lot before she could respond.

She felt her skin where he'd touched her and couldn't help but smile like crazy. She hadn't been this happy in a long time. Maybe not since she'd split up with Erik. If only her mom and dad could see this day. See that she had been able to reconcile with him and get married. If only they'd be there to hold their grandchildren.

A dark-haired man with facial hair and onyx-colored eyes approached. He wore a black suit with a white shirt, and he carried Asher on his shoulder. Her heart melted over the sweetness the pair made. What was it about a strapping guy like Reed tenderly holding a baby that got to her? Such a juxtaposition, she supposed.

"You look exactly like Erik described you." He introduced himself. "I hear you and Asher have already met."

She nodded. "It's nice of you to give me a ride. I'm kind of a last minute addition."

"One that has my wife smiling non-stop. She won't admit it, but Erik has a special place in her heart. She loves all her brothers, but she said there's something special about him being the baby. And of course, the only one who looks like her."

"I think the feeling goes both ways."

Asher started to fuss, and Reed jiggled him. "What say we take off so Little Man can fall asleep in his car seat."

They stepped into the beautiful August sunshine with a soft breeze helping to cool the temperatures in the eighties.

Reed clicked open an SUV with a remote and settled Asher in his seat.

She went around and climbed in, and by the time she did, he had the vehicle running and the air blowing, though it was hot. He got them on the road, and Asher's head tipped in sleep.

"Is parenthood everything you thought it would be?" she asked.

"No!" He shot her an embarrassed look. "Sorry, that was a little over the top. They tell you how much it's going to change your life. How everything becomes about this little person, but you still aren't prepared. And I've got it easy. I'm not responsible for all the feedings like Sierra is."

"I can only imagine."

"I'm guessing because you're here today that things are good with you and Erik again."

She couldn't contain her smile.

"All right, then." He grinned. "It should be a fun evening for the both of you."

"It will be." She looked out the window before she gave away her announcement.

"You going to miss working for the Bureau?" he asked.

"Being part of a great organization, yes." She looked back at him. "All the red tape and paperwork, no."

A dark eyebrow rose, and he looked intimidating, as many FBI agents did. "How do you know Veritas doesn't have even more?"

"I suspect Maya runs a tight ship without a lot of redundancies."

"Yeah," he said. "I was just messing with you. I always hate it when we lose someone good. The slackers seem to stay for life, but good people get scooped up by the private sector."

"I wouldn't have left except for wanting to be here in

Portland and the local office isn't large enough here to support my job."

"The things we do for love." He grinned at her.

Heat rushed over her face, and she looked out the window again. She should just keep her mouth shut, but she had one question to ask him before she clammed up. "What's it like to join the Byrd family?"

He cast her an inquisitive look. "Honestly?"

"It goes no further than this vehicle." She nodded and mimicked locking her lips.

"It's terrific and terrifying." A wry smile found his face. "I'm not big on a lot of talking, so you can imagine my overload when the whole family gets together. But the love, camaraderie, the concern for each other takes over, and I'm more than glad I said I do to Sierra."

He tapped his thumb on the wheel. "But if you're thinking of saying I do as well, just know that you're saying it not just to Erik but to the entire Byrd family too."

Erik didn't like how his mom had cornered Kennedy. She didn't look upset, but it was just a matter of time before Kennedy broke under pressure and admitted their engagement. Erik didn't want to spoil this day, so he headed through the crowd in her direction.

Toni clasped his hand. "I know you're on a mission, but I just wanted to be sure you tell Kennedy that I'm going to throw my bouquet soon if she wants to get in on it."

"I'll be sure she knows."

"I'm glad you two are back together," Clay added. "Maybe we'll be here for you two soon."

"I better go." He gave both of them a quick hug and slipped into the crowd again before he said anything to take away from their day. As he approached, Kennedy locked gazes with him, and their secret burned in her eyes.

His mother spun. "Oh, good. You won't believe it, son."

"What's that?" He did his best to keep a level tone.

"Kennedy agreed to come to family dinner tomorrow night."

"That is, if you want me there," Kennedy quickly said.

He took her hand. "Of course I do."

"Oh, I see." His mom's lips curled up in a broad smile. "I hoped it would be this serious, but now I can see it is."

He cast her a questioning look.

"The way you two look at each other. We'll have another wedding real soon if I'm not mistaken." His mom's smile widened.

Erik stepped closer to his mother but kept hold of Kennedy's hand. "I'm not confirming or denying anything. But I am asking you to ignore us until after Clay and Toni's big day is over. They deserve to be the center of attention."

"Your kindness is touching." His mother squeezed his shoulder. "I'm not sure what I did to deserve such fine sons, but I am most blessed."

"Now don't go all mushy on me, Mom. Go gush over Clay before they leave."

She nodded. "To be continued at dinner tomorrow night."

Erik wanted to groan, but he was blessed to have a mother who loved all of them so very much. He looked at Kennedy. "She means well."

"I know, and I look forward to having her in my life." She grinned. "On most days, anyway."

Erik drew her close for a hug. "Toni is going to throw the bouquet, so we should head over there."

"I'll let someone else catch it. I don't need it. I've already got the man I want to spend the rest of my life with."

Hearing the words made his breath hitch. "You don't have to catch it, but should still go over there or people might wonder why you aren't."

"You're right." She started in the direction of the exit, tugging him along as they wound among round tables set with crisp white linens and littered with cake plates and forks.

She stopped next to Malone in the back of the twenty or so young women.

Malone glanced at them and rolled her eyes. "This is a waste of time for me. I doubt I'll ever get married."

Erik had learned that, as outgoing as Malone was, she was also a very private person, never talking about anything outside of her career and Reed. Erik wouldn't ask why she didn't think she would marry, but Kennedy stepped closer to her. "Mind if I ask why not?"

Malone frowned, and her perfectly plucked eyebrows rose. Erik expected her to blow Kennedy off, but she met her gaze instead. "I have too many people who need my help to find time to be a wife or even a mother."

Kennedy seemed to mull over her answer for a moment. "I applaud your cause. It's very noble. But you deserve happiness too."

Her frown deepened. "A topic I don't want to get into today."

Toni and Clay approached the women, who all looked eager to catch the bouquet.

Toni smiled at them. "Thank you all for coming. I pray your dreams come true like mine did." She shot her husband a burning look, and Clay blushed.

Erik understood. These women who'd come into their lives brought such indescribable emotions that the guys couldn't contain them. The public acknowledgment of a look like this one could make any one of them blush.

Toni turned around. "Okay, ladies. Here it comes."

She lifted her arms and did a few practice movements, then let the bouquet fly. The woman had quite the arm, and the flowers soared over the group toward the back. Kennedy bumped her hip into Malone, who eased over and the bouquet fell into her hands.

Applause broke out, but she looked at the arrangement as if it was a live snake coiling around her fingers. "But I...I don't."

She shook her head and looked at everyone around her. "This doesn't mean anything. It's just a silly tradition."

Erik spotted his mother making a beeline in their direction. He would step in front of Malone to protect her, but he didn't want to make a scene.

His mom curled an arm around Malone's shoulder. "It looks like you need to sit down."

"I think I do," Malone said. "I don't believe in what this means, but it's thrown me for a loop."

Something Erik had never seen with this strong attorney.

"Let's go have a talk about it." His mother led Malone among the other women to a nearby table.

Kennedy slid her arm into his. "You think your mother is matchmaking?"

"Absolutely." He looked at Kennedy.

"Then she has her work cut out for her," Kennedy said. "Malone had a mighty fierce response to the flowers like even thinking about marriage made her sick."

Kennedy inched closer to Erik. "I'm glad we're over that."

"Me too."

"Your trust issue is gone too, right?"

"It is." He took both of her hands and smiled at her. "I know you'll never intentionally hurt me."

"I won't. I promise." She moved closer, and he caught a pleasant whiff of that flowery perfume again. "And no secrets either. None. With our freedom from WITSEC, that is all in the past."

He slipped his arms around her waist. "And no more disappearing."

"My feet are firmly planted wherever my soon-to-be husband plants his."

He smiled at her, his heart alight with fire. He couldn't ignore the need to kiss her any longer, and he pressed his lips against hers. Firmly but quickly, he let her know how much he loved her. When he looked up, a dreamy smile slid across her face.

He groaned and pulled her into his embrace. "Don't plant them too deeply, honey. Because when you marry a Byrd, you'll be expected to soar."

∼

Thank you so much for reading Night Watch. If you've enjoyed the book, I would be grateful if you would post a review on the bookseller's site. Just a few words is all it takes.

And you'll be happy to hear that there are more books in this series!

Book 1 Night Fall – November/2020
Book 2 – Night Vision – December/2020
Book 3 - Night Hawk – January/2021
Book 4 –Night Moves – July/2021
Book 5 – Night Watch – August/2021
Book 6 – Night Prey – September,/2021

I'd like to invite you to learn more about the books in the

series and my other books by signing up for my newsletter and connecting with me on social media or even send me a messsage. I also hold monthly giveaways that I'd like to share with you, and I'd love to hear from you. So stop by this page and join in.

www.susansleeman.com/sign-up/

~

NIGHT PREY - BOOK 6

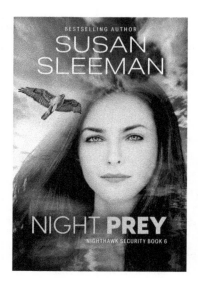

She lived for upholding the law...

Defense attorney, Malone Rice, doesn't want to go to her fifteen year class reunion. Attending means running into her former high school flame, now Portland police detective, Ian Blair. But when the committee decides to honor her for her pro-bono work with homeless teens, she knows it would be churlish not to attend. She will have to go and make the best of it.

But now the law won't save her.

As expected, Ian attends the reunion, but what Malone doesn't expect—could never expect—is that Ian would find her standing over their classmate's dead body. Or that she would still have feelings for the once bad-boy of their high school. Ian's struggling too, between arresting Malone for murder and his age-old attraction to her. He walks a tightrope, until evidence surfaces that the real killer's still out there, and Malone becomes his prey. Can Ian overcome his feelings to focus and uncover the truth before the killer strikes again and Malone ends up dead?

PRE-ORDER NIGHT PREY!

NIGHTHAWK SECURITY SERIES

Protecting others when unspeakable danger lurks.

Keep reading for more information on the additional books in the Nighthawk Security Series where the Cold Harbor and Truth Seekers teams work side-by-side with Nighthawk Security.

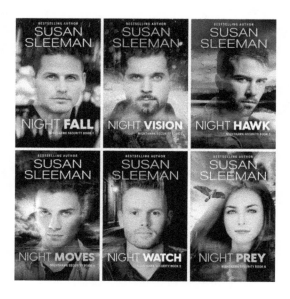

A woman plagued by a stalker. Children of a murderer. A woman whose mother died under suspicious circumstances.

All in danger. Lives on the line. Needing protection.

Enter the brothers of Nighthawk Security. The five Byrd brothers with years of former military and law enforcement experience coming together to offer protection and investigation services. Their goal—protecting others when unspeakable danger lurks.

Book 1 Night Fall – November, 2020
Book 2 – Night Vision – December, 2020
Book 3 - Night Hawk – January, 2021
Book 4 –Night Moves – July, 2021
Book 5 – Night Watch – August, 2021
Book 6 – Night Prey – October, 2021

For More Details Visit -
www.susansleeman.com/books/nighthawk-security/

THE TRUTH SEEKERS
People are rarely who they seem

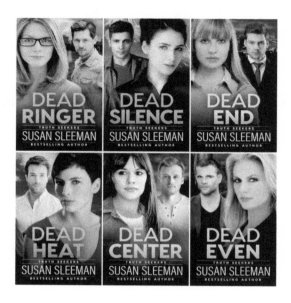

A twin who never knew her sister existed, a mother whose child is not her own, a woman whose father is anything but her father. All searching. All seeking. All needing help and hope.

Meet the unsung heroes of the Veritas Center. The Truth Seekers – a team, that includes experts in forensic anthropology, DNA, trace evidence, ballistics, cybercrimes, and toxicology. Committed to restoring hope and families by solving one mystery at a time, none of them are prepared for when the mystery comes calling close to home and threatens to destroy the only life they've known.

For More Details Visit -
www.susansleeman.com/books/truth-seekers/

BOOKS IN THE COLD HARBOR SERIES

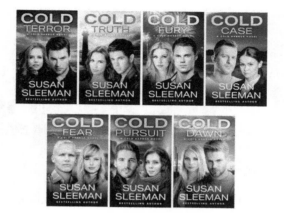

Blackwell Tactical – this law enforcement training facility and protection services agency is made up of former military and law enforcement heroes whose injuries keep them from the line of duty. When trouble strikes, there's no better team to have on your side, and they would give everything, even their lives, to protect innocents.

For More Details Visit -
www.susansleeman.com/books/cold-harbor/

HOMELAND HEROES SERIES

When the clock is ticking on criminal activity conducted on or facilitated by the Internet there is no better team to call other than the RED team, a division of the HSI—Homeland Security's Investigation Unit. RED team includes FBI and DHS Agents, and US Marshal's Service Deputies.

For More Details Visit -

www.susansleeman.com/books/homeland-heroes/

WHITE KNIGHTS SERIES

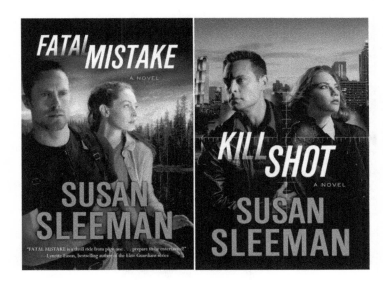

Join the White Knights as they investigate stories plucked from today's news headlines. The FBI Critical Incident Response Team includes experts in crisis management, explosives, ballistics/weapons, negotiating/criminal profiling, cyber crimes, and forensics. All team members are former military and they stand ready to deploy within four hours, anytime and anywhere to mitigate the highest-priority threats facing our nation.

www.susansleeman.com/books/white-knights/

ABOUT SUSAN

SUSAN SLEEMAN is a bestselling and award-winning author of more than 40 inspirational/Christian and clean read romantic suspense books. In addition to writing, Susan also hosts the website, TheSuspenseZone.com.

Susan currently lives in Oregon, but has had the pleasure of living in nine states. Her husband is a retired church music director and they have two beautiful daughters, a very special son-in-law, and an adorable grandson.

For more information visit:
www.susansleeman.com